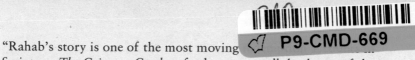

Books by Jill Eileen Smith

THE WIVES OF KING DAVID
Michal
Abigail
Bathsheba

WIVES OF THE PATRIARCHS
Sarai
Rebekah
Rachel

THE LOVES OF KING SOLOMON (ebook series)
The Desert Princess

DAUGHTERS OF THE PROMISED LAND
The Crimson Cord

The CRIMSON CORD

RAHAB'S STORY

JILL EILEEN SMITH

Revell
a division of Baker Publishing Group
Grand Rapids, Michigan

Published by Revell
a division of Baker Publishing Group
P.O. Box 6287, Grand Rapids, MI 49516-6287
www.revellbooks.com

Printed in the United States of America

Library of Congress Cataloging-in-Publication Data
Smith, Jill Eileen, 1958–
    The crimson cord : Rahab's story / Jill Eileen Smith.
        pages ; cm — (Daughters of the promised land ; Book 1)
    Summary: "The breathtaking story of the prostitute who risked everything
to protect two Israelite spies before the battle of Jericho"—Publisher.
        ISBN 978-0-8007-2034-6 (softcover)
        1. Rahab (Biblical figure)—Fiction. 2. Women in the Bible—Fiction. 3. Bible.
Old Testament—History of Biblical events—Fiction. 4. Jericho—History—
Siege, ca. 1400 B.C.—Fiction. I. Title.
PS3619.M58838C75 2015
813'.6—dc23   2014036586

Published in association with the Books & Such Literary Agency, Wendy Lawton,
Central Valley Office, P.O. Box 1227, Hilmar, CA 95324, wendy@booksandsuch.biz

15 16 17 18 19 20 21   7 6 5 4 3 2 1

To M'shiach Adonai, the Lord's Anointed One, Messiah—
my Rock, my Strength, my Redeemer—who redeemed
Rahab so we could see a picture of mercy and of grace.
Thank you.

PART 1

And Joshua the son of Nun sent two men secretly from Shittim as spies, saying, "Go, view the land, especially Jericho." And they went and came into the house of a prostitute whose name was Rahab and lodged there . . .

Before the men lay down, she came up to them on the roof and said to the men, "I know that the LORD has given you the land . . . Now then, please swear to me by the LORD that, as I have dealt kindly with you, you also will deal kindly with my father's house, and . . . that you will save alive my father and mother, my brothers and sisters, and all who belong to them, and deliver our lives from death."

Joshua 2:1, 8–9, 12–13 ESV

1

Rahab draped the pale blue scarf over her head and shivered in the predawn chill. Her two sisters, Cala and Adara, took some convincing, but in the end, they had followed her on the short walk to the city's public gardens in search of the dead carcasses of the female *coccus ilicis*, the crimson worms prized for their deep scarlet dyes.

"You know the king's servants have probably already stripped the trees bare," Cala said, resting a protective hand over the growing babe within her. "And Tzadok was not too happy to have me leave him with just a blanket for warmth when I left our bed."

Gamal never noticed whether Rahab shared their bed anymore. How quickly his ardor had cooled after the war that left him both injured and a national hero for saving the prince's life. Yet how could a single battle cause so much change?

Shame heated her face, and she quickly ducked her head

lest Cala notice. Surely she had done something to displease him. Surely her childlessness had forced him to seek lovers in the streets and drink in the taverns at night.

Your daughter is very beautiful, my lord. The memory of Gamal's words that day during her fifteenth summer invaded her thoughts. He had accompanied his father to her father's home to seek her hand in marriage. How tall and proud Gamal had looked, standing like the soldier he was with one hand behind his back, the other resting on his close-cropped dark beard. Dark hair peeked beneath a leather helmet, and a slight smile tipped the corners of a strong, round jaw.

Her heart had beat faster at the sound of his deep yet gentle voice, and though she hid in the shadows in the connecting room, she heard every word of the exchange, the bartering. Gamal's father had the prescribed bride-price, and Gamal, a soldier in the king's guard, earned a good living. Rahab would be well cared for in her new home.

How short-lived that promise.

The familiar twinge of envy filled her in one glance at Cala's protruding middle. In five years of marriage she had not produced a son for Gamal, or even a daughter, though a daughter would not have pleased him. Perhaps she should be searching for mandrakes or performing fertility rites at the temple to procure a child instead of searching for worms that might bring her profit to feed her husband's gaming habit. A child would remove the sting of her shame and give her someone to love. A child might cause Gamal to look on her with favor again.

"Your thoughts are very far away, my sister," Cala said, drawing up beside her as they walked along the mud-brick streets now where palm trees lined the boulevard. "I know that look." Her voice dropped to a whisper, and they both glanced Adara's way.

Rahab shook her head. "It is nothing." Though in truth it was everything. She could not create a child any more than she could find the elusive mandrakes. And she was not about to offer sacrifices or prostitute herself to the temple on the whims of false hope.

"Has Gamal hurt you again?" Cala rested a hand on her arm, forcing Rahab to stop and meet her gaze. Cala knew the truth of his hidden abuse, something Rahab could not tell her mother or father or brothers.

Rahab looked beyond her sister, feeling the sudden touch of the morning breeze like a forgiving kiss. She drew in a slow breath, strangely strengthened. She glanced once more at Adara, then leaned close to Cala. "He is always angry," she said quickly. "The prince's edict arrived yesterday afternoon. They want an accounting by week's end and Gamal is not ready." She walked on, remembering the panic in his eyes. "Scarlet linens bring a high price in the markets." She *had* to find a way to repay Gamal's debt, to earn his respect. She glanced at Cala. "I have to try."

Rahab looked at Adara, whose young eyes were wide with curiosity. "I have to try what?" Adara asked.

"I have to try to find these worms so I can create scarlet threads and sell them to feed my family." She smiled at Adara, on the cusp of womanhood, still innocent and carefree and irresponsible. Something Rahab had not felt since the day Gamal returned from war, three years before, but wanted desperately to preserve in her baby sister for as long as she could.

"That's not all that you told Cala. What does the prince

want with Gamal?" Adara's thin brows narrowed, and her lip jutted in her typical pout. "I'm not naive, you know."

You are far more naive than you realize, dear sister. "I know you aren't, my sweet, but I don't have time to explain it all right now. Please. I need your help to find these worms. Their carcasses will be white and we will have to scrape them off the trees."

Adara's shoulders drooped, but she turned her attention to the nearest tree, her whole energy caught up in the hunt as though they were searching for buried treasure.

Which they were. Rahab moved deeper into the grove and slowly scanned the trunk of an oak tree. If only there were a god of worms, she would pray to him or her and offer a sacrifice of the few hoarded pieces of bronze and silver she kept hidden in a jar in their bedchamber. Precious metals she had earned from her weaving but that would not even come close to paying off Gamal's debt.

She had to find enough worms to make the prized red dye and make it in abundance.

She could not even consider another option.

⁓⁓⚓⁓⁓

Rahab shuddered, feeling the weight of Gamal's cursing the following evening. "What good are you to me if you cannot produce even the smallest lump of silver?" He tossed both hands above his head in a frustrated gesture. "A wife that cannot produce heirs could at least find some way to increase her husband's fortunes. You are a worthless whore!"

She ducked her head, waiting for the blow that did not come, yet his words did not miss their mark. How swift his barbs—sharp daggers to her soul. She heard his pacing limp thump against the woven mats she had lovingly made to keep the floor packed and smooth. They had once lived in a house in the wealthier section of town, with a large private courtyard in a home of stone floors and many rooms. One they shared with his family.

But the king had greatly rewarded Gamal for his action in battle, for the day he had thrown himself in front of the prince and taken the arrow that should have ended the prince's life. Gamal had used some of that reward to rent a house closer to the main thoroughfare. A smaller dwelling, but one Rahab had taken great joy in making their own. One free of his mother's nagging tongue.

"My luck is changing tonight, Rahab. I'm *this* close to winning"—he pinched his fingers together to emphasize his point—"but I need silver to put in the pot." His voice had softened as if he had suddenly forgotten his tirade. Did he think she could so easily sweep aside his accusing words to give him what he wanted?

She straightened, drawing on courage she thought she had lost. "The games are slanted against you, Gamal. Wouldn't it be better to wait just awhile? Give me time. I can give you more if you can just be patient."

The blow came too fast for her to duck this time. Tears stung her eyes, matching the sharp sting against her cheek.

"Don't tell me to be patient. I have given you years!" She knew in an instant they were no longer talking about silver but sons. Did he not consider the fact that if he spent more time with her instead of the foreign women he had come to favor, she might at last produce a child? But of course, the fault was hers alone. Always hers.

She flinched as his hand drew close again, and he fingered a lock of her hair as if turning a new thought over in his mind. "There is a way you could repay me." He let the comment hang in the air between them until she slowly, fearfully met his level gaze.

She swallowed, recognizing the scheming gleam in his eyes. There was always some new plan, some way he devised for her to please him, though none ever did. Did he want her to visit the temples as she had considered the previous morning?

Horror filled her, and she wanted to pull away from him, to curl into a corner and hide like a young girl again in her father's house. Shaking overtook her, and she clasped her hands to her arms, trying to still the sudden cold.

"I've had men ask after you," he said after too many breaths. His dark eyes searched hers.

She stared at him wide-eyed but could not find her voice.

He shook his head and gave a brittle laugh. "Of course, I tell them where they can take their suggestions." He lifted her chin with two fingers, possessive. "I need you to be quicker with the cloth, or find some other way to get me gold."

So now it was gold he wanted? *I am doing all that I can.* "Yes, my lord."

"It's the only way we can get out from under our debt," he said as though trying to convince her.

Your debt. How he loved to include her in his foolish choices. And yet . . . if she had been all she should have been as wife to him, would he have needed to pursue women or drink or games to find relief from the pain she caused? The question haunted her, as it did every time he left the house at night, leaving her alone. Every time she crawled into their

bed without his company. Every time he looked at l
disdain.

She blinked, hating the tears that threatened. One moment she wanted to fall at his feet and weep, begging him
to forgive her. But sometimes in the next breath, sudden
violent emotions would overtake her. If she had dared, she
would flail her arms against his proud chest and scream in
his face.

*Why can't you return to work as a guard? Why can't you
be kind like my father and brothers, like normal men?* The
words barely held on the tip of her tongue, but to say them
would incur an even fiercer wrath. Surely his former commander, Dabir, now the king's advisor, would allow him to
work in one of the positions that required less marching. He
could guard the king's prisoners or sit at the gate, inspecting
the merchants as they entered.

But Gamal had allowed the king's praise and his forthcom-
ing gift to make him lazy, and he had wasted all he had been
given until he was the one indebted to the king rather than
the king indebted to him.

She jumped at the jarring sound of the door slamming,
caught off guard that Gamal would leave without another
word to her. She shook herself from her conflicted thoughts.
How she hated that man! And yet how much she longed to
please him.

She touched her cheek, briefly wondering if it had started
to purple. Her brothers would kill him if they knew what
he did to her.

But she could not allow his blood on their hands, despite
what he was. He was still her husband.

A sigh escaped as she walked to the door to secure the latch.

Rahab stared into the flickering lamp some time later, too weary to rise. She had been up well before dawn and had worked at combing the flax to prepare for dyeing ever since Gamal had left, and now wanted nothing more than to fall into bed and succumb to blessed sleep. Her paltry efforts would not bring silver to Gamal's pockets any sooner for her late hours, but somehow keeping her hands busy helped stop her mind from racing through all manner of future fears.

She startled at a light rap at the outer door. Surely her nerves were overly heightened. She stilled, listening. Probably a wandering drunk tapping on the posts of her gate as he passed.

The knock came again, louder, incessant, and Rahab felt a sense of dread. Dare she answer with Gamal still out? What if it was someone from the gaming house come to tell her that Gamal had been hurt in a fight, or worse . . .

She would not let her thoughts trail there.

But the knock continued, refusing to be ignored. She rose slowly and crept to the inner door, peering into the gathering dusk. Moonlight streamed into her courtyard, illuminating two men. On closer inspection, she noted the king's insignia on the guard's helmet and breastplate. She hesitated, trying to make out the face of the other man, when he raised a fist to knock once more.

Dabir? Gamal's former commander still held sway over the troops, but he had risen in power to advise both Prince Nahid and the king. What was he doing at her door in the dark of night?

She hesitated again. Dare she answer? Gamal was not here to defend her.

16

She nearly scoffed at that last thought. Gamal had not defended her honor in years.

Indecision warred in her exhausted mind. Her lighted lamps gave her presence away, and to refuse to answer an emissary of the king . . . She stood a moment more until at last, hands trembling, she lifted the latch.

"My lord." She bowed. "What can I do for you?"

"Rahab?" Dabir bent low, took her hand, and lifted her to her feet. The look in his dark, narrow eyes and the touch of his strong yet gentle fingers fairly scorched her. He led her into the room and closed the door, leaving the guard at the gate. His lazy smile made her blood pump hard.

What was he doing here? She pulled her hand free of his and took a step back. "Has something happened to my husband, to Gamal?"

He stared down at her, his eyes roaming, his look possessive, causing her skin to tingle as though he still held her hand. Silence filled the space between them, and she searched her mind for something to say, something to make him go.

"Your husband is fine. The last time I saw him, he was carousing and eyeing a prostitute before he passed out on the floor. The owner of the gaming house thought to throw him into the street, but I convinced the man to let Gamal stay and sleep it off."

Rahab closed her eyes, blinking back tears of rage . . . and defeat. Gamal probably lost another bet and then drank himself into unconsciousness—again. He deserved to be thrown into the street.

"Why then have you come?" If he knew Gamal's whereabouts, then his only reason for coming here was . . . She met his gaze, caught the edge in his smile.

"Gamal owes the crown a lot of gold, Rahab. If he is tossed into the gutter and dies, he is of no use to us."

"Of course not." *That doesn't explain why you are here.*

"Is that a bruise on your cheek?" Dabir's question startled her. He moved slowly closer and gently touched the spot Gamal had slapped. She gasped. "Did he hurt you?" He drew back, his dark brows drawn low. "If he laid a hand on you . . ."

She shook her head and looked away. "I fell. That is all. I'm fine." She found his concern strangely disconcerting.

He stood without moving, and she sensed him assessing her. At last he stepped closer, placed two fingers beneath her chin, and gently drew her gaze to his. "I would never hurt you, Rahab." His look held such kindness, such desire, she struggled to pull in a breath.

"I'm fine," she said again. Her breath hitched as his finger traced a line along her jaw. "Gamal does not hurt me." But she could not meet his gaze.

He stepped closer still and cupped her injured cheek. "We both know that's not true, Rahab. I have heard him go so far as to offer you to the highest bidder, just to stay in the game."

Another gasp escaped. No words would come. She stared at him.

"I would not let him go through with such a thing," he said, his voice warm, his words honey. "You are fortunate that I frequent the gaming houses. Another time I might not be there to stop such a thing." His finger trailed the path from her ear to her throat.

He tugged her nearer, his lips soft, gentle, molding her to him. "I can give you so much more than Gamal ever could, Rahab." His breath grew hot against her cheek. "He would never have to know."

Rahab's lips tingled with another lingering kiss, and she could not stop the desire, the deep longing for more. To be loved and cherished, as Gamal once cared for her. She closed her eyes against the memory and allowed his kiss to deepen. "He cannot know," she whispered between breaths. "Unless . . ." Horror struck her with such force she drew back, breaking his hold, trembling. "Did Gamal sell me to you for a night?" Of course he had. Why else would a man of Dabir's standing want her?

Her stomach twisted at the memory of Gamal's threat a few hours earlier. *I've had men ask after you.* She crossed her arms, shielding her heart and her body from his words.

Dabir cocked his head, studying her, his gaze understanding, his smile congenial. "Dear, sweet Rahab. I am not a man who pays a drunkard for time with his wife." He lifted a hand toward her, but she took a step backward. He lowered his arm, accepting. "But you . . . you, my dear, are a treasure Gamal should not own, a woman of passion and beauty. The mere thought of you has often robbed me of sleep and invaded my dreams."

"Men visit the harlots at the temples to appease their dreams, or go to the gaming houses for the women of the night, but that doesn't mean I want to be one of them." Her shaking grew.

His soft chuckle incensed her. "My darling Rahab, you are much too beautiful to be a common harlot."

She looked away, all comments frozen within her. *Your daughter is very beautiful, my lord.* Gamal did not say those things now. His lack of desire for her had caused her to fear she had lost her beauty due to her barrenness, that she now appeared gaunt, like the ones at the edge of Sheol.

"If you have not paid my husband for a night with me, why are you here?"

"I think you know the answer to that question, Rahab." And she did know, but she did not want to face it.

"Am I to become mistress to the king's advisor to repay my husband's debt?" She was alone with him, unprotected. How could she stop him from doing as he pleased?

"Not if you do not want to." He lowered his dark head, his shoulders drooping ever so slightly in a gesture of defeat.

She watched him, pulled in a long breath, and slowly released it. She swallowed, summoning courage. "You would leave if I asked it of you?"

He lifted his gaze again, and she sensed his power . . . and his vulnerability. "I would not force you."

So he did not purchase her, and he was not forcing Gamal's debt on her.

Dabir's rich robes swished as he took two steps closer to her. He stopped, stretched one ringed hand toward her. "I would give you myself, Rahab. I would show you all the pleasures Gamal has forgotten."

She looked from his outstretched hand to his aristocratic face. The lines along his brow showed concern, his strong jaw determination.

"I will not allow Gamal to hurt you ever again." His promise held a tiny thread of hope, and yet what could he do but cause ill to her husband?

"I would not have you harm him." She searched Dabir's face and did not pull away as his fingers slowly encased hers.

"I will not harm him." He tugged her closer. Exhaustion filled her, and she did not have the strength to resist. His arms came around her, and his kiss barely skimmed her lips.

Gentle fingers rubbed circles at her back, and his kiss slowly, tenderly deepened. "Come with me, Rahab." His feet moved in the rhythm of a dance to the door of her chambers. With the ease of a warrior, he lifted her into his arms.

Common sense whispered warnings. *Fight back. Flee.* But he had captured her with kindness, leaving all courage behind her.

Dabir stood over her some time later, tying the belt of his robe. She lounged among the bed pillows, feeling warm, accepted. She folded her hands beneath her chin, a smile ghosting her lips. Longing rose to ask him to stay, to come again. But one glance at the moon's bright glow through her window told her Gamal would soon return, fall into bed with her, and assume she slept.

She clutched the sheets to her and sat up. "Please, my lord, would you hand me my robe?" He had tossed it onto a nearby chair.

He looked at her and chuckled. "You weren't so shy an hour ago, my love." He cupped her cheek and bent to kiss her. "Get it yourself."

She balked at his tone, uncertain. But she did as he said, dressing quickly.

She walked with him to the door. When would she see him again? But she could not ask it. Dare not think it. He had come, and she had given him what he wanted. That was the extent of it.

He pulled a small packet from the pocket of his robe and handed it to her. "For you. Don't show Gamal."

She took it but did not undo the strings to the wrapping.

"Open it."

She searched his face, saw him smile again in that gentle, coaxing way.

She fumbled with the strings until his hands came beneath hers to steady them. At last she pulled free the finest length of scarlet fabric she had ever seen. Never in her lifetime could she duplicate such richness.

"I cannot accept this," she said without thinking.

His frown made her stomach flutter. "Of course you can. It is a gift."

"But I did nothing to earn it."

"Precisely why it is a gift, my dear." He tipped her chin. "But you did earn it." He smiled down at her with the gaze of one who has known more than he should. "Keep it."

His parting kiss left her shaken.

2

The comb shook in Rahab's clenched hand the following afternoon as she pulled it through the flax spread over the bed of sharp nails. Once the flax was combed, she would at last be able to spin the fibers into linen threads. But her nerves were as brittle as the drying stalks had been, and the sunlight warming her back where she sat in the house's inner courtyard could not curb the chill rushing through her at Gamal's frantic pacing. He knew. Somehow he had discovered her night with Dabir.

His silence as he paced only confirmed her thoughts.

She watched him from the corner of her eye, forcing herself to continue the task, feeling as though the air around her might snap and break into tiny shards like broken pottery. He whirled again, this time stopping to place a clay tablet in front of her.

"Have you seen this?"

She stopped her work to glance at the royal seal on the clay. The pictures were clear. It was a royal summons with her husband's family crest in the request section. "Is this not the summons that came earlier this week? Prince Nahid wants an accounting. But you still have three days."

He stared at her. "Are you blind? Did you not hear the knock on the door or see the king's messenger? Look at the number stamp. The request is for today."

Today? Her stomach knotted, and bile rose up the back of her throat. This was Dabir's doing. But what did they want with Gamal so soon?

"He never sends an official summons," Gamal said, pacing away from her once more. "He *always* sends a messenger who stays long enough to tell me where to meet him."

It was forever *never* and *always* with him. Neither of which were true, proven by the first edict the prince had sent only a few days earlier. "Are you ready for this meeting?" She picked at the flax again and drew in a steadying breath.

"Of course I'm not ready." Even his limping strides were too long for the narrow court, and he cursed as he turned, heading back her way. "If you had done as I asked last night, I would have enough to pay down the debt today. But you failed me, Rahab, and my luck didn't hold. So now where am I supposed to come up with so much silver?" His look pierced her.

Done as he asked? About the silver or . . . what? But he had not sent Dabir or he would mention it now. She pictured the scarlet cloth now tucked safely away with her hoarded silver and bronze and felt suddenly ill with the weight of choice. Did she have the right to hide such things from her husband? Did not everything she earned belong to him?

But you did earn it. Dabir's words mocked her.

I've had men ask after you.

Her head throbbed with confusion. If she gave Gamal the

scarlet cloth Dabir had given her, he could sell it to appease the prince. But then he would ask where she got it. He would know her work was not nearly as good as the fine linen that belonged in kings' palaces.

"Prince Nahid has not pressed you for payment before," she said, trying to stall his rising anger. "Perhaps this accounting is to compare your records with his. Perhaps he can even be persuaded to postpone the debt."

"I don't want it postponed, Rahab. I want it canceled outright." Gamal stopped in front of her again, towering over her where she sat, his tall form dwarfing hers, his dark eyes simmering with pride and arrogance.

"Why would the prince cancel such a large debt?" She kept her voice even but scooted back from him just the same.

He studied her, as Dabir had done the night before, and she was sure he could read into her heart. Could he see the guilt she was trying desperately to hide?

"He wouldn't," Gamal said at last. "Not without a good reason."

The crimson cloth flashed in her mind's eye again, and this time she sensed it was some kind of omen or direction from the gods. "I may have something that will persuade him." She stood before she could change her mind and rushed to her bedchamber, closed the door, and quickly retrieved the jar from the hole in the floor beneath the mat. She tucked the cloth in the pocket of her robe and hurried to right the mess she had made. She would not give him everything. But the cloth should fetch a large sum, if Gamal was shrewd enough to barter for the highest price. She returned to the courtyard, her heart racing with uncertainty, silently praying that Gamal would believe her.

"And just how can you help me?" His scowl showed deep lines along his forehead, and she realized in that moment how much the years and the strong drink had aged him.

"I've been working day and night to finish this. It isn't as big as I wanted, but the color is perfect and should fetch a high price in the market." She held out the cloth to him, tasting the lie's bitterness, and sank to the bench, her energy spent.

He snatched it from her and slowly turned it over in his large hands. Her heart beat double time, and she studied her feet, not daring to more than glance into his startled face.

"You *have* been holding back on me, wife." His sneer held a triumphant edge as he turned the cloth over in his hand. "With cloth of this quality"—he looked at her—"we will make our fortune yet."

She swallowed the solid lump that had formed in her throat. "It takes a long time to make such fine quality." Her words were barely above a whisper, but she knew even if she shouted he wouldn't hear her.

He bent low at her side and touched a strand of her silken hair that had slipped from beneath her headscarf. "You are the only good thing the gods ever gave me." He cupped her cheek, tilting her chin up. "So beautiful . . ."

Her stomach knotted to hear him say such things. Did he really think so? And here she had given herself to another man in his absence, throwing his love aside without forethought.

He gently touched her swollen, purpling cheek. "I should not have slapped you." His voice choked, as though his heart were breaking with the weight of his admission. He coaxed her to meet his gaze. "I won't do it again, my love. I promise."

She nodded, unable to speak, equally unable to keep the tears from slipping from her eyes. He brushed them away with his thumb and leaned close, his breath smelling of garlic and herbs, not the usual wine or strong drink he carried even on his clothes.

"I will make it up to you, my love." He kissed her softly, his words full of promise, filling her with guilt. She should tell him the truth. Tell him the cloth was not hers. Tell him of Dabir and how the cloth was payment for her "services." Though even she could not believe that had been Dabir's true intent. He cared for her. She sensed it.

Gamal stood then, still clutching the cloth. "I will be back in time to take the money this will bring to the prince," he said, his smile warm, inviting. He offered her a hand. She took it and stood, allowing him to encase her once more in his arms. "So gifted," he whispered against her ear.

"Gamal, I—" But he hushed her with a finger to her lips, then gave her a parting kiss.

She touched the place where his lips had been and watched him limp through the gate. She had almost told him everything. In her effort to thank him for his kindness to her, she had nearly ruined the moment.

A deep sigh escaped, and her body involuntarily shook. What would happen if Dabir found out she had given Gamal the cloth? And how on earth would she make anything so fine to appease Gamal in the future?

***

Rahab glanced at the position of the sun overhead, her heart skipping a beat at how fast time had moved. Gamal should have been home long ago. Only two reasons would have kept him away. Either he had not yet sold the material, or he had been waylaid at the gaming house.

Unless someone had assaulted him and stolen his silver.

Fear quickened her blood at the sudden sound of marching feet coming her direction. She laid aside the flax comb and stood, quickly brushing flax residue from her robe, then hid in the shadows along the wall. She turned toward the sound, saw the king's men stop at her gate. Where was Gamal?

Loud pounding hit the outer door. "Open in the name of the king!" The guard's shout curled a tight fist in her middle. The squeaking of leather hinges coming from the back of the house caused her to turn. She caught sight of Adara peering from the sitting room into the courtyard. Her young sister didn't mind scaling the back wall and entering through their little-used door. But what was she doing here now?

The pounding outside of her door continued. She backed farther from it and slipped into the house, hoping they had not seen her, and met Adara, silencing her with a finger to her lips.

She bent low to avoid exposure from the window and pulled Adara to the floor. "What are you doing here?" she whispered.

Adara's eyes grew wide as she stared at Rahab's cheek. "What happened to you? Why is your face purple?"

Rahab touched the spot where Gamal had hit her and secured the scarf over it. "It is nothing." She touched Adara's arm. "Please, don't tell Father." Though right now she wished for her father and brothers to rescue her from this house, from her life.

Adara startled at the incessant banging, louder now. "Are you going to just ignore them?" Her voice remained as hushed as Rahab's.

"They want Gamal, not me, and he's not here."

A frown creased Adara's face. "Why do they want Gamal?"
Rahab studied her sister. How much dare she tell her?

Gamal's voice cut through the noise of the king's men,
and Rahab quickly stood, Adara with her. "Go home now.
Tell Father and our brothers that Gamal has been summoned
to the Hall of Justice. I'm going to go with him." She raised
a hand to stop Adara's protests. "Just go." She shooed her
back the way she had come, then hurried to the gate where
Gamal stood arguing with the guards.

"Did you receive the summons from Prince Nahid?" the
lead guard asked.

Gamal nodded. "Yes, just this morning. But the first notice said I had three more days. Why this sudden rush and
change of plans?"

"And your accounts are ready?"

"I know what is owed." Gamal's confidence worried her,
but she held her tongue. There was nothing to say to such
a lie. The amount owed changed with each new debt he incurred. "But I do not have enough for this month's payment.
I need more time."

Had he not sold the cloth?

The guard leaned close to smell Gamal's breath. "And yet
you can afford to drink so early in the day?" He shook his
head. "The crown prince of Jericho requests your presence
in the Hall of Justice. Now." The two guards near the door
each took a step to the side to allow Gamal to walk between
them. "You will come." The speaker glanced through the
gate and caught sight of Rahab. His brow lifted in interest.
"This is your wife?"

Gamal looked at Rahab, his expression defiant yet wary.
"My wife was not the one summoned." His voice held little

29

conviction. He limped forward without a backward glance at her, but the guard stopped him, blocking his path.

"Your wife will also come." His command brooked no argument, and Rahab begged the moon god Yerach, and whatever other god might be listening, to keep her husband's mouth shut. Better she go along than for Gamal to get himself in greater trouble by showing disrespect to the prince's guard.

Gamal stood fidgeting while Rahab grabbed her cloak from a peg by the door and hurried after them. She ducked her head toward the guard, then walked behind her husband in silence.

The columned hall where the guards led them stood at the front of the debtors' prison, where men slept when they were loaned out to work the king's fields or flocks or quarries or worse. Some stayed only long enough to be sold to passing merchants, if the debt was high enough or worthy enough to command such measures.

Rahab leaned against a tall marble pillar at the back of the audience chamber, clinging to her cloak, cinching her scarf tighter at the neck to cover her bruised face. A warm, late spring breeze moved through the open windows to stir the room's still air, but Rahab felt only the chill of fear as she watched the guards grip Gamal's forearms and force him to his knees in front of Prince Nahid, seated on a chair of ornate wood and gold. His formal dress of rich robes and the golden circlet crown on his dark head worried her. This prince had power. Would he use it against her husband, against her?

Behind the prince and to his right stood Dabir, dressed in all his royal finery. His presence here should have comforted, but his expression toward Gamal only added to her fear. And her guilt. If she hadn't given herself to him, would Gamal have been called here three days early?

Her stomach twisted like a wound spindle as the guard who had led them here stepped forward.

"Gamal, son of Bakri, awaits your judgment, my lord," he said.

Prince Nahid rested both hands on the carved arms of his chair and looked down at Gamal, who still knelt, head bent toward the shining mosaic tiles, his shoulders slumped. In that moment, Rahab wanted to rush forward and pull him into her arms and, for the second time that day, beg his forgiveness for believing Dabir's honeyed words. To assure her husband that she would never desert him, that things would work out.

But Dabir's glare held her shivering where she stood.

"Gamal, my friend." The prince's tone held surprising kindness. "Have you brought the records of your accounts?"

Gamal did not look up. "I am afraid, my lord, that my accounts are not in proper order. I need time—"

"You have had three years, Gamal. And my records show that your debt is clearly out of hand." The prince drummed the fingers of his left hand on the chair's arm.

"Forgive me, my lord, but I fear the injuries to my leg have affected my thinking. The daily pain . . . Sometimes the drink helps, sometimes it clouds my judgment." Gamal looked up then, and Rahab caught a glimpse of him wincing as he clutched his bad leg with one hand. Irritation pricked her. He was lying. Gamal rarely complained about the pain, and sometimes the limp barely showed. The only thing clouding his judgment was his own lack of common sense and arrogant pride.

"Your judgment is more than a little clouded, Gamal. You

owe the king's coffers nearly twenty years' worth of silver. Twenty years, Gamal. My life is not worth that much." Prince Nahid's heavy brows furrowed, and the grim set to his square jaw revealed age lines along the corners of his mouth. He was still young, probably in his late twenties, a handsome man.

Gamal rose up on one knee and boldly met the prince's gaze. "On the contrary, my prince. Your life is worth far more. Your father thought so when he offered me such generous gifts after the battle." The reminder of the king's reward was aimed precisely as Gamal intended, no doubt. But Rahab saw little warmth in the prince's eyes.

"I think your memory is also clouded, Gamal. For you have taken my father's generosity and spent far beyond your means. Your debt to the crown has gone beyond the reward for my life." He crossed his arms. Rahab held her breath, fearing to release it lest in doing so she lose what little grasp she still had on her self-control.

"Please, my lord, if you just give me more time . . ." Gamal's voice sounded thin and strained as it lapsed into silence.

"Time is not on your side, Gamal." The prince cleared his throat. "I am ordering the confiscation of all you own. You will be escorted to debtors' prison until we can find suitable buyers to take you or until you can work off your debt in the king's stone quarries. Your wife will be sold as well."

Rahab stuffed a fist to her mouth, unable to stifle a soft cry, but the sound went unheard as Gamal's cries rose above hers. He fell to the tile floor, face in his hands, weeping.

"Please, my lord, I beg you, do not hold this thing against your servant. If you will have mercy on me and cancel the debt, I promise I will make it up to you." His voice broke on a sob as guards stepped closer. They stopped at the prince's upraised hand. "Please, remember the kindness done to you by your servant, and if you will release me from this bond, I will never again mention the king's reward in your presence, nor consider myself worthy of anything else from your hand. Only please, have mercy on me!"

Rahab pulled the cloak tighter, clenching her jaw to keep it from trembling. Did the moon god hear the prayers of gamblers begging release from debts they owed? Or was it some other whose amulet she should have purchased who deserved her sacrifice? Her sister would know. Why hadn't she asked her long ago?

Bile rose in the back of her throat as she watched the prince stare down at her weeping husband. Why did he wait? What point was there to watching a man humiliate himself?

She grew faint as the full force of Prince Nahid's words hit her. What did it mean to be sold into slavery? What would she do? Who would purchase her? The images in her mind's eye were not pleasant.

My darling Rahab, you are much too beautiful to be a common harlot. Dabir's words mocked her now. If she were sold, no one would see her weaving skills worth nearly as much as her beauty.

She moved farther into the shadows, silently cursing the gods for making her desirous to men, suddenly wishing she could fly away like a bird and disappear where no one could find her.

"Stand up, Gamal."

The command snapped her thoughts to the prince once more.

Gamal rose slowly, using both hands to hold on to his bad leg to gain his balance. He stood and wiped his eyes, shoulders slumped, head bowed.

Silence descended in the hall as Prince Nahid sat, arms crossed, his gaze raking her husband. What was he doing now? Did the prince enjoy this game of torture?

"I will cancel your debt." He rested both hands on the arms of the chair. "See to it that you do not squander my mercy."

The room closed in on Rahab, the breath sucked from every pore as every man stood still, processing the prince's words. A moment later a gentle breeze returned, touching Rahab's cheeks, freeing her from the prison of her fear. Had she heard correctly?

Gamal's weeping returned, and he fell once more to his knees. "Thank you, my lord! You are the greatest of princes. May you live forever!"

"Help him up and take him home." Prince Nahid's lips twitched, but he did not smile, and Rahab did not miss the hint of skepticism in his eyes, nor the complete scowl on Dabir's square face.

Two guards stepped closer to Gamal and lifted him from the tiles, half carrying him toward the doors near where she waited. He met her gaze as they approached, his expression a mixture of relief and something she could not define. If she did not know better, she might think Gamal thought everything had turned out exactly as he'd planned.

3

Rahab stood at the bronze kettle set over the fire, dipping her spun thread into the red dye. She had spent yesterday with her sister, gathering poppies for the scarlet color, as she could not find enough crimson worms to produce the color in large amounts. Poppies weren't nearly as rich a shade, but the yellow anemones for the golden threads winding through the garments should add to the color's lack.

A sigh lifted her chest, and she tightened the scarf over her nose to mask the smell of the dye combined with the leftover scent of the retted, drying flax coming from the roof. Weaving had its happier moments, but these were not her favorites. Her only consolation came in knowing she could provide food for their table, to feed Gamal's belly, even if she could not console his moods. She watched him from the corner of her eye, a caged mountain goat, always butting his head where it didn't belong.

"I'm going out," he said after his third look into the pot that held the dye. He scrunched his face and whirled about, no sign of his limp, and stomped toward the gate. "I'll be back in time to break bread."

He slammed the gate and turned toward the center of town. Toward the gaming houses. Did this city never sleep? The seedier businesses stayed open long past the sun's setting and opened shortly after dawn. If a man wanted to drown his worries in barley beer or strong drink, they were more than happy to comply.

She turned from stirring the dye once more to step into the house, away from the sun's glaring heat. Gamal had known not a moment's peace in the week since the prince's pardon.

If he was not careful, he would ruin everything.

"Rahab?" She startled at the sound of Gamal's voice. Back so soon?

She hurried from the house to the courtyard and met him near the gate.

"Is something wrong, my lord?" She glanced at the bubbling dye and grabbed the stick to stir it once more.

He snatched his staff from where he had left it leaning against the wall. He couldn't very well pretend to limp without it.

"I need silver. Where did you put the coins you earned from your last sale of these things?" He pointed to the loom in the opposite corner, where a wide swath of cloth stood partially finished.

"I spent it on food and on flax to make more linen and baskets. I gave you the rest last month." As much as she would tell him of it.

His nostrils flared with thinly veiled anger. He walked into the house, stomping about, moving furniture, rummaging through their things. There was nothing left worth selling.

He had already bartered away their wedding gifts, and though he won a few gambling matches now and then, he would lose even more the next night, always digging his hole and theirs a little deeper.

Please, don't let him look under the mat. She had taken to offering silent prayers to the air around her. For though the moon god had apparently freed Gamal from the prince's anger, he had not changed Gamal. Her husband was as difficult as he'd ever been, all gratitude lost within the first day of his reprieve.

Gamal's curses reached her ears. She poked the wooden prong into the bubbling dye again and lifted the threads. Satisfied with the shade of crimson, she carefully pulled the dyed flaxen threads out of the simmering pot and placed them in a similar pot of tepid water to cool. The tapping of Gamal's staff stopped behind her.

"When will you be done with that? How soon until you can sell more of it?" His desperate tone revived the worry she had unsuccessfully laid aside. She lifted the last of the fiber into the cooling pot.

"Why do you need silver so badly, Gamal? Our debt is canceled and we have food to eat and a house to live in." She straightened, facing him. "We have each other. What more do we need?" She gentled her tone, but a chill worked through her at his suddenly charming smile.

He took a step closer and reached for her hand. "A man wants to provide well for his family." His gaze swept over her, and the flicker of sudden longing filled his gaze. He hadn't forgotten a man's need for sons, but the reminder only added to her ever-increasing guilt. "And this house is too small."

She stared at him, but words failed her. *She* had failed him.

To remind him that they did not need a bigger house for two people would be to remind him of her worthlessness.

He leaned close to her ear. "Did you not see the grand columns of the king's halls? Why can't a man like me, a man who saved the prince's life, be afforded similar pleasures? We deserve more, Rahab, and after I convinced Nahid to cancel the debt, I knew the gods were smiling on us again."

Cold fear shook Rahab, though the heat of the fire and warmth of the midday sun made beads of sweat break out on her forehead. She met Gamal's gaze, pulled her hand from his grasp, and wrapped her arms about her. "No . . . it isn't right." Her words, a mere whisper, were not lost on Gamal.

"Of course it's right." He took a step away from her, his glare piercing. "Why don't you ever believe in me, Rahab? No man always wins at the tables, but some have made enough to buy their wives jewels and build bigger houses on King's Row. I can finally do the same for you, and you throw it back in my face?" The pitch of his voice rose with his ire, every word punctuated.

She stole a look at him again, holding herself slightly away, afraid he would slap her. But he whirled about, slamming his staff against the stones as he walked toward the gate instead. "I will get the silver, Rahab, and make my fortune." He threw a look over his shoulder. "You'll see."

Rahab stumbled over to a nearby bench and sank down, huddling beneath the shelter of her own crossed arms and hooded veil. How could Gamal not see the dangerous end to his plans? Had Prince Nahid's mercy meant nothing at all to him?

She watched him pass through the gate, his curses lingering in his wake.

Tendaji hefted a sack of newly threshed wheat over his shoulder, forcing himself to be grateful for such an abundant harvest. Sweat from the afternoon's heat still glistened on his skin, and the weight of the sickle hung from his belt. But his mother would eat and that was good. *Please, let her eat.*

When she was gone, he would stop caring.

If only Kahiru had lived.

He fought the urge to shake his fist at the sky. The moon god did not care about a Nubian's grief. Most of the people of Jericho had little use for him or his family, especially since Kahiru had been lost in childbirth, taking their son with her. Kahiru, a Jericho-born Canaanite, had not cared about the color of Tendaji's dark skin. She had cared about him, had loved his family, especially his mother.

He swallowed the grief, hefting the sack to his other shoulder. She'd been so small, so beautiful. What had she ever seen in him, big brute that he was? He sighed at the memories, the harsh, blaming looks that followed her death. As if he had somehow caused it.

And now his mother had succumbed, had let the grief of too much loss fill her belly in place of food. Perhaps there was only so much pain a body could hold and still breathe.

He had seen too much pain.

Kahiru's face filled his mind's eye, though it did not linger. The memories were fading with each passing year . . . Their son would have been walking by now. And had he lived, Tendaji would have taken him often to the fields to learn to handle the bow and arrows. As all Nubian boys learned long before they truly became men.

He glanced at the half moon not yet fully visible in the fading sunlight and nearly spat in the moon's face. What good were prayers unanswered? What use a god who did not hear?

He rounded a bend leading to a small house on the farthest edge of town, struck by its crumbling mud-brick walls. Weariness made every muscle weak as he dumped the sack onto the cracked courtyard stones and sank onto the bench, wondering if it too would betray him and give way under his weight. A clay basin leaned against the wall, and tepid, brackish water sat in a cistern for him to wash his feet. He closed his eyes, imagining for the briefest moment what it would be like to have someone else care for his needs.

To have Kahiru back again.

A *hobble-clop* coming from the street drew him up short. He straightened and stood, turning away from the sound. No one would intentionally visit him here.

But the thumping clop of a limping man made him turn again toward the courtyard. "Gamal?" He blinked, certain he was mistaken.

"It is I, as you can see." He came closer and stopped.

"What brings you to my humble home, Gamal?" Wariness filled him. He had not seen Gamal since the war. Only his wife had come to pay her respects when Kahiru abandoned him to Sheol. "Won't you sit and take your rest?" His courtesy won over caution as he motioned to one of two benches that circled a cold hearth at the edge of the small court.

"I have not come to visit." Gamal's tone was hard, and the light from the setting sun bathed his face in shadow. Tendaji felt the skin on his neck prickle. Gamal was a friend. He relaxed his stance.

"Well then, how can I help you?" Had something happened

to Gamal's wife or another family member? Sudden empathy filled him. How well he could relate.

"I came to collect the silver you owe me. I need it now." Gamal's hand fisted around the staff he leaned against.

Tendaji heard movement inside the house and prayed his mother's caregiver would not take that moment to come outside to greet him. If his mother heard this commotion, she would worry, and she was already too frail.

"My earnings are few, Gamal, and I owe a debt to Mama's physicians and caregivers."

Gamal looked at Tendaji, his expression and the disdain it carried all too clear. "You owe a debt to me as well. A debt far older than the one you have now."

Tendaji took a step backward. "I don't have it. I'm sorry." He glanced at the sack of grain. "Do you need food? Is someone ill? If I can help you, I will."

Gamal seemed unfazed by Tendaji's offer. "I don't want your apologies. I want your silver." His deep voice dropped in pitch. Suddenly he lifted the staff and shoved it against Tendaji's chest, pushing him against the wall of the house. "You will give it to me now, or I'll take you to debtors' prison."

Tendaji grabbed the staff, trying to free it from jabbing his ribs, but Gamal had the leverage of surprise and only pushed the end of the staff harder. Tendaji had underestimated Gamal's strength.

"Please!" Pain shot through him, and he felt a rib crack. Anger, swift and fierce, choked him. What was wrong with the man? Tendaji tried again, this time forcing the staff from Gamal's grip.

But Gamal closed the distance, both hands coming around

Tendaji's throat. "Pay me what you owe!" His words were barely audible through gritted teeth.

Tendaji struggled to breathe, fighting to break Gamal's hold, but Gamal's whole body now fell against Tendaji, holding him against the wall. He fought for air, trying desperately to shift his weight to lift a knee and shove Gamal from him, when suddenly Gamal let go. Tendaji dragged in a breath, then another. Gamal stepped back a pace, and Tendaji bent forward, hands on his knees, straining for a breath deep enough to replace the air he'd lost.

But before he could get his bearings, Gamal's thick arm came around him, his hands tightening on both shoulders. He tried to drag Tendaji forward. Tendaji connected a fist to his jaw. Gamal reeled back, lost his balance. Tendaji scrambled free.

Gamal shot forward. Grabbed Tendaji's arm, wrenching him closer. "You are coming with me to the judges. If you will not pay me now, I *will* collect every coin from the overseers." The words hit Tendaji with the force of a punch. He did owe Gamal the money. He was in his rights to demand payment.

Tendaji stilled, ceasing his struggle. "Please, Gamal, if you send me to debtors' prison, there will be no one to care for my mother. Give me time."

"You have had three years. Your time is up." His big hand clamped down on Tendaji's arm, and in that moment Tendaji knew it would do him no good to fight. Mama would suffer if he killed the man, and where else could a fight lead?

"Can I say goodbye to my mother? Please?" He could almost hear her desperate weeping when he did not return.

"She'll hear about your whereabouts soon enough." Gamal

dragged him toward the gate, and this time Tendaji did not argue.

⁓⁓⁓⚜⁓⁓⁓

They neared the Hall of Justice, but the hour was already past for an audience with the financier. Gamal's pace grew quicker, and Tendaji's already exhausted legs could barely keep up. When they reached the guards at the prison, Gamal shoved Tendaji forward. He stumbled, and Gamal gave him another shove, pushing him to his knees.

"This man owes me a month's worth of silver and cannot pay it. I'm handing him over to you until he pays me in full."

Tendaji's stomach churned as fear sliced through him. He had not eaten in hours and would not likely see a meal in this dark place. And yet, suddenly he did not care. Except for his mother, it mattered little what happened to him. He could die in this place. Would that reunite him with Kahiru?

Rough arms grabbed Tendaji as the scribe at the guard's gate handed Gamal a clay tablet. "Come back tomorrow, and the magistrate will work out the terms of the man's sentence. You will be paid when he earns his keep."

"I'll be here."

Tendaji heard Gamal's heavy, limping footfalls recede behind him as the guards escorted him through the prison gates. When the guard shoved him into a windowless room and shut the door, his depression deepened. He felt his way along the dark walls. Finding no place to sit or sleep, he carefully sank to the dirt floor and buried his head in his hands. Perhaps he deserved this somehow.

He silently let out a string of curses on the moon, his father, Gamal, himself. And death for taking all he held dear.

4

Rahab ladled stew into a second clay bowl as she heard Gamal slam the door and whistle a welcoming tune. She had not heard the sound of his music in . . . she could not remember how long. A sense of relief filled her. He must have simply gone out to clear his mind, to realize what good fortune they had already received. She poked her head from the cooking room to the entryway.

"I held supper for you." She set the bowl on a low table and moved to retrieve a fresh loaf of flatbread.

Gamal sank down onto the wooden bench, one of the few pieces of furniture he had not sold, and took the bread from Rahab's hands. He ate in silence, and she waited, knowing him well enough to keep her questions to herself.

"Sit with me and eat," he commanded after requesting a second bowl.

She handed it to him, set her own bowl on the table, and took the bench opposite him. She dipped her bread into the stew and chewed slowly. The silence grew.

"Tomorrow I will have the silver I need," he said at last. He lifted a brow, his look holding challenge.

The relief she'd felt quickly vanished. She lowered her gaze in respect. "How is that, my lord?" She had not seen him take anything with him to sell. Perhaps he had found work, though at this hour she could not imagine who would hire him.

He reached across the table and lifted her chin to force her to look up, his smile unnerving. "I went to collect an old debt. The man couldn't pay, so I took him to debtors' prison." He leaned back and put his hands behind his head, obviously pleased with himself.

Rahab searched her mind for who could possibly owe Gamal money that he had not already claimed to feed his gambling habit. "Who?" she finally asked, setting the piece of flatbread she was about to eat onto the table, no longer hungry.

"Someone from my war days. It's been three years. If I counted interest, which I intend to do, he owes me a great deal more than he borrowed." Gamal took up the bread and dipped it once more into his stew, as if the conversation were a normal day's discussion. "So what did you do all day?"

Rahab stared at him. He did not intend to tell her? "I worked on dyeing linen, weeded the garden, and ground the grain for the bread." Her voice sounded as deflated as her hopes.

Gamal nodded, seeming not to notice. "Good. That's good." He chewed in continued silence.

Rahab worried her lower lip, drawing on courage she did not feel. "Are you speaking of Tendaji the Nubian, my lord?"

Gamal tensed, slowly lifting his head. "What if I am? It doesn't matter who, dear wife. Getting my hands on the silver is what matters. The magistrate will give me a down payment on the man's work, and I will continue to collect for at least a year. Maybe more."

Rahab's stomach grew queasy. She pressed a hand to her middle to still the feeling. By his lack of admission, she sensed Gamal's guilt, however insincere. He knew Tendaji still grieved the loss of his wife and son, if the rumors were true—and Cala was seldom wrong on town gossip. And now his mother was gravely ill. Surely Gamal knew.

"I told you, Rahab, our fortunes are changing. Things are going to be looking up from now on." He picked at a tooth with a fingernail, removing a piece of parsley that had lodged between two slightly crooked teeth.

"I hope so, my lord." She looked at him, but he did not meet her gaze, and she suddenly realized by his rigid posture that the subject was closed. Gamal did not care about the Nubian's grief. Gamal thought as little of the darker-skinned peoples as Prince Nahid did, whose disdain was well known. Rahab had never understood their prejudice but knew better, after years of Gamal's moods, than to say so.

But the thought of what her husband had done to the poor man sickened her already upset stomach. Was Gamal's memory so short that he could forget the prince's mercy toward him? How could he go and be so cruel to someone else in return?

Gamal wiped his mouth on a linen cloth and pushed the bench back. She rose with him and cleared his dish the moment he left the room. He avoided her gaze as he walked toward the bedchamber, his limp barely evident. He would not expect her to follow so soon and would probably be snoring by the time she put the food away. Though it was barely night, he would sleep, then rise and leave her for the gaming house, even without the silver he so craved.

The best thing she could do was to stay out of his way. But she also knew as she watched his retreating back that she could not let him do this to an innocent, grieving man, despite the color of his skin. She must find a way to help free Tendaji, whatever it cost her.

———✦———

After a restless night, Rahab slipped out of bed before dawn. She retrieved all of the silver and bronze she could spare from the jar beneath the mat and tucked them into a hidden pouch in her tunic, then set about mixing the wheat flour with oil and starter, setting it to rise. Her sister Cala should be awake soon, and Gamal would not miss her. He would sleep half the morning after the amount of beer he drank last night, and she had wondered when she awoke in the dark of night if a woman's perfume was not also among the many scents her husband carried. Had he been with another woman? A common harlot? Or someone he loved?

An involuntary shiver shook her as she pulled the iron kettle from the fire and set herbs in a clay cup to brew into a strong, dark tea. She had no room to condemn Gamal when the fingers pointing back at her carried the memory of Dabir. They were a sad pair, she and Gamal, each pretending to care for the other.

When had her love for Gamal waned?

She stilled at the sound of palm fronds blowing in the early morning breeze outside their window. Tendaji's cell likely had no window, and her husband slept in the next room, not caring for the condition of the man. How could Gamal do such a thing to a friend? And what would happen if Dabir heard of Gamal's actions?

Guilt filled her as she glanced at the sky. To even think of Dabir felt like betrayal. A loyal wife would not have slept with another man. Though why she thought so, she did not know. Everyone in Jericho could tell tales of unfaithfulness, and they were told with pride, not shame. Why then did she feel such guilt?

Dabir could help Tendaji. The thought tickled the edges of her mind, and for a fleeting moment, she toyed with the idea of going to see Dabir rather than Cala. But Dabir might not appreciate the assumption that she expected favors from him now. He despised Gamal. And she was not so hateful as to see her husband sold into slavery as a result of her loose tongue.

The brewed tea tasted bitter, but she let it rest on her tongue before swallowing, then set the cup on the wooden shelf near the clay oven, grabbed her cloak, and left the house.

The early light of dawn cast pink shadows over Cala's home, and birds chirped their greeting at Rahab's approach. A low fire glowed in the main courtyard where Cala already had a kettle of water set to boil, though there was no sign of Cala herself. Rahab opened the gate, cringing at the squeak, hoping the noise would not wake Tzadok. She stepped through and held the gate, moved it slowly back into place, then took a seat on one of the stone benches and waited. Cala came from the cooking room, carrying two jars.

Rahab stood. "I need to talk to you." She took one of the jars from Cala and carried it to the bench.

"You're up early." Cala settled her pregnant body onto the opposite bench. An iron griddle sat on its prongs near the fire, and she pulled it to her to set about grilling flatbread. "Pour some of that here."

Rahab obeyed, half grateful for someone to tell her what to do, then set the jar in its niche in the stones. "Gamal has done something . . ." She stopped. Dare she tell even Cala?

"Has he hurt you again?" Cala's round brown eyes filled with concern.

Rahab looked away, touched a hand to the cheek that still held tinges of purple. "No. He didn't hurt me." She swallowed, then glanced around, assuring herself they were alone. "Gamal took Tendaji to debtors' prison last night."

Cala's eyes grew wide. "The Nubian?"

Rahab nodded. "The one who befriended Gamal after he was first injured during the war. But then Tendaji's father died, and he was the one who needed help. So Gamal loaned him some silver. He wasn't gambling as heavily in those days." She glanced beyond Cala toward the house and sighed with relief when she saw no sign of Cala's husband.

"Tendaji lost more than his father, if the gossips are right," Cala said. They shared a knowing look. "So what happened? Gamal threw Tendaji into prison . . ." Cala's hands had stilled from mixing the wheat and oil.

"Let me do that." Rahab's own hands suddenly needed a task, and Cala readily handed her the bowl.

"Did Gamal ask him to repay the debt?"

Rahab squeezed the dough between both hands. "Yes. Gamal has it in his head that his luck has turned and all he needs is some silver to make our fortune. How can he not see that the cancellation of our debt was an amazing mercy on the part of the prince? Why does he seek to put us right back where we were?" She blinked at the sudden moisture in her eyes and looked at her sister. "Is there something wrong with me that he is not content to live as normal men? Why must he always risk all we have? And now this!"

Cala rubbed a hand over the place where the babe grew within her, her look thoughtful. "It's not your fault, Rahab. You did not choose Gamal, and you could not know how such recognition after the war would change him. But you are not the reason Gamal gambles or takes such risks. And nothing you can do will change him."

"If I had borne him a son, he would not take such risks." She ripped a piece of the dough from the mass and stretched it flat. When it baked, it would puff into soft bread, the kind Gamal preferred.

"Even a son would not make Gamal into a caring husband and father. A good man is good without a reason." Cala touched her arm, her gaze emphatic and kind. "You know this, Rahab. Do not let him make you feel worth nothing."

Rahab nodded, pushing her guilt aside. "You are right. If Gamal was a good man, Tendaji would be in the fields this morning and caring for his mother this night."

Cala drew in a breath. "What can we do? How will he care for her from prison?"

Rahab shook her head. "I do not know. But someone needs to go to the magistrate and seek Tendaji's release." She touched the place at her side where the precious metals lay hidden in the pocket of her tunic. "I've brought some silver and bronze . . . Perhaps I can pay for Tendaji's release."

Cala frowned, stretching her dough into a flat circle. "You cannot do such a thing. Why not just give Gamal the silver yourself then?"

"Gamal would still demand what is owed from Tendaji.

He would not need to know where this came from. But if I go . . . I don't know if they will do as I ask."

Cala's thoughtful gaze traveled to the house behind her. "Tzadok could go. If you give me the coins, he could see to Tendaji's redemption. But that may not be enough. Now that Tendaji is there, even silver will not get him out unless Gamal forgives the debt."

"Maybe Tzadok could talk to Gamal." Rahab's hopes were quickly waning.

Cala laughed, but the sound carried no mirth. "Don't take this wrong, dear sister, but Tzadok hates Gamal. Besides, you know Gamal won't listen." She tossed her dough onto the griddle and placed it over the fire. "The only thing to do is to go to the magistrate and tell him what Gamal has done. Tell him Tendaji was imprisoned without cause."

"But Gamal did have a cause, at least in the eyes of the law."

"Not a good one."

"Since when is owing someone silver not a good cause to go to debtors' prison?"

"Since when is debtors' prison ever good? Why are you suddenly defending him?"

Defeated, Rahab sighed.

"I'm sorry." Cala touched Rahab's arm.

"No, you're right." Her stomach twisted into an uncomfortable knot. "I thought Prince Nahid would surely send Gamal to that place just a few days ago. But he forgave the debt."

"Something Gamal should be celebrating by going out to find real work." Cala clucked her tongue, reminding Rahab of their mother's habit.

"He claims to try." Rahab handed Cala the bowl with the remaining dough ready to bake. "I'd better go."

"What are you going to do?"

Rahab stood, brushing the dust of the flour from her cloak. "I don't know."

"Can I tell Tzadok? Do you want him to take the coins to the magistrate?"

Rahab weighed the request but a moment, then shrugged. She didn't care what Cala or anyone else did anymore. She could not fix her husband's bad choices or change his personality. But she did not have to like it.

"Tell Tzadok what you want," Rahab said. "As for the coins, let me think on it." She trusted her sister, but she wasn't so sure she trusted Tzadok. "I'm going to check on Tendaji's mother and do what I can."

"Here, take this." Cala placed the unbaked loaves in a clay bowl and handed them to Rahab. "Let me know if his mother needs more."

Rahab took the bowl, hoping Tendaji's mother had fuel for a fire, then turned to leave. She glanced at the sky. Gamal would still be in bed. She had time if she hurried.

By the time Rahab reached the opposite end of town, the sun had fully risen, and with it a crowd had formed in the streets. She ducked her head, avoiding the scrutinizing looks of men on their way to the fish market. Tendaji lived in the poorer, smellier section of town, and Rahab held an edge of the cloak to her nose as she drew closer. She made a few discreet inquiries, asking which house belonged to the Nubian, and soon stood at the gate, despairing to find the house in such disrepair. Could Gamal not see the man was poor? Disgust ripped through her again, and she had to tell herself to unclench her fists, breathe slowly, and deal with Gamal later.

She walked through the gate that stood slightly ajar, scanning the courtyard. A sack of grain stood near a crumbling bench and a cracked cistern of tepid, insect-covered water. Near one wall a large staff lay forgotten. Rahab stepped closer, recognizing the carvings. Gamal would never have left his staff behind without a reason. He prized this gift from the king, and Rahab often wondered why he hadn't sold it off long ago. She picked it up, turning it in her hands. Gamal and Tendaji must have scuffled for him to drop it. How had Gamal overpowered the stronger, younger Nubian?

She set the staff on the bench and walked carefully over broken stones to the door. She knocked twice and waited. Footsteps came from beyond the door, then stopped.

"Who is it?" A woman's voice sounded thin and frightened.

"I am a friend of Tendaji's. Is his mother all right?"

The door opened a crack and the daylight illumined the woman, who looked to be a little older than Rahab.

"Forgive me. I do not mean to intrude." Rahab handed the woman the bowl. "They aren't baked yet, but they are fresh."

The woman peeked into the bowl with a skeptical, curious eye, then, seemingly satisfied, took it from Rahab's hands. "Let me put these on to bake so you can take your bowl with you." She moved into the room and looked over her shoulder. "Come in."

Rahab followed her into the cooking room. The house was dark with some of the rooms still shuttered, but the small room where the woman led her held welcome morning light.

"How is Tendaji's mother?" Rahab stopped at the

threshold, suddenly wanting to leave. If Gamal found out she had come . . .

"She was frantic last night after what happened, as you can imagine! I had to coax her to drink some herbs to finally get her to sleep." The woman looked at Rahab. "She's dying, you know. But I fear if her son is kept in prison, she will die far sooner than she would have. He is all she has."

Rahab nodded, unable to speak past a lump forming in her throat. "I am very sorry this happened."

The woman's eyes narrowed, and she drew closer to Rahab. "Who did you say you were again?"

"A friend of Tendaji's. My husband and I have known Tendaji for many years. We should have done more to help him."

The woman looked her up and down, then turned back to her work, placing the loaves on the griddle set above a low fire. Rahab should have baked the loaves before she came. Was everything Tendaji owned falling apart?

A swift desire to flee this place came over her. How could she look at Gamal after this? "I should go." She tamped down her rising panic, hoping her voice sounded calm.

"You do not wish to wait to eat these with us?" The woman met Rahab's gaze. "It was kind of you to bring them."

"No, thank you. I can't." She backed from the room, then turned about, heading to the door.

"You forgot your bowl."

Rahab stopped. Cala wouldn't miss it, and Tendaji's mother could use something newer. "Keep it." She hurried through the door to the courtyard, catching sight of Gamal's staff as she walked. She paused, looking down on it. Maybe the caregiver could sell it and use the coins to help get Tendaji out of prison. But could she trust this woman to do right by Tendaji?

Snatching it up, she hurried through the gate. She would take it to her sister and let Tzadok sell it to help pay Tendaji's debt. That, added to the coins in her pouch, should come close to reaching the redemption fee. Gamal would miss his prize, but he did not deserve to keep it!

5

Cala greeted her at the gate as if she'd been waiting for her.

"I'm sorry, I left your bowl with them. They had nothing and—"

Cala held up a hand. "Forget it. Just come inside." She gripped Rahab's wrist to tug her forward, but Rahab gently broke her hold.

"I can't. Gamal will surely be up by now, and he will wonder where I am."

Cala shook her head. "No he won't." She looked beyond Rahab toward the street.

"Why not?" She followed Cala's gaze. "Are you expecting someone?"

Cala reached for her wrist again, her grip firmer this time. The look in her eyes sent a shiver through Rahab. "What happened?"

"You need to come in and sit down."

Rahab numbly obeyed. The walk to Tendaji's house had taken longer than she thought, but the sun was not even halfway to the midpoint yet. She could not have been gone long. What could have possibly happened in such a short time?

She walked with Cala into the sitting room, and Cala shut the door. "You'll be safe here."

"Safe?" Fear shot through her. "What are you talking about?"

Cala motioned to a pair of cushions and took a seat beside her. She clasped Rahab's hand in her own. "Tzadok heard what you said."

Rahab frowned. "I told you that you could tell him. So?"

Cala looked briefly away. "So I told him . . . and it made him so angry I thought he would burst something inside of him." She released Rahab's hand and tucked a strand of light brown hair behind one ear. "You know Tzadok hates Gamal, but worse, he likes Tendaji. He just kept pacing and saying Gamal's actions were unconscionable."

"They are," Rahab whispered, the memories of Tendaji's home singeing her conscience.

"Tzadok is a man of action. You know this." Cala looked away as though the truth about her husband shamed her. "I asked him what we should do, thinking he could go privately to the authorities. But Tzadok, he . . ."

"He what? Just tell me, Cala." Rahab felt her fear and impatience rising with each beat of her heart.

"He went immediately to the authorities, telling some of his friends along the way. By the time he got to see the magistrate, a large crowd was with him. The chief financier, Dabir, listened to Tzadok, and, well . . ." She glanced toward the door. "He just left here a few minutes ago after coming to warn me. The king's guards are at your house now, apprehending Gamal."

Rahab touched her trembling lips. Her mind whirled with images of her husband weeping before the prince, of Dabir's scowl as he watched. They would not have mercy on him a second time.

"I must go to him." She slowly rose, holding her sister's gaze.

"You can't. Please, Rahab." She put a hand to her back and pushed up from the cushion. "If they punish Gamal, they could come for you too. Tzadok will tell us what happens. Please, wait with me." Her pleading tone made Rahab waver.

"I shouldn't have told you." She looked at Cala's stricken face. "Why didn't Tzadok work this out quietly?"

"He told me it would not have mattered. Once he told Dabir, the thing Gamal has done would not remain quiet. You know this. He sees the way Gamal treats you, Rahab. Tzadok is not without feeling. He is doing this to protect you."

"He can't protect me, Cala. Dabir knows where we live, where you live. He knows everything about this kingdom. And if he knows, the prince does too." Memories of the night Dabir had wooed her filled her mind. The familiar guilt quickened her heart, but in the next moment a thought kindled. Perhaps Dabir could be convinced to release Tendaji and Gamal . . . if she gave him something of value in return.

"I have to go. There may be something I can do." She released a shaky breath, knowing full well that she was walking toward all that she despised.

Cala gripped her arm once more, clinging to her. "Please, listen to me, Rahab. Nothing good will come of you going."

"I have to know. I have to see for myself." She paused, meeting Cala's gaze. "If you would support me, come with me. Together we will be safe."

"We will be safer in the house."

"No place is truly safe." She held out a hand. "Come. Let us see what is to become of my husband."

~⚜~

Dabir stood near Prince Nahid's cushioned chair while the prince paced the length of the antechamber outside of the audience chamber in the Hall of Justice. That the prince was angry and irritated worked well with Dabir's goals, but he did not tell him so. Time enough to unveil his plans. Now was the time to appease and to convince the prince to undo the mercy he had shown Gamal last week. What a travesty that had been!

Dabir clenched his hands into fists behind his back, telling himself at the same time to calm. One wrong word could tip the prince's decision in the wrong direction, costing more loss to the throne and, most importantly, costing him more than his weight in fine gold.

"The crowds are growing restless, my prince. Shall I bring in the ungrateful wretch?" Dabir unclasped his hands, crossing them instead over his chest in a relaxed pose. He hid a smile when Nahid slowed his pacing and collapsed into his chair.

"I canceled his debt, Dabir. I showed Gamal more mercy than any man in this kingdom, and he repays me by throwing another man in prison for a much smaller sum? How could he do this to me? He's made me look like a fool."

"Nay, not at all, my prince. Gamal's actions only make him look foolish and worthless, not you. If you hang the man and release the prisoner, you will be a hero to your people." And grow richer taking all that belonged to Gamal

59

in the process. But Nahid would care more about his image than his coffers.

"I cannot hang Gamal." He stood again, walked to a window, and pushed the curtain aside to peer into the outer court. "The crowd keeps growing. I have to do something or we will have a riot to contend with."

Dabir moved a step closer to the prince, still keeping a distance. "Then you must do something to appease them. If you will not hang Gamal, then send him to the torturers until he pays the last amount." Nahid did not answer, but Dabir recognized this as his way of thinking, of deciding his best course of action. "Assyria is said to have perfected the art of torture."

"I cannot send him to such torturers." The prince turned on him. "The man saved my life!"

"Then sell him to the wealthy merchants of Syria who frequent our town. You would never have to see him again, and they would pay a high price for one so large and young."

"Gamal limps in pain. What good would he be to them?"

"I believe, my lord, that Gamal does not hurt nearly as much as he claims."

The prince held his gaze, assessing. "You think he lied to me?"

"Without doubt, my lord."

The prince turned to gaze again at the crowd. "I will sell him at auction to the highest bidder. What the Syrians do with him is of no concern to me."

Dabir nodded. "A wise choice, my lord." He paused for effect. "Might I add that you should consider that to gain the full benefit from the man, you must sell his wife and all that he has, as you would have done if you had not canceled his debt."

The prince let the curtain fall closed and slowly turned to face Dabir. He stroked a hand over his clean-shaven chin. "You are right as usual, Dabir." He straightened his back and walked with purposeful strides to the door of the audience chamber.

Dabir stepped forward. "My lord, if I may." He waited as the prince turned.

"What is it?" He looked slightly irritated, but not impatient.

"I would like to buy Gamal's wife."

Nahid lifted a brow but said nothing.

"She and I . . . that is, I will be glad to pay her part to cover Gamal's expenses, if she is willing to please me."

Nahid courted a slow smile. "I underestimated you, Dabir. I would have not thought you capable of such . . . delightful unfaithfulness."

Dabir took a step back and touched his temple. "I would not have thought so myself, but Rahab is . . ."

"Very beautiful?"

Dabir nodded and Nahid laughed. "Have Gamal brought to me now. Soon you shall have your little mistress."

Men and women spread into the crowded streets, making it impossible to reach the steps of the Hall of Justice. Shouts erupted from all sides, and Rahab strained to understand the words.

"What are they saying?" Cala had a tight grasp of Rahab's arm and leaned toward her ear to be heard.

Rahab tilted her head to listen and drew Cala closer as they weaved through a group of women, excusing themselves as they went.

"Free the Nubian! Death to the betrayer!" Others picked up the shouts until they grew to a full chant. The betrayer could only be Gamal. Rahab's stomach twisted in dread.

She pushed her way closer, dragging Cala behind her until at last she found a spot near the bottom of the steps where the overhanging roof created a swatch of shade. The chanting nearly drowned out all ability to hear, but one look at Cala told her what her sister was thinking. If Gamal were brought out to face this mob of accusers, they would hang him on the spot.

She moved like an unseeing one, vaguely aware of Cala still clutching her arm.

"Where are you going?" Cala hissed in her ear.

Rahab scanned the street, watching the mouths move, but their voices could not penetrate the fog that had suddenly blanketed her.

"Rahab! Listen to me! We shouldn't be here." Cala's frantic tone and the pain of her nails digging into Rahab's arm got her attention.

"What?" She shook herself, but the detached feeling would not leave. She faced her sister. "I have to get to Dabir. I can't let them do this to Gamal."

Cala looked aghast. "You can't." She tightened her grip, though Rahab tried to shake free. "Rahab, you aren't thinking clearly. If you go to Dabir, they will capture you. Do you honestly think even he will listen to you? You are a poor wife of a worthless man. And what if they order Gamal's death? Do you think you will go unscathed?" Cala tugged her away from the steps, but Rahab held her ground.

"I have to, Cala. Dabir and I . . . that is . . ." She stopped, heat creeping up her neck. She was nothing to Dabir.

"You think because you spent one night with the man he owes you something?"

Rahab darted glances around them and leaned closer. "I never told you that."

"Yes, you did."

Rahab searched her mind. "I don't recall it."

"Perhaps I heard it at the well. You can be sure Dabir spoke of it or Gamal heard it. There are no secrets in this walled town." Cala touched her middle, and Rahab suddenly realized she should not have brought her here.

"Go home, Cala. You should not have come." The chanting of the crowd grew to a deafening roar. Surely the prince would do something to stop them before a riot broke out.

"I'm not leaving you," Cala shouted above the din.

Rahab wove them closer to the raised porch where the prince or the king often conducted final judgments. She glanced at the blocked double doors to the Hall of Justice and the guards flanking the surrounding portico. She would never reach Dabir now. But she pulled them closer to the porch, where at last trumpets sounded and flag bearers preceded the prince, Dabir at his right hand.

Behind them, guards lifted the arms of a prisoner whose robe had been stripped from him, his arms and feet shackled with heavy chains. Rahab barely recognized him with his long hair now shaven and his beard gone. The chanting ceased.

"Gamal, son of Bakri, why did you despise my mercy and do this thing?" Prince Nahid's tone held no warmth, and Dabir's expression no pity.

Rahab's stomach churned with worry too deep for words.

"It is no longer in my power to spare you, Gamal. As you have no defense for your actions and I am loath to demand your death, I order you to be sold at auction to the highest bidder, along with your wife and all that you have. Take him to debtors' prison to await his outcome."

Cheers erupted from the crowd as guards surrounded Gamal and lifted him from the floor. There was no time for apologies or goodbyes.

Cala slipped an arm around Rahab's waist as if to hold her up. "We must go." She tugged again when Rahab did not respond.

Cala shoved past and around shouting men and dancing women, until at last they broke free of the city's town square. Cala stopped at last on a quieter street in the shade of a date palm, one of many lining Jericho's boulevards. She released her grip on Rahab's arm and put both hands on her knees, drawing breath.

"We shouldn't have come," Rahab said, though her voice seemed oddly unlike her own. "I should have listened to you."

Cala straightened. "It is better to know than to wonder. No matter how bad the outcome."

Rahab nodded. "They will come for me soon. Dabir will make sure of it." The memory of his pitiless frown would not abate, blocking every good feeling she had known for the man.

"Then we will hide you from them."

Rahab stared at her. "There is no place Dabir's arm does not reach."

Exhaustion lined Cala's face, and Rahab suddenly realized it was her sister who needed to hide, to rest.

"Come. Before I do anything else, I am taking you home."

6

"We can't let them take her." Cala spoke, arms crossed, before her husband and Rahab's father and brothers. Rahab stood in the shadows with her mother's arms pressed tight around her waist as though she would never release her. "It's not her fault that Gamal ruined her life. She tried to stop him!"

"What do you expect us to do, woman? We can't stop the prince's edict. She will be sold along with Gamal." Tzadok glanced Rahab's way but looked quickly beyond her, his guilt evident. If he had kept his mouth shut, Gamal would not have been taken into custody.

"Gamal has brought ruin on his mother and father, his wife, and all of us." Her father Sadid's quiet words caused even the birds to still their chirping outside of the window of her sister's house, where everyone had gathered.

Tzadok turned to face Rahab's father, his bearing tall and proud. "Gamal's debt is his own. They can't force it upon any of us."

"How foolish you are, my son, to think the king and his son

incapable of anything. They can do whatever they please."
Her father straightened, the lines of his face drawn into
deep grooves, revealing a lifetime of work and worry. Rahab
couldn't bear to see him suffer so on her account.

She squeezed her mother's shoulders, then extracted herself
from the woman's frightened grip and came to kneel at her
father's side. "Abba, do not fear for yourselves because of me.
I will speak to Dabir and offer him whatever he wishes to
keep you out of it." She patted his knee and smiled, despite
the look of doubt that still lingered in his eyes.

She stood and faced her brothers. "I will do all I can to
protect you." Dabir's scowl flashed in her mind's eye once
more, and one glance at Cala told her they both doubted her
ability to do as she'd promised.

"When are they auctioning Gamal?" This from her brother
Hazim.

"At dawn." Rahab glanced at the window. The sun edged
near its setting place, its orange glow like a brilliant gem.
Perhaps she could reach Dabir even yet tonight.

"We must hide you, Rahab. Our men can keep you safe."
Adara's innocent voice spoke as she quietly emerged from
the shadows. She looked to their father. "Please, Abba, do
something to help Rahab. This is not her fault."

Rahab glimpsed the quick flash of memory in her father's
gaze, the look of guilt he still bore. After Gamal had grown
distant, even hostile, toward her family, her father had re-
gretted his choice of husband for her. Though he had never
voiced his thoughts, she knew it in every unguarded moment
when Gamal was in his presence.

She walked to Adara's side and touched her arm. "Little
one, do not fret so. I can take care of myself."

"You are a woman! No woman is safe alone." Adara straightened, revealing the beginning curves of one grown. What would the crown do to her sister if Rahab did not stop them? They must not even know of her existence.

"I am a woman of age, dear Adara. When you marry, you will understand." She touched her sister's shoulders and looked into her eyes. "You must keep quiet about Gamal. Do not tell anyone that you even know him."

"But they already know." Her wide eyes showed increasing fear.

"They will forget." She bent to kiss Adara's forehead. "Promise me."

Adara nodded, but she did not look convinced.

"Rahab is right," their father said. "She knows how to handle difficult men." His gaze met Rahab's in an understanding look of acceptance. "I am simply sorry she has had to learn to do so."

She knelt at his side and again touched his knee. "So you will let me go to Dabir?"

"I have no doubt he will find you whether you go to him or not."

Rahab nodded. "Which is why I will go home now and wait for them to come. If they come here, none of you will be safe." She stood, straightened her cloak, then bent to kiss her father's cheek. As she turned, she felt herself swept into her mother's clinging embrace. A soft whimper escaped her mother's lips, but a moment later she released her with a worried sigh.

Cala came to her next, then Adara, then her sisters-in-law, each quietly weeping, forcing Rahab to blink away the emotion that threatened them all. Even her brothers, Hazim,

Azad, and Jaul, and her brother-in-law Tzadok touched her shoulder in a parting gesture.

She stayed in the shadows as she made her way by the moon's light to her home. No lamp greeted her as she entered her court, and dusk cast eerie shadows over the stones. The door creaked on its leather hinges, and a sense of dread swept through her as she entered the dark interior alone. She had rarely stayed away from home so late, and if she did, Gamal had always accompanied her. Memories of their early years filled her, of days when Gamal had carried her laughing over the threshold, kissing her face, her neck, both of them slightly drunk with too much wine. Tears sprang to her eyes as she stumbled over the rug Gamal had probably kicked when they arrested him.

She clutched the wall and moved slowly until she found one of the cushions in their sitting room and sank onto it. How long until they came for her? She tilted her head to listen, bristling at every footstep that moved past her house.

Darkness fell over the room, and no more than a sliver of moon rose to offer light through the narrow windows. She forced her weighted limbs to rise and walked to the cooking room. Rummaging for a piece of dry bread left over from the morning's repast, she realized she was not hungry and could not eat it even if she wanted to. If only she could run away.

The thought brought the slightest ray of hope as she considered and discarded a number of ways she could disguise herself and sneak out of the city. She could use the coins still tucked into her belt to bribe the guards to let her through. But the memory of her father's worried frown stopped her short. If they could not find her, her family would suffer. She would not allow that.

Exhaustion overwhelmed her. She dragged herself to the bed she had shared with Gamal and flung herself among the covers, longing to weep, but longing more to sleep, to forget.

Hours later—for she must have fallen into a fitful sleep—sharp stomping carried to her through the shuttered window, and her heart skipped a beat at the staccato rap of a fist against her front door. She sat up, her head spinning from grogginess and hunger.

She pressed a hand to her middle and forced her shaky legs to stand. Her cloak still wrapped about her, she cinched it tighter, then drew in a calming breath and opened the door.

The king's guards stood in her courtyard, armed with clubs and swords as if she were a common criminal.

"What can I do for you?" Rahab lifted her chin, though her voice shook.

"We seek Rahab, wife of Gamal." The guard who spoke seemed incredibly young to Rahab, though she herself was only twenty.

Rahab swallowed a distasteful retort. "I am Rahab." She would not allow them to see her fear.

"Wife of Gamal?"

She nodded. She suddenly had no desire to make this easy on them.

"You are to come with us. Now." The guard's commanding tone sounded older than his years.

She glanced into the dark house behind her, wondering if she would see it again. She should have rescued the rest of the silver from the floor and given it to her sister to keep for her. But there was no use worrying about such things now beyond her control.

"Come. No need to gather anything. Your belongings are the king's property now, and he will dispense of them." Guards approached her, one on either side, and clutched her upper arms.

She attempted to free herself. "There is no need to force me. I'm coming." But they did not release their grip.

The street was dark save for a few torches in neighboring courtyards and the lone torch carried by one of the guards leading the way. She was dragged, barely able to keep up with their marching feet, back to the very place she had been with Cala that morning. The Hall of Justice.

⚜

Rahab turned on the narrow cot in the dank cell. She had not realized the Hall of Justice had such rooms beneath its surface until the guards locked her away in one. The single torch that stood in the hall outside the stone gate flickered, casting the barest of shadows along the dirt floor. A mouse gnawed something in a corner of the room, and Rahab pulled her feet beneath her robe, barely daring to touch anything. She did not normally fear the insects or night sounds, but to be underground in the dark . . . She shivered, clinging to her cloak, grateful they let her keep it. Why had they not listened and taken her to Dabir?

She slept fitfully and jumped at approaching footsteps. A guard unlocked the door to her prison. "Come," he said, his bark sounding unnaturally loud in the enclosed hall. Rahab jumped up and followed close behind, praying with every step that he would not stop.

Dawn nearly blinded her as they reached the surface and stepped into the public courtyard of the government buildings. A wooden platform had been raised in the center of the court, and men dressed in fine clothes from Jericho and abroad, merchants in colors she did not recognize, filled the area around the platform.

Guards entered the court from the area of the debtors' prison, leading a group of scraggly prisoners. Rahab squinted, searching. There. Her pulse jumped in recognition. Gamal followed near the end, head hanging in humiliation. She looked away, ashamed at what he had become, furious with what he had done to them, to her family. She clenched and unclenched her fists, barely reining in her rage. If he were near, she would claw his face with her nails and spit at his feet.

She drew in a breath, telling herself to calm, and searched the crowd for Tendaji, grateful when no sign of the black man appeared. Perhaps they had freed him to care for his mother. She took some small comfort in that hope.

The crowds grew as the guards led her to a holding area near the platform. She was not bound as Gamal was and glanced briefly about her, wondering if she could slip past the guards and get lost in the crowd. But one eyed her too closely and seemed to find his only concern to be her safety. There was no escape from this indignity.

"How much will you give for this one?" the auctioneer shouted to the crowd, pointing to a gaunt-looking man old enough to be her grandfather if he had lived. "Come now, he's stronger than he looks." The man laughed and slapped the slave's bare shoulder.

The bidding ended quickly for one so useless, and the rest of the line of men paraded before the onlookers. When

Gamal's turn came, Rahab could not take her eyes from him, willing him to look her way. But his gaze remained downcast as Syrian merchants circled him, poking, prodding.

"Thirty pieces of silver for this one." The Syrian's offer was generous, though it did not even come close to covering Gamal's debt to Prince Nahid.

Rahab stood stiff, her heart beating with the kind of dread that turned her limbs to water. She could not do this.

She turned to the guard standing nearest her as Gamal was led away in chains with the Syrian merchant, not once looking to see if she stood near enough to watch. "Please," she said to the guard, "I must speak to the king's advisor, Dabir. He is a personal friend."

"Your husband was a personal friend to the prince and that made no difference, miss. I'm afraid Dabir is not available to speak to you."

"Has anyone spoken to him to ask?" She could not give up so easily. She offered the guard her most beguiling smile. "Just a moment of his time is all I ask."

The guard hesitated. "Look, miss, I'm just telling you what I was told. Dabir said to bring you here. He is speaking to your father and brothers even now."

Alarm shot through her. Nothing good would come of such a meeting. "All the more reason I need to see him."

The guard shook his head. "Dabir gave strict orders. You are to be sold to the highest bidder." He took her arm as the auctioneer called for the female slaves. "Come on then. Looks like it's your turn."

Rahab blinked back tears as she allowed the guard to lead her onto the platform. Half-naked women stood in a row, their eyes vacant as though death had already claimed them. Perhaps in slavery it already had.

Rahab cinched her robe tighter, praying to every god she could imagine to allow her to keep her clothing and her dignity.

Dabir sat behind a large oak table, his high seat giving him the ability to look down on those who stood before him—this time Rahab's father and brothers. He fingered his close-cropped beard and narrowed his eyes as he looked them over. The father seemed worried. Good. The brothers, wary. Also good.

Dabir cleared his throat. "As you are aware," he said, addressing Rahab's father, "your son-in-law Gamal has incurred an enormous debt to the crown, and when that debt was forgiven, he scorned the prince's mercy and did not turn from his wayward scheming." He paused, allowing his words to sink in, watching the men shift from foot to foot. Impatient. Afraid. He hid a smile.

"Unfortunately, even his sale to Syrian merchants has brought in only a small portion to cover his debt. And his wife did not fare much better." He ran his tongue over his moist lips, then took a drink from the wine cup next to him. "Therefore"—he wiped his mouth with the back of his hand—"the rest of Gamal's debt will be divided between his parents and each of you until it is paid in full. You may still work your farms or businesses or whatever it is you do, but a portion will be paid monthly to the king in addition to your taxes."

He leaned back in his chair, taking in their surprised, horrified looks. Would they protest? But after a moment of silence, he added, "Be grateful you and all you own are not immediately sold to cover this man's debt. And next time, I would make very sure your daughters do not marry fools."

Rahab's father merely nodded, though the weight of Dabir's words seemed too heavy for him to carry through the door. Had he made the penalty too harsh? Should he have told them that once Rahab belonged to him, the debt would easily be paid? She was worth the price of untold rubies in his mind.

But as he watched them walk silently from his office, he allowed himself a small smile. No, keeping them under his thumb was better than leaving them alone. It would ensure Rahab's submission to his plan to keep her as his mistress . . . and so much more.

He stood abruptly at the thought. Rahab should be on the auction block by now, and his servant had better not mess up the bidding. He could not afford to have her sold to someone else. She was his, no matter what it cost him.

7

Vulgar comments and the shouts of the bidders filled Rahab's ears, despite her desperate attempts to block them. She shivered, grasping for her cloak that was not there. They had nearly ripped it from her, though the guard who seemed to be her constant shadow had not allowed them to take her tunic. She told herself she should be grateful for this kindness, except for the deep hatred, the anger that swelled within her against Gamal, against Dabir. She should not be here. This was not her fault.

The last calls for more silver stopped, and a cheer erupted from a man she did not recognize. The guard who flanked her returned her cloak and took her to a man whose close-shaven beard and make of clothing set him apart as one of Jericho, a servant of some high rank.

"You purchased me for your master, is that it?" she asked as the man led her from the crowd, through the back alleys toward the king's palace.

"You will find out soon enough." The man continued on at a hurried pace, until she recognized familiar halls, the very halls that led to the chambers of the king's advisor. Could it be?

Her heart kicked over with a mixture of dread and hope. When they stopped at one of the chamber doors, she saw the markings of the king's advisor carved into the wooden plaque that hung by leather straps to the right of the entrance. The door opened, and the servant stepped back, allowing her to precede him.

Dabir slowly turned from the window, where he could look down on the king's main courtyard. His gaze slid over her, possessive, the flicker of longing in his dark, narrowed eyes. The door clicked shut behind her.

"So you have paid the price to own me, Dabir?" She stood studying him, barely containing her heart's bitter cry. No. She must find a way to turn this around to her advantage. She would not be slave to this man as she had been to Gamal. She would not let him destroy her spirit. Somewhere in the night in the dank prison cell, she had chosen to believe her sister. She was not worthless as Gamal had said. Maybe her barrenness was a sign of the gods' displeasure with him, not her.

Dabir stepped closer but did not attempt to touch her. "I must admit, my dear Rahab, that I could not bear the thought of you carried off with a Syrian caravan. I will say, though, that your husband has made things quite convenient for us." He shook his head and tsked his tongue. "Such a fool you married, my girl." He fairly purred the words as he stepped nearer still, his gaze fixed on hers.

He cupped her cheek, and she tilted her head, looking away.

"Am I to be your slave then, Dabir?" *Or just your unwilling mistress?*

His touch was gentle on her cheek, and he tipped her chin up so that she was forced to look into his eyes. "*Slave* is such a harsh word, my dear." He sifted his fingers through one long strand of her unkempt hair. She had had no opportunity to bathe or change her clothes since spending the night in the cell.

"Nevertheless, spending the night in a prison gives one that impression, my lord." She offered him a rare glimpse into a vulnerable gaze, then quickly lowered her eyes.

His arms came around her then, and he leaned close. "I am sorry for the poor accommodations, my love, but it had to be done." He softly kissed her, but she could not return it. She was in no mood for love.

He held her at arm's length, studying her. "The truth is, Rahab, I have wanted you for a long time, and I saw my chance. I paid a great deal of silver to have you, and I daresay it would have cost me more if I had allowed them to show you as the other female slaves are shown. Your beauty is impossible to contain, my dear."

Her stomach twisted at the reminder of those moments when too many men had stood gawking at her, raising the bids higher and higher. She should be grateful Dabir wanted her so badly. But not like this. Not when the guilt of their affair and the pain of all Gamal had put her through was still so raw.

"Does this mean I am no longer married?" How could she remain married to a man who in all respects had abandoned her?

He stroked her cheek, looked deeply into her eyes. "Gamal is no longer your concern, Rahab. He will not be coming back. I would not expect him to live long in a land that puts their slaves to hard labor."

She knew this. Should have known it when she glimpsed the Syrian traders. But memories of the early days rushed in on her. *Your daughter is very beautiful, my lord*. She closed her eyes.

"I know, my love. I know." Dabir pulled her close and stroked her back. He must have assumed her expression was one of sorrow over Gamal's loss. But as the memories faded, she knew she would not grieve Gamal. Not after all he had put her through. No. She grieved the loss of her freedom.

"What is to become of me?" she whispered against Dabir's rough cheek, taking advantage of the moment of his kindness to ask what might later become too difficult to say.

Dabir kissed her cheek and brushed the hair from her face. His dark eyes held a glint of longing and the pride of one who has gained a priceless prize. He took her hand in his and squeezed her fingers. "Come, sit with me and I will tell you." He gave her a lazy smile and tugged her toward a cushioned couch that lined one of the walls of the spacious room. He positioned her to face him.

"I have bought a house along the outer wall of the city," he said, lifting his square chin in that telltale pride. "The neighborhood is much safer and better than where you are living now. You will have servants and guards, and an allowance to spend however you please."

She lifted a brow but said nothing.

He looked at her, stroked a strand of her hair. "I have plans for you, Rahab. But now is not the time to share them with you." He took her hand again and helped her to her feet. "You must be hungry." He led her toward the door. "I will take you to your new home, where you can eat and bathe and sleep. I will visit you tomorrow to explain what you are to do."

***

Rahab stood before a wooden gate, its scrollwork rivaling that of some of the finest homes in Jericho. A guard opened it for her and nodded to Dabir, and a female servant met them in the courtyard to wash their dusty feet. Inside, the rooms were large, spread with tapestries, and sconces held the flame of torches along the walls. Intricately carved furnishings, the kind Gamal would have sold and gambled away, graced each room with elegance.

"Well, my dear Rahab, what do you think?" Dabir turned in a circle, his arm taking in the spacious sitting room. Every vase, every pillow, every detail seemed in perfect place.

"I think it is wonderful," she said, her voice soft, breathy. "But I am afraid to touch anything."

Dabir laughed and came toward her, pulling her into his arms. He swung her around, still laughing. "Touch all you like, my dear girl. This place is for your use." His smile seemed genuine, but Rahab could not stop the sense of wariness that fringed the edges of her mind.

"Will you show me the rest?" She could tell he was eager to show off all he was offering her. But . . . what of his wife?

"Of course." He took hold of her elbow and gently led her into a large cooking area, where a woman stood at a wooden table chopping vegetables. "This is Kifah. She will cook whatever food you like."

Rahab stared, seeing herself in such a role just yesterday. She glanced at Dabir, calculating his motives and purpose for her. He wanted more than he was saying.

She followed him to a small sleeping chamber, then to a larger one, then to several more. Was he expecting her to run an inn? Or would he dare to want children by her?

"You're terribly quiet, my dear." He swiveled to face her and caught her in a light embrace. "Surely you have a thought in that beautiful head of yours?" His bright smile did not warm her.

She hugged her arms to her chest and glanced around the opulent room. What must the chambers in the palace be like if a normal house could boast so much?

"I don't know what to say," she said, meeting his ardent gaze. "How did you . . . I mean, this is too nice for someone like me, Dabir. Surely your wife and children—"

"Live in a home far better than this one." He pressed a gentle finger to her lips. "Did you not realize the wealth and power I wield? Surely you are not ignorant of my position." He studied her, and she lowered her gaze against his scrutiny.

"I knew you were advisor to the king." She looked at him and offered a weak smile. "I did not realize how close an advisor or how well the kingdom paid you."

His arms came around her then, and before she could think, his lips claimed hers, as they had the night he wooed her. "Well, it is time you realized it." His dark eyes narrowed slightly, and she caught his sudden shift in mood. He touched her hair and twirled a strand around his finger. "You are mine now, Rahab."

The knot in her stomach tightened, fed by his obvious need to control her.

"Does your wife know about me?" She watched him, wondering if this was a wise question. "I only wonder how I should act if I should meet her at the market."

"You will never meet my wife at the market. The servants

do her work." He sounded petulant, and she imagined a woman who sat lazily on a garden bench or upon her bed all day doing nothing.

"Am I allowed to go to market, my lord? I do enjoy picking my own fruits and fabrics. I will learn to weave the finest linen you can imagine." She smiled brighter now and placed a hand against his chest, coaxing, praying for this small amount of freedom. "I would do my part to please you, Dabir. I could not bear to sit about with nothing to occupy me."

He considered her a moment, as though the question was more difficult than she thought it should be. "When I am sure I can trust you, and possibly with a guard accompanying you, then we will discuss it. For now, the servants will go to market, but you are free to weave or spin or do whatever you desire—inside these walls."

So she was a prisoner as surely as she had been in that cell the night before. But she did not say so. "Thank you for your generosity, my lord." She gave him what she hoped was a grateful smile. She should be thankful to him. After all, he had rescued her from slavery to foreign merchants.

But as she lay alone in her bed after he had finished with her that night, she could not stop the aching loneliness, the awful truth she had known since she married Gamal. She was a slave. As she had been a slave in her marriage, now she was slave to this pompous, wealthy man, who was as much a fool as Gamal. A different type of fool, but pride and greed always produced fools, no matter what level of success they achieved.

She had simply been traded from one fool to another, hopelessly bound to their desires.

8

Evening shadows danced with the flickering torches in Rahab's sitting room, where Dabir lounged on one of her plush couches. Not a speck of dust swirled above the lamps nor dared to land on the polished wood of the tables. Three months in her spacious prison had nearly driven her mad with the desire to do something, *anything*. But most of the daily womanly tasks, including the polishing of his expensive furniture, had been given to servants, and she had had no visitors except Dabir. A deep ache for her family settled within her.

"I acquired a new villa today," Dabir said, drawing her to look at him. He crossed one ankle over the other and clasped his hands behind his head. "It's quite nice, actually, though of course I will hire men to change things to my liking." He smiled. "I'll have to take you there sometime."

She picked up an embroidered pillow and ran a hennaed finger over the delicate fabric. "What plans do you have for this one?" She met his gaze, showing interest, though his purchases had begun to weary her, especially his prideful arrogance as he bragged his way through the telling of the details. But she had learned well how to play the role he demanded. To do otherwise . . . She blinked. Dabir could be abusive in ways Gamal had not even considered.

"I haven't decided yet. I may rent it out for a time. Or I may acquire another mistress." His smile, meant to cause her distress, did the opposite. Another mistress would mean more freedom for her—away from him. But she could never let him think she was anything but his devoted lover. She rose gracefully and came to kneel at his side.

"Have you wearied of me so soon, my lord?" She touched his knee and looked into his calculating gaze, showing him the vulnerable expression she had long ago perfected. What a pretender she had become!

He cupped her cheek, and she knew by the longing in his eyes that her act had its desired effect. "Would you miss me, my girl?"

She lowered her eyes, feigning respect. "I can barely wait for the hour of your visit, my lord. If there is something I have done . . ."

He lifted her chin. "You have been everything I expected, Rahab. You have nothing to fear," he said, though she knew he lied as easily as she did.

"Thank you, my lord."

He pulled her onto his lap, and she sifted her fingers along the edges of his beard. "Whose villa? Did the family come under hard times?"

Dabir traced a line along her jaw, his breath catching as she drew nearer, kissing him. "The man took his family and moved north."

Rahab felt his arms surround her. Her kiss lingered. "Why would he leave?" she whispered. "Jericho is so well protected."

Dabir stiffened and pushed her slightly from him, his gaze hardened. "The fool heard a rumor about those wandering Israelites coming to attack Canaan, so he took his family, sold everything he could, and fled." Her heart beat faster at the intensity that suddenly filled his face, reddening his cheeks. This was a subject that always heated Dabir's ire, and she realized too late that she should not have asked the question.

"Where does he think he will go? What city has stouter walls?" she said, hoping to appease him. She stroked his arm. "Besides, everyone knows the Israelites are a bunch of slaves who can't find their way out of the wilderness."

He looked at her, his body slowly relaxing, the tension easing. "No one can breach these walls, Rahab. And no one can escape them without my notice."

She saw the threat beneath the mask of his charm, but she leaned closer, teasing his ear. "Who would want to try, my lord? You are the great Dabir." She let her warm breath touch his neck. "I trust he sold his villa to you at a more than reasonable price?"

His laughter brought a sigh to her lips. He would forget his anger now. Relief coursed through her as he set her on her feet and rose, taking her hand. "But of course, my dearest. Do you think I would give him what it was worth?" He kissed her then, harder than she liked, but she did not flinch.

She fingered the hair above his ear. "So tell me what else happened today?" She knew how to play his game and forced herself to continue the role.

He chuckled again, pulling her so close she could barely breathe. "How you try to thwart me, my dear girl." He ran his finger over her painted lips. "I am in no mood for games tonight." He lifted her with ease and walked toward her bedchamber, lowering her onto the bed beneath the canopy. He placed his hands on either side of her and searched her gaze. "But I will tell you this . . . I received an invitation to the king's ball to celebrate the Feast of Keret today. I have been asked to pick the woman who will play the king's virgin daughter to 'marry' the prince during the feast."

"How wonderful for you, my lord." She touched his cheek, then played with the fringe of his tunic. "Who will you pick?"

His sudden silence caused her to meet his gaze.

"Your younger sister is a beautiful virgin."

Rahab's heart did a painful flip, and she felt the blood drain from her face. *No!* "My little sister is still a child, my lord." *Please, Yerach, do not let them take Adara.* She must offer a sacrifice . . . *something.*

"She is nearly a woman. She would do for the feast."

His smile unnerved her, and she found it difficult to breathe. How had she not seen this coming? Pure hatred for the man nearly choked her. She closed her eyes, fighting for control of her emotions. She swallowed hard. Looked into his dark eyes.

"I beg you, my lord." She paused, summoning control from a place deep within. "Please do not ask this of her. She is innocent and knows nothing of the ways of men."

"That is the definition of a virgin, my dear. This is a great honor for her, to 'wed' the prince of Jericho." He brushed the hair from her face, and for the first time she felt nauseated at his touch.

"Let me take her place." The words were out before she could think another thought.

"You are by no means qualified, my dear." He chuckled, even as he lay beside her on the raised bed.

She turned, forcing every true emotion from her, and sidled closer to him. "But is this not a part to play? I can be anything you ask of me, my lord. I daresay I would know from all you have taught me how to please the prince." Though the thought of the man who had sent her husband into bondage did not bring her pleasant feelings. Dealing with his advisor was already a struggle. How would she continue to deny her feelings and give herself to yet another man?

But she could not let them take Adara.

"Do you think it a small thing for me to give you to another, Rahab?" He acted offended, and for the brief moment their gazes met she sensed honesty in him. Did he actually care for her? The home he had provided flashed through her thoughts. He did like to give her things.

"I would never think of giving my heart to him, Dabir." She stroked his arm. "You know that it is you alone I love." She smiled and kissed him before he could respond, desperate to prove her lying words. "I would not disappoint you, my lord. The prince would thank you, perhaps even promote you at the end of the feast. Anyone else would surely disappoint him." Her heart beat faster. She dared not even speak her sister's name lest he lose his focus on her.

"You drive a hard bargain, my sweet." He gave in to her kisses and closed his eyes. He would not speak of it again, despite her desperate need to pull a promise from him. But experience had taught her how far she could push him.

So she did as she had always done since the day Dabir had purchased her—submitted to his choices and pretended to be someone she was not.

A week later, on the sixth day of the yearly Festival of Keret, Rahab awoke to the deafening march of soldiers stomping the circular streets of Jericho. They had repeated the same silent parade for the past five days. On the seventh, tomorrow, they would shout and dance in the streets, blaring trumpets and clashing cymbals and fairly shaking the earth beneath them. And at the end of it all, she would "marry" the prince, as she had begged Dabir to allow her to do.

If only she had not been forced to make such a choice.

She rose from her bed, pushing anxiety from her heart for the hundredth time. She could do this. She *must* do this, for Adara's sake. But though she had once appreciated his mercy, she did not like Prince Nahid. And she thought the ritual of Keret a farce meant to appease the desires of men more than the needs of the moon god. But even her father had insisted that the land's fertility was at stake. Had the decision been given to him, he might have offered Adara in her place.

What if Dabir changes his mind? The thought greeted her again, as it had every dawn for the past week, with the first sound of the soldiers and the silent parade of her fellow citizens following solemnly behind the prince, Dabir, and most of the royal court. What if he had spoken to her father about Adara and pulled a switch on her at the last moment?

She drew in a long, slow breath. *Stop.* She could not continue to worry.

Tomorrow. One more day and she could stop fearing Dabir's treachery.

But in her mind's eye she saw the look of malice in Dabir's eyes as he watched Gamal on his knees, pleading for his life. And the gleam of greed when he looked at her, at moments he thought she did not notice. Dabir wanted more from her than he had yet let on. She knew it in a place deep within her, in a place she did not want to visit.

Dabir was capable of evil beyond what she could imagine.

Sweat drew a thin line along her brow, even as a chill swept over her. What had she agreed to do? Why had Dabir given in to her so easily? He had brought up Adara on purpose. Had he done so to get her to unwittingly do his bidding?

But why? Why share her with the prince?

She sank back among the covers, her stomach suddenly heaving. Something was wrong.

With each staccato march of the soldiers, her dread grew.

<hr />

At dawn the following morning, the familiar march began once again. This time they would circle the city seven times. She rose quickly from her bed, greeted with the rich scent of spikenard, a gift sent to her from Dabir for the evening's festivities. Sweet delicacies awaited her at a small table in the corner of her chamber, but her stomach revolted at the thought of food. Tonight she would be escorted to Prince Nahid's chambers dressed as his consort. Their union, if the gods were merciful, would bring a fruitful harvest to the land.

What if it also brought about a real child in her womb?

The thought stirred the desire she had lived with every day of her marriage. But three months with Dabir had proven her barrenness was not Gamal's fault. Why had the gods not looked on her with such favor?

You are a worthless whore. Gamal's words rang as sharply as they had four months before.

She rose stiffly, forcing all thoughts of a child, of whatever womanly longings she had once possessed, from her heart. She could not dwell on them. If she did, they would consume her.

Time dulled with the incessant marching.

As the hour approached, servants came to dress her hair and fitted wide circles of silver filigreed earrings into the holes in her ears. The white tunic dipped low at her neckline, and a long slit below her waist easily showed one long leg. A sheer scarlet robe did little to cover what the tunic exposed. One look in the long silver mirror caused her face to flush nearly as crimson as the robe.

She was dressed as a priestess, not a princess. A king's daughter was to be the part she played. Unless . . . Her earlier fears surfaced like rushing water in a dry wadi. Dabir had lied to her all along. Hadn't she always known it? Would she arrive at the banquet to find Adara dressed as a princess ready to be given to King Keret/Prince Nahid?

Her skin tingled with rage, but in a moment, a breath, the rage gave way to the too familiar shame. She pulled at the tunic, trying to raise it above her nearly exposed breasts, to no avail.

A knock on the outer door startled her, and before she could ponder her conflicting thoughts, Dabir stood before her, arm extended.

"My dear Rahab, how lovely you look tonight."

She merely nodded, her throat too dry for words.

He chuckled. "You seem quite taken with yourself in that mirror." He stepped closer and grasped her hand. Raising it above his head, he motioned for her to twirl about. "Ah yes. The fit is perfect, my dear."

For a harlot. Though she did not say so.

"If you please the prince tonight, then tomorrow night we

will begin to expand your services." His smile and calculating look brought the heat, the rage, to the surface again. He viewed tonight as her unveiling to all of the wealthy men of Jericho, men who would happily line Dabir's pockets if she pleased the prince.

"I see." She looked away from his scrutiny.

"This is part of your debt, Rahab. You knew you had to earn your keep eventually." He held her at arm's length.

She lowered her head.

Silence filled the room until his coarse laughter broke its barrier. "You did not actually think that I was giving in to your pathetic begging to save your sister, did you?" He lifted her chin. "You did!" His continued laughter burned her like hot sand on bare skin. "I thought you wiser than that, Rahab."

His words felt like one of Gamal's slaps against her cheek. Her heart beat too fast, and she closed her eyes, grasping for dignity.

"No," she whispered at last. "Of course I did not think so." But she had hoped. What a fool she had been.

He studied her. "The truth is, Rahab, that Prince Nahid has shown interest in you from the beginning. When he invited me to pick the virgin, he said it in such a way that I knew it was not truly a virgin he wanted this time. This is why you will play this role and wed him tonight. After that, we will see what shall be done with you."

"And if he is not pleased with me?" The question blurted from her, and she wished she could pull it back. She already knew the answer to that question.

Dabir looked at her for a long moment. "I have no doubt in your ability, my dear." He ushered her from her chambers toward the waiting chariot. "Rest assured," he said, bending close to her ear as they moved through the gate, "that you do not want to cross me. This is for us, Rahab. Together we will build a great fortune."

How like Gamal he sounded!

She would never be free of the greed of fools.

9

Dabir held Rahab's elbow as they walked past the king's audience chamber into the anteroom where she would await her summons.

"The guards will escort you to stand behind the king as King Keret approaches. Do as I taught you and all will be well." He left her then without so much as a backward glance.

Rahab wrapped both arms about her, surprised that Dabir had allowed her a multicolored cloak to be worn over her sheer clothing. At least for now she did not feel as though she were a slave at auction again. But as the noise from the audience chamber grew and Prince Nahid's voice rose above the throng to demand his bride, her pulse quickened.

She glanced at the guard who stood watch at the side door. Sweat dampened her palms, and she realized too late that she should have eaten earlier when she'd had the chance. Now she felt nearly faint with hunger, anticipation . . . and fear.

"It's time," the guard said, dragging her wayward thoughts to what lay ahead.

One step at a time. She had little choice if she hoped to

live past this night. To go against Dabir or to even attempt to run from her fate could land her back in that dank prison cell or worse. She had no wish to end her life. Not yet. Not when hope of redemption, of working her way out of this awful debt, still seemed possible.

She followed the guard through the antechamber door into a glittering room where sconces were lined up on either side from the throne to the main door. Marble steps interlaid with gold led to a golden throne where the king sat facing his son, Prince Nahid.

"King Pubala," Prince Nahid said, using the fictitious name of the legendary king, "I demand that you grant me your daughter Hariya to become my wife, to obtain a son by her."

"Who are you to demand anything from me?" his father, the king of Jericho, responded, playing the role.

"It is I who am conqueror. While you slept, my soldiers have marched upon this city. You are in our debt, oh king." At Prince Nahid's words, soldiers climbed the steps to the throne and surrounded the king.

Rahab felt a slight nudge, forcing her to step from behind a purple and golden curtain. Guards gripped her upper arms and escorted her to stand before King Keret.

"Hariya?"

"Yes, my lord," Rahab said, lowering her gaze, then bowing at his feet.

He reached for her hand and lifted her up, intertwining their fingers. "Now you shall become my wife."

She nodded, saying nothing, as Dabir had instructed her. Prince Nahid led her through the wide hall to the open doors. Courtiers clapped and minstrels played flutes and harps, while the steady beat of distant drums filled the palace courtyard.

The prince did not stop as they descended the steps of the palace, leading her, with the crowd following, to his apartments on the opposite side of the large square court. At the door to his own chambers, he turned her to face him.

"Oh Hariya, how beautiful you are." He smiled, and it almost seemed genuine.

"Thank you, my lord," she said, bowing low again, then returning his smile.

The crowd cheered as the prince removed her striped cloak. Whistles and a few remarks she wished she did not understand came from some of the men standing closest. Nahid took her hand and turned her to face the men, who now forced their way past the women to the front of the throng.

"My bride!" the prince exclaimed with too much enthusiasm.

Rahab stiffened, tamping down all emotion. The tunic and scarlet robe did little to hold her dignity, but she lifted her chin, courting a hint of defiance. She *was* beautiful. She knew it from the many hours she had spent staring at her reflection to please Dabir.

But as the men continued their ribald comments, she felt her defenses crumbling one stubborn thought at a time. Prince Nahid turned her in a circle once more, then swiftly pulled her into his arms and kissed her in sight of all. "Let us take this inside, shall we?" he whispered against her ear.

"Yes, my lord." She shivered and wrapped her fingers tightly against his and followed him into his chambers.

⚜

"You will think me a fool to tell you this," Prince Nahid said once the door to his bedchamber shut behind them. "But I did not originally intend to take you as they expect."

He sank onto a low couch and stretched his legs in front of him, crossing them at the ankles.

Rahab stood on a soft woolen rug, hands clasped in front of her, eyes downcast. "I do not understand." Hadn't Dabir insisted that the prince wanted her?

"That is, I do not normally sleep with the virgins."

Silence settled between them, broken only by the distant drums and the sounds of men and women dancing in the courtyard outside the prince's window. So Adara would have been safe with him? But no one would believe that she was truly still a virgin, and her life in the home of a husband would have been forfeit.

Rahab sighed softly. "But I am not a virgin." Despite the humiliation it had cost her, she had made the right choice.

"No, you are not." His voice was both gentle and commanding. "Look at me, Rahab."

She glanced up from studying her feet, noticing the hand he extended that beckoned her to sit beside him on the plush cushions. She came slowly, warily.

He took her hand and rubbed his thumb over her palm. She swallowed and closed her eyes, willing her emotions into submission. She could not stop him from doing what men would do, but she dare not give her heart to him. She was nothing to him. And he was nothing to her.

His fingers moved up her arm, and she could not stop the tingling. He cupped her cheek and then kissed her temple, his hands probing. Dabir would expect her to comply, to willingly give herself to this man for the simple fact that he was the prince of Jericho.

Her stomach knotted, reminding her that this man had ruined her life, had sold her into slavery. She stiffened.

He pulled back and held her at arm's length.

"I am sorry about Gamal," he said. She startled at this sudden turn of thought and met his gaze, saw the sorrow in his dark eyes. Was he lying just to force her to melt in his arms?

"You are kind to say so, my lord." She could not so easily accept such words.

He searched her face, slowly letting his gaze take in the rest of her. "Dabir was right. You are indeed very beautiful."

She shivered again at his touch, felt his fingers slide over her shoulder once more. His kiss gentled as he drew her closer.

"If you but say the word, I will purchase you from Dabir."

She blinked, stared into his earnest dark eyes. "Purchase me, my lord?" If he'd wanted her so badly, why did he allow Dabir to claim her in the first place? Dabir's face flitted in her mind's eye, purpled with rage. She was his investment. *This is for us, Rahab. Together we will build a great fortune.* But at what cost to her?

"I would pay what is owed to Dabir in order for you to give me an heir." He twisted a strand of her hair, then carefully released the combs, letting the full length of it tumble about her shoulders. He leaned in, his hot breath on her face, his lips claiming hers, possessive, determined. Was he serious?

She caught her breath as he drew back to search her face. "Does this please you?" he asked.

That he should care to please her at all made no sense. "Forgive me, my lord, but how can the child of a slave be of any importance to you? Would not your other sons hate him and try to destroy him?" She had heard tales of such things happening in other kingdoms from Cala.

He leaned against the couch again, pulling away from her.

"I am the son of a slave woman, Rahab. Did you not know this?"

She lifted a brow, surprised at the revelation. "No, my lord. I was not aware." A thousand questions filled her mind. If his mother was a slave, how did he hold such a place of prominence in the kingdom? Awareness suddenly dawned as she recalled Cala's comments to her one afternoon.

"You have only sisters." She looked at him. Saw his face darken, followed by a curt nod.

He stood abruptly and walked to the window but did not part the curtains. She sat where she was, uncertain what to do next. He turned but did not move toward her, extending his hand instead. She rose and came to him.

"I never sleep with the virgins," he said with greater emphasis this time, "at these festivals. It is always expected, but I refuse to put these unsuspecting young girls into a harem to be forgotten as my mother was." He paused. "Despite the fact that she produced a male heir when my father's wives could not, he dared not give her the favor she deserved, lest he anger the kings of the nations of his wives." His smile grew thoughtful, and he sifted his hands through her undone hair. "When the feast ends, I quietly send the virgins home."

Rahab processed his words. "But you cannot send me home."

He shook his head. "But I can take you from Dabir. I would treat you kindly."

"I don't know what to say, my lord." Did he know Dabir's plans for her? She bowed at his feet. "I am my lord's servant."

His arms came around her and he pulled her to him. His kiss lingered. A soft groan escaped him as he led her to his canopied bed. But her mind could not focus on the

97

love he wanted from her, despite his kind words. At least she had preserved Adara's innocence, for hers could never be regained.

⁓⁘⁓

Dabir watched Rahab from across the room later that evening, after the marriage between herself and King Keret. He covered a smile with his linen napkin as his gaze caught the prince's satisfied look. Rahab had surely pleased him most thoroughly, if Dabir knew the prince at all. And who better than he understood the prince's mind? With the prince's endorsement, Rahab might just be the most lucrative investment he had yet made.

He leaned against the cushioned couch, sipping his wine. He had planned this well. Rahab would need more protection now. Two strong eunuchs should do, or one impressive in size. He swirled the liquid in his cup, contemplating his options. He startled at the prince's approach and scrambled to bow at his feet.

"Do not trouble yourself, Dabir. You nearly spilled the wine over your robe." The prince's tone held candor and a hint of amusement.

Dabir straightened, heat creeping up his neck and filling his face in a rush. "I am sorry, my lord. I was lost in thought and did not hear or see your approach."

Prince Nahid sat beside Dabir on the farthest end of the plush couch. "I want to purchase Rahab from you."

Dabir straightened and clutched his cup, studying the elaborate spread of food before him, scrambling to collect his thoughts. What nonsense was this? He swallowed, forcing his anger to calm. This was Rahab's doing.

He looked up, met the prince's amused gaze. "I don't understand, my lord. You assured me that Rahab was mine."

"I changed my mind." He studied one manicured finger. "I find her quite pleasing." His smile seemed cocky and too self-assured to Dabir's thinking.

"As I expected you would, my prince." He smiled and nodded. He could not let this man, prince or not, do this to his plans.

Prince Nahid gave a slight nod of acknowledgment, his gaze aimed in Rahab's direction. After a lengthy pause, the prince looked Dabir in the eye. "I will cancel her debt and return the money you paid for her. She will become my servant."

Dabir's middle tightened against the blow of the prince's words. "I'm afraid your words confuse me, my lord. Rahab is worth far more as a consort than a free woman."

The prince's gaze narrowed but did not waver. "I do not intend to free her, Dabir. I intend to produce an heir by her."

This was unexpected. Perhaps not Rahab's doing at all. Dabir's mind raced, calculating, unwilling to submit this loss. "You are aware, my lord, that the woman is barren?" It was a risk to say so, as he could not prove it, but he would make sure it was true before the prince took her. He swallowed, his pulse racing in time with his thoughts.

The prince looked at him strangely. "I was not aware." He accepted wine from a servant and drank deeply before speaking again. "You are sure of this?"

Dabir nodded, not daring to release any sign of relief. "Gamal had her for five years, my lord, and they had no children. I have been to her bed many nights for at least three months, and still she carries no child."

"And you are sure this is not of her own doing? Women have ways of preventing a child."

Dabir nearly squirmed under the prince's scrutiny. "I am certain Rahab wanted to give Gamal a son, as all wives are wont to do, my lord. But in five years with Gamal," he emphasized again, "she did not conceive a child." He stroked his bearded chin and lifted his gaze to the prince.

The prince looked across the room to where Rahab still sat at the bridal table. "She is exquisite," he said, his tone wistful. "Together we could have created fine sons."

Dabir offered a sympathetic sigh. "I am indeed sorry, my lord. If you would still wish to have her, please, I give her to you as a gift. She is of no use to me if she cannot please those closest to you. And they will not desire her if you find her wanting." A flicker of regret accompanied his offer, but he knew he had to take the risk. He could not fight against the king's only son without ending up at the end of a stake or sold as Gamal had been.

"No," Prince Nahid said, though his gaze did not meet Dabir's. "If she has not conceived in all that time with two different men, then I cannot take the chance that she will be able to do as I'd hoped. Besides, she is right. I do have other sons."

He had spoken to Rahab of this? Dabir gritted his teeth. She would use such knowledge against him, given the chance. If she had the prince's ear . . . he would have to tread lightly and appease her, slave or not. He needed her to play her part well. Threats alone would not garner her favor. He must sweeten his coffers with honeyed words if he were to add gold to them as well.

"However," the prince said, interrupting his thoughts,

"I want her exclusively for a month." He held Dabir's gaze without flinching. Dabir would get nowhere if he attempted to argue against him.

"Your presence will make her all the more appealing, my lord." Dabir smiled.

"I thought you'd see it that way." The prince accepted another goblet of wine from a passing servant. "I assume you have her well protected."

Dabir fingered a date pastry but did not eat it. "I have given it consideration."

"Have you someone in mind?"

Dabir shook his head. "I thought to use one of the eunuchs I employ, but none are impressive enough to attack a would-be nemesis. There is the man her husband accused who started this whole mess."

"The Nubian?"

"The same." He'd forgotten the man's name, but it would take little trouble to discover it.

Prince Nahid's brows drew close in a frown. "I don't like Nubians, Dabir." He touched the place where his beard hid the scar that had nearly ended his life in Jericho's last war, fought against Canaanite rivals and mercenary Nubians.

"I realize that, my lord, but from what Rahab has told me, this one fought on our side. He was Gamal's friend."

"Gamal had a strange way of treating his *friends*." The prince stood then, and Dabir rose with him.

"Shall I pursue the Nubian then, my lord? He seemed strong enough, and at least his kind would have little interest in Rahab."

"He could not afford her." The prince laughed, a derisive sound. There was definitely no love in the man's heart for the darker race.

"All the more reason he could be a good protector. And he knows where he could end up if he crosses us." Dabir waited the space of many heartbeats and watched as conflicting emotions crossed the prince's face.

At last he nodded. "All right, Dabir. Do as you wish." Dabir bowed his thanks.

Prince Nahid strode away without acknowledgment.

10

Tendaji hefted his irrigation sickle and hoe over his shoulder and strode through Jericho's gates with the rest of the field workers. Some of the men around him whistled as they walked, no doubt thinking ahead to a good meal prepared by a wife, surrounded by children. Others, he knew, sang or whistled in anticipation of the drink that would drown their sorrows for another day.

Tendaji kept to himself, hanging back from the crowd as they allowed the king's guards to inspect their seed baskets. Fear hung in the city's air, hovering just above the songs of the men. And the guards' nerves were heightened. Tendaji read it in their hardened faces beneath heavy leather helmets.

"Any news of the Israelites?" Tendaji asked as the guard sifted through his limp goatskin sack that had carried almonds and cheese for his midday meal.

The guard sized Tendaji up, then shrugged. "Nothing notable to report. The last merchants that came through here said the Israelites had moved their camp closer to the Jordan.

They'll never get across during flood season, but come the heat of summer, we could see some action against them." The guard waved Tendaji through with a nod. "They won't get through these walls, though." He laughed, but Tendaji sensed the bravery was forced.

He continued into the city, walked past the closed-up merchant stalls, and passed several more blocks until he turned to the poor section and his crumbling home. He entered the courtyard and lit the lamp from the torch that burned continually near his gate. The house was cold and dark, and the heaviness he always carried with him when he returned here hit him like a fresh, overpowering wave. His mother was gone, and he could no longer afford the services of a servant to wash his feet or fix his meals. He would never be anything more than servant of the king, working the king's fields, feeding the king's greed.

He set the small clay lamp on a stand in the corner of the room, then sank onto a worn wooden bench, dropped his tools to the dirt floor, and bent forward, his face in his hands. His stomach growled in protest, as it had been doing for hours since his simple meal. There was little left in the cooking room, and he'd sold the goat to pay for the final visit from the physician. What he wouldn't give for a large mug of strong drink to forget. To wallow in the grief he had known too long. First his father, then Kahiru and his son, and now his mother. How was he supposed to survive in the world, friendless, without family, and alone?

The gnawing in his stomach would not ease. He searched the wicker baskets hanging from the beam above his head in the cooking room. Happy memories mingled with ones of loss as he managed to put together some toasted grain and the last of the goat cheese. He fingered the coins in the belt at his waist. He would have to leave the fields in time to stop at a market on the way home tomorrow.

If only he could go to sleep and not awaken.

He swiped at unmanly tears, startled at a knock on his outer door. No one visited him. But his hesitant feet carried him to the door just the same. A slit in the wood showed two armed palace guards standing in his courtyard. A knot filled the space where his hunger had been. He opened the door a crack and peered out.

"Yes?"

"Are you Tendaji the Nubian?"

The knot doubled, and the muscles along his back tightened. He straightened, determined not to show his sudden fear. "I am Tendaji."

"By order of Dabir, advisor to the king, you are commanded to come with us."

This could not be good. But it would do no good to protest.

As he followed the guards, lights from the homes of his neighbors flickered in tall torches near the street, giving at least some illumination besides the moon to guide their way. The streets took many turns before the poor section gave way to the shops and homes of those in higher society. Houses set along the city wall were among the best protected—if a man could afford such a thing.

The Hall of Justice loomed ahead as they made yet another turn onto the King's Highway. The palace sat above and behind it, its golden towers gleaming in torchlight.

"This way," one of the guards said as he pointed to a hallway just inside the government building. The slap of leather against the tiles was the only sound, keeping time with the questions swirling in his head. Why did Dabir want such a meeting with him now?

At last they stopped before an ornate door that stood partway open. One of the guards knocked and poked his head in. "We have the Nubian, my lord."

"Good. Good. Send him in."

The guard stepped back and allowed Tendaji to pass him. He entered a brightly lit, paneled room, with one wall housing a window and another an expensive tapestry. A large table separated him from Dabir, who sat like a king on a raised dais behind it.

"Tendaji, my friend, come in. Sit." He pointed to a stiff wooden chair placed before the wide table. Tendaji sat, sensing even more than seeing Dabir's power. He noted the man's multicolored robe with threads of gold interlaced in clear stripes down the sides. Except for the lack of a golden crown on his head, Dabir was the image of royalty. Tendaji mentally compared his threadbare clothing and had to force himself to sit tall, lest he give in completely to this obvious intimidation.

"What can I do for you, my lord?" He studied the man's crossed arms and narrowed gaze. He seemed almost ill at ease, as though he did not trust Tendaji.

"It has come to my attention that you could use some financial aid. Rumor has it that your mother's ill health, peace be upon her, drained your earnings. Am I correct?"

Tendaji stiffened, unsure why his financial business should matter at all to this man, but he went along with the conversation. "You are correct."

"I am sorry for your loss."

He lowered his gaze. "Thank you, my lord."

"She was all you had left in the world, am I also correct

in this?" Dabir uncrossed his arms and placed his hands on the table.

Tendaji nodded. "Yes, my lord. My father passed on many years ago, and my wife died in childbirth after I returned from a rotation of duty."

"You were in the king's army then?"

"For a short time, yes."

Dabir seemed to consider this, while Tendaji waited, hands clasped in his lap, studying the blunt edges of his nails.

"I have a job to offer you, Tendaji, if you will consider it. The pay is good, as long as you do your job well, and you will sleep in a home far nicer than the one you do now. Your meals will be provided, and you will no longer need to work the fields. Does this interest you?"

Tendaji looked up and raised a brow. "I am curious as to what you find in me that is worthy of such a duty, my lord."

Dabir's smile was subtle, as though he knew a secret no one else shared. "You are strong and loyal, Tendaji. Your loyalty to your mother speaks a great deal about your character. And you know how to use a weapon, if indeed you spent time in the king's service."

Tendaji nodded. "Yes, my lord."

"Then are you interested?"

"What is it that I would be doing, my lord?" He was highly interested, but not without knowing what pot of hot oil he was jumping into.

"You would be personal guard to my newest asset. Rahab." Dabir's gaze held his, unwavering. "You know of whom I speak, Tendaji?"

"The wife of Gamal?" Rahab was not a common enough name to be anyone else.

"The same. Since Gamal's debt grew so large and came to such an unfortunate end, we were forced to sell him to Syrian traders. But his payment was not enough to cover his debt, so Rahab has entered into an agreement with us to pay it back." Dabir's look held challenge, and Tendaji knew this was not a man to be crossed.

"Is Rahab's life in danger then?"

"Let us just say that she provides a service that can bring about unsavory patrons. You must guard her against such men. And you must go with her wherever she goes. She is not even to go to market unescorted. We do not wish to see anything happen to her . . . or to you."

Tendaji sensed the threat behind Dabir's smooth smile. "I would keep her safe." He had always liked Rahab. Though he did not like the implication of what this man was forcing her to do.

Dabir's smile widened. "I thought you might see it that way. So then we have an agreement?"

Tendaji stood. "Yes, my lord. Just tell me what I need to do."

Dabir remained seated but summoned the guards. "Take this man and see that he is fed and fitted with proper clothing. Then show him to the guest rooms on the palace grounds. I will take him to Rahab in the morning."

11

Rahab stretched beneath fine linen covers, wanting to continue the dream, her thoughts languid. The poppy-laced tea she drank after her final guest had left and Tendaji had bolted the door behind him always left her mornings in a state of lethargy. But she didn't care. Let her sleep the day away. It was better than facing herself in the silver mirror and continuing the lie.

Three months had nearly passed since Dabir had forced her into this life, and once Prince Nahid's month had ended, more men than she could count clamored for an hour in her arms. She should have known the prince meant none of his grand promises to purchase her for himself, to free her from Dabir's plans for her. Gone was his desire to sire an heir through her. He seemed content to use her and leave her to seek her own rescue. If indeed such a rescue could be found.

She tossed the pillow over her head, the dream a lost memory now. Unfortunate that she could not live night and day on the narcotic tea. If she could only forget . . . forget the lewd, vulgar, sometimes cruel men. Why had Prince Nahid ended his exclusive visits? Why throw her to the dogs of his court?

She pulled the covers to her neck and closed her eyes. Light slipped into the room around the edges of the shuttered windows, brightening the curtains that shrouded her bed.

Oh, for the chance to escape her life.

The door creaked open, and soft footfalls of a servant entered her room. The scraping of a tray against the wooden table told her that food awaited her. A moment later, the servant took the bronze urns to empty the night's contents and shut the door without a word.

Rahab drew in a deep breath and swung her legs over the side of the bed. Despite the bath she always required before bed, she still felt stained, dirty in places no one could see. She placed shaky feet on the tiled floor, found her soft doeskin slippers, and emerged from beneath the curtains. A queasy feeling settled over her the moment she stood up. She grabbed the back of a chair and eased herself onto it, taking several deep breaths, waiting as she had for the past month or more for the feeling to pass. Had she become so disgusted with her life that each thought of it made her sick?

She gripped the edges of the chair and forced herself to stand. She had to be strong. Weak women never accomplished anything. Weak women never learned to control their circumstances.

She exhaled a breath she'd held too long, reminding herself everything was temporary. Eventually she would find a way to escape or earn enough to buy her freedom. As she had done with Gamal, she had quickly learned to do with Dabir, hiding silver beneath the floor. Dabir would not own her forever. Of that she was certain.

A knock at her door brought her thoughts up short. She walked toward it and opened it a crack.

"Mistress?" Tendaji stood at attention, his gaze not quite meeting hers. It occurred to her that he was the only man who had ever treated her with respect. She opened the door fully.

"Come in, Tendaji. I am dressed." She stepped aside, but he stayed where he was and shook his head.

"I do not need to enter, mistress. I simply came to see if you needed my services. Can I get you anything from the market or the vendors?"

She looked at him until he met her gaze. Kindness filled his dark eyes. Regret over what she could not control washed over her. Gamal would still be here if he had not betrayed this man.

"Thank you, Tendaji, but I don't think so. I am not feeling well today."

"Shall I send for your sister?"

Rahab had not seen Cala in months. Such loss suddenly added to her queasiness. She nodded, too emotional to speak.

"I will hurry, mistress." Tendaji turned and fairly ran from the house before she could respond.

The thought of his loyalty strangely comforted her . . . but a moment later, her stomach churned again and she barely reached the clay pot in time to empty its contents.

<hr />

"You have all the signs of pregnancy, my sister." Cala sat on the edge of one of Rahab's elegant stuffed chairs a short time later, acting as though she feared Tzadok would appear in the room at any moment.

"He's not going to find you here, Cala. And besides, Tend-aji will warn me if anyone knocks on our door."

Cala drew a breath. "He doesn't allow me to come." Her gaze skittered from Rahab's face to look about the room again. "This all belongs to you?"

Rahab folded her hands in her lap, forcing back the bitter words she held for Cala's ridiculous jealousy. "It belongs to Dabir. He allows me to use it."

Cala nodded but did not meet Rahab's gaze. "Mother and Adara send their love."

Emotion swelled, and Rahab could not speak for a moment.

"Father won't let them come to visit, though Adara has threatened to sneak away to spend time with you. I fear that child is much too curious."

"She is not a child. She needs to wed."

Cala did not argue the point. "Do you know who fathered your babe?"

Her babe. She had not thought of this sickness as a person. "I thought I was barren." Even Dabir had said so when he suggested she visit the palace midwife for the silphium plant to be sure she stayed that way. But Rahab had refused, and somehow he had acquiesced. "This is not possible," she said, reinforcing what she knew had to be true. "There must be another explanation. Could I be dying?"

"I seriously doubt that." Cala came to kneel at her side and touched her knee. "Just because you never conceived with Gamal and Dabir does not mean the fault lay with you. Perhaps the problem was with them."

"Men are never to blame." The words came out harsh, like her life.

Cala nodded. "That is only their pride speaking. It is possible for a man to be the one whose seed will not take root in a woman."

Rahab stared at her, unbelieving. And yet . . . could there truly be a babe growing within her? She met her sister's concerned gaze. "If there is a child," she said, "I do not know the father. I have been with too many men to count in the past three months. Prince Nahid came the most." Even after his month had ended, he seemed taken with her. How often she had listened as he spoke of his wives, his children, even his fears of war. But he didn't stay. He never stayed.

She looked down at her hands, twisting the fabric of her robe between sweaty palms.

"Will Dabir let you keep it?"

A servant knocked, then entered the room with steaming cups of mint tea.

"I don't know," Rahab said after the servant left again. She took a cup and blew on the steam, then set it on a low table beside her. "I don't think he will be happy."

Sympathy filled Cala's expression. "But if the child is the prince's? Did you not tell me he wanted an heir to come from you?"

Rahab shrugged, suddenly listless. "How could I prove such a thing? He wanted me when he thought I could be only his and give him more sons. But he has sons. Any child I would bear would mean nothing to him."

Cala frowned, touching Rahab's arm. "Surely the prince sees something in you he desires, Rahab. I cannot believe he would cast you aside if you sought him out." She slowly stood and took her place again in the chair opposite Rahab. "I would keep the baby for you, if Tzadok would let me."

"He would never allow such a thing and you know it."

Cala's expression held sadness. "He is not as kind a man as I had hoped," she said softly. She glanced about the room again, as though making sure they were still alone. "I think Dabir makes him feel powerless, and Tzadok likes to control."

"All men seek control." Rahab folded her hands in her lap, studying the patterns her servants had painstakingly created with orange and maroon henna.

"Not all men."

Rahab looked up.

"Father does not grapple so hard to appear powerful. But we are all staggering under the weight of Dabir's demands."

Stunned, Rahab leaned into the chair, wishing it would swallow her. "He lied to me then." What did she expect? "He has placed Gamal's burden on all of you?"

Cala nodded. "Life has not been easy for any of us. Though I know you have suffered the most."

"All the more reason Tzadok would never let you keep my child," Rahab whispered. "He or she would be a constant reminder of the shame I have brought on you all."

Cala's silence followed. She did not contradict what they both knew was true. But Rahab could not shake the maternal instincts growing ever stronger within her. Suddenly she did not care who had fathered the life within her. She wanted this child. She needed him or her more than she had ever needed anyone in all of her life. Someone to love and to love her in return. Flesh of her flesh.

"I don't know how I'm going to do it, Cala," Rahab whispered, "but I need to keep my baby."

Cala smiled. "I will do anything I can to help you."

"I know you will."

But after Cala returned home an hour later, Rahab knew this was something she would have to work out alone.

⁓⁓⁓⁓♔⁓⁓⁓⁓

Rahab paced her sitting room two months later, her heart racing, her nerves frayed. She had waited as long as she could, her condition confirmed by her mother and the local midwife. A condition she could not keep secret any longer. Even now her belly had begun to fatten, and Dabir had mentioned it the week earlier, suggesting she was indulging in too many delicacies. Kifah had immediately begun to ration her portions, which proved challenging as her appetite grew more and more ravenous.

And now he stared at her from the cushioned couch in her sitting room, his body gone rigid with the news. "This is impossible. You are barren."

"Apparently not anymore." She stopped moving long enough to look at him. "I want to keep my baby." She held his gaze, challenging him.

Dabir scowled, and he slowly stood to face her. Silence thickened the air. His nostrils flared, and he stepped closer, his breath hot on her face. "How long have you kept this from me?" His hand connected with her face in a hard slap.

Tears sprang up, her attempt to blink them away futile. She took a step back, a hand to her burning cheek. "I wanted to be sure." She slinked farther back, suddenly hearing movement behind her.

"Everything all right, mistress?" Tendaji's voice brought welcome comfort, though he could not protect her from Dabir.

"Everything is fine, Tendaji." Dabir's tone held its telltale threat. "Leave us."

Tendaji nodded and backed away. "I'm here if you need me, mistress."

Dabir raised a brow at the Nubian's unexpected challenge, but settled his gaze once more on Rahab as Tendaji left the room. "Don't even attempt to lie to me, Rahab. How long?"

"Please forgive my impertinence, my lord," she said in her usual attempt to appease. "I have been barren so long. I had to be sure." She looked up, allowing him to see her tears. "I am about three months along."

Dabir sucked in a breath as though the length of time surprised him. He walked to the window, his back to her. Silence pulsed like dread before a coming storm.

"You cannot keep it," he said at last. "Your debt is too great, and we would lose too much time and money waiting for you to birth it."

"I will take on more clients until the babe becomes obvious. I will double the visits once it is born." Urgency filled her tone despite her attempt to remain calm.

He looked at her, his smile calculating. "If you are so willing to take on more men, you can do that now, without the babe."

She lost the ability to breathe for a dizzying moment, hating the way his words pierced her.

"No, please, Dabir." But she was begging now, and no kindness filled his gaze.

He stepped closer, gripped her arm. "If you do not visit the palace midwife by week's end to rid yourself of this . . . this burden, I will take you there myself. And believe me, Rahab, you will regret it if I am forced to do so."

"He is gone, mistress," Tendaji told her moments later. He found her staring listlessly out the window in the city wall, longing to escape to the fields and hills beyond. "Did he hurt you?"

Rahab released a shuddering breath and turned to face him. "Can I trust you, Tendaji? Will you keep my secrets even from Dabir?"

"Every day for any reason, mistress." His fierce look surprised her. Dabir had given Tendaji lucrative employment. Was she foolish to trust him? But she had no one else strong enough to do what she must.

She motioned for him to shut the door, then spoke close to his ear. "Dabir does not wish me to keep my child. He is sending me to the palace midwife by week's end to . . ." She choked on a sob. "To destroy it." Her hushed words sounded loud in her ears.

Tendaji's brows knit, and his expression darkened his already black skin. He studied her for so long she feared he wouldn't speak, would walk away. And why not? He had lost his wife in childbirth. Why should he care if Gamal's wife was allowed to keep hers?

"I will not let him hurt you, Rahab." He glanced at the closed door. Her gaze followed. She could not trust that another servant might not have her ear to the wood, listening, spying. They both stepped nearer the window. He closed the shutters. "I will take you to the hills and we will escape to Nubia. You can birth the child there," he whispered. "And then I will take you wherever you wish to go."

She stared at him. "If Dabir catches us, he will kill you and still take my baby."

His look did not waver, and she wondered what thoughts went through his head. Dabir had underestimated this man. A man who had nothing left to lose. "Dabir will be lucky to win such a battle, mistress. Until a man knows deep grief, he cannot even imagine revenge."

12

Dabir cursed as he paced his chambers in the Hall of Justice that evening. He should go home to his wife and children, but worry brushed the edges of his thoughts, and he knew he could not leave this place until he formulated a plan. He sank onto his cushioned chair and put his head between his knees. How was it possible Rahab had conceived? For the briefest of moments he imagined what a child of theirs might look like.

He abruptly stood and paced again, glancing as he did so in the silver mirror hanging to the side of the tapestry behind his desk. He wasn't bad looking, if he did say so. And coupled with Rahab . . .

A sharp breath caught in his chest. *Impossible.* She was barren. He had known her for months . . . to no avail. Not that he hadn't hoped. His wife's son, the brat, was an imbecile, not worthy to be called his. Not worthy to inherit all he had obtained.

Ah, but a son of Rahab's . . . he could have rivaled all of

the princes in Jericho, even in all of Canaan! Her beauty and his charm would have made it so.

Obviously, however, this child was not his.

Whose child?

Prince Nahid had spent over a month at her side. What if the child were his, as the prince had once suggested? If Nahid discovered the truth and Dabir forced an end to the pregnancy . . . He shuddered at the thought of the tortures the prince could command.

A deep sigh escaped, followed by a grueling yawn. He was so very tired. But he could not go home. The prince had requested he dine with him tonight, and there would surely be talk of Rahab. Dabir wiped a hand over his mouth. He must take care not to drink too much and to watch his tongue. The less Prince Nahid knew, the better.

Dawn had barely crested the eastern ridge the next morning when Rahab wrapped herself in a heavy veil and cloak and followed Tendaji through Jericho's quiet streets. They had spent the night gathering and packing the fewest items they would need and could conceal in the packs of a donkey, which Tendaji would purchase on their way out of town with the coins she had hoarded. No time for goodbyes to her family. They were safest if they did not know.

She smelled the market before they turned onto the lane that led to it. Camel dung mingled with the scents of spices and fish and fresh-baked breads—their normally pleasant smells nearly overwhelming. She glanced around at the familiar merchants, noting Tendaji had stepped aside to speak to a caravan master who was unloading his wares.

"Care for some of the bread, miss? Baked it fresh this morn, I did. Looks like you could use some color in those cheeks." A semi-toothless female merchant held out a loaf of flatbread to her. "If you buy one, you can take your pick of another for half the price."

Rahab's stomach turned and growled, and suddenly the bread smell overtook the others. "Yes, please." While she normally would have haggled over the price, she absently handed the woman some coins, snatched the bread and one pastry, and took a greedy bite.

The woman laughed. "So . . . hungry after all, eh, my girl? You're much too thin, you know. Not enough meat on them bones for a man to get his hands around."

Rahab ignored the comment. The men she entertained seemed to have no problem wrapping their groping hands around her. Her eyes burned with sudden moisture. What was wrong with her? She was not a woman given to useless tears.

"There, there. I mean you no harm." The woman seemed truly stricken that she had offended a customer.

Rahab shook her head. "No, you said nothing wrong." She wiped crumbs from her mouth. "The bread is very good. Thank you." She ducked her head and turned away before the woman could say more.

"If you are ready, we can go." Tendaji came up beside her, holding the donkey's reins, and gently touched her elbow to guide her through the crowded street.

When they were some distance from listening ears, she glanced at Tendaji. "Thank you for helping me."

He gave a slight bow but said nothing. Urgency guided their steps as more markets opened and people swarmed the streets. The sooner they could get past the guards, the better.

They continued down the mud-brick streets in silence. Jericho's open gates loomed ahead, its guards flanking the stone archway. Rahab felt the clasp of her veil, making sure it was secure. She would cover her eyes if it was possible to still see, but the fabric of her veil was too thick and dark.

Tendaji led the way, sickle over his shoulder. He spoke to one of the guards.

"Name," the guard demanded.

"Tendiah."

The man jotted his name on a clay tablet. "Purpose?" He looked up, and Rahab caught his scrutiny of Tendaji and herself as well. She stood very still, barely breathing.

"I am the king's servant setting out to work the harvest." He gestured behind him, taking in Rahab and the donkey. "My wife has come to help with our small garden patch near the wall."

The guard looked at her. She lowered her gaze, fearing he might recognize her despite her heavy covering. "Your wife's name?"

Tendaji did not hesitate. "Hadirah."

The guard recorded her name as well, then, after searching the donkey's nearly empty sacks, motioned them through. Rahab did not truly breathe until they were at the edge of the wheat fields.

"We made it," she whispered. "But the guards on the wall will surely see if we head to the hills. Perhaps we should go toward the Jordan instead."

Tendaji looked at her, his smile slightly amused. "Mistress, the Jordan is at flood stage. How do you expect we would cross it? Besides, the Israelites are on the other side. We would be leaving one danger and entering another."

She released an exhausted breath. She had slept little last

night, and though the sun was barely up, she felt its coming heat beneath her clothes. She longed for her bed. No. Not her bed. She longed to return to her innocence, before Gamal ever walked into her life.

"Come," Tendaji said, interrupting her thoughts. "Few are in the fields yet. We will do as we discussed and skirt the edges of the field. The wheat is tall enough to hide us from the guards on the wall." He took the donkey's reins and tugged. She followed in silence.

By the time the sun had risen halfway in the sky, they had reached a copse of trees a fair distance from the king's fields. Rahab sank to the ground beneath the shade of a large terebinth tree.

Tendaji tied the donkey's reins to a branch and knelt at her side. "I wish I could suggest that you ride, but that would look suspicious until we are beyond sight of the city walls, especially when you are supposed to be traveling closer to the gardens near the walls."

She nodded. "I know." She tucked a loose strand of hair under her veil. How she longed to rid herself of the restrictive material. "Thank you."

"I have done very little, mistress."

"You have risked your life."

He shrugged. "My life is worth nothing."

She looked at him. "It is to me, Tendaji. I am sorry for all of your losses. If we succeed, this will be the greatest kindness you could ever do for me." She glanced heavenward, wishing there were a prayer she could offer on his behalf.

"We probably should not rest here long." Tendaji rose then and retrieved some almonds from the sack at the donkey's side. "Eat." He handed them to her.

She took them with a grateful nod, and he helped her up. She ate in silence as they continued to walk toward the hills. If they could reach the burial caves, they would be safe for the night.

But as the day lengthened and the hills seemed no closer, Rahab realized they should have somehow left under cover of night. Jericho's guards were still within sight as they paced the walls and searched the distance. By now surely one of her servants had run to Dabir with the news that she and Tendaji had not returned from market.

Fear slithered up her spine, causing a hitch in her step. She caught herself and rested a hand on the donkey's saddle to keep her balance over the uneven terrain. If Dabir was as clever as she knew him to be, he could be on their trail and overtake them before nightfall.

But she did not voice her fears. Tendaji had risked too much, had too much faith in his plan. She trudged on, praying he was right.

"She's what?" Dabir stared at the cook he had hired to serve Rahab, a middle-aged woman who had little scruples and loved the coins her spying added to her pockets.

"Gone, my lord." The woman rubbed her hands together and would not meet his gaze. "The Nubian left with her for market this morning before dawn—"

"Before dawn? No markets open that early." He massaged the back of his neck, his anger rising.

"Begging pardon, my lord. But some of the bread makers do, to catch the workers as they leave for the king's fields." She straightened as though her courage had suddenly risen.

"Rahab never arises before the sun is at its midpoint." He knew, for he had checked on her more than once and found her still abed. Especially now. Women always slept more when they carried a child.

"Well, she left *this* morning, my lord, with the Nubian. And they had not returned at dusk when the first customers began to call."

"And you are just telling me this *now*?" He dragged a hand over his beard and stood, towering over her. He should have her beaten.

"Forgive me, my lord. I was not at the house the whole day. After I fixed the noon meal, I left to tend to my own family. When I returned to prepare the prostitute's evening meal, I found the earlier food untouched and no sign of either of them." Despite the stiffness of her spine, she twisted the belt at her waist, again refusing to meet his gaze.

Dabir studied her for too long, feeling suddenly weak, though his rage simmered to boiling.

"Go home," he barked, no longer able to abide her presence. Incompetent fool!

But as she hurried from his chamber, he forced his thoughts away from the woman's failings to his own. Obviously, he had underestimated both the Nubian and Rahab. He walked to the window, looked over the town square where people still waited for an audience with some high official or another. It had to be the babe that sparked this. Women were ridiculously possessive when it came to their children.

He whirled about and clapped his hands. "Guards!"

The door opened, and two young guards instantly appeared and bowed low.

"It appears the Nubian and my servant Rahab the prostitute

have fled Jericho. You are to find them. Now." He let the last word register on their startled faces. "If you do not bring them both to me alive by morning, you will be hanged in the marketplace as a warning to all who thwart the will of the king's advisor."

"How will we know where they went, my lord?" one dared to ask. Fool.

"How do you think you would find such information? Ask the guards at the gate. Take men with you. If they have left the city, search in all directions a day's walk from here. If they have not, search every house in Jericho. Leave no stone uncovered." He paused, assessing them, wondering if any man in Jericho was truly competent. "They may have been disguised. Make sure the guards at the gate have full descriptions of them."

"Yes, my lord. It will be as you say, my lord."

He dismissed them without a word and went back to pacing. It would do no good for him to go with them, nor was he up to such a trek. But he could join the guards on the city wall. Perhaps they had seen something and simply failed to report it.

He cursed as he left his chamber, certain that if Jericho ever came under attack, the men of the city would cower like women in their beds. They were all fools, if a Nubian and a woman could so easily deceive them.

13

Rahab sank to the dirt floor of the burial cave, every limb aching with relief. Dusk had deepened, and Tendaji sat near the front of the cave, keeping watch. The donkey knelt not far from where she sat, and she slowly stretched out on the ground, not even caring that the stone crevices at the back held the bones of her ancestors. Somehow she would probably pay for disrupting such a place, but it was the least likely place Dabir's men would look for them.

And she had no doubt they would look. By now her presence was surely missed, and Dabir had probably swallowed his tongue sputtering curses at the men and women he employed. She closed her eyes and sent a silent prayer toward the heavens that no one would suffer on her account.

If the moon god heard and answered, she would name her son Yerach after him, devote her life to his service. *Please, I do not make an idle promise. Let me escape Dabir and keep this child.*

She settled on Tendaji's cloak and used her own as a

covering, grateful for his kindness once again. Faith had never been easy for her, and even now she prayed on the fringes of doubt. Why should the moon god answer a prostitute? She did not have a single thing to offer in sacrifice except her unborn child.

And that she would not give. A sick feeling washed over her. Child sacrifice was the highest gift one could give the gods. But the whole purpose of her prayer was to save the child, not give him up.

Turmoil churned her stomach. She rolled onto her side and tried to shut out the disturbing thoughts. But sleep would not come.

"Rahab." Tendaji's whisper and slight shaking of her shoulder jolted her awake. Was it morning?

"What is it?" Her body ached, and she could barely force herself to sit up.

"Guards roam the hills. We must move farther into the cave."

Alarm shot through her, and suddenly she had no trouble rising. She sprang to her feet and grabbed Tendaji's cloak, handing it to him. "Dare we go farther into such a cave?" The dead would surely resent the intrusion.

"We have no choice," he said, tight-lipped.

She followed his lead without a word, the donkey between them. But the donkey seemed to sense the odor of the more recent dead. The stone Tendaji had rolled from the cave was one that had not sat sealed as long as the others, making it easier to move. But the smell as they wandered deeper into the cave grew putrid. The donkey stopped and brayed.

Rahab stroked its nose. "There, there," she said softly. "You don't have to keep going." She looked at Tendaji. "We can't. They will hear us if he grows stubborn." She inclined her head toward the animal, which had taken two steps back and strained at the reins to turn and head toward the entrance.

"We will have to let him go then. Help me grab everything from his back." Tendaji untied the saddle and tossed it in a corner, and the two of them tucked every provision they could carry into the pockets of their cloaks. Tendaji led the animal to the cave's entrance where the stone stood slightly ajar and allowed it to run free, slapping its bottom to direct it to leave them. The donkey moved a few paces and stopped, refusing to budge.

Tendaji mumbled under his breath words in his Nubian tongue. Rahab huddled against a wall, shivering. Men's voices drew nearer. Tendaji left the opening and joined her, taking her hand in his and tugging her again toward the wrapped corpses. "Stubborn animal won't leave."

"He will give us away," she whispered.

"Yes."

They moved in silence until they had gone as far as they dared. If they got locked in here, they would soon become like the men and women resting on the stone slabs.

Rahab placed a protective hand over the place the babe grew. *Please, Yerach.* But she felt as though her prayers did not move beyond the cave's walls.

Voices grew louder and closer. They had entered the cave. There was no doubt now.

Rahab stood rigid, hoping the shadows would hide her. If only she had time to unwrap one of the dead bodies and encase herself in the grave clothes.

But as the sound of heavy feet clomped toward them and a torch lit the area not far from where they stood, she knew it was too late. They were caught. Yerach had not heard.

⁓⁓⁓

Dabir's hand connected with her cheek once, twice, bringing swift tears to the surface. "Did you honestly think you could escape without my notice, Rahab?" He glanced at Tendaji, whose hands were tied behind him, on his knees at her side. "And you! Such betrayal is reprehensible." He spat in Tendaji's face, then looked at his guards. "Take this man and strip his virility. He wanted to spare the prostitute's child? He shall remain childless all his days."

"No! Please, Dabir. Tendaji did nothing but obey me. Please do not punish him." Rahab's pleading brought another slap to her cheek. Dabir yanked her up from her kneeling position and motioned to the guards, who grabbed both her arms and carried her through an adjoining door. But not before she caught the shock registering on Tendaji's face, his dark skin paling.

Two burly guards lifted him with ease, as though the man had lost all strength to fight, as the anteroom door shut in her face. "Tendaji!" She screamed his name over and over, at last dissolving into tears. "He did nothing wrong!" But her angry tirade went unanswered, and the sounds coming from beyond her small prison grew silent.

She wanted to die.

The door swung open moments later, with Dabir filling the archway. He stomped forward, grabbed her bound hands, and dragged her back into his chamber, tossing her onto his plush couch. He towered over her and grabbed a strip of leather hanging on his wall, a whip that she always thought ornamental, to intimidate those who sat before Dabir's judgment.

"The Nubian will return to guard you after he has recovered," Dabir said through gritted teeth. "Fortunately, eunuchs make good guards when the prize is a weak woman."

The sting of the lash came down on her calves. "Lest you think you can run from me again."

She could not stifle a cry as he beat her again and again. Rahab's stomach grew queasy. Was this how he intended to make her lose the child?

"Please, my lord, forgive me." Her voice cracked on hoarse tears.

He dropped the whip even as he stared down at her. Silence was broken only by his heated breathing. "What am I to do with you, Rahab?" His angry tone now sounded hurt. "I trusted you." He turned away from her then and walked to the window. She curled into a ball, weeping, her bound hands protecting the babe.

He stalked back to her, straightening to his full height. "I should have known you would run when I insisted you could not keep the child. How can you even want the thing when you don't know the father? Prostitutes don't raise children!" He pushed her aside until she fell onto the floor, then sank onto the couch in her place. "Will you say nothing in your defense?"

Every nerve ending hurt from his beating, but she knew she dared not ignore him. He had made his power over her very clear. She looked up briefly, then lowered her eyes in a gesture of respect. "I should not have disobeyed you, my lord. I did not want to hurt anyone."

"But you did, Rahab. Surely you knew Tendaji could not go unpunished for helping you."

She closed her eyes, her tears salty on her tongue.

"I have no choice, Rahab. You have left me no choice." He sounded angry, and yet the wounded tone came through once more. "If you'd wanted a child, you should have told me long ago. Perhaps other arrangements could have been made."

He sounded so magnanimous, but she had listened too long to his lying tongue. "If other arrangements can be made, then let me carry this child to term. Even if I must give him up, let me give him life." She couldn't bear to let them do what she had heard from Cala's gossip. Temple prostitutes who managed to become pregnant were forced to drink bitter waters to expel the child from them. The ordeal left most to choose any means possible to prevent any further pregnancy.

Moments slipped past as Dabir stared down at her. "It is not possible," he said after many breaths. "Too much is at stake. You already know this."

Too much money to be lost, which was why even his beating was so careful. He knew she would heal from both the miscarriage and the bruises together.

He stood and gripped her bound hands, lifting her up. "Come." He turned her about and led her through the halls, down several more corridors toward the king's harem, to the palace midwife. He stopped at the door and checked her bonds, tightening the rope until she winced. "I do not trust you, my dear."

He knocked on the door and spoke quietly to the woman, who took Rahab's arm in silence and led her to a back room. "She can return home in three days," the woman told Dabir.

Rahab heard his retreating footsteps but caught sight of the guard he left standing near the woman's door.

"It's quite a mess you're in, young one." She tsked her tongue and shook her head, her expression sad. "It's harder the longer you wait."

"I don't want this," Rahab said, her voice cracked like broken pottery.

The woman's gaze held sympathy as she patted her arm. "I know. But there is nothing I can do."

Rahab sat on the cot the woman indicated while she set about mixing a brew of herbs. "If the gods are smiling on you, this might not work," she said, glancing at Rahab. "In that case, I will tell the king's advisor there is nothing to be done but wait until it is born. Pray the gods have mercy."

Rahab felt the slightest flicker of hope at the woman's words. But all thought of the gods whisked the hope from her. If the gods favored her, if Yerach had done as she asked, she would not have been caught, Tendaji would not suffer the fate Dabir had assigned him, and she would be free.

But as she drank the bitter water, she prayed just the same.

─────✦─────

Rahab awoke still groggy from the effects of a drug-induced sleep. She rolled onto her side and rose up on one elbow. What day was it? She closed her eyes against the onslaught of a violent headache and rested her head once more on the pillow.

The room was one she did not know, and for a moment she could not recall where she was. Sunlight streamed through low windows, and movement in the room caught her eye. The palace midwife. Memory rushed in on her with awful clarity.

"So you are awake at last. Good."

Rahab squinted against the glare and tried to hide her eyes from the woman. She pressed a hand to her flat middle. So the herbs had done their work. The thought tasted acrid on her tongue. She turned away from the woman. "Leave me be!"

The woman stood silent a moment, but Rahab refused to face her. "It is my duty to see that you come through the ordeal without complications. Dabir considers you a great asset, Rahab. I am here to be sure you make a full recovery."

"Dabir can go to the pit," she spat under her breath. Overwhelming hatred for the man nearly choked her.

"I am going to pretend I did not hear that last comment, mistress." She cleared her throat as though she felt somehow uncomfortable. "I have ordered a meal of fresh herbs and cheese and fruit to help you regain your strength. And I have put healing balm on your wounds." She paused. "I don't know what you did to deserve that man's wrath, but he obviously still wants you in his service or he would not have gone to this much trouble." She touched Rahab's arm, but Rahab shook it off.

"Think what you like," the woman said, her voice kind. "But you are worth far more than you know." She headed toward the door. "When you are done pouting, come out and have something to eat."

Her footsteps receded, and Rahab waited, relieved when at last the door shut and the room grew quiet. She sagged against the thin cot, no longer able to keep the pain held tight within her. Pain that went far deeper than the wounds Dabir had inflicted. Memories of the cramping and fear, of the tears she could not stop, would not be put off. She had kept silent during most of the suffering, but now . . .

Now, as the silence lingered and the room remained empty,

she gave in to the crushing emotion. *Oh god, oh god!* How could Yerach have allowed this to happen? Even her silent prayers, as the woman had suggested, had not caused the herbs to fail.

She rocked forward and back, tucking her knees beneath her, drawing herself into the position of a newborn babe. *Let me die. Please let me die.*

But her prayer, like every other she had ever uttered, went unanswered, and the wound in her heart bled with every tear.

14

Rahab sat listless at her dressing table three months later, while another new maid dressed her hair in jeweled combs and draped dangling earrings from her ears. Once she had healed, Dabir had increased the number of men she was required to entertain each week, which left her little time after sundown to ready herself. Sometimes she even allowed the occasional visitor during daylight hours to give herself time to recover.

She was a role player, acting with each new man as though she truly cared for him. She played on their fears, then soothed their bruised egos, all the while knowing she meant none of it. She was dead inside.

Especially since Tendaji had returned to her a broken man. Though not really a man but a eunuch, his courage and determination—even his hatred of Dabir—apparently gone. As Dabir had ruined her, he had destroyed Tendaji's manhood.

She wished she had never been born.

The servant finished the work on her hair without a word, for Rahab could not abide frivolous talk with women who came and went as often as she changed her garments. Rahab stood and out of habit smoothed the faint wrinkles out of her purple robe. She moved slowly to her chamber door toward the outer courtyard. She found Tendaji where she expected to, standing at the gate as he had always done.

He glanced up at her approach, the light gone from his eyes. "Can I help you, mistress?" His voice sounded flat, and where he had once held compassion for her, there was no resemblance of it in his gaze now.

"I came to see how you are doing, Tendaji." She paused, thinking how foolish she sounded. "That is, I wanted to tell you how very sorry I am for getting you into such trouble. I should never have told you about the babe . . ." Her voice trailed off, and she studied the tiles at her feet. "If you ever want to leave, I will understand. I will not stop you." She looked up but glanced beyond him, unable to hold his gaze.

"It was my choice to take you away from Jericho, Rahab. I knew the risks."

"You did not know Dabir's cruelty as I did. I should not have expected to escape him." She looked into Tendaji's eyes, surprised to find the hint of compassion flickering there. "He has kept my family living in fear since Gamal's foolish acts. Even my sister is no longer allowed to visit me."

She turned to go, her heart like a stone within her.

"Did you betray me to Dabir? Did you even hint at our plans to escape?" Tendaji's quiet words stopped her cold. So even he did not truly believe her.

She turned once more to face him. "When would I have done such a thing? We were never apart."

"We were during the hours you spent in your bed and I guarded the gate."

"And you will recall that no one visited during that time." He had every right to hate her, but his distrust pained her.

"There were servants." He glanced beyond her as though he expected one to appear even now.

Realization dawned. "I wanted my baby, Tendaji. Why would I have ever done such a thing? Do you think me so evil that I would seek to hurt you or my babe . . ." She swallowed hard. "Who will never see the light of day?"

His face softened as her words settled on him. He nodded. "Then Dabir acted quickly once the servants discovered we were gone. He found us too easily. One or more of your servants spies on you for him."

"I have always known it," she said, holding his gaze. "Why do you think I feared to trust even you?"

He nodded, then looked away, and she knew instinctively that his new status had yet to settle with him, and he could not abide the embarrassment given his lost manhood.

Silence passed between them, but it held less anger.

At last Tendaji leaned close to her ear. "One day Dabir will regret what he has done." He straightened, unsmiling, but one look into his eyes told her he had not lost all courage. Revenge could carry him far.

She touched his arm and nodded, then walked away. She made her way to her chambers and closed the door behind her.

At the window where she and Tendaji had plotted their escape, she looked out over the valley toward the Jordan, toward the camp of Israel, then searched the hills in the opposite direction. They had gone far in a single day. But not far enough.

If only they could have made it. But now, with added ser-vants—Dabir's spies—her prison remained stronger than ever. Worse, she had sacrificed her virtue, putting her soul in bondage. She needed rescue from herself, for she hated all she had become.

PART 2

The king of Jericho was told, "Look, some of the Israelites have come here tonight to spy out the land." So the king of Jericho sent this message to Rahab: "Bring out the men who came to you and entered your house, because they have come to spy out the whole land."

Joshua 2:1–3

Hezron the father of Ram,
Ram the father of Amminadab,
Amminadab the father of Nahshon,
Nahshon the father of Salmon,
Salmon the father of Boaz.

Ruth 4:19–21

15

Rushing waters sped over protruding rocks and tree limbs in the Jordan, overshadowing this narrower place in the river. Salmon stood at the edge, sensing Mishael's nervous presence at his side.

"The overhanging branches almost meet in the middle. We should be able to hold steady to them to cross," Salmon said, glancing from the slippery rocks below to the sturdy tree branches above.

"God will be with you. Be strong and courageous." The elder, their leader Joshua, stood behind them, one hand on each of their shoulders. "Once you have crossed, wait to join a caravan of merchants to enter the city. They should not be able to tell you apart from any other travelers. At least we can hope for that much." He paused and they turned to face him. "Once you are in the city, do not draw attention to yourselves. Just act like travelers and listen to what the people are saying. Lodge there if you can." He handed them a bag of silver.

Salmon took the bag and nodded, his faith rising with

Joshua's confident tone. "We will do as you have asked. And make no mistake, we will not fail." Not like the spies Moses had sent to see this land. He would not live with their regrets or their consequences.

He glanced at Mishael. "Let's cross this river and get to Jericho."

On the other side of the river, Salmon ungirded his robe and retied his sandals, which had been dangling about his neck. He pulled the turban from his pocket and tied it with a leather strap, while Mishael did the same.

"That was easier than I expected," Mishael said, brushing the last of the dirt from his feet. "Let's hope getting the information we need is as simple."

Salmon looked toward the formidable walls of Jericho, still half a day's walk from where they stood. "How hard can it be?" Though his thoughts carried the same concerns.

Salmon and Mishael searched the bank for branches large enough to use as walking sticks, hacked some of the dangling stems from their edges, and started walking.

"I hope we don't have to use these or the daggers in our belts." Mishael thumped the ground with his new staff and gave Salmon a mischievous smile. "I could whack a few heads with this, though—don't think I couldn't."

Salmon laughed. "I have no doubt about your ability to whack heads, my friend." The thought brought to mind the times when they would wrestle as young boys.

"Zimri always beat you." Mishael spoke as though he had read his thoughts.

"I let him win a few times." His smile quickly faded as he

remembered Zimri's end. How could the man have allowed a Midianite woman to seduce him? He shook his head, the very idea one he simply could not grasp.

"You should have put him in his place. Perhaps then he wouldn't have been so arrogant." A quick glance at Mishael told him they shared the same memory. And loss.

"Our God is an exacting God," Salmon whispered, praying he had not offended the Almighty. "That is, it is a fearful thing to purposely disobey Him."

Mishael picked up a stone and cast it a great distance. "We should have invaded Midian and pulled Zimri out before he could act so foolishly."

"Or stood guard at his tent and threatened him even if he just needed to relieve himself outside the camp?" Salmon scowled and shook his head. "No one can control another man forever, my friend. Not even you." He smiled, then slapped Mishael lightly on the back. "Let us do our best to be more faithful." He glanced toward Jericho's forbidding walls. "And not let a woman seduce us into such false worship to cause the whole camp to suffer." Twenty-four thousand people had died in a plague because of Zimri's sin with Kozbi, daughter of a Midianite leader.

The reminder sobered him, and apparently the normally talkative Mishael too, for they walked along in silence until they came to a place to camp near Jericho's thick gates. Hidden among a copse of trees, they waited for an approaching caravan.

At dawn the next morning, several caravans approached. Salmon and Mishael slipped in among them, immediately picking up a conversation with the servants among the crowd.

"What wares have you brought with you today?" Mishael

asked one of the Midianite traders, whose dark turban and standard etched on the sides of the donkey's carts told both men his heritage.

The man gave Mishael and Salmon a hard glance, as if trying to place them. "I have seen you before. Are we neighbors?" The man scratched a dark, short-cropped beard.

Salmon ran a hand over his own beard, silently praying that the length of the edges would not give them away. For though they had discussed shaving their beards to fit in with the rest of the Canaanite men, Salmon could not bring himself to do so. To break even one of the laws of Moses would prove him unrighteous, unfaithful. Like his father before him, who once stood as a prince in Judah. He could not follow that path.

"We are travelers from Shittim," Mishael said. "We are on our way toward Babylon by way of the King's Highway."

"Stopping for supplies at Jericho?" the man asked, his brow lifted, too curious.

Salmon nodded, holding up a limp goatskin at his side. "I'm afraid we have more coins than food. It is hard to eat silver." He laughed, glancing at Mishael, who joined him.

"And look, here we are at the gates already," Mishael said, pulling away.

Salmon followed his friend, then glanced back at the Midianite. God had now declared these people enemies of Israel, despite their link to Abraham through his concubine Keturah. Midian had even given Moses shelter and a wife, but the incident with Zimri and Kozbi had changed all of that previous goodwill.

"You don't happen to have any fresh bread among those wares, do you, my friend?" Salmon asked in parting, knowing from a quick view of his goods that he carried tools, not food.

The man shook his head. "No, not to sell. My loss," he said, smiling. "God go with you, my friend." He tipped his fingers to his head, a parting gesture.

Salmon looked at Mishael, wondering if he had anything to say about the man's use of God's blessing, but his friend's gaze had settled on the gates looming before them. Midianites would invoke the Baals, but some might still believe in Abraham's God, as Moses' father-in-law had.

"Do you have a plan?" Mishael asked, drawing Salmon's thoughts to their task at hand. "What reason do we give for entering their fair city?" He bent near Salmon's ear, though the crowd had grown so noisy, he need not have bothered to whisper.

"We tell them the truth. We are here to collect supplies for our journey to Babylon."

"And we may need to know a good place to lodge for the night," Mishael added, a smirk covering his normally handsome face.

"I am not even going to ask you what that smirk intends, my friend." Most lodging houses belonged to prostitutes in cities such as Jericho. A place where Zimri had been snared by Kozbi, though she had not been a prostitute but a Midianite leader's daughter.

"Don't worry." Mishael rested a hand on Salmon's shoulder. "Women are the last thing on my mind."

The Midianite caravan moved through the gates, and Salmon and Mishael slipped in among them as though they were part of it. The guards glanced at them. Salmon nodded a greeting but kept walking. Mishael followed.

A second group of guards stood at the inner gate. This time they were stopped.

"State your business." The guard seemed young and wary.

Salmon met his gaze and smiled. "We are but travelers, my lord." He lifted his empty sack. "Our supplies have run low, and we are trying to catch up with our brothers, who set out a day ahead of us on our way home to Babylon." He let the sack fall to his side. "We simply wish to buy supplies from your merchants."

The guard nodded and waved them through.

Salmon walked into a shop where a man stood at a table of freshly baked flatbreads seasoned with various spices. "How much?" he asked, pointing to one with rosemary leaves sprinkled over it.

The man looked him over as if sizing him up. "You are not from around here."

Salmon shook his head. "No, we are just passing through. We were separated from our countrymen, and it has taken longer to return than we expected." He pointed again to the bread and held out a small piece of silver. "Will this cover it?"

The man's eyes widened, but he also seemed pleased. "It will suffice." He picked up the loaf, glanced at Mishael, then added a second. "For your friend."

Salmon bowed. "Thank you." He took the loaves and handed one to Mishael. "Can you tell me where we can find lodging for the night? We will leave in the morning but thought we might enjoy the pleasures of Jericho for a day." He smiled, sniffed the loaf, and released a deep sigh. "I haven't tasted my wife's bread in months." He glanced at the man, trying to determine his reaction.

"Out on a raiding party, were you?" The man's eyes held the slightest hint of calculation. "We've heard rumors of those Israelites." He leaned closer and glanced around as though his words were the choicest of secrets. "People are afraid of them. Have you run into them in your travels?"

"Why would they be afraid of them? They are on the other side of the Jordan and its banks are near to flooding. Besides, they are wanderers." He waved a hand in dismissal. "What possible harm can they do?"

The man looked at Salmon as though he had lost all sensibility. "Have you not heard of their God? There are rumors . . . stories of how He delivered them from the Egyptian Pharaoh, how He parted the sea, how they killed those two kings of the Amorites, Sihon and Og?"

Salmon nodded. "I've heard such tales. But that was years ago. They've been wandering in the wilderness for forty years. I don't think you have anything to fear."

The man looked like he wanted to believe them, but Salmon still saw the skepticism in his eyes. He touched the man's shoulder. "Don't worry, my friend." At the man's nod, he added, "Now about that lodging?"

The man's smile held the hint of a smirk. "How much are you willing to pay, and what kind of lodging?"

"Just something—"

"Something that will give us a fair taste of Jericho's better life," Mishael interrupted.

The man laughed. "Then I would recommend you try to get an appointment with our town's finest woman of the night. Only the richest men can afford her, and she is the consort of the prince himself."

Salmon's middle tightened. A prostitute, as he expected.

"Where is this residence, my friend?" Mishael asked when Salmon said nothing.

"The house of Rahab. It is built into the wall in the wealthier section of town, not far from the palace itself. She has a big Nubian guard who stands watch at her gate. If you take the road along the wall, you can't miss it."

"Thank you, my friend." Mishael elbowed Salmon.

"Yes, thank you." He bowed once more and backed away, his bread still untouched, but Mishael's was half gone.

Salmon gripped his staff in one hand and tore off a hunk of bread with his teeth. "So, now we shall see just how much a prostitute is willing to tell us without seducing us." They would not be like Zimri.

He stalked off, leaving Mishael to catch up with him.

16

The walk through the city of palms took time, and more than once they found themselves taking a wrong turn down a street with little light. The sun had already passed the midway point in the sky, and still they had not found the prostitute's house.

"Are we lost?" Mishael pulled a handful of almonds from his pocket and handed a few to Salmon.

Salmon glanced at the sky and toward the city walls. "Not exactly lost. Not yet." He hated to admit such a thing, but as the sun continued toward the west, his stomach rumbled and worry settled in his middle. "Let's check this street. The man said we couldn't miss the place."

"At least we've gotten a good idea of what the city looks like. Perhaps those wrong turns were providential." Mishael reached for another handful of almonds.

"You might want to ration those." Salmon glanced at the sack of dates he carried. "We might need these for many days to come."

"Can't you hear my stomach roaring? It's like thunder inside of me!"

Salmon laughed. "You complain too much." He spotted the prostitute's house a few moments later, but held Mishael back when he continued as if he would simply approach without forethought. "What are we supposed to say to her?" The very thought of speaking to a prostitute turned his stomach.

"If she is as popular as the merchant said she is, let's at least see if we can secure an appointment with her first. Then we will worry about what to say." Mishael lifted a brow. "Unless you would rather spend the night in the streets. How much sleep do you think you'll get in the open in a wicked city?"

"I don't expect to sleep at all regardless." Salmon glanced behind them, grateful to see they were relatively alone. Neighbors were not within hearing distance, even if Mishael should learn to keep his voice down. "Come on then. We can speak to the Nubian."

Salmon led the way to the prostitute's gate and found it locked. He rattled the knocker and waited. "Maybe they are sleeping?" he whispered to Mishael.

"At this hour?" Mishael looked doubtful. A moment later, a tall, dark-skinned man approached the gate.

"What do you seek?" He looked down at them, his gaze taking in their appearances before settling on their faces.

"We are travelers, here on business." Salmon cleared his throat. "We seek a night's lodging with your mistress. A merchant in the marketplace recommended her to us."

The Nubian looked them over again, then shook his head. "I'm afraid the merchant is mistaken. This is not an inn. My mistress does not keep men through the night. They pay for time with her. They do not stay."

Disappointment and relief mingled in Salmon's heart. He glanced around, then lowered his voice. "I can pay her well. For a few moments of her time then. We will seek lodging elsewhere." He hated himself for what he was suggesting, though he had no intention of actually using her services. Why did he even care? And yet . . . had God led them here? What better place to gain information from than a woman who slept with the city's highest officials?

The Nubian looked dubious but held up a hand. "Stay here." When he walked into the house, Mishael stepped closer to Salmon.

"How are you planning to spend that time with her?" His look held uncertainty, even fear. Zimri's demise was too recent to treat this mission with anything but caution. "You wouldn't actually touch her, would you?"

"Of course not!" Salmon shifted from foot to foot. "If she will see us, we will question her. That is all."

Salmon glanced at the sun, now past the midway point, then leaned against the stone pillar that held the gate firm. At last the Nubian returned, unlocked the gate, and bid them enter. Salmon followed the taller man into a sitting room covered in scarlets and purples, with cushioned couches and plush embroidered pillows. Oriental tapestries hung from whitewashed walls, and alabaster vases sat on low tables. The prostitute lived well.

"Sit," the Nubian said, pointing to the couches.

Salmon glanced at Mishael, but one look at the Nubian and he obeyed, sitting uncomfortably on the edge of the seat. They waited in silence long enough for Salmon to have counted a thousand sheep.

"What's taking her so long?" Mishael whispered.

Salmon shrugged, but he could tell by the look in his friend's eyes that he was as anxious as Salmon to be about their business. It would be dusk soon, and they needed to get back to the city gate and find a real inn to stay in. Sitting here was wasting time.

His heart beat faster at the thought. He stood. "This was a mistake." He motioned to Mishael to come and headed toward the door.

"Going so soon? My, my, but you foreigners are an impatient lot." A rich, sultry voice came from behind him. He turned and took in the sight of her. His breath stuck in his throat. The woman was simply beautiful. He had expected rich adornments in her hair and jewels dangling about her body. He had expected rich, patterned clothing, but though her robe was scarlet, her tunic was white, and she wore a simple scarf over her head.

She stepped closer to him. "I am Rahab, and this is my home. Tendaji, my guard, tells me that you seek lodging. Surely you are aware that my services provide much more." She tilted her head, her look curious, not seductive.

"We are aware that you are the consort of princes and wealthy men."

"Neither of which you appear to be," she said, glancing from Salmon to Mishael, who now stood beside him. "So tell me, what really brings you to see me?" She motioned to the couches and sat in a plush chair opposite them.

Salmon glanced beyond her. "Is this room secure? Will our words be heard by your servants?"

She looked thoughtful but a moment, then shook her head. "Had you asked me that a few months ago, I would have said yes. My employer kept me his prisoner until the prince got word of what he had done to me." She looked away as though the thought still pained her, but her expression quickly changed and she faced them once more. "Since then, I have come to an agreement with my employer and dismissed all of the servants but Tendaji and hired my younger sister as my maid. No one else in this town can be trusted." She looked toward the window. "My house is still watched, but they do not enter without my permission."

Salmon nodded. "That is good."

"So why have you come to me if not for my services, which Tendaji tells me you can afford." She crossed one leg over the other, exposing her bare foot.

Salmon looked away, embarrassed. "We are simply visitors to your city on our way to Babylon. We came for supplies and to spend the night before we attempt to catch up with our brothers. It seemed wise for us to learn what we could of your city while we are here." He met her gaze, unflinching, studying her reaction. "When a merchant suggested you knew more than most, we decided to start here." He smiled, though inside he chided himself that lies should fall so easily from his lips.

Rahab uncrossed her legs and tucked them beneath her, as if sensing his discomfort in her presence. "Tell me your names. Where are you from?" Her brows narrowed the slightest bit, and Salmon thought her too intelligent to be a prostitute. Why had some man of this city, even the prince himself, not married this woman? What an asset she would be to a kingdom. Yet how he could tell that by one glance, he did not know. She must have cast some sort of spell or curse on him.

"I am Mishael," his friend said before Salmon could rein in his thoughts. "And this is my friend Salmon."

"Interesting names. You say you are headed to Babylon?" She rested her chin in her hand. Even her nails were plain, not painted, as he'd expected them to be. As Kozbi's had been when he helped bury her body.

"We have business there." Mishael spoke for him again. Salmon met his gaze, getting the message that he clearly hoped Salmon would speak up and take over this conversation.

Salmon studied her. "You are not dressed as a prostitute."

She raised a brow. "You seem quite aware of what my profession requires."

Heat filled his face, and he looked away from her gaze once more, thoroughly embarrassed. He *must* get hold of his wayward thoughts. She waited, watching him, and Salmon debated within himself whether to tell her the truth.

Her forehead knit with the tiniest of scowls. "Clearly you need something from me, my lord. If it is not my services, then please, either tell me or do not waste my time." She shifted gracefully and stood.

Salmon jumped to his feet. "Can we trust you? Do you keep the secrets of your patrons?"

Rahab searched his face but did not smile. "Normally my patrons pay for my silence." But as Salmon reached to pull out several pieces of silver, she waved his actions aside. "To simply talk is free." She motioned toward a side door. "Come."

Salmon followed, Mishael at his heels. She led them to an inner courtyard and a stairway leading to her roof. They walked in silence until they reached a small enclosure facing the city wall. Rahab opened a half door and showed them inside.

"I know by your clothing and beards that you are not from around here," she said softly. "And I can tell by your eyes that you are not truly headed to Babylon. So tell me the truth. If you want my silence, tell me why you are here."

Salmon nodded. "We have come from beyond the Jordan. We are Israelites."

She looked at him, and he thought her beauty would poison him where he stood. No wonder Zimri fell captive to Kozbi.

He straightened, narrowing his gaze. "Do the men of this place speak of us?"

She glanced through the top of the half door, seemingly to make sure they were still alone, then leaned closer. Too close. Salmon's breath hitched, but he held steady.

"Most of the men of the city fear you," she said. "We have heard the stories of what your God did to the Pharaoh of Egypt with the plagues, and to the kings of the Amorites, Og and Sihon. And even though you wandered in the wilderness and plagues have befallen you, the fear of you has not abated. In fact, it has grown stronger in recent months, as if people fear invasion." Her gaze held first Salmon's then Mishael's.

"They would be right to fear our God," Mishael said softly. "He is a great and powerful God, and He does not abide sin. Not even from among His own people."

Salmon looked at her. "One of the plagues you speak of took twenty-four thousand of our people because one of our men took a Midianite woman."

Rahab drew in a breath, clearly troubled. "So your God does not allow for outsiders to enter your camp? He would kill you for taking one in?" She seemed to take a sudden interest in her feet.

The scent of her perfume wafted in the small room, and Salmon drew a hand over his face, trying to block its potency. "Not for taking in a foreigner," he said at last. "If a foreigner chooses to follow the ways of our God, they would not be shut out. It was because our people had been seduced to follow the lifeless gods of the Midianites, the Baals of Peor, and worshiped them instead of the one true God, that our God became angry and sent the plague on us."

She still studied her feet and clasped her hands together. "Your God is a powerful God."

"Yes," Salmon said, wondering at the soft awe in her voice.

She sighed, then glanced at him but could not hold his gaze. "What is the purpose of your visit here?"

She appeared to struggle with something, but Salmon could not deduce what it was from her expression.

"Our God is giving us this land. We have come here to spy it out."

She drew a sharp breath, but a moment later, she nodded and sighed, as if she had been expecting this very thing. "It is what our leaders have feared. Now their fears will come upon them."

"Yes." Sadness accompanied his admission in that she would suffer along with the city. He did not explore why a prostitute should matter to him in that moment.

"May I ask one question?" Her voice held longing, a need to know.

"Of course." Salmon glanced beyond her toward the other rooftops. No one lingered near to overhear them.

"Why would your God do that? Why take something from its rightful owners to give to a group of wanderers?" She fingered her veil, then clasped her hands once more.

Salmon wondered again if this woman could be trusted, but he sent a silent prayer heavenward and hoped that Moses' assurance that God would be near them when they prayed would actually prove true.

"God is the rightful owner of all land," he said quietly. "He promised the land of Canaan to our ancestor Abraham many years ago. But our forefathers had to go through a time of great testing and punishment for our disobedience to Him. Now at last, God has made a way for us to see His promise fulfilled."

Silence followed as she seemed to ponder his words. "And He is giving you Jericho first, is that right?"

"You could say that."

"You will find these walls hard to breach," she said, straightening, confidence suddenly lifting her chin. "I can assure you that it will not take long for word of your presence to reach the king, but I will not be the one to tell him. As I said, my house is watched. Even now, despite our secrecy, men will know that you are here, and they will send guards to question me. They do this with every foreigner."

Mishael touched Salmon's arm, his expression strained.

"Can you give us a place to hide until we can escape the city?" Salmon asked.

Footsteps sounded in the distance, and Rahab stepped from the small enclosure and bid them stay where they were. The Nubian met her at the top of the stairs.

"We shouldn't have come," Mishael whispered once she was out of earshot.

"Well, we're here now." He looked at his friend. "It wouldn't hurt to pray."

Rahab appeared at the small half door. She motioned to mounds of flax a short distance from them, spread out on her roof to dry in the sun. "The king's men are at my door.

Hide beneath the flax until I can send them away. Then I will return to you." She pointed to a corner of the roof that was hidden in shadows and turned to go.

"Rahab," Salmon whispered.

She looked back at him.

"You will not betray us?" They would somehow scale the outer wall, despite the deep drop, and risk injury if he thought he could not trust her. "Promise me."

She offered him the slightest hint of a smile. Her beauty nearly took his breath. "I promise. On my life, I will send the guards away. Then I will return to you."

She hurried down the steps while Salmon and Mishael buried themselves in stalks of prickly flax.

Rahab slipped into her room and stood before the mirror. Her simple attire would never do, especially if Dabir happened to accompany the king's guards. She searched her wooden chest for an embroidered robe and quickly pinned up her hair, leaving a few strands loose beneath the veil, then added earrings and one of the many necklaces Dabir had given her. Her sister was better at applying the kohl to her eyes, but Rahab had already sent her home.

Satisfied at last, she strode to her sitting room, where Tendaji waited near the door. "Dabir is leading ten of the king's personal guards. Shall I let them in?"

She shook her head. "No. I will come with you to the gate." She led the way, and Tendaji followed close on her heels.

"Dabir, how good it is to see you." She offered a coy smile, then glanced beyond him as though she just now noticed the torch-carrying guards. "But . . . what is this? Have I done something wrong?" She played the part of a truly anxious woman, longing to please, giving him what she knew he wanted with one well-placed look.

Dabir gripped the barred gate and rattled it. "Let me in, Rahab. The king has sent us."

"What does the king want with me?" Memories of Dabir's offices, of his whip surfaced, and she could not stop the sudden tightness in her middle. If not for Prince Nahid's rescue once he'd learned of the beating . . .

"You beat Rahab? Why would you do such a thing, Dabir?" Prince Nahid had paced her sitting room while Dabir sat nervously on the edge of her couch. Rahab had stood to the side, trembling at the rage she had sparked with the word *babe*.

Dabir's face paled, but he held his chin up, and Rahab sensed an elaborate lie awaited her ears. "She escaped, my lord. The Nubian took her to our ancestral burial caves, of all places, and she admitted the plan was hers from the beginning. I had no choice but to teach her a lesson." He cleared his throat at the prince's glaring hatred.

Rahab swallowed hard. She had never seen such anger in the prince's eyes in all the time she had known him.

"You will never touch her again, Dabir. If I find out you have caused her even a hint of pain, I will have your body impaled on a stake in front of the Hall of Justice. Do you understand?"

Dabir nodded but did not speak.

"Say it, Dabir."

"Yes, my lord." He clasped his hands in front of him, and in that moment Rahab almost felt a hint of compassion for the man. But the emotion did not linger, swiftly replaced by the burning anger that always accompanied the memories of the midwife, of her child.

"The king has sent for you if you are harboring Israelite spies." Dabir's comment drew her back to look into eyes full of malice. She took a small step backward.

"I don't know what you are talking about." Her heart hammered in her chest, but she held still, silently praying to the God of Israel to keep her calm. Did their God hear the prayers of a foreigner, whom He seemed to despise?

"The king says, 'Bring out the men who came to you and entered your house, because they have come to spy out the whole land.'" Dabir looked beyond her to Tendaji, then back to hold her gaze once more. "We know they came to you. They were seen entering Jericho, and the bread merchant says he pointed them here. So bring them out so that we may take them to the king."

"Yes, the men came to me," she said, "but I did not know where they had come from. At dusk, when it was time to close the city gate, they left. I don't know which way they went. Go after them quickly. You may catch up with them." She held Dabir's gaze, unflinching.

He looked at Tendaji. "Does she speak the truth?" Menace emanated from Dabir's heated gaze, but Rahab felt Tendaji also stiffen and straighten beside her.

"She speaks the truth. Two foreign men came just before dusk. They did not stay long." He crossed his arms and took a step closer to Rahab.

Dabir looked quickly from one to the other, then whirled on his heel. "After them!" he barked to the ten guards with him. They rushed ahead, but Dabir hung back. He glanced at Rahab. "We will find them," he said, his voice smooth as oil. "And if you are not telling the truth, it will not go well for either of you."

"I am telling the truth," she said, her mouth set in a determined line. "If I had known they were Israelites, I would have turned them over to you before they could escape. They deceived me. But I would expect nothing less."

Dabir gave a slight nod, then left toward the direction of the palace. He would not dirty his hands searching for the spies. He would leave that to the king's guards, who would pay dearly if they failed.

17

Salmon shifted uncomfortably beneath the stalks of flax, fighting the urge to sneeze. Voices drifted up to them from Rahab's outer courtyard below, and after what seemed like hours, quiet descended, and Salmon took the risk of emerging from under the flax.

"I think they're gone," he whispered to Mishael. "We need to get out of here."

"Don't you think we should wait for Rahab? She said she would return."

Salmon considered the thought. It appeared she had indeed kept her word and sent the king's men away, but to what end? Would they return with greater numbers and surround the house? He rose and crept to the parapet, peeked over the edge, and looked down at the steep drop to the ground below. He turned and hurried back into the shadows at the sound of footsteps on the stairs.

Rahab appeared, her form only slightly illuminated by the half moon. He noticed the adornments in her ears and the way her hair draped in delicate ringlets beneath a veil she had pulled back. He glanced away, angry at the way his heart beat faster as she approached. How could he even think of allowing his feelings to betray him in the presence of a prostitute?

She drew alongside him and motioned both of them closer to the small room they had used before. "Please." She waved a hand toward the now dark room.

Salmon looked at her, not fully trusting her. "You first."

She raised a brow, then seemed to understand his fears. She stepped inside, and Mishael followed. Salmon stood in the arch but swung the door partly closed.

"It is safer to speak in here where the sound will not travel across the rooftops," she said.

"Did you send them away?"

"Yes." She lowered her gaze, and for the briefest moment, Salmon felt compassion for her. What had led her to this life?

She lifted her gaze and met his, her look vulnerable, almost pleading. "I know that the Lord has given you this land," she said, "and that a great fear of you has fallen on us, so that all who live in this country are melting in fear because of you." She glanced to Mishael, then looked at Salmon once more. "We have heard how the Lord dried up the water of the Red Sea for you when you came out of Egypt."

Salmon nodded, saying nothing.

"The rumors have grown in strength over the years," she continued, "and lately, with the tales of the movement of your tribes toward the Jordan, everyone's courage has failed because of you." She glanced beyond him as though the next words were hard for her. "Though my people do not believe it, I know that the Lord your God is God in heaven above and on the earth below." A sense of awe filled her dark, liquid eyes.

She held her hands in front of her in supplication. "Please swear to me by the Lord that you will show kindness to my family, because I have shown kindness to you. Give me a sure sign that you will spare the lives of my father and mother, my brothers and sisters, and all who belong to them—and that you will save us from death."

Salmon studied her, seeing honesty in her gaze. He glanced at Mishael, caught his slight nod, then faced Rahab. "Our lives for your lives," he said. "If you don't tell what we are doing, we will treat you kindly and faithfully when the Lord gives us the land."

She drew in a breath and released it. "Thank you." She let her hands fall to her sides, relief evident in her eyes. "Come with me. I will let you down through the window in my room."

At Salmon's look, she smiled. "Do not worry. You will not be tainted by entering it. But the window is the biggest one along the wall to allow you through."

He nodded and stepped out of the rooftop chamber. They waited while she closed it behind her, then followed her, crouching as they walked down the stairs. They passed the same courtyard and hallways and entered her private set of rooms. There was no sign of the Nubian, and Salmon hoped that did not bode ill for them or her.

She walked to a wicker basket and pulled a scarlet rope from its depths. "Can you tie a secure knot?" She handed one end to Salmon and pointed to the post attached to the curtain-draped bed, then fetched two pouches and filled them with almonds and figs. She gave one to Mishael, who tied it to his waist, and held the other out to Salmon.

Salmon secured the rope, though just touching the bedpost made him squirm, then took the pouch from Rahab, taking care not to touch her fingers in the exchange. He nodded his thanks. Rahab looked at him oddly, then carried the other end of the rope to the window, opened the shutters, and tossed it out. She peered from side to side, then turned to face them.

"The king's men will head toward the Jordan in search of you. Go to the hills so the pursuers will not find you. Hide yourselves there three days until they return, and then go on your way."

Mishael grabbed the rope and tugged. "It should hold." He climbed onto the ledge to lower himself slowly down. Salmon watched him but a moment, then faced Rahab.

"This oath you made us swear will not be binding on us unless, when we enter the land, you have tied this scarlet cord in this window, and unless you have brought your father and mother, your brothers, and all your family into your house. If any of them go outside your house into the street, their blood will be on their own heads—we will not be responsible." He stepped closer to the window as Mishael disappeared from his view. "As for those who are in the house with you, their blood will be on our head if a hand is laid on them. But if you tell what we are doing, we will be released from the oath you made us swear."

"Agreed," she said, lifting her chin. "Let it be as you say."

Salmon climbed onto the ledge, his grip tight on the rope. He glanced up at a touch on his shoulder. "Thank you," she said, quickly removing her hand. "Go in peace."

His face heated with the shock of her touch. He lowered himself quickly to the ground where Mishael waited, then glanced back one more time before they took off running.

Rahab was retying the cord around a shutter post, where it continued to dangle from the window.

⁓⚜⁓

Rahab stood at the window until the two men of Israel were long out of view. The night breeze turned cool, and she mildly wondered if they would make it past the burial caves and into the hills. She should have warned them to go far enough. She shivered and closed the shutters. Of course they would. They were not children. No. Her cheeks heated at the memory of the way the one, Salmon, had looked at her. He was a man through and through, and he clearly disdained her profession. Hadn't he told her of the foreigners, the Midianites, who were God's enemies? Jericho's people were no different.

She walked to her bed and sat on the edge, staring down at her unpainted hands. She should have allowed Adara to draw the henna patterns along her nails. Her first patron should be arriving soon. But she found she suddenly did not care. What would happen if she turned the men away? Dabir was too busy worrying about the Israelites to check on her again. And if he wanted silver for her services, she could draw on the stash she had hidden beneath the floor.

She rubbed her forehead to forestall a headache. How weary she had become of her life. Of the men who became as pitiful as selfish children the moment they walked into her chambers. So needy. So demanding. So weak.

She closed her eyes, seeing again Salmon's disapproving scowl crease his handsome Israelite brow. Those dark eyes, hooded beneath dark bangs that escaped below his tan turban. Her heart had skipped a beat at the first sight of him, but she had ignored it. And she was wise to continue to do so. Even if by some great miracle she escaped Jericho's downfall with her life, neither Salmon nor any Israelite man would have anything to do with a prostitute. She was dung in their eyes, foreign. Forbidden.

But if Israel truly gained victory over the warriors of Jericho, she could be free of Dabir, of this life she loathed. And there was no reason to doubt a God who could part the Red Sea.

She drew in a breath and slowly released it. There was also no reason to continue to entertain patrons if she did not care to do so. Especially after making the spies such a solemn promise. The thought of strange men or even repeat customers touching her . . . she could not bear it.

Have mercy on me, she pleaded, unable to even lift her head to the skies, fearful she might think Israel's God and the moon to be one. Did such a mighty God hear the cries of a prostitute?

She straightened and stood, then met Tendaji at the door near the courtyard, informing him that she was not available for visitors.

18

If things go as we told her, and Rahab lives through the taking of Jericho . . ."

At Mishael's words, Salmon glanced up from the stick he was whittling. "What about her?" Rahab was the last person he wanted to talk about right now. But he couldn't seem to get her out of his thoughts.

"Where will she go? What will become of her family? Once we destroy their town and their people, we will have to take them in. Won't Rahab have to marry one of our people?" Mishael's expression held confusion mingled with his telltale concern as he met Salmon's gaze. He quoted Moses' words. "'When you go out to war against your enemies, and the Lord your God gives them into your hand and you take them captive, and you see among the captives a beautiful woman, and you desire to take her to be your wife . . .'"

Salmon looked at Mishael askance. "No one in Israel is going to want to marry a prostitute."

Mishael glanced beyond the low fire toward the mouth of the cave. "Can our God not redeem a prostitute?"

"They are defiled, Mishael. Prostitution defiles a land. Do you not remember Zimri and Kozbi?"

"Captives of war can repent and be joined to our tribes."

"You're assuming that just because she wants to save her life that she has repented and wants to leave her soiled work." Salmon heard the bitter tone in his voice.

"I did not doubt her sincerity." Mishael's quiet words silenced Salmon's response. Let Joshua decide her fate. Was it not he who had Yahweh's ear? Why should Salmon care what happened to Rahab or her family?

"All that matters is that we get back to Joshua and give a good report." He set the flint knife down. "And hope the prostitute keeps her word."

"If she does, Joshua might think it best for someone to marry her if she is to stay among us," Mishael said again.

Salmon scowled at his friend. "Or she lives like a widow outside the camp. Stop troubling yourself over a woman who means nothing. Her fate is God's, not ours."

Three uneventful days later, Salmon climbed to the top of the hill above the cave and scanned the horizon in each direction, his gaze landing on the gates of Jericho in the distance. No sign of the king's men filled the valley.

"It appears they've given up," he said when he joined Mishael again near the cave's mouth.

Mishael tucked his flint knife into his belt and girded his robe to make walking easier, as Salmon had already done. "Are you ready then?"

Salmon nodded. He was more than ready to return to the Israelite camp.

They skirted a wide path from Jericho, avoiding any hint of the sentries' notice, keeping to the tree lines and traveling most often by night. Salmon pushed himself, anxious to return, to plan how best to take the city. War strategies were always the best remedy for wayward thoughts.

Two nights later, he plopped beside Mishael on the banks of the Jordan near the place they had crossed nearly a week earlier. "What happens if Joshua doesn't approve of our deal with Rahab?" The thought had troubled him the closer they got to the river's edge. He had given his word, but a part of him had wagered that she would not keep hers, freeing him from the guilt of bargaining with a prostitute.

"He will approve. Why wouldn't he?" Mishael tied the straps of both sandals together and put them around his neck.

"She is a *prostitute*. He wouldn't expect us to make such a bargain." Weariness crept over him, but he bent forward to untie his sandals as well. Every muscle ached with the day's trek, fueled by the guilt, the worry. "I should never have promised her."

"She did not give you much choice. She helped us escape and did not give us away. Doesn't that count for something with you?" Mishael's normally congenial tone turned angry. "Why do you beat yourself up so? She saved our lives. We will save hers. So be it."

Salmon did not respond as Mishael stood and reached for a low-hanging branch. Salmon draped his sandals over his neck and came up behind him. The river was narrower at this spot, and not so deep they couldn't swim if their feet slipped on any moss-covered rocks. Mishael's sure footing gave Salmon's weary body strength to continue.

"Don't fall in," Mishael called as he grasped the tree on the other side. "I don't want to have to fetch you out."

Salmon grasped the same branch moments later. "Be grateful you didn't have to. I would have had to dunk you."

They both crawled up the embankment and sat a moment, panting from the exertion.

"Be kind to her when you tell Joshua the tale."

Salmon's gaze snapped to Mishael's. "I am always kind."

"You disdain her. And your thoughts toward her are not kind."

"So now you have the ability to know my thoughts?" Salmon met Mishael's gaze, then quickly retrieved his sandals and tied them on his feet. "We need to go. It will be too dark to find Joshua's tent among the throng."

"Just don't forget what I said." Mishael fell into step beside him, and the two passed the Tent of Meeting and came to Joshua's door soon after.

"How did it go?" Joshua reclined on a mat across from them in his sitting room, his smile serious and unassuming. "I see you made it there and back unharmed."

Salmon nodded. "Yes. The trip was . . . interesting."

Joshua looked from man to man. "Tell me everything."

Salmon talked throughout the meal they shared, with Mishael interjecting here and there, until they came to speak of Rahab.

"So you stayed with a prostitute?"

"Not exactly stayed," Salmon said, feeling his defenses rising. "It became apparent that a woman of her profession, one with the ear of the king, would have information that could prove useful. We merely questioned her."

"And she proved to be quite helpful to us," Mishael said.

Salmon glanced at his friend. "Yes. Yes, she did." He

held Joshua's gaze. "While we were talking with her, the king's guards appeared at her gate. Someone had reported our presence to him, and Rahab said the guards watched her house closely. She hid us from them and sent them off another way. Then she let us down through her window by a rope."

Joshua clasped his hands in front of him. "A brave woman. One of obvious faith."

"Or she is very good at saying what she must to get her way." Salmon looked down, half ashamed of the judgment he felt toward her. He drew a slow breath and once more met Joshua's gaze. "She made us promise to spare her and her family when we come to take the land."

"And did you?"

"Yes, my lord, on the condition she keeps her end of the bargain." Salmon set his empty clay bowl on the tray in front of him and wiped his mouth with the back of his sleeve. "So far, everything she has said and done for us has come to pass."

"The Lord has surely given the whole land into our hands," Mishael added. "All of the people are melting in fear because of us."

"According to Rahab," Salmon added. "Though I think because of her unique situation, she is more aware than most."

Joshua nodded but said nothing for the space of many breaths. "The Lord is in this," he said at last. "He used this woman to spare your lives. When we take Jericho, we will do the same for her." He stood then, and the men stood with him. "Get some sleep. Tomorrow we will travel back to the Jordan."

The journey from Shittim to the Jordan took longer for their large company than it did for just two men. By the third day, Salmon found himself in Joshua's tent once more.

"As heads of your tribes," Joshua said, "go throughout the camp and tell the people: 'When you see the ark of the covenant of the Lord your God, and the Levitical priests carrying it, you are to move out from your positions and follow it. Then you will know which way to go, since you have never been this way before. But keep a distance of about two thousand cubits between you and the ark—do not go near it.'"

Twelve men nodded their agreement.

"Tell the people to gather here near my tent before nightfall. Any questions?" Joshua's gaze swept the group. "Good. When you have finished, report to me."

Salmon left the tent and glanced at the sun, blinking against its glare. He had wanted to ask where the priests would be leading them, but he had been with Joshua long enough to know that when the time was right, he would tell them what they needed to know.

"I should have sent another of your tribe to do the work today, my friend," Joshua said hours later when Salmon returned, sweating and mopping his brow with a swatch of linen cloth. "You look as though you have barely slept since you returned from Jericho."

Salmon rubbed the back of his neck. "I've slept."

Joshua raised a brow.

"Just carried along by some fitful dreams, is all." Salmon felt Joshua's scrutiny as he met the man's gaze. "And anxious to be on with the next step of our journey." It was partly the truth. He itched to pursue the land Adonai had promised them. He could not tell Joshua that a beautiful prostitute had invaded his waking and sleeping.

Other heads of the tribes trickled into the tent, and Joshua bid them sit to eat and rest in its shade.

Joshua's wife Eliana and their two daughters brought trays of cheeses and figs and pistachios newly picked from nearby trees, and placed them before the men. Talk of war and strategies for taking Jericho were tossed about until the sun had moved to near dusk.

Joshua motioned for the men to precede him out of the tent where a crowd had gathered, their numbers too great to count. He stood before the group and raised his hands for silence. "Consecrate yourselves," he said, "for tomorrow the Lord will do amazing things among you."

What sorts of amazing things? The question burned in Salmon, even as a sense of humility filled him. How did a man consecrate his mind from wandering to forbidden places?

The thought burdened and angered him as he followed the crowd to gather what was needed for his trek to the river at dawn. To wash and don fresh clothing seemed so outward, as though even a foreigner could do so and fit right in with the rest of their tribes. But what soap, what hyssop could cleanse a person from all that held him captive? What cleansing could purify the hidden places of his heart?

—————✦—————

"Take up the ark of the covenant and pass on ahead of the people," Joshua told the priests the morning after their purification. "When you reach the edge of the Jordan's waters, go and stand in the river."

Salmon stood far from the priests, as Joshua had commanded, watching as the men carried the ark on long poles that rested on their shoulders. They passed through the crowd, who had kept a wide berth around them. When the priests had passed out of earshot of Joshua, he turned to the crowd and raised his arms.

"Come here and listen to the words of the Lord your God," he said. "This is how you will know that the living God is among you and that He will certainly drive out before you the Canaanites, Hittites, Hivites, Perizzites, Girgashites, Amorites, and Jebusites. See, the ark of the covenant of the Lord of all the earth will go into the Jordan ahead of you." He glanced at the men closest to him, eyeing each one in turn. "Now then," he continued, "choose twelve men from the tribes of Israel, one from each tribe. And as soon as the priests who carry the ark of the Lord—the Lord of all the earth—set foot in the Jordan, its waters flowing downstream will be cut off and stand up in a heap."

Salmon felt a tap on his shoulder and smiled as Mishael came up alongside him. "Everyone knows you are a leader in Judah. You should be one of the twelve."

Salmon shrugged one shoulder. "Caleb is the elder among us. And I do not deserve to be a leader any more than the other men." Never mind that his father had been a prince in Judah. His wayward thoughts toward Rahab of late had taught him not to think so highly of himself. Surely a truly consecrated man would keep his thoughts as pure as his body.

"Maybe not, but Joshua picked you in the past. In case you

haven't noticed, he has chosen younger men to lead." Mishael fell into step beside Salmon as the priests continued forward.

"That's because there are no old men left except for himself and Caleb." But perhaps Caleb did not want such duties, though he did often sit in on meetings when they strategized for war.

"Well, whether you like it or not, Joshua has picked you more than once, and the men I've talked to agree with his choice."

Salmon glanced at his conniving friend and almost thought to reprimand him with an offhand remark, but thought better of it. Purity of heart also meant purity of tongue. Oh, what a wretched man he was!

"The Jordan is still at flood stage," Mishael said, as though Salmon did not already know it. "Do you really think Adonai will stop the waters as He did for the people when Moses led them through the Red Sea?"

Salmon considered the question, not wishing to speak too quickly. Did he believe it? Or would he only believe it when he saw it happen? "If Joshua says Adonai will do this, then I believe him. The Lord is with Joshua as He was with Moses." He glanced heavenward, then toward the sounds of the Jordan, which was barely hidden by grasses and underbrush. "But this will be a sight to see."

The priests carrying the ark stopped at the water's edge, and all of the people stopped with them, keeping their distance. Together, as if they had rehearsed how they would manage the slippery bank, the priests each put one foot in front of the other and touched the water's edge.

Salmon strained to see upstream, though if he were closer to the priests he could get a better view. But even from his place behind them, he could see the waters receding from the middle of the river. The swatch of dry land grew wider and wider as the waters piled up high so far upstream that Salmon could not see where they stopped. The priests carrying the ark stepped into the middle of the river. When the space around them grew wide enough to let the people pass in safety, the entire camp of Israel crossed the Jordan on dry ground.

Salmon moved with the tribe of Judah to the edge of the bank. The sound of the river pulsed in the distance, a thing leashed. Had it only moments ago flooded the riverbed? Yet his feet did not sink into muck, the ground so dry dust clung to his sandals.

Awe filled him as he looked to his left and right, straining for a glimpse of the waters. But trees and a bend in the river blocked his view. He glanced at Mishael, tempted to run to the other side and race down the bank for a closer look. But the crowd pressed in on them. Salmon's heart beat to the tune of heady silence and reverent fear.

When the last Israelite sandal touched the other side of the Jordan, Joshua called the twelve leaders together. "Go over before the ark of the Lord your God into the middle of the Jordan," he said. "Each of you is to take up a stone on his shoulder, according to the number of the tribes of the Israelites, to serve as a sign among you. In the future, when your children ask you, 'What do these stones mean?' tell them that the flow of the Jordan was cut off before the ark of the covenant of the Lord. When it crossed the Jordan, the waters of the Jordan were cut off. These stones are to be a memorial to the people of Israel forever."

The head of Judah's tribe, Salmon turned toward the river once more and led the group of twelve men back onto the dry riverbed at the prescribed distance from the ark. Rocks lined the river's floor, some large, some ground to pebbles and sand. Salmon dug around a large boulder and hefted it onto his shoulder, then turned back to where Joshua and the people waited.

He slowly lowered the huge rock and placed it near Joshua's feet. One by one, eleven other tribal leaders did the same.

"Come out of the river," Joshua called to the priests.

They moved as one man. As their feet left the riverbed to touch the grassy banks, a thunderous roar shook the air, submersing all other sounds. Water crashed over the Jordan's bed, whooshing near the place where Salmon stood, its foaming silver spray like a wide yawning mouth. Flood stage returned in full force. But not one of them had been left or drowned in its fury.

19

Rahab sat before her dressing table as dusk fell over the town, and Tendaji lit the torches in the courtyards. Her sister Adara pulled a shell comb through her long dark hair, fussing with a knot at the end.

"Ouch! Don't tug so hard."

"Well, next time tie a scarf over your head when you sleep, or wear it in a braid. You toss too much and it gets all tangled." Adara pulled gently this time and freed the knot at last.

"I hate sleeping in a headscarf. And I can't help it if I toss and turn." She loathed the way her voice lifted to a whine. She cleared her throat. "That is," she said in a more cultured tone, "I like things as they are. Just be careful with the tangles, please."

Adara drew the comb once more through her hair and began the work of pinning it in place. "Who do you see first tonight?"

Her question caused the familiar longing to be free of this life to surface in full force. Rahab had canceled her customers for nearly a week, but too soon her silver had depleted and

Dabir demanded an accounting. She could not ignore her life or refuse to continue the work he demanded. If she did, he would suspect something. She could not risk the life of her Israelite rescuers even to save herself many more weeks of pain. The thought left her listless.

She glanced at her too-curious sister, wishing not for the first time that her father would find her a man and betroth her. "Does it matter? They are all egotistical children." *Please, God of Israel, don't let my sister end up doing what I do. Don't let Dabir even consider the idea.* She took great care that Adara left long before any men arrived.

"Surely some are more pleasing than others," Adara said. "You used to care for Dabir."

Rahab's stomach tightened. "I was a fool to ever flirt with Dabir. I never cared for him."

"Prince Nahid is handsome," Adara offered. "Surely the handsome ones aren't so bad."

The image of Salmon's handsome face appeared in Rahab's thoughts. Would life be different with someone like him? She closed her eyes against the worrisome image. A man like that would never look twice at a woman like her. She was excrement—or worse—in his eyes.

"You're awfully quiet tonight." Adara twirled a long strand of hair into an imported ivory clip, a gift from Prince Nahid.

"Just thinking." Rahab glanced at her reflection in the silver mirror. How long until the Israelites arrived to take the city? Surely they would come. She must prepare her family for the invasion. But how? She had imagined and discarded all manner of arguments—all futile. They would not agree to stay under her roof for even one night.

And yet she must find a way. She turned in her seat and faced her sister.

"Obviously, you have something to tell me." Adara was young but too bright for her own good.

Rahab nodded. "I do, and you must listen carefully." She took her sister's hand, drawing the comb from her fingers and setting it aside. "You must go home after this and speak to Father and Mother. You must convince them and Cala and Tzadok and our brothers and sisters-in-law to come to my house and stay with me."

Adara's eyes grew wide, her look disbelieving. "You can't be serious." She took a step back, though she did not pull her hand from Rahab's. "Surely you have been drinking too much of the poppy tea, my sister, if you think for a moment that Father would just leave everything to stay with you." Adara's brow furrowed, her expression troubled. "He barely tolerates me working here." Her gaze flitted beyond Rahab. "He will be angry if I do not return to him soon."

Rahab pulled Adara closer in a gentle but firm grip. "Please look at me, Adara." When the girl complied, she continued. "I cannot explain it to you now lest I break a confidence and a promise." She glanced toward the window and took a quick look around the room. Empty. But she lowered her voice just the same. "I will come myself to speak with them soon, but you must warn them that danger is coming, and if they want to save their lives, they must stay within my walls."

Fear crept into Adara's expression as Rahab released her grip. She backed farther away and sank onto Rahab's corner chair. "What kind of danger?" she whispered.

Rahab moved to kneel at her sister's side. "Can I trust you?"

Adara bit her lower lip and nodded. Rahab studied the

girl, then recalled Salmon's warning. *If you tell what we are doing, we will be released from the oath you made us swear.*

Rahab drew in a breath at the memory. "I am sorry. I wish I could tell you the whole truth, but if I do, I will risk our safety." What would she do if her family would not come without a detailed explanation? "You must just do as I say. Make them listen. Get them to come. And tomorrow or the next day, when I can get away, I will come to them myself if I must."

"Father will not want that," Adara said, straightening. "If you come, you must not be seen. He is embarrassed by you."

The words stung despite their ring of truth. Rahab stood and smoothed the length of her robe. "Embarrassed or not, if they want to live, they must come." She turned then, snatched up her earrings, and looped them into holes drilled into her earlobes. "Go home," she said without facing her sister again.

"Rahab, I'm sorry," Adara said, placing a hand on Rahab's arm.

Rahab looked at her, then pulled her close. She loved her sister, no matter what her father thought of her. Even the men she entertained hated her on some level they would not admit. She hated herself for the same reasons.

She kissed the top of Adara's head. "Go home," she said again. "Father will worry. Just please, do as I have told you." She turned then and walked into the sitting room as the first knock sounded on the courtyard gate.

⁓⚓⁓

"Have you heard?" Dabir paced her sitting room the following evening, his agitation palpable. "Everyone is talking about it." He sank onto her couch, elbows on his knees, his gaze beyond hers. "The waters of the Jordan just parted. Just like that! No feat of engineering could stop rushing waters and make the ground dry in an instant."

He stood again, and Rahab forced her mouth into a thin line to keep from smiling at his discomfiture. Dabir looked like a prancing peacock, ruffling his feathers. But this was no mating dance he did. The proud Dabir clearly struggled to mask his fear. If he weren't so unpredictable and volatile, she could almost laugh at his agitated movements. Instead, she rose gracefully from her plush chair and walked closer.

"Dabir, my sweet," she purred in his ear. "Jericho's walls are thick and strong, are they not? Have you not told me many a time that no one can breach them?" She stroked a hand along his bare arm, but he stiffened instead of relaxing as he usually did.

"The terror this has evoked in this city . . . The generals cannot even get one man to take up arms and go out to meet them, to cut them down before they can come to attack us or bar us from leaving. We can't live forever without trade." He spoke as though he had not heard her.

"Surely we can shoot at them from the walls. Perhaps our men just need time."

He faced her. "Time for what? Their fears have only grown these past months."

"But the walls are so thick—"

"Yes, they are. Unless someone who lives along the wall opens their window and allows them entrance." By his look she could tell he was calculating the possibility of that happening.

"The windows are too high in the walls, my lord. And even if they got through the first set of walls, they would have to breach the second to get through to the palace. You are quite safe, I am sure." She stroked his arm again, but he brushed her off.

"I should send men to bar every window." He took in the room. "Perhaps I should start with yours." His piercing gaze told her he remembered too well her attempt to escape the city. But she had not used her window. And he could not know, unless he had seen the scarlet cord, that she had helped the spies. What would she do with her family if Dabir continued to visit? Surely he would suspect something.

She shrugged one shoulder and met his gaze. "Perhaps you should." She felt her heart skip a beat, hoping he wouldn't notice her discomfort behind her coy smile. "But," she said, drawing closer to him, "did you come here only to tell me about Israel, or did you want my attention in some *other* way?" She traced a finger along his square jaw and close-cropped beard, then leaned in and kissed him. She wrapped her fingers through his and gently tugged him toward her chambers.

He resisted a moment, his look serious as though he were trying to read her thoughts, until she kissed him again. Then he followed her without a word.

───※───

Rahab awoke as the sun reached the midway point in the sky to find Dabir sitting at a table near her window. He normally did not stay the night, but once she got alone with him, she could not make him leave, disappointing several customers. She glanced at the shuttered window, relieved to see that he had not bolted it, nor did she see any sign of the scarlet cord near him. He sat, hands clasped in his lap, but as she swung her legs to the side of the bed, he came to sit beside her.

"I want you to come to my home. Stay with me until this fear is past." He touched her cheek. She flinched as though he had slapped her. He dropped his hand, and she glimpsed his uncertainty.

She blinked and yawned, masking her earlier reaction. She rose and pulled a thick robe from a peg along the wall and wrapped it around her. More than a week had passed since the spies had left, promising to return. How long?

She drew in a breath and straightened, forcing herself to walk with graceful strides toward where Dabir now stood in the middle of the room.

"I want you to get your things and come with me now," he said.

Her pulse raced, though she smoothed her expression to pretend that it didn't. She touched his chest. "But what of your wife, your children? Surely they would object to my presence." She caught the slightest doubt flickering in his eyes. Good. Persuading a doubtful man was far easier than a confident one.

He clasped his hand around hers and pulled it to his lips, lightly kissing her fingers. "You would stay in the guest house. The arrangements could continue as they are, but you would be close, where I could keep you safe."

Imprisoned, not safe. She met his gaze. The doubt she'd glimpsed had disappeared.

"I won't accept anything but your compliance, Rahab." His look held determination, and a sick feeling settled inside of her. She walked from her chamber into her sitting room, closer to Tendaji, who stood at his usual guard post. Her sister had yet to come to fix her hair for another night's work, and only the cook could be heard putting food on a tray for her.

"I cannot go with you, Dabir. I would not feel safe if I left my home." She spoke with her back to him, meeting Tendaji's hooded gaze across the room. She turned to face Dabir but took a step back. Alarm fused with wrath in his narrowed eyes, and he moved swiftly toward her and gripped her arms in his big hands.

"You cannot? Since when do you tell me you cannot obey me? It wasn't a request, Rahab. You will pack your things now and come with me until the Israelites are destroyed." He dragged her back toward her room and shoved her inside. She stumbled and fell to her knees. "Start packing."

She pushed her hands into the plush rug and slowly rose, glancing once at him. What could she do? The urge to look toward her window came over her, but she resisted. If she could close the door, she would use the rope and drop to the ground and run until she found the Israelites. With their help, she could rescue her family and see Dabir destroyed. But she knew in a heartbeat she could never run fast enough to outwit Dabir.

God of Israel, help me. The naturalness of the prayer surprised her.

She glared at Dabir, her own anger fueled by his outright audacity. "Fine. I'll come." But she would not stay. She stood, walked to the door, and slammed it in his face, latching the leather hook to bar him easy entrance.

Let him try to follow. Let him try to beat her. She didn't care.

Silence descended as she waited for the door to burst open and Dabir to come after her. But it was his laughter outside her chamber that caught her ear. "The prostitute wants her privacy? How very noble of you, Rahab." A slight pause. "Just make it quick."

She did not respond. But she went to her chest and stuffed several tunics and robes into a leather sack just the same. She glanced around the room, noting all of the items she used to paint her face and body into something men would want. How was she supposed to fit it all into baskets or sacks without spilling the precious powders and ointments? She needed time and at least one donkey to cart it all across town to Dabir's palatial home. But any moment now, Dabir would kick the door in and she would have no more excuses.

But even the sure knowledge of his wrath could not motivate her. She slowed her efforts. Let him wait.

The sounds of pacing and muffled curses came to her through the closed door. Moments later, Dabir's fist beat upon the wood. "You're taking too long, Rahab. Let's go!"

A swift grunt and *oof* followed, along with a sickening gush that turned her stomach. Tendaji? Dabir? Or had the Israelites already come and broken their promise?

Surely not.

But a headache assaulted her, and fear nearly crushed her. She dare not look. She must look. Indecision drew battle lines within her as her hand trembled on the latch.

20

Tendaji half lifted, half dragged Dabir's body through the gate to Rahab's courtyard. His heart beat double time, and the strength he had thought stripped from him now pumped hard through his veins. How he hated this man. He looked down at the bloody neck where he had quietly slit Dabir's throat. He would have to clean up the blood on Rahab's rugs and floors when he returned, but first he had to find a place far from here where Dabir's body would not easily be found.

He glanced through the second courtyard gate toward the street that ran along the front of Rahab's home, for once grateful for the Israelite threat. The city's fears had caused the men and women to huddle indoors. Even the marketplace had grown quieter since the gates had been barred. Though the Israelites still camped on the plains near Gilgal, the kings of the Amorites and Canaanites had lost all courage to face them. No caravans crossed from their kingdoms into Jericho. The city and the surrounding area were as quiet as a tomb.

Tendaji stood a moment, trying to decide his next move.

Jill Eileen Smith

He startled at the sound of padding feet coming from inside the house. Rahab stood in the arch of the door, visibly shaken.

"Rahab."

She swallowed as if finding her voice. "You are alive."

"Yes." Did she think Dabir had been the one to kill him?

Her smile wobbled, but she nodded vigorously. "You can't leave him here."

He looked at her. "I know."

She glanced at Dabir's grotesque face, slick with blood, and closed her eyes.

"At first I was going to drag him through the streets to bury him somewhere, but there are no tombs in the city," he said, trying to distract her thoughts from what must surely seem sickening to her.

"We need to get him outside the city to the caves."

"We cannot leave the city. The gates are barred." Did she not know this? But at her nod of acquiescence, he realized she was still trying to process what he had done.

"He was an evil man," she said, meeting Tendaji's gaze. "Thank you for protecting me from him." Though she could not know that his reasons were for far more than her protection.

"We could bury him beneath the stones of the courtyard," she offered, though she seemed uncertain.

Tendaji shook his head. "He does not deserve any type of proper burial."

"No, he does not." Her breathing grew steadier as she held his gaze with no hint of chastisement for his actions.

"I could toss him through your window. We can tell the king or the prince that he jumped to his death in fear of the Israelites."

She nodded again. "Dabir *was* afraid, as are all the rest of the men of Jericho. It was why he wanted to take me with him to his home. To keep me *safe*." She spat the word as though it were a curse.

She turned then and walked through the house toward her chambers. Tendaji lifted his burden again and followed her past the bloody rugs in the sitting room, trailing blood all the way to Rahab's window.

"Open the shutters," he said, at last dropping his burden to the floor under the window, "and look to see if the guards are near."

Rahab did as she was told and tilted her head out, looking up to the right and up to the left, then down to the ground. "All clear."

She turned back and helped him lift Dabir's dead weight onto the ledge, then quickly took Dabir's turban and pulled the edges down to cover the wound. Then with one last look into the vacant eyes of the man who had maimed him, Tendaji pushed Dabir over the side and closed the shutters before he could hear the crushing thud of flesh and dirt.

⁕

Salmon glanced toward the walled city of Jericho as he trudged up the hill toward the large terebinth tree where Joshua waited. Gibeath Haaraloth, the hill of foreskins, stretched before him, and his hands were still sticky with the blood of circumcision of the men in his tribe. Exhaustion weighted his steps as he approached the tent where Joshua stood. His heartbeat quickened at what awaited him. Joshua looked up as he neared the shade of the tree.

"Ah, my son Salmon. I should have sent others to help

you, considering Judah is our largest tribe." He extended a hand, and Salmon placed the flint knife in Joshua's palm. "Step closer into the shade." He motioned to an area where a small tent had been placed to offer privacy. Salmon obeyed.

"Do you understand the purpose of this act, my son?" It was a question Salmon had asked hundreds of times in the past few hours.

"Yes, my lord. To fulfill the covenant God made with Abraham," Salmon said, lifting his chin. He was of Abraham's seed, a rightful heir to the land Yahweh had promised.

Joshua knelt at Salmon's feet, the flint knife in his right hand. Salmon closed his eyes, bracing for the jolt of pain. "How well you know the answer, my son," Joshua said, causing Salmon's pulse to jump as he looked into the man's soulful gaze. "But I will ask you again before I do this. You are a prince in Judah. Do you truly understand why our God commands all Israelite men to undergo this ritual? For if it is just to keep an outward covenant because you must, you are missing our God's intent."

Salmon's face heated, his mind a muddle of unanswered questions. Why did God command such a thing? And why had his father not obeyed the command when Salmon was still an infant in arms, as the law prescribed?

The tip of the blade pricked his skin, and the jolt of pain he'd anticipated shot through him. The deed was completed before he could formulate a response to Joshua. A servant offered Salmon a jar of healing ointment, and Joshua dropped the foreskin into a hole in the dirt and buried it.

Joshua rose, his hand extending the flint knife back to Salmon. "Experience will teach you the reason for the covenant we keep, Salmon. You have spent the day asking the questions. But until you felt the edge of the blade yourself, you could not fully know the cost of the covenant. As you go to your tent to heal, think about these things. Ask our God to give you insight, my son."

Salmon nodded, unable to speak past the lump in his throat. He limped past Joshua, wishing for a walking stick or shepherd's staff, not sure he had the strength to make it down the hill to the sea of Judah's tents spread before its base, where the men in his tribe lay on their mats, unmoving.

Pain nearly crippled him as the terrain grew seemingly rockier with every step. How had he not noticed these annoyingly jarring stones beneath his sandals? He stopped, hands to his knees, dragging in a breath. As he slowly straightened as best he could, he glimpsed the walls of Jericho in the distance. Walls with windows and the house of one beautiful, helpful prostitute. How many men would have thought twice about visiting her bed if they had undergone such personal, private pain?

Was that the answer Joshua intended him to see? But Joshua didn't know how wayward his thoughts had been of late. He shuffled forward, the shock of every movement like a fiery touch. If he'd taken a wife, what would she say to him if she could see him now—so weak, so vulnerable?

―――※―――

"The day after tomorrow is the fourteenth day of the month," Joshua said a week later, as his wife passed around a tray of sweets and his young daughters served Salmon and the other heads of tribes cups of watered wine.

"You want us to celebrate the Passover," one of the men said, his cup held loosely in one hand.

"As we should have done in obedience every year since we escaped Egypt." Joshua's gaze moved from man to man. "But as you all know much more fully now, your forefathers were not an obedient people. If they had been, each of you would have been circumcised on the eighth day of your birth."

"And saved ourselves a lot of discomfort," another said, eliciting chuckles from the group.

"That night of Passover in Egypt was no small thing," Joshua said, drawing Salmon's attention. "Our people hovered beneath the blood sprinkled on the doorposts and lintels of our homes, with sandaled feet, staffs in hand, unleavened bread eaten in haste. Terror floated in the skies above, and the screams of the Egyptian people sometimes still invade my dreams."

Salmon's heartbeat slowed, his thoughts sobering. Before the experience at Gibeath Haaraloth, he had itched to take his sword and plunge into Canaanite lands. His hands had trained since his youth for war. But now . . . He met Joshua's gaze. Circumcision had changed him. He'd been vulnerable. Unprotected. Had the Canaanites known what Israel's God had commanded of His men, they could have swooped down on the whole regiment of fighting men and wiped them out with hardly a whimper in return.

"I want you to go throughout the camp," Joshua continued, "and tell each household to prepare for the Passover. Choose an unblemished lamb for the sacrifice. Smaller households may share with others so that none is wasted. After Passover, we will harvest the grain and eat from the land."

They talked of the coming feast rather than war and ate of the treats Joshua had supplied, then moved as one to do his bidding. Salmon felt a hand on his shoulder and held back to accept Joshua's parting kiss. "I would make you my right-hand man, Salmon. As I was to Moses, so you shall be to me. Will you accept this calling?"

Salmon looked into Joshua's lined face, seeing the trust the man placed in him. Trust he was not sure he deserved. He swallowed, aware of a sudden shift in emotion. "I would be honored," he said. "If that is our God's wish."

Joshua ran a hand over his graying beard. "I will admit, it is my wish, but I also believe God sees our hearts and with yours He would be pleased."

"I fear I am far from being a man that pleases Him, my lord." He studied the woven rug beneath his feet. "I know my wayward thoughts too well."

Joshua cupped his shoulder. "You will find your courage challenged and your faith failing at times, my son. But our God is a patient God, a merciful God. One who gives courage to the weak, to those who trust in Him—even with their wayward thoughts." He smiled and Salmon lightly returned it.

"He is a true God and one worthy of our trust," Salmon said. Circumcision had taught him that much.

"Then I can count on you?" Joshua asked.

Salmon nodded, wondering just where such a calling would lead him.

21

Rahab startled out of a sound sleep. Steady pounding of the earth's surface and the jangling of warriors' armor fairly shook the walls of the city. Had they entered the gates?

She sat up. She must get to her family. Convince them to come now!

Tangled covers seemed to fight her efforts. Her heart thumped hard as she opened the shutter and peered from her window to the sea of men below.

First priests carrying a golden box, then men dressed as military leaders, then soldiers tromped in straight lines around the circle of the town, saying not a word. Just as her townsmen had done during the Festival of Keret several months earlier.

Israelites. Were their actions mocking Jericho's feast honoring the moon god?

A wave of fear and excitement moved through her. Israel's God had mocked the gods of Egypt. Surely He was powerful enough to do the same to the moon god of Canaan. The god the people of Jericho also worshiped.

She glanced at the scarlet cord, relieved to see it still held secure. A breath she'd held too long escaped as she stepped back and closed the shutter up tight. She must make her father see that there could be no more waiting.

Although Adara had tried to convince the family to move to Rahab's home, they had refused. And once news of Dabir's apparent suicide spread, the town had lost all hope. Even Prince Nahid refused to visit her. No men ventured from their homes to hers. Except for the cook and Tendaji and a stray cat that had found its way to her courtyard, she lived alone. She looked down as the cat, back arched, rubbed against her bare leg. She bent to pick him up. The poor thing had been scrawny, nearly starved when she found him. And the cook had protested feeding the animal. Cats, especially black and brown like this one, she'd said, were evil tools of the gods. Only the Egyptians held them in high regard.

"You're not a tool of evil, little one." She kissed the cat's brown nose and stroked the dark stripes down his back. "No more than I am." Her words trailed off. What was true of her could not be true of such a small, charming creature.

He rewarded her with a kiss against her check, and she felt an uncommon motherly bond to the animal, as though he understood her and needed her, like she'd needed the babe she'd lost.

"Do you need me?" she whispered against his cheek. His loud purr was her reward. But a moment later he buried his head against her arm, as though she could protect him from the strange silence . . . the sounds of steady, heavy marching, but missing a battle cry.

"Are you afraid?"

His purr ceased, and she realized that even this animal was not safe from Israel's invasion if he did not stay within her walls. Soon there would be a breach, and since she did not know when, she must convince her family to come to her for safety today.

"Perhaps you could convince them." She spoke to the cat but knew she was really speaking to herself, bolstering her courage. "I will leave you with Tendaji, for I do not trust that the cook won't put you in a soup and feed it to me. Perhaps when I return you will have many arms to hold you."

She set the cat on the end of her bed, patted its head, then hurried to dress in her plainest garments and old, dull robe. She must not be recognized as she took the streets to her father's house. But she must hurry and bring her family back with her before it was too late.

The sun was halfway between dawn and the day's midpoint when Rahab knelt before her father, arms outstretched, pleading with him to listen to her. "Father, please, come stay with me. We are surely safer together than separate."

Her brothers laughed outright at her words, causing a sinking feeling to settle within her. "Why should an entire household move to stay with *you*, when you are one woman alone?" Tzadok said, his expression carrying its familiar frown. "I have no intention of living in the home of a prostitute."

Silence followed his caustic remark until an argument broke out between her brothers and sisters. Her mother came to stand behind her father, placing a hand on his shoulder as though to infuse him with her strength. Rahab noted the deep lines along her father's weathered brow, her pulse suddenly quickening at the realization that he was indeed not as strong as he had been the day she married Gamal.

"What possible reason can you give us for coming to stay with you?" her brother Jaul asked, breaking her train of thought. "Are you privy to something the rest of us do not know?"

She rose slowly and let her gaze sweep the room, resting on each of her brothers. "Men tell me many things they would normally keep to themselves." She swallowed the impossibility of keeping the truth from them yet trying to convince them to see things her way. She had to convince them without revealing Salmon's secret.

Help me, God of Israel. If only Salmon had not insisted they stay within her walls.

She straightened. "Did you not think it strange the way they marched in silence in one complete circle around the city? Just like we do during Keret's festival? If my guess is right, they will do the same again tomorrow. Perhaps they will take until the seventh day to attack, as our festival lasts a week, but we cannot be sure. What if they challenge us on the third day to surprise us?" She watched their skeptical faces, their doubt evident. And why should they listen to her, a prostitute?

She reined in the desperate need to beg and plead with them, instead kneeling again at her father's side. "I cannot force you, Father. But I have plenty of room, and my home stands along the wall. If they invade the city, we could escape from the window in the wall." Though she knew they ought to see through such impossibility, she could think of nothing else to say to convince them.

Her father's gaze shifted to hers, softening. He cupped her cheek with a veined hand. "My dear Rahab." His expression filled with sorrow, as though his thoughts carried him to another time and place.

"Father," Rahab said again, her tone more urgent this time. "Just because the Israelites have stopped marching for today does not mean they will not return tomorrow. They *will* return. They are going to take this city."

She stood and turned in a circle to include her brothers in her plea. "You can think what you want of me, but you have heard what their God did to stop up the Jordan River in the midst of flood stage. You have heard of the miracles He performed in Egypt and seen how the men of the city won't even leave their homes for fear. Well, they are right to fear a God so powerful. I fear Him."

"If their God is so powerful that He could destroy Egypt and stop up the Jordan, what good does it do to band together?" her father said. "We are all doomed."

"Then let us be doomed together," she said, longing to reinstill hope in her father's hopeless eyes. "But I do not think we are doomed," she added, leaning forward to kiss his cheek. "I believe in their God, Father. If He is as great as the tales tell, then come with me and let us encourage each other while we wait."

She watched her father's changing expressions, his indecision palpable. At last he stood. "We will come with you." To the household he said, "Gather your things, only what you can carry, and let us go and lodge with Rahab."

The following morning Rahab awoke to the same marching beat, only this time, Adara clung to her in the bed they shared, as though they were both young girls.

"Why do they not shout like normal warriors?" Adara poked her head from beneath thick linen sheets. "Are they truly acting out the part of our festival?"

Rahab patted her sister's arm, reminded of her innocence. "I can only assume what they are up to, my sweet. But I do believe they will break through these walls. It is only a matter of time."

"You do not know that for sure." Adara rose up on one elbow. "Do you?"

Rahab noted Adara's raised brow and slowly nodded.

"The spies promised you, didn't they?" Adara's dark eyes grew round. "Why didn't you tell us?" she whispered, glancing toward the closed door.

"You speculate too much, my sister. Even if they had given it, since when have you known me to trust any man's word?" *Only when a handsome stranger is able to take my breath with a look.*

But no, she was not so fickle as that. She had heard the stories of their God, seen the fear in the eyes of the men of the city. She rolled on her side to face her sister.

"You used to trust men." Adara met her gaze, searching.

"I trust Israel's God, not their men."

"But if the Israelites did not promise you, how do you know their God will accept you . . . or us? Why would He save a prostitute?"

The words, though said in innocence, stung.

"He has no reason to," she whispered, pulling Adara into her arms lest she see her doubt, her fear. "But I believe He can. If He is merciful."

Adara pulled slowly away, jumped from the bed, and walked toward the shuttered window. "I have never heard of a god who is merciful without a calculated reason." She touched the shutter and glanced at Rahab. "One peek?"

Rahab chuckled, then came to stand at Adara's side. "Suddenly you are brave?"

Adara shrugged. "I've never seen an Israelite," she whispered. "Are they very different than we are?"

Salmon's handsome bearded face filled Rahab's mind, the memory as sharp as it had been every day since she had helped both men escape. "Not very different." Somehow she could not bring herself to describe them to her virgin sister.

Adara looked at her and began to unlatch the shutter. "Just a quick glance?"

Rahab nodded. But before she could pull the shutter open, her mother burst into the room. "What are you doing? Do you want them to see you? Close that at once."

Rahab stepped back from the window, and Adara hurried to her mother's side. "It's not Rahab's fault, Mama. I asked to look."

Her mother's scowl brought heat to Rahab's cheeks. A moment later her father's large frame filled the archway. "Their priests carry a gold box on long poles ahead of the company. And men march before it with the horns of rams, yet they do not blow the trumpets. This is not like our festival. What foolishness is this?"

Rahab felt his gaze bore into hers, as though she should somehow know the secrets of Israel's plans. "I do not know, Father."

He shook his head in disgust and strode from the room. Her mother followed, taking Adara with her. Rahab hurried after them, fearing they would leave and go home after only one night. But relief filled her as she saw them go to the cooking room and accept food from the cook. The cat licked scraps from a bowl in the adjacent courtyard near where Cala stood. Her sister met Rahab's gaze with a guilty one of her own.

"He was hungry, and I felt sorry for him."

Rahab smiled. "I intended to feed him. But how did he get out of my room?" She'd been sleeping with the animal for days but, in the hustle of settling her family, had forgotten him.

"He was scratching at the door, and I was awake with Raji, so I let him out. Where did you find him? Tzadok thinks cats are cursed."

Rahab scowled. Tzadok had an opinion about everything, but she did not say so. "He showed up in our courtyard one day. I have yet to name him."

Cala nodded. "I like him. He's so scrawny, though. Do you think he'll live?"

Rahab picked the cat up after he'd finished eating and stopped to lick his paws. "He's a fighter. If he doesn't get crushed in the battle, we must keep him inside with us." She looked at her sister. "Will you help me?"

"If I think of it. With the men underfoot and Raji nursing at odd hours, I don't know. Better ask Adara to help you." Cala turned at the sound of her young son crying. "I should go."

Rahab stroked the cat's back and held him close, wishing it were her baby she held and not just a homeless animal. She nodded at Cala, who walked toward one of Rahab's bedrooms. But a moment later she turned back.

"Thank you for doing this for us," she said. She placed a hand on Rahab's shoulder. "I know Father and Tzadok and our brothers blame you, but I know it was not your fault—all that happened to you. To us. Thank you for suggesting this final time together." She put a fist to her mouth to stifle a sob. "At least if we die, we die together." She hurried off to care for her child, while Rahab sank onto one of the plush chairs in her courtyard, still holding the cat.

The marching had ceased for the second day, but the thought was not comforting.

22

On the seventh day, the march began with an armed guard leading seven priests carrying seven trumpets and blowing the rams' horns with short blasts. They walked ahead of the priests who carried the ark of the Lord. The rear guard followed the ark, and Joshua stood at the head of the troops who came behind. Heavy footfalls accompanied the trumpet blasts around Jericho's walls. Once, twice, until at last the seventh time ended at the city gates.

The trumpets sounded again, this time long and loud. Joshua turned and faced the fighting men.

"Shout!" His voice carried on the silent wind. "For the Lord has given you the city! The city and all that is in it are to be devoted to the Lord. Only Rahab the prostitute and all who are with her in her house shall be spared, because she hid the spies we sent."

Salmon's heart beat with the heavy rhythm of the march and the added rush of coming battle. So Rahab would be spared. He found a mixture of anxiety and relief in that knowledge and drew himself up straighter, determined. He would keep his promise to her, lest he anger his God and his leader. But he would not allow her to tempt him into sin. She was still a Canaanite, after all.

And a prostitute. He shoved aside his inner battle as Joshua's voice continued.

"But keep away from the devoted things, so that you will not bring about your own destruction by taking any of them. Otherwise you will make the camp of Israel liable to destruction and bring trouble on it. All the silver and gold and the articles of bronze and iron are sacred to the Lord and must go into His treasury."

As Joshua's words ended, the army gave a deafening shout. Salmon looked toward the city walls, saw the scarlet cord hanging from Rahab's window. A roar, like that of the river Jordan when God unleashed its fury from the hold He had placed on it, crashed around him. He watched as the thick bricks of the outer wall crumbled downward and formed a perfect ramp. Had Israel spent weeks building it, they could not have created a better rampart.

The rumble continued until every last brick collapsed, except for the part attached to Rahab's home. Battle cries drowned out all other sounds as the men charged the city.

Rahab stood in the center of her sitting room, surrounded by her family. Cala's baby had not stopped crying since the first trumpet blast, but when the roaring sound of crumbling bricks came, he buried his head into Cala's chest and barely whimpered.

"They have broken the walls," Tzadok said, peering through the window to the courtyard where Tendaji stood, still barring the gate. "We should go out there and fight them."

"You can't!" Cala's voice was low, like a growling she-bear. "I will not lose you."

Her husband glanced at her. "What makes you think we will die? What makes you think we will not kill them?"

Rahab's brothers joined the argument, suddenly acting like a pack of wolves pacing her sitting room.

"Tzadok is right. We would be fools to just sit here and die." Azad nearly kicked the cat in his pacing.

Rahab scooped the cat into her arms and moved to the doorway to block their way, but they pushed her aside with ease. She turned, the words forming on her tongue to beg them to stay, but stopped at the sight of Tendaji blocking the entry.

"Rahab has asked you to stay. You will stay," he said, command in his voice.

"Who's going to make us? You?" Tzadok's mocking tone made Rahab want to slap him, but she held her peace and pulled the cat closer.

"If that's what you require." Tendaji's look turned menacing. "Do you truly think Dabir jumped to his death?"

For once, Tzadok had no response.

"Dabir was a fool," Tendaji said, "but he did not die a fool's death. Take care that you do not do the same."

Rahab's brothers stepped back, the threat clear, while Tendaji returned to the gate to stand guard. Relief filled her as she watched her family settle onto couches and chairs, all huddled together, listening to the carnage outside. One thing was certain. The wall had fallen all around them, but her house remained standing. If she did not believe in the God of Israel before this, she did now.

Tendaji drew in a breath and slowly released it. If Rahab's brothers had not backed down, he did not know what he would have done. He was no match for all of them, and he could not kill them as he had Dabir. He had no stomach for such a thing without just provocation.

He leaned against the wall behind the locked iron gate, watching Israelite soldiers enter the houses of Rahab's neighbors. Screaming came to him from up the street, a woman crying and cursing the man chasing her. Tendaji watched as she hiked her skirts to better outrun him, but he could tell she would not get far in bare feet and carrying a heavy sack over her shoulder.

Don't be a fool, he nearly shouted at her, but he knew she would not hear from this distance. He glanced back at Rahab's family where they huddled. He could help this woman, pull her inside to safety.

He undid the bolt and slipped through the gate's opening, closing it quietly behind him. The woman drew closer, but her pursuer was gaining on her.

"Come with me," Tendaji shouted. "You will be safe here." He stepped into the street and moved toward her, reaching for her hand. "Leave your burden." But she refused to do so.

Before their hands could touch, she stumbled, her lifeblood spilling onto the ground at his feet. Tendaji stood dumbstruck. He had not seen the other Israelite come from the side alley. Fear and disgust rose with his bile, and he nearly wretched.

"You would kill a mere woman?" he shouted, anger rushing through him. He turned to run back to the safety of Rahab's courtyard, but then fell to his knees as the pain of a sword sliced through his back and came out his gut, spilling his blood on the stones in front of Rahab's house.

Joshua climbed over the ramp the wall had created and met Salmon and Mishael coming toward him. The smell of death rose all around them, and silence filled the space where the shouts and screams had been.

"We have done as you commanded, my lord," Salmon said, sheathing his sword. "We have yet to go throughout the city to be sure, but by all accounts every living thing is dead."

Joshua nodded. "Good." His solemn gaze held penetrating sorrow. To destroy a people did not bring joy. But they had exacted judgment as God had commanded. Salmon found no pleasure in the work.

Joshua ran a hand through his hair and looked toward the one house still standing along the wall. "Go into the prostitute's house and bring her out and all who belong to her, in accordance with your oath to her," he said.

Salmon glanced at Mishael, then back at Joshua. "It will be as you say." They turned and walked quickly down the bloodied street. Bodies lay strewn along the lane, and when they approached the familiar gate, Salmon saw the Nubian guard who had protected Rahab and kept their secret lying facedown, his blood pooling around him.

Mishael shook his head. "Why did he not stay in her home?"

Salmon shrugged. "Only he knows, and he is not here to tell us."

They stepped gingerly around the man and pushed the

gate open, which was surprisingly unlocked. A crying child greeted their ears, and the sounds of shuffling grew in the sitting room.

Salmon knocked on the closed door. "Rahab?"

Silence followed, but he heard soft footfalls cross the room. The door opened, and Rahab, holding an animal—was that a cat?—looked into his face, sheer relief evident in her dark, unpainted eyes. How beautiful she was. If only . . . But he let the thought fall away.

"Come with us, all of you. We are about to burn the city."

Rahab faced her family. "Gather only what is necessary. This is our chance to start anew."

Salmon noted a few dark looks from some who could only be her brothers, but the women in the group showed tears of relief. The old man, possibly Rahab's father, carried a look of utter defeat. Salmon didn't blame him. And yet, he just wanted to get them out of the city and settled outside Israel's camp.

"Hurry," he said, trying hard to be patient.

Rahab came first, still clinging to the cat, and Mishael went ahead of them out the courtyard gate.

"Don't look around," Salmon said quietly to Rahab. "It will only give you nightmares." As seeing the bodies of Zimri and Kozbi had done for him.

But Rahab stopped at the sight of Tendaji and sank to her knees. The cat squirmed to leave her arms, but she tightened her hold. "Tendaji! No!" Her voice wavered. "Why did you not stay inside?"

Her soft weeping and the way she touched the Nubian's cold hand moved him. Suddenly she did not seem like a prostitute anymore, but a woman who had lost someone she loved.

Salmon knelt at her side and gently gripped her arm, tugging her to come away from death. "Come," he said softly. "There is nothing to be done for him."

He placed a calming hand on the cat's head, pulled Rahab gently to her feet, and guided her with one hand at the small of her back, too aware of the curve of her waist beneath the simple tunic. He glimpsed a woman not far from Tendaji, cut down in the act of running. Perhaps Tendaji had tried to save her. He prayed Adonai would have mercy on the man's soul, though he knew there was nothing to be done about that now.

At last they reached Joshua's side, and Salmon introduced Rahab to their leader.

"You are the prostitute who saved the lives of my men." Joshua's comment was not a question, but Rahab nodded regardless. "Thank you for sparing them. As you have done for them, we have done for you. These men will take you to the area outside of our camp where you can set up a camp of your own. They will see to any needs you have."

Rahab glanced for a long moment at the pet in her arms, then lifted her chin and met Joshua's gaze. "Thank you, my lord. I hope from this day on, I will no longer be thought of as a prostitute. I want to pledge allegiance to Israel."

Joshua nodded. "Such an occupation is not allowed in Israel," he said frankly. "We will discuss your future in a few days."

He dismissed them to give orders to put the silver and gold and bronze and iron into the treasury of the Lord's house, then put the city to the flames. Salmon led Rahab and her family to the outskirts of Israel's camp.

She faced him as he was about to turn back to join his men. "What I said to your leader . . ." She paused as if searching for words. "I meant it. I will do whatever is required to follow your God."

Skepticism warred with wanting to believe her as Salmon searched her earnest gaze. "The men of your family would have to be circumcised to join us."

She lowered her head but a moment. "I do not know if my family will accept that." She looked up. "But regardless of what they choose, I want to obey your God, the God who saved us."

Salmon nodded. "Joshua will explain to you what must be done," he said, suddenly anxious to leave. "I will come for you to meet him in the morning."

Later that evening as smoke curled from the city to the sky, Salmon pondered Rahab's request. The law did make provisions for captive brides. The problem would be finding someone willing to marry a prostitute. Former prostitute, he corrected himself, and yet he could not get the stigma of that fact from his mind.

Light from the moon shone down on the celebrating camp as a group of warriors gathered around Joshua. Mishael sidled up alongside Salmon, both of them looking toward what used to be Jericho.

"Too bad for all of those people," Mishael said, his voice unusually solemn. "I mean, I know they were under God's curse because of the detestable things they did and the worship they promoted, and I know He intended us to exact His will . . . but it's still hard to watch."

"Most of the men are happy about the victory." Salmon met his friend's gaze. "But I agree with you." Battle was not at all as he had expected. Watching the life flow from a man, woman, child, or animal, all at the end of his own sword . . . He looked heavenward, wishing Adonai would wash him clean of the memories.

"It's not like I expected," Mishael said, shaking his head. "I'm glad we were able to save Rahab, though."

Salmon glanced at Mishael, a strange foreboding growing within him. "Are you considering offering to marry her?"

Mishael looked at him strangely. "Me?" He laughed. "It hadn't even crossed my mind—not for myself." He gave Salmon a pointed look. "I thought she seemed perfect for you."

Salmon scoffed. "You want me to marry a prostitute?"

"Can you not overlook the sins of her past? She is a woman whom Adonai deemed worthy to save."

"Why me then? Why not you?" Salmon felt his defenses rising.

Mishael gave him a sidelong glance as the crowd grew near Joshua's tent. "I was thinking about her younger sister." He smiled, that mischievous grin that always said less than Salmon wanted to know. On the walk to the outskirts of the camp, Rahab had introduced her family. Mishael must have noticed Adara, the unmarried younger sister in the group.

"You're hopeless," Salmon said as they both turned to join the ranks at Joshua's tent.

Joshua climbed up on a large stone and raised his hands for silence. The crowd quieted.

"Look toward Jericho, all of you," Joshua said with a loud cry. "And hear my words." He paused as the men faced Jericho's smoldering remains. "Cursed before the Lord is the one who undertakes to rebuild this city, Jericho. At the cost of his firstborn son he will lay its foundations. At the cost of his youngest he will set up its gates."

Silence followed Joshua's remarks. Slowly, the crowd dispersed, Joshua's words sobering.

"You want company tonight?" Mishael asked as Salmon headed toward his tent alone.

Salmon shrugged. "Sure. As long as you don't snore."

Mishael laughed. "I can't promise that, but I'll try not to kick you in my sleep."

"Good. Then tomorrow you can come with me to Rahab's camp and escort her to Joshua." Salmon ran a hand through his hair at the thought. "Then we will see what is to be done with her."

PART 3

By faith the walls of Jericho fell down after they were encircled for seven days. By faith the harlot Rahab did not perish with those who did not believe, when she had received the spies with peace.

Hebrews 11:30–31 NKJV

Likewise, was not Rahab the harlot also justified by works when she received the messengers and sent them out another way?

James 2:25 NKJV

Nahshon the father of Salmon,
Salmon the father of Boaz, whose mother was Rahab,
Boaz the father of Obed, whose mother was Ruth,
Obed the father of Jesse,
and Jesse the father of King David.

Matthew 1:4–6

23

The smoke from Jericho's burned-out city carried an acrid, sickening scent toward the Israelite camp, and Rahab stood in her tent watching the last of the curling blackness reach greedy fingers toward the heavens. The pink light of dawn seemed out of place against the backdrop of such destruction.

She blinked away the ever-present emotion, seeing in her mind's eye Tendaji's broken body. Had her cook suffered the same fate? But of course she had, for she had refused to stay once the shout of Israel's warriors was heard from outside Jericho's gates. The loss, the shock of it all, had overtaken Rahab's family as the flames rose higher. But for fear of the triumphant Israelites, the women had wept quietly, without the normal mourners' loud cries and tears. She hugged herself, feeling the soft skin of her arms, still struggling to accept the fact that she had been spared.

Why—when she deserved judgment? For despite Dabir's part in forcing her into prostitution, she had acted her part willingly. She could have refused and rotted in one of their prisons. If Dabir hadn't beaten her to death first.

The truth was, she had done what she had to in order to live. To save her family. And herself.

The admission did nothing to wash the scars from her memory. Just as the baths she had required at the end of each evening with some sniveling customer had done nothing to rid her mind of what they did to her, what she allowed them to do. Worse, with a handful, perhaps only one—Prince Nahid—she had allowed herself to care, to enjoy his attention.

She closed her eyes for the briefest moment. Judgment *had* come on those men even as it should have come on her, and yet here she stood. She was free to start a new life, a respectable life.

The thought should have pleased her, did please her, but . . . Salmon's look of disdain, the one he tried to hide, surfaced in her mind, and she wondered if anyone would let her forget what she'd been.

She glanced up at the sound of male voices coming from the Israelite camp. Fear curdled her middle. Would such men seek out her services even against their God's wishes? Was she safe even here?

But as the men drew closer, she recognized Salmon and Mishael. She drew in a breath, forcing calmness into her spirit. Tendaji would have protected her. Could she count on Joshua and these two men to do the same?

She left the door of her tent and walked with graceful steps to meet Israel's two spies. She bowed at their feet as they approached.

"Rise, Rahab," Salmon said, and his voice carried a hint

of emotion she had not expected. "There is no need to bow to us."

She rose quickly, smoothing her skirts. "I only wished to express my gratitude to you both." She flushed, unable to hold either man's gaze. "Thank you, again, for saving my family."

Salmon cleared his throat. "We are happy to have done so. Without you, we would not be standing here."

She looked up at that, searched his face. Silence fell between them until Mishael chuckled. "I think we have all said enough thank-yous. Now how about we get on with what we came for?" His smile held a mischievous glint, and Rahab tilted her head and lifted a brow.

"And what would that be, my lord?"

"We came to take you to Joshua." Salmon turned and gestured toward the Israelite camp. "Is there anything you need to do first?"

Rahab thought a moment. To walk through the camp with just two men . . .

"I would like to bring my sister Adara, if you can wait while I get her." She prayed her sister was not still sleeping.

The men nodded, and Rahab hurried toward her tent, which Adara had shared the night before. "Adara?" She spoke softly, looking around the darkened tent, relieved when she saw her sister step from behind a partition, tying the belt of her robe.

"What is it?"

"Oh good. You are awake."

"It is hard to sleep on the ground, and besides, I heard you talking and peeked outside. What do those men want?" Adara's wide eyes were filled with curiosity and a sense of excitement.

"They came to take me to Joshua, their leader. If you are willing, I would like you to come with me." She glanced beyond her sister a moment, surprised at the heat again filling her face. What was this sense of humility, of shame?

"I would be happy to come with you." Her smile brightened, calming some of Rahab's unease.

"Good. Run and tell Father and Mother where we are going. And hurry. I do not want to keep them waiting." Rahab left the tent, knowing her sister's desire for adventure would cause her quick obedience.

A few moments later, Salmon and Mishael led Rahab and Adara into Israel's camp, with her oldest brother Azad joining them. Perhaps her father was more protective than she realized, though Rahab knew it was for Adara's sake that Azad followed them.

"I am surprised they ever let you act as my maid," Rahab whispered to Adara, out of Azad's hearing. "Or sleep in my tent."

Adara gripped Rahab's arm and leaned close. "They only fuss over me because I am the youngest. But I know how to get my way when I really want it." She twisted her baby finger through Rahab's and smiled. "Father is not so hard to reason with. He is just angry at what all those men have done to you. And he doesn't trust the Israelites."

Rahab nodded. "I think their leader, Joshua, is a good man."

They grew silent as the men continued leading them past curious onlookers, both men and women. Rahab pulled the headscarf closer about her neck, ducking her head, not wishing to be seen . . . to be judged.

At last they came to a large tent at the head of the tribe of

Ephraim, not far from the Tent of Meeting. Salmon stopped at the fire pit in front of the awning and called Joshua's name. The old man emerged from his tent, took in their appearances in one glance, and welcomed them into his home.

"I am glad you have come." Joshua beckoned Rahab, her sister, and her brother to sit on plush cushions along one wall, while Salmon and Mishael remained outside the tent.

"Thank you, my lord." Rahab attempted a wobbly smile, her nerves heightened at the fear of what he might say.

"You said you wanted to pledge allegiance to Israel."

She nodded, not daring a look at either brother or sister. "Yes."

He seemed to consider them and her comment but a moment. "Very well. If that is the case, this is what our law requires and what you must do to become one of us."

———

Rahab walked in silence with her brother and sister, ignoring the curious gazes of the Israelites, feeling the heat of her brother's anger at each circumcised male they passed. Salmon and Mishael had not joined them on this return trip, and she was glad of it. Joshua's words were too much to take in, and the thought of what was required of her, of her family, was humbling.

"These people are barbarians!" Azad said as they finally reached the outskirts of the Israelite camp and the safety of their father's tent. "They want all of us"—he pointed to the men in Rahab's family—"to be circumcised in order to celebrate their feast days with them, to become one people with them." He crossed his arms, staring each one down. "I, for one, want no part of such a thing."

Rahab watched her brothers nod their agreement, and suddenly the room of her father's borrowed tent erupted with loud, swift bickering. Rahab took Adara's hand and tugged her to follow, leaving the men to argue alone.

"Shouldn't we find Mother and Cala and tell them what Joshua said?" Adara's dreamy expression told Rahab far more than her words. Had she not understood Joshua's words?

"Father and Tzadok will tell them. Besides, the rest does not apply to them. Only to you and to me, if we are willing, or if one of the men of Israel wants us." She glanced at Adara's stricken look. How quickly her expressions changed. She must learn to mask her emotions if she was to survive in a world where men ruled. "We are captives, you understand."

They entered Rahab's dark tent, but Rahab had no desire to lift the sides. It would only bring the sounds of bickering closer.

"Perhaps we should go for a walk to the river. The Jordan's whooshing will drown out the sounds of our men." Adara stood at the threshold, her gaze beckoning.

Rahab glanced at her few belongings. She did not even have a spindle and distaff with her, nor her tools for weaving flax. But then, the flax on her roof had burned along with the city.

"It is good to walk." Though her feet already hurt from walking as much as they had through Israel's camp.

They slipped past the tents of her family, all gifts from Salmon's and Mishael's people. They owned so little. And they owed their life to Israel. How could they survive unless they followed the laws of Israel's God and became one with their people?

"I didn't like the part about shaving my hair," Adara said softly as the roar of the river drew closer. "I don't mind trimming my nails." She held up a hand where the henna still coated the tips of her fingernails, then looked at Rahab and twirled her fingers through long strands of dark hair. "But how humiliating to be shaven!" She looked down at her clothes and fingered her multicolored robe, one that she had taken great care to create at Rahab's side while Rahab worked the flax into linen. "What would we wear if we put these aside?"

"I imagine the husband who would claim you would provide new clothing. At least they would allow a headscarf when we leave their tents." Rahab felt anew the humility, even humiliation, this God would exact from her. She already felt shame from all she had done. But His ways were humbling in a way she had not before experienced.

"I suppose the purpose of these things is to help us put aside our past, to start anew, with new hair, new clothes, new faith." Rahab tucked her arm through her younger sister's. "Do you want to join with Israel? I was speaking for myself when we talked with Joshua. I would not expect any of my family to follow me if they truly did not want to."

"The cost is high," Adara said, looking out over the river, her voice carried away on the wind.

"Too high?" Rahab wondered the same thing. Could she do what was required? But then, who would have her? She would not be required to follow the law of captive bride unless a man came forward to claim her, to want to marry her. She could remain on the outskirts of the camp and survive on her own. Perhaps her father would move them to another city or town.

"Not too high." Adara's words brought Rahab's thoughts up short. "Not if Mishael were the one asking." Color heightened her sister's cheeks, and Rahab took a step back to better look into her eyes.

"You only just met the man." Whereas Rahab had been unable to forget Salmon from the first day the spies had come to her home.

"You have spoken of them both in favorable terms more than once, my sister." Adara smiled. "Besides, he is very handsome, is he not?"

Rahab shook her head. The girl had no idea of the ways of men, and how one who could seem so kind could end up so cruel.

"Do you think Salmon would marry you?" Adara's question startled her. She met her sister's honest gaze.

"Why would you think such a thing? He has shown no interest in me. If any feelings have come from the man, they are definitely not the amiable kind. He disdains me." The realization, the memory, of how he had nearly cringed when she touched him as he climbed from her window filled her mind, blotting out the kindness he had shown when he tried to keep her from kneeling beside Tendaji's broken body.

"I see the way he looks at you." Adara bent to retrieve a smooth stone from beside the river and tossed it in, watching it plop. "He may not realize it yet, but he cares for you, Rahab."

Rahab glanced from Adara to the river. "Why should he care about a prostitute?" Why should God have saved her in the first place?

"You are too hard on yourself." Adara stepped closer and touched her arm. "If Israel's God found you worthy to save and spared our lives for no reason other than we are your family, then that says more about you than us." A solemn expression came over her youthful face. "I believe in their

God, Rahab, even if Father does not. No matter what our men want to do, I want to obey the God of Israel along with you." She squeezed Rahab's arm in a possessive, sisterly gesture.

Rahab blinked back the sudden threat of tears and pulled Adara into her arms. "Thank you," she whispered in her ear. "If it comes to that, I would be glad to have you near—to rock your babies on my knee."

"And I will attend to yours as well," Adara insisted. "Do not fear, Rahab. Someone will marry you and love you for yourself. They will not use you as Dabir did."

Or Gamal. Or Prince Nahid. Or countless other men. What she wouldn't give for someone to love her for her.

But even Salmon could not be what she wanted. Of that she was certain. She had lived too long and seen too much to think that any man could give her that kind of unconditional, forgiving love.

"I will be content if you are happy," she told Adara. She slipped her arm through her sister's, and together they walked back to the bickering of her father's camp.

24

Rahab and her sisters walked to the Jordan to draw water a week after the burning of Jericho. She had heard nothing more from Salmon or Mishael or Joshua—only the constant arguments of the men in her father's household. The river was not as high as it had been, allowing them to hear the voices of the women of Israel as they approached.

"Don't look at them," Cala said, shifting away from the chatter of the older women who bent near the river to wash their clothes. "They always scowl at us as though we have no right to be here."

Rahab glanced at the Hebrew women, caught the curious looks of some, the obvious disdain of others. She met Cala's gaze and nodded. "Let's move farther downstream."

Adara swung a clay jug to her shoulder and straightened her back, walking with a purposeful, graceful swing of her hips, her chin tipped upward.

Rahab laughed softly, then leaned closer to her younger sister. "You're going to make them like us less than they do."

"That's just the problem," Cala said, kneeling to fill her jar at the water's edge. "They will never accept us. You have heard what the men are saying. How can we ask them to submit to some barbaric practice to stay with a people who despise us?"

"I don't think they despise us." Rahab looked toward the women again, their heads huddled close as if they gossiped. "They don't know us."

"They don't want to know us." Cala stood, lifting the heavy jug to her head and balancing it with one practiced hand.

They walked back the way they had come toward their small makeshift camp. At least the cat had stayed. She noticed him sleeping in a patch of sunlight just outside her tent. How long before he ran off?

"Father is thinking of leaving soon."

Rahab stopped at Cala's words, the weight of her own jug suddenly heavy on her head.

"How soon?" She wasn't surprised. But somehow she had hoped . . .

"Tonight. Or tomorrow. I'm not sure. But they will leave when the sons of Israel are sleeping, lest they try to stop us." Cala looked at Rahab, her dark eyes narrowed. "You won't tell them, will you?"

Rahab shook her head. "Why would I do that? You are my family. But I will miss you."

Adara turned, her eyes wide. "You would not join us?"

Rahab studied them both, two sisters dear to her heart. How could she bear to have them leave her? "I cannot leave."

"Why not?"

"I promised my allegiance to Israel's God."

"So serve Him in another place. Why stay here with people

you don't know?" Adara's voice rose in pitch, clearly agitated. "I don't want to go without you."

"Why go to another place where we know no one? At least here we know Salmon and Mishael and Joshua. And their God spared us. Where would we go that could possibly be any better?" Rahab set the cold jar on the ground at her feet, and her sisters did the same. "Their God is giving them the whole land of Canaan. All the kings fear them. Where does Father think to go that will be any safer than we are here?" She couldn't believe they had kept this decision from her.

"Father wants to head to Egypt." Cala lowered her gaze as if suddenly fascinated with her sandaled feet.

Rahab glanced from Cala to Adara. "I suppose Tzadok supports this."

Cala nodded.

"Will you stay with me?" She faced Adara. "Or has Father insisted you join them?"

Color flushed Adara's face. She glanced beyond Rahab. "I would stay with you. I would marry an Israelite. But Father will hear none of it." Moisture touched her lashes, and she held Rahab's gaze.

"Mishael would have asked for you, I think." Though Rahab only said so on instinct, based on all she had known of men.

"And I would have accepted." Adara looked briefly away, then stepped closer and fell into Rahab's arms. "Oh Rahab. Can't you convince Father to let me stay with you? Can we ask Joshua to arrange a marriage before Father leaves? We are Israel's captives, after all, aren't we? We can't just walk away."

Rahab patted her sister's back. "We are captives in a sense, but not in the normal way, since it was our lives for theirs.

And Joshua isn't likely to try to take power from Father. He is your protector."

"Then he is your protector too. You must come with us." This from Cala, surprising Rahab with the strength of her words.

Rahab slowly shook her head. "Father gave up protecting me a long time ago." She looked toward the Israelite camp and back toward the river, where she caught a glimpse of one of the women watching them. Was she being a fool to want to stay? Would such women ever accept her? And how could she stay without her sisters?

"Can you at least talk to him? He listened to you once before. Maybe he will listen again. Maybe Joshua could make him listen." Adara's tone grew desperate, her feelings for Mishael only too evident in her bright gaze.

Rahab held Adara close, then released her and lifted the jar once more. "Azad heard the requirements the same as we did for pledging allegiance to Israel. Our men are appalled at such a request." She understood why, though she could hardly explain it to her virgin sister.

"But why?" Adara asked, clearly troubled. "How is that any worse than having your head shaved?"

Rahab released a heavy sigh, groping for the right words. "It brings only emotional pain to shave a woman's head," she said slowly. "For a man, it brings physical weakness, pain, and a blow to his pride. Trust me, dear one, it is much worse."

"Tzadok said he heard tell of Israel's ancestors killing a whole city of men who'd agreed to be circumcised. Once they succumbed, while they were still weak, Israel attacked them. Tzadok—he doesn't trust them." Cala lifted her chin in a sudden show of pride in her husband's decision. "After hearing that tale, I don't either."

Silence followed the remark, and Rahab glanced at Adara, wondering how strong her feelings for Mishael would prove to be. She didn't really know the man. Though she said she believed in Israel's God, she was so young and impressionable. It was too much to ask her to choose between her whole family and Rahab.

"It sounds like you are already convinced then." Rahab looked at Cala, who gave a slight nod.

"If Father leaves, I will not put up a fight."

Adara squirmed under Rahab's gaze. "Will you?" Rahab asked.

Adara walked slowly, saying nothing at first. "I don't want to." She blinked back tears. "It would be perfect if you would just come with us."

How oblivious her sister was to anything but her own thoughts, her own pain. "I could say the same to all of you. Just stay. It would be safer here." Did they have any idea how hard it would be to travel the mountains and wilderness to get to Egypt? "Don't you remember what the Egyptians did to Israel? And what their God did to the Egyptians?"

Adara stared at Rahab, but Cala just shrugged. "We weren't there. These are stories of old. Many things could have changed in the telling over the years."

"For a God who just recently parted the Jordan as He did the Red Sea and who just saved us from a city He let Israel destroy, I cannot help but wonder why you think the past tales are not as real. Besides, why believe one tale and not another? You seem quick to accept Israel's treachery toward the circumcised, yet don't believe the stories of Egypt's enslaving them or of the plagues?" Were her sisters really that naive?

"All I know is that Father and Tzadok and our brothers don't like it here. If they go, we have no choice but to go with them." They stopped near their tents, each setting their jugs in small depressions in the ground. "We should bake the flatbread for travel. Tzadok said to be ready at a moment's notice."

Rahab nodded, then embraced each sister. "I hope you will say goodbye before you leave." She swallowed, emotion threatening.

Adara clung to her. "Please speak to Father for me."

Rahab kissed her forehead. "I will try, dear one. But I seriously doubt there is anything I can do."

Salmon dug his staff into the earth, keeping to the sides of the road where the moonlight flickered beyond them, casting both himself and Mishael in darkness. The town of Ai lay just beyond the next ridge, but they would wait until daylight to enter with the rest of the merchants, as they had done in Jericho.

"Let's not make the mistake of staying too long this time." Mishael sank onto the ground in front of a shallow cave tucked into the hill overlooking the city. "We can't be sure of finding a friendly prostitute again." He chuckled, but Salmon merely nodded.

"Or a friendly merchant, for that matter." He did not meet his friend's gaze but rather closed his eyes and leaned against the cave wall, pretending to want sleep.

"You can't possibly be tired already." Mishael picked up

a flint knife and piece of wood he had found along the path and began to shave the edges.

"I don't feel much like talking, is all." The truth was he could not shake the image of Rahab from his thoughts. What was to become of her? It troubled him that he cared even a little. How many men had known her? What had led her into such a vile life?

Mishael whistled a soft tune, breaking his attention. He opened his eyes, caught the laughter in his friend's gaze. "Don't feel like talking? Or can't stop thinking about a certain beautiful captive?"

"She's not a captive. She saved our lives, so we saved hers."

"The people treat her like one. My sister tells me that whenever Rahab and her sisters come to the river for water, the women of Israel stare at them, gossiping and scowling." He flicked a piece of wood from his robe.

"So tell your sister to befriend them. Why allow her to put up with that?" Heat crawled up the back of Salmon's neck at the thought of what he would like to say to some of those women.

"I have little control over my sister's words and you know it. What woman in Israel ever keeps her tongue silent when she is among the gossips? If my sister befriended Rahab, what do you think will happen to her? She will be shunned."

"And yet you would marry Rahab's younger sister Adara. You are fickle in your convictions, my friend." Salmon shoved aside his irritation.

"You are an enigma to me, Salmon. First you say, 'Who could ever marry a prostitute?' Then you tell me I should make my sister befriend one." His brows narrowed as his scrutiny grew. "Look me in the eye and tell me you do not care for Rahab."

Salmon met Mishael's gaze, but he could not hold it.

"I knew it." Mishael's laughter was too self-satisfying.

"I do not care for Rahab." Salmon forced the words through suddenly dry lips.

Mishael's laughter stopped. Silence followed as they looked at each other. At last Mishael shrugged, as though through with the conversation. "Your loss, my friend."

Salmon looked away. "I'd like to see you marry someone who has known more men than she can count."

Mishael tucked the flint knife into the pouch at his side and stretched out on the ground, hands behind his head. "Perhaps I will." He rolled over, his back to Salmon, the conversation clearly at an end.

Salmon stared at his friend's relaxed pose. Mishael was just baiting him, as he and Zimri and Mishael had baited each other throughout their childhood. He couldn't marry Rahab any more than Salmon could.

And yet as Salmon closed his eyes, it was Rahab's vulnerable face that appeared in his mind's eye . . . with that scrawny homeless cat tucked into her arms.

He must have slept, for dawn woke him with much the same thoughts as he'd had hours before. Mishael had already doused the embers of last night's fire.

"How long have you been awake?"

"Not long." Mishael glanced at him. "You ready to head to town?"

Salmon rose and stretched. "Yes."

They left camp and headed south toward the plain, where the gates of the small city stood open before them. "How shall we handle this?" Mishael asked.

Salmon tapped the earth with his staff. "Same as before."

Mishael nodded. Salmon felt the slightest tension between them. "Look," he said when the silence stretched on too long. "I know you think me conflicted about Rahab, defending her one moment, shunning her the next. But I can't marry a prostitute, no matter how much she might have changed." He paused, glancing at his friend. "So if you find her worthy, you have my blessing."

Mishael stared into the distance. The gates of the city drew closer. "I will think on it."

Somehow the thought that Mishael preferred Adara but would consider covering Rahab's shame tasted sour on Salmon's tongue. Would to God he had such courage. The woman had captivated him with more than her beauty. She was smart and resourceful and she loved her family. And that silly cat.

All qualities he would want in a wife.

If only her past didn't keep coming between them.

25

Rahab awoke before dawn to the sound of loud purring in her ear. She blinked and rubbed her eyes. What day was it? Unnatural silence greeted her. Of course, everyone would still be abed. She glanced at the cat that had perched on her chest. "Perhaps the cook was right about you, you little beast. Why did you wake me?"

She rolled over on her side, trying to ignore the animal. But the absence of the predawn activity she should have heard grew deafening. She tossed the covers aside and stood, wrapped a robe about her, and walked slowly to her tent's door, heart pounding. She peered into the gray light and looked from right to left. There was no sign of her family. The tents, the water jars, even the few goats the Israelites had given them were gone.

Shock broke through her foggy thoughts, and the dew tickled her feet as she walked. "Adara? Cala?" Had no one the decency to say goodbye?

She stifled a soft cry and placed a hand to her throat as she walked the length of the small area where each tent had stood. How far had they gotten? Did they wait until they knew she slept?

Twin daggers of betrayal and hurt pierced her, bringing with them a physical ache so deep she had to remind herself to breathe. With the breath's release came a simmering rage. How could they do this to her? She had saved their lives!

She looked south, toward Egypt. No sign of Adara or even of her family's small caravan in the distance. They must have left during the darkest heart of night. *Oh God, what am I supposed to do?* Was there no one trustworthy, no one who wanted her?

Soft fur rubbed her calf, followed by the cat's familiar purr. A moment later, he hopped up into her arms. Round green eyes looked directly into hers as if to say, "I didn't leave you."

She held him close, wetting his fur with her tears.

⁕

Rahab tried to sleep again, to no avail. At last she rose, tidied the small tent of her few belongings, and pulled the cat into her arms. "Don't worry about the people," she whispered in his ear. "Just hang on to my robe, and I won't let you go." She couldn't leave him alone. He might not wait for her, or worse, he might be torn to pieces by some wild animal. She covered her hair with a veil, shielding the cat like a babe in arms, and headed toward Israel's camp.

She passed several women talking in a group near some of the tents, but their conversations stopped abruptly as they saw her approach. She glanced their way and nodded, her stomach tightening with their lack of response. She sighed, mentally shaking herself. It did not matter what they thought of her. She was here now, and she would seek Joshua's protection.

The camp seemed to stretch on forever, and she searched her mind for the path Salmon had led them over a week before. At last she spotted Joshua addressing a group of soldiers. "Be strong and courageous and take the city," she heard him shout as she grew close. "The spies have agreed that not all of us need to go up, for the city is small. So go now, and defeat Ai in the name of the Lord."

Rahab glimpsed Salmon and Mishael among the group that turned and marched away at Joshua's orders. When the last man left the camp, Rahab forced her feet to continue forward until she stood within arm's length of Joshua.

"My lord, may I speak a word with you?" Her voice sounded distant, and she could not help the dead feeling inside of her. The hope she'd felt when Israel had rescued her family, when men had actually kept their word, failed her now.

Joshua turned, his lined face smiling at her as though she was already one of them. Of course, she wasn't. "How can I help you, Rahab?" He motioned her to enter the sitting room of his tent, then called to his wife to bring water to drink. "Please, sit."

Rahab found a cushion and settled the cat in her lap as she lowered herself to the floor. She smiled at Joshua's wife Eliana, a woman much younger than Joshua himself. She noticed the slice of fresh cucumber floating in the clay water cup. She sipped. "Thank you."

The woman nodded and smiled, then spotted the cat. "Well, who is it you have here?" She knelt at Rahab's side and gently touched the cat's head. His purr followed. "What a friendly little thing." Eliana looked from the cat to hold Rahab's gaze. "We are so glad to have you as one of us now. I hope you will consider spending some time with my girls and me."

The offer took Rahab off guard, but she managed a slight nod. "Thank you. That is very kind."

"Not at all. You are a hero in this camp. If not for you, we would never have had the advantage to take Jericho." She smiled again, then sat in a corner and picked up her spindle and distaff.

Joshua gave his wife an affectionate look, then faced Rahab. "Now, please, tell me what I can do for you."

Rahab swallowed, drawing on courage she did not feel, calmed by Eliana's kindness. "It appears, my lord, that my family has left the protection of Israel. They broke camp and left by cover of night while I slept."

"Oh, my dear girl, how awful for you!" Eliana said, her expression filled with genuine sympathy. She glanced at her husband. "You must come and stay with us, of course."

How was it this woman seemed to know her very thoughts? "Thank you again, mistress. That is very kind of you."

"Call me Eliana." She nodded to Joshua.

"Of course Eliana is right, Rahab. You cannot live alone outside the camp. It isn't safe."

"But to live among you, a woman alone . . . is that safe, my lord? Will your men keep their distance from me?" She met his gaze and knew he understood her meaning.

"If any one of my men sought you out as the men of your city once did, he would be punished. Our God does not abide adultery, Rahab. He is pleased when we marry and are fruitful and multiply."

"I could live in my own tent then?" She stroked the cat's head and could not meet Joshua's gaze.

"As long as you pitch it near my wife's. No one will touch you under my protection."

"Thank you, my lord."

"Call me Joshua, dear girl. I am not your master. Only one God is master of all."

Rahab nodded, though she found the comment curious, even confusing.

"But I wonder if I might ask you a question," Joshua said quietly, sipping on a cup of water.

"Of course. Anything." She would not pretend or lie in giving her answer as she had become so adept at doing.

"Why would you choose us over your own family?" He paused. "I realize you feel a devotion to us for saving your life. But family ties are strong, and the bonds of father and daughter hard to break. Why would you not remain under your father's protection now that you are free?"

She studied the outlines of the cat's dark and varying shades of brown, slightly tightening her grip, tugging him gently closer to her heart. Was the animal her new shield against pain? But of course, the little thing had no power to keep her from the wounds of men and women.

"If you would rather not tell me, you have no obligation to do so," Joshua said after her lengthy silence.

"No, no. I do not mind," she said quickly. "You must understand. I love my family." Her voice caught on the memories of their absence, and suddenly she felt completely alone.

Eliana laid her distaff and spindle aside and came once more to kneel at her side. "If you are not ready, we do not need to know your secrets, Rahab. Just know that you are accepted. Whatever happened with your family or in your past is past." She looked to her husband, who gave a slight nod. "One day I will tell you about our sacrifices, and then perhaps you can confess the hurt to our God and be made whole once more." She patted Rahab's knee.

"I have not been whole since I married an unworthy man." She suddenly realized that the memories of Gamal, Dabir, and the others were still too fresh to share with strangers. Even kind strangers.

"You may set your tent in the circle of mine," Joshua said, "near Eliana's. I will see to it that no man comes near you. You will spend your days serving my wife, helping her to prepare food and clothing for some of the younger unmarried men or care for the widows among us. Does that please you?"

"Yes. Thank you." She swallowed the perpetual emotion, wondering where the stoic lying prostitute had gone. In this place, with these people, she felt nothing like that now. "I will go and gather my things."

"I will send my daughters to help you."

She nodded and waited for him to call his daughters, left the cat with Eliana on the promise of her swift return, then walked with the girls to her tent, feeling as though perhaps something would at last be right with her world.

26

The city of Ai loomed before them, an insignificant town with less than half the men Jericho had possessed. Salmon glanced at Mishael and smiled. They would be home in time for the evening meal if all went as they expected. They divided the three thousand men into three groups, one coming after the other. Caleb's nephew Othniel led the first group, then Mishael the second, and Salmon brought up the last of the men.

They came around from behind a large copse of trees, expecting to walk right through the open city gate. But as Othniel's group approached, arrows shot down at them from the wall. Soldiers from Ai stormed through the gates, chasing them back.

Salmon commanded his troop to circle around the city, but Mishael's group was caught in the chase all the way to the stone quarries. Seeing the gate shut up behind the warriors, Salmon and Othniel pursued the men of Ai. But more soldiers appeared, coming from the trees, and as Salmon reached the quarries where Mishael's group was already trying to make their way down the slopes, Salmon ducked into a shallow cave with a few of his men, his courage drained.

"How is it possible they are striking us down?" This from one of his men. "We outnumber them two to one."

Salmon shaded his eyes against the sun's glare and looked down on the men trying to maneuver the slopes. His heart stopped, then went into a full gallop as he watched an arrow from a soldier of Ai arc and dip straight toward Mishael.

"Mishael, run!" But Salmon was too far away to be heard. Time seemed like a distant enemy as he broke free of the cave and raced down the hill toward his friend. As he reached Mishael's side, saw his crumpled, broken body, he let out a war cry that shook the stones surrounding them. He readied his bow and shot back at the approaching handful of soldiers, shouting at his men to do the same.

But as each one looked around at their losses, they fled like children running to their mothers. Salmon took a bold step closer to the men of Ai and nocked another arrow. The men of Ai did the same, both sides standing there waiting for the other to strike.

"Go home, Israelites," one of them shouted. "Your God may have given you Jericho, but you will not defeat us."

Salmon glanced around him, wanting to shout back that their God could defeat them with twelve men instead of three thousand. But as the men of Ai turned back toward their city, he did not loose his arrow, and he did not say the words. He turned instead, defeat filling him, picked up Mishael's body, and walked toward home.

⚜

"We lost thirty-six men," Salmon told Joshua later that afternoon. "Including Mishael." His voice broke, and silence followed the remark.

244

Rahab strained to hear more as she knelt in the women's half of Joshua's tent, crushing mint leaves and adding them to the water she had drawn earlier from the Jordan.

"We don't know how they knew we were coming," one of the other leaders said, "but somehow they were ready for us. They met us at the gate, and some were waiting in the forest."

"We spent the afternoon looking for a cave big enough to bury the bodies." Rahab could still hear the wobble of emotion in the timbre of Salmon's deep voice.

The room grew quiet again, until at last Joshua spoke. "Send for the elders of the people. I will go before the ark of the Lord and they will join me. Perhaps our God will hear our prayers and show us why we were defeated."

Salmon followed Joshua across the compound to the place where the ark of the Lord rested. Joshua tore his tunic, and Salmon and the rest of the elders did the same. They sprinkled dust on their heads and fell facedown on the ground before the Lord.

As dusk descended, Joshua's voice broke the silence. "Alas, Sovereign Lord, why did you ever bring this people across the Jordan to deliver us into the hands of the Amorites to destroy us? If only we had been content to stay on the other side of the Jordan!"

Salmon's heart felt like a heavy weight within his chest. Joshua's doubt and anguish mingled with the scent of Mishael's blood, which Salmon would never be able to wash from his hands. Such defeat seemed impossible with the God who had parted the Jordan and caused Jericho's walls to tumble. And yet, here they were, fresh from the awful task of burying their dead.

"Pardon your servant, Lord. What can I say, now that Israel has been routed by its enemies? The Canaanites and the other people of the country will hear about this, and they will surround us and wipe out our name from the earth. What then will you do for your own great name?" Joshua's voice wavered, and Salmon's throat ached with the need to cry out, *Why?*

Stillness, unnatural and eerie, followed Joshua's prayer, but moments later a rumble like thunder moved above their heads, and Salmon strained to hear above the roar.

"Stand up!" a deep voice said from the darkening clouds. "What are you doing down on your face? Israel has sinned. They have violated my covenant, which I commanded them to keep. They have taken some of the devoted things, they have stolen, they have lied, they have put them with their own possessions. That is why the Israelites cannot stand against their enemies. They turn their backs and run because they have been made liable to destruction. I will not be with you anymore unless you destroy whatever among you is devoted to destruction.

"Go, consecrate the people," the voice continued. "Tell them, 'Consecrate yourselves in preparation for tomorrow, for this is what the Lord, the God of Israel, says: There are devoted things among you, Israel. You cannot stand against your enemies until you remove them.'"

After a few more instructions, the clouds lifted and the voice departed. Salmon rose on shaky legs and looked toward Joshua, whose face was both aglow and hard as flint.

"Go among the people and do as the Lord commanded.

Each one must wash their clothes and consecrate themselves. Tomorrow we will go through every tribe, every family, until we find who is guilty," Joshua said.

Salmon did not wait for dismissal, nor speak a word to any man. Fear and anger mingled, rising like a storm within him. Mishael had died because some fool had disobeyed their God?

But as he marched toward the camp, he stopped short at thoughts of the temptations he had considered, of Rahab. Could the disobedient one be him?

27

Rahab spent the rest of the evening washing her garments along with the rest of the women in Israel, kneeling at the Jordan until every last piece of clothing was washed clean. She had said little to Joshua's wife during the solemn consecration and returned to her tent to find sleep impossible. Could she be the cause of Israel's defeat? Was her desire to join them a source of anger to their God? Perhaps she should have been devoted to destruction along with her people, and the fact that they had spared her . . . did that make her guilty of this great loss?

She shivered at the thought, telling herself it wasn't true. Joshua had spared her because she had helped his men. Still, perhaps Joshua had failed his God by saving her. Or perhaps her family leaving Israel's protection was the cause.

She rose against the chill of night and wrapped her cloak about her, padding softly past the sleeping cat, and stepped into the moonlight. The camp lay in quiet slumber around her. Only the distant howl of a wolf or jackal disturbed the silence. She left her torch in its stand outside her door and crept quietly around the circle of tents surrounding Joshua's.

Worry weighted her spirit, and she felt the stirrings of doubt in her soul. Memories of Jericho's broken walls—everything fallen except her house—rose in her thoughts. Surely God alone had done such a thing. Surely He had meant for her to live because she had put her trust in Him. Hadn't He?

She rounded the bend, heading back toward her tent. Sounds of weeping met her ear, and she wondered if the tears came from the tent of one who had lost a loved one in the war. Did Mishael's family live near here? She was suddenly grateful Adara was not here to witness Mishael's loss. If she had married him, she would already be widowed.

The thought unnerved her. She could not imagine her little sister having to live through the things she had suffered in losing Gamal.

But whoever was guilty of angering Israel's God—what kind of judgment would they suffer? Jericho's burning embers filled her mind's eye, and her feet were suddenly no longer sluggish. She lifted the edge of her cloak and hurried as quickly as she could back to her tent.

Dawn came too early, and Rahab rose with the women of Joshua's household to prepare the morning meal, but Joshua and the elders ate nothing as the tribes gathered in the center of the camp. Rahab stood in the shadows as Joshua called the tribes one by one, in order of birth. Reuben, Simeon, Levi, Judah.

"The Lord has chosen Judah," Joshua said, his face rugged and stern. "All of the clans of Judah, come forward."

Rahab glanced at the group, Salmon's tribe. Fear slithered through her, a living thing, as she watched Salmon walk with the tribe to face Joshua. Would Salmon be punished for his promise, the promise that had saved her life? She had coaxed it from him, had bargained for it as easily as she had told so many lies to the men who shared her bed. All for the sake of her freedom. But at what cost to Salmon, to Israel? She placed a hand on her middle, trying to quell the sickening drcad.

Joshua looked the men over, then closed his eyes as if listening for direction. "The clan of Zerah, come forward."

Rahab released a shaky breath as she watched Salmon step back. She did not know the clans of Israel, but apparently Zerah was not Salmon's ancestor. Which meant he could not be guilty of promising to save her. She searched quickly around for a stone to sit upon, fearing her legs would not hold her.

Joshua repeated the process, listening for the Lord's choice. "The family of Zimri, come forward." The men of Zimri's family stepped in front of Joshua one at a time, man by man. At last Joshua continued. "Achan son of Karmi, the son of Zimri, the son of Zerah, of the tribe of Judah, the Lord has chosen you. Now, my son, give glory to the Lord, the God of Israel, and honor him. Tell me what you have done. Do not hide it from me."

Achan's face turned ashen as though he would faint. He lifted his hands in supplication and fell to his knees. "It is true! I have sinned against the Lord, the God of Israel. This is what I have done: when I saw in the plunder a beautiful robe from Babylonia, two hundred shekels of silver, and a bar of gold weighing fifty shekels, I coveted them and took them. They are hidden in the ground inside my tent, with the silver underneath."

Joshua glanced at Salmon and Othniel. "Go and find the items."

The space of too many heartbeats later, with Achan weeping on his knees, Rahab watched as Salmon and Othniel brought the items to Joshua. Her breath caught. The robe had belonged to Prince Nahid. Her heart thumped hard as she remembered. He had worn it with pride on the day of the Feast of Keret, when he had "married" her. Mishael had died for a robe? One she could have duplicated if they had asked.

Sorrow filled her as Salmon and Othniel laid the rest of the items on the ground before all Israel, spread out before the Lord.

"Thus says the Lord." Joshua's voice rang with power over the camp, and Rahab shivered at its strength. "'Whoever is caught with the devoted things shall be destroyed by fire, along with all that belongs to him. He has violated the covenant of the Lord and has done an outrageous thing in Israel!'"

Joshua's gaze took in the whole camp, then landed on the elders closest to him. "Gather everything and bring Achan, son of Zerah, his sons and his daughters, his cattle, donkeys, and sheep, his tent, and all that he has to the Valley of Achor."

Rahab watched as the men quickly obeyed, lifting a weeping Achan and grasping the hands of his family. High-pitched wails came from his daughters and curses on Achan from his sons. Rahab watched, dumbstruck. Were they really going to destroy all?

Joshua's wife and daughters followed the crowd to the Valley of Achor, and Rahab was swept along with them, her curiosity making it impossible for her to stay away. What kind of God would spare a foreign prostitute and destroy some of His own people?

⚜

"Why have you brought this trouble on us?" Joshua asked as the crowd stood on the hillsides of the Valley of Achor, Achan and his family and belongings huddled together in the center of the small valley. "The Lord will bring trouble on you today."

Salmon looked on, willing his limbs to stop trembling. When Judah had been chosen, he had feared—he still could not quite accept the relief he had felt when he discovered his clan was not among the guilty. His father was descended from Perez, one of Judah's twins by Tamar; Zerah was the other twin. He sighed. So promising to save Rahab had not angered God or caused this defeat.

Still, how easy it would have been to want to keep some of the spoils of the wealthy Jericho. He shuddered to think that he could have succumbed to the same temptation.

He looked up at the sound of a high-pitched shriek. The first volley of stones had hit their marks, bruising Achan and his sons and daughters. Salmon looked on, numb, unable to force his arm to throw the rock in his hand. Were they not all guilty of coveting things similar to what Achan had taken? If not for the tangible evidence, no one but God would have known. No one but God could read the hearts of those exacting His judgment now.

But Mishael had died because of this man.

And yet, as the feeling of vengeance rose upon him for his friend's sake, he could not look into the valley below without remorse for his own sense of utter failure. He had pledged to obey the law of God. To accept that law meant accepting both the blessing and the cursing that came with it. If only blessing were all that ever followed Israel's actions. How much easier it would be to create a god he could manage, one who did not demand something so impossible as *do not covet* a neighbor's possessions.

He looked down at Achan, seeing himself. What a wretched man he was!

He glanced over his shoulder and glimpsed Rahab not far from him, standing behind Joshua's wife and daughters. More cries came from the valley below as men circled the rim. He turned, forcing weighty limbs to carry him closer. *Forgive me, Adonai. I find this law . . . so difficult.*

But he stayed with the men out of obedience, casting stones down on Achan until the last voice fell silent and the torches were tossed below, turning everything Achan had held dear to ash.

Salmon stepped back to join Joshua and the other elders of Israel. No one spoke. How did one discuss something so weighty? He had done as he'd been told. But his feet moved as through a sluggish, muddy stream. Fear gripped him, and for the briefest moment he understood how his father must have felt when judgment from Moses told him he would die in the wilderness. All because he had put fear above faith.

Salmon fell to the rear of the group, feeling those same fears grip him now, his thoughts churning. He cast a glance behind him toward the women and children but saw no sign of Rahab. He wasn't surprised. Israel's God probably made even less sense to her.

Had she known the man who had worn that robe?

The sudden thought came from some dark place within

him, the place that could not forget the past—and could not forgive his father or Zimri and now Achan, men whose acts had harmed so many.

He picked up his pace to join the elders, no longer wishing to be so close to the women. What Rahab knew or did was no concern of his.

Rahab sat with Joshua's wife and daughters near the central fire pit later that evening, grinding grain for the meal, grateful for the quiet. And yet a part of it unnerved her. Noise, even the squabbling of children, would dispel the sounds in her head, the cries of Achan's family. But the women worked in silence, and Rahab could not keep her thoughts from wandering back to that awful moment when she watched Salmon throw his first stone. Of course, he had killed the enemy in battle, but this judgment did not make sense. Was Israel's God like the exacting vengeful gods of Canaan's pantheon? Had she traded one faith for another only to find it the same? And yet, clearly Israel's God held more power.

She looked up as the sound of male voices drew closer. Men walked slowly toward Joshua's tent, Salmon coming at the last. He glanced in her direction and raised a brow as if he was surprised to see her there. She gave him a polite nod, then bent over the grindstone again, the noise drowning out the words of the men.

She looked through slightly lifted lashes to see Salmon and the elders enter Joshua's tent. Good. She did not have to speak to him. She was not sure how she would respond if he sought her out. She was still so confused by him, by his God, by justice and mercy. If a man or woman broke the law in Jericho, they worked until they had repaid their debt. Very seldom were they granted mercy there. Memories of Gamal's short-lived grace entered her mind. If Gamal had not been such a fool, perhaps she would have tasted mercy the rest of her life.

"Rahab?" Eliana spoke, jarring her thoughts to the present.

"Yes, mistress?" She stopped the grindstone and brushed the dust from her hands.

"Please, it's just Eliana." She smiled, easing some of Rahab's concerns with her genuine acceptance. "I wondered if you would take some of the mint water to the men in the receiving room. I'm sure they are thirsty after such a day as this."

Rahab stood and wiped her hands on the sides of her robe. "Of course. I am happy to oblige." She was willing to help, to repay Joshua through his family, but the lie that she was happy to do so tasted bitter.

She entered the tent with the jug of mint water and poured some into several clay cups, then carried them to each man, keeping her eyes downcast. When she reached Salmon's side, she quickly placed the cup near him for him to reach without encountering her touch. Such contact would only embarrass him and mortify her.

"Thank you," Salmon said, the soft timbre of his voice jolting her.

She nodded without meeting his gaze, then quickly backed away and hurried from the tent, feeling as though his words had scorched her. She must stop this nonsense, this foolish attraction to the man. Salmon could not possibly care even a little for a prostitute.

She returned to her duties at Eliana's side, gathered up

the flour, and took it to the area to the side of the tent where the brick oven stood. There she kneaded the flour and water until her arms ached, wishing the action could undo all of her past, all of her restless thoughts.

But as the bread baked on the brick stones, she felt no better than she had since her family had left her, despite Joshua's family's acceptance. Abandoned and alone, even in the midst of thousands of people.

28

Salmon sipped the mint water Rahab had handed him, his gaze following her but a moment, then he looked quickly away. Why did she act as though she could not even approach him? Had he offended her? Silent chastisement followed that thought. What did it matter what she thought of him?

"The Lord spoke to me this afternoon," Joshua said, interrupting Salmon's musings. "The Lord said, 'Do not be afraid, do not be discouraged. Take the whole army with you, and go up and attack Ai. For I have delivered into your hands the king of Ai, his people, his city, and his land. You shall do to Ai and its king as you did to Jericho and its king, except that you may carry off their plunder and livestock for yourselves. Set an ambush behind the city.'"

Salmon thought of their previous attempts to do just that. Why should this time be any different? But he did not voice the question. He could either try again and risk a second defeat, or fear loss and not even try. For Mishael's sake, he had no choice.

"I want you to call the men to arms. In the morning we will travel to the place of ambush between Bethel and Ai. There I will give you the Lord's instructions." Joshua looked from one man to the next, twelve leaders, one from each of the tribes of Israel. "Any questions?"

Salmon glanced at his comrades, but the sobering activity of the morning seemed to silence each one.

"It will be as you have commanded, my lord," Salmon said. "We will go now and call the army to be ready for battle at dawn."

Joshua met Salmon's gaze, then took in the group. "Be strong and courageous, all of you. Achan's treachery hurt us all, but we have dealt with him and those who shared in his guilt. It is time to go out and obey the Lord and take this city."

As the men rose and left Joshua's tent, Salmon turned at a touch on his shoulder. "When you are finished," Joshua said, "return and take the evening meal with us."

Salmon nodded. "Thank you, my lord." He stepped into the fading sunlight and looked around the work area of Joshua's tent, but saw no sign of Rahab. Why was she spending time near Joshua's women? Where was she living?

He walked away, thinking to ask Joshua later that evening, but as he headed in the direction of his tribe, he spotted her sitting at the door of a small tent, working flax with her hands. The cat she cherished lay curled at her side.

⁓⚜⁓

Rahab looked up at the sound of men hurrying past her tent. She had not stayed with Joshua's wife Eliana after the encounter with Salmon, however minor it had been. The sight of him sitting with Joshua and the elders was too great a reminder of powerful men . . . of Jericho . . . even those of Syria who had taken Gamal away. *Gamal.* How long it had been since her thoughts had strayed to him.

Was he still living?

Why did she even care about such a thing? Tzadok had hinted that the Syrians would sell him to torturers, and Dabir had insisted Gamal was dead, though he'd had no written communication to show her to prove that his words were not just another one of his many lies. Dabir would say the moon was square and make men believe him when he was at his most charming. And she, to her great shame, had wanted to believe him about Gamal—in fact, had often believed him.

She drew in a breath as memories washed over her and grief settled in her heart. For the first time since Jericho's fall, she saw her aching loneliness for what it was. She'd been abandoned by everyone she loved. Why had she stayed in Israel? Egypt was not so bad that she could not have survived. Her family would have protected her. She could have proclaimed herself a widow and allowed her father to pick a new husband for her.

Who would pick a husband for her here?

She shook herself. She did not want another man. Men were untrustworthy.

She glanced up, sensing someone watching her. Salmon. Now what did he want? She waited, knowing it would be impolite to ignore him.

"May I help you?"

He stood a moment without a response.

"I thought you were with your family outside of the camp." He studied her, his gaze somber, curious.

"My family moved on to Egypt," she said, looking at the half-finished flaxen basket in her lap.

"When?" His voice had dropped in pitch, and she glanced up again, sensing his genuine concern. She supposed he deserved an explanation for saving her life.

"About a week after you rescued us. My father and brothers could not abide the strict rules of your God." She held his gaze. "So they left."

"But you remained."

"Yes."

Silence followed her remark, and he gave his head a little shake as if trying to understand. "Why?" he said at last. "They are your family."

She stroked the cat and looked beyond him, fighting the sudden emotion his comment evoked. "Your God saved my life. I could not leave one so powerful."

Salmon stared at her, but his expression revealed little. "He is a God of blessing and of cursing, as you saw today."

She nodded, recalling Achan's weeping. "It should have been me in Achan's place." She straightened, setting the basket aside. "So I have seen your God's mercy to the undeserving."

Salmon nodded. "Your faith is great, Rahab." He took a step back, looked as though he might say something more, then simply nodded and walked away.

Rahab watched him go. He was wrong. If he knew her thoughts, he would know what little faith she clung to. This God of Israel was beyond her understanding. And she was not sure she wanted to understand.

Salmon held a cup of red grape juice to his lips. They had not lived in the land long enough to turn the juice to wine, but the taste of the fresh juice was one he savored, after so many years of the same diet of manna, quail, and water in the wilderness.

The women had left them alone, and dusk had descended over the camp. "I should go to my tent and rest, but I am finding that meal has made me feel too good to move. Thank you for inviting me, Joshua."

Joshua nodded, sipped from his own cup, then wiped the red stain from his beard with the back of his hand. "You are welcome to eat with us anytime, my friend. I know it cannot be easy without a family of your own." Joshua looked at him, his gaze thoughtful, and Salmon felt the unfamiliar desire to squirm like he had done when his father spoke to him as a child. "I wonder," Joshua said, setting the cup beside him on a low table, "if you have given any thought to marriage. I know we have been busy with war these several years, and many men have put off taking a wife, but it is not good for a man to be alone."

Salmon rubbed the back of his neck. "Mishael would have agreed with you." A stab of grief hit him at the memory of Mishael's teasing laughter. "But I have not found a woman who has sparked my interest."

"Have you considered Rahab?"

Salmon startled as though the woman had walked into the room. He shook his head. Had Mishael put the idea in Joshua's mind before that last battle?

"It is hard to consider a woman who has known so many men," he said, his gaze glancing off Joshua's, unable to hold it.

"God is able to forgive even the most proud and sinful among us, my friend." Joshua's look held fatherly comfort and a knowing of secrets Salmon wished he understood.

"God may be able to forgive, but I am finding that I do

not possess His ability." Salmon glanced toward the tent's opening, but no woman stood visibly listening.

Joshua did not respond immediately. "Give yourself time, my son."

Joshua's smile unnerved him, as if somehow God had told him the secret dealings of Salmon's heart. But God did not reveal men's secrets like that, did He?

The disturbing thought followed him as he took the path to his tent.

Three days later, Salmon watched from a perch halfway up a large terebinth tree as Joshua led the rest of Israel's army and set up camp north of Ai, with the valley between them and the city. To the west of the city, between Bethel and Ai, another group of about five thousand men were also waiting in ambush. The plan was a good one, leaving no way for the men of Ai to escape without someone to block their path.

"Things will go better this time," Othniel said to Salmon as he descended the tree. Though Salmon had always preferred Mishael's company, Othniel was not only Caleb's nephew, he was one of Israel's greatest fighters.

"I know." Salmon glanced toward Ai, where the sound of merriment came from the merchants' section of town. "I just wish Mishael had lived to see this."

Othniel nodded. "The loss of so many was sobering."

Salmon regarded the stocky man, his square jaw with its determined set, his beard hanging low, yet recently trimmed to within the allowed specifications of the law. Salmon ran a hand along his own scraggly beard. He hadn't viewed his appearance in any type of mirror in weeks and couldn't imagine how decrepit he looked.

"The gates are opening," Othniel said, drawing away from the cover of the trees.

Salmon followed. "The king of Ai has spotted Joshua in the valley."

"And so it begins." Othniel pulled his sword from the belt at his side and readied his hand.

"Joshua and his men are fleeing." Salmon sent a silent prayer heavenward that the men of Ai would pursue as Joshua had hoped.

"And there they go." Othniel glanced at Salmon as the two stood near some of the thousands of men hidden behind the city.

They watched in silence as the city emptied out, the doors left open behind them. "They expect to return victorious." Salmon's blood pumped hot through his veins.

"Then they will be sorely disappointed." Othniel grinned. Both waited a moment longer, watching for Joshua's signal. At last they spotted it. Joshua's sword stretched out toward Ai.

"Let's go!" Salmon shouted to the men behind them.

They raced toward the open city, swords in hand, and cut down every living person within it. This time they took the animals and spoils with them as they left. Then as they had done with Jericho, they set Ai on fire and slipped away to join the battle with Joshua.

Rahab looked up from the familiar grindstone at the sound of bleating sheep and goats and distant whoops of celebrating war heroes. Eliana set aside the grain sifter and stood. "Come." She smiled and extended a hand to Rahab. "Let us greet the returning men."

She called to her daughters to join them, and her voice carried an excited lilt, but Rahab couldn't muster the same feeling. Conflicted emotions warred within her. Who was this God Israel served who gave victory or defeat, who even taught men strategies of war? Her faith in Him seemed so broken and weak, and despite the words of allegiance she'd proclaimed to Joshua, she could not help feeling as though she did not belong here.

"Aren't you coming?" Eliana brushed the last bits of chaff from her skirt and glanced at Rahab. "It is customary for the women to sing the praises of the men and of our God for His victories over our enemies."

Rahab stood and met the woman's gaze. "I am finding it hard as a daughter of Jericho to not think that your people still think me your enemy."

Eliana's face softened, and she reached a hand to touch Rahab's arm. "I know this is hard for you, Rahab, especially without your family near. But you are one of us now. And I can see that it is time I introduced you to more of the women so you realize just how well they think of you."

Rahab's eyes widened ever so slightly. "The women barely look at me as I pass. They stop their conversations, as though afraid I might overhear." She met Eliana's gaze. "They act as the women of Jericho did who thought themselves far above me."

Eliana's daughters rushed to her side at that moment. "Are we going?" one asked.

The other grabbed Rahab's hand. "Come on! This is one of the best chances we get to dance with the unmarried boys."

Rahab met Eliana's gaze above the girl's head as the two were carried along with the throng of women. The noise of the crowd grew as they neared the edge of the camp, where the returning army approached.

"Can we find Abba?" the youngest daughter asked Eliana.

Eliana nodded, laughing. "Those girls," she said as her daughters rushed off. She sighed. "Too soon Joshua is going to have to find husbands for them." Her look held kindness. "As he would gladly do for you, my dear girl." She patted Rahab's arm as more women swarmed around them.

"Those days are gone for me, Eliana," she said, bending close to her friend's ear. "And the truth is, I do not know whether my husband Gamal still lives. Am I not bound to him if he does?"

Some of the women glanced her way and smiled, surprising her. "Isn't that the prostitute Rahab, who saved our spies?" she overheard one say.

"I heard she was very brave," came the voice of another.

Eliana touched her arm, made her pause. "I do not know the answer to that question, but I will surely ask Joshua. Our spies could certainly search it out."

"Whether I am married or not," Rahab said, looking about lest anyone overhear, "I am barren. No man wants to marry a prostitute who cannot give him sons."

Eliana's round face filled with compassion. "Nothing is impossible with our God, Rahab," she said, pulling her close in a motherly embrace. "Never lose hope."

Rahab nodded, suddenly unable to speak or sing. She blinked away the emotion she felt far too often of late. The crowd grew larger, and the men were jubilant as they entered the camp. Flocks of sheep and goats and donkeys and cattle were driven to hurriedly enlarged pens outside the camp, and the women greeted their men, all who were in dire need of bathing, with dancing and an occasional stolen kiss.

Rahab watched the spectacle, spotting Salmon in the crowd laughing with a few of the men, then turning to listen to something Joshua was saying. She wondered for the briefest moment what it would be like to dance for him, to have him swing her around in a joyous hold, and to later kiss her with tenderness, true and genuine.

She released a breath, telling herself she imagined too much, and slipped from the crowd before Salmon could catch a glimpse of her watching him. There was no sense in entertaining such thoughts. For despite Eliana's suggestion, she could not imagine any man wanting her, least of all a spy who despised all she'd been, all he thought she would always be.

⁓~⚜~⁓

Salmon awoke the next morning fighting to remember where he was. Fitful dreams had invaded a night that should have been restful and sweet. But though the victory of Ai was complete and rewarding, the cost of losing Mishael dampened his joy. He should have come home arm in arm with his friend, singing the victory songs, praising Adonai together.

Why him, Lord? Why not me?

Mishael had done nothing worthy of death. And why should he and thirty-five other men pay for Achan's greed? Why did the innocent end up caught in the sins of the guilty?

He rose from his cot, rubbed sleep from his eyes, and

in the dark tent quickly donned his clothes. Thoughts of Rahab surfaced as he scrubbed tepid water over his face. Why did the guilty end up saved from the punishment they deserved?

He shook his head, watching as water droplets sprayed across the small room. Blood still clung to his skin from the battle, and he needed to wash clean in the Jordan before he walked with the elders and all Israel to Mount Ebal to offer a sacrifice to the Lord for His grace in granting victory.

He grabbed a clean tunic, his robe, hyssop, and soap and stepped into the predawn light, headed to the river. The women of the camp were just awakening, many moving in the same direction to gather the day's water from the Jordan. Salmon took a different path to avoid them, to a place secluded among a larger copse of trees.

The questions he'd awoken with churned in him as the icy waters chilled his bare skin. He sank beneath the surface, scrubbing with the hyssop until his body tingled and the dried blood no longer stained his arms and legs. How was God both judging and yet merciful? How could one be expected to obey His laws, yet another be granted pardon without even knowing those laws existed?

He scrubbed harder, then suddenly realized he was making the skin raw. He stopped abruptly and tossed the hyssop branch to the bank, then dunked and soaped his hair, scrubbing and dunking several more times, trying to blot Mishael's broken body from his mind. His death was the hardest to understand. Why could God not have told Joshua of Achan's treachery before they risked the deaths of so many men? Why only after those men had died did God reveal the truth?

Anger surged through him, and he shoved his body out of the water, grabbed a thick piece of linen, and dried himself. Finally dressed and outwardly cleansed, he headed back to camp. But his heart still felt dry and dirty, as though the blood of his friend clung to each beating vessel. And no piece of hyssop in all of Canaan could reach deep enough to rub it out.

29

Shortly after the morning meal, Rahab listened in the shadows of Joshua's tent as he addressed his family, the elders, and all of his servants. "We will take three days to consecrate ourselves and gather whatever we need to travel to Mount Ebal and Mount Gerizim. There we will offer sacrifices to the Lord, as Moses the Lord's servant commanded us to do."

He dismissed them then to do what apparently they already understood must be accomplished, but Rahab stood still, not knowing whether to go or stay. Was she to accompany all of Israel on this trip? Or was she an unwelcome guest who would stay behind with the tents?

As the elders, including Salmon, filed out of Joshua's tent, Rahab sought Eliana. "What would you have me do?"

Eliana turned to face Rahab, her smile sober. "Forgive me, Rahab. I should have explained this to you sooner." She took Rahab's arm and led her to the women's area. "We are to travel to the valley between the mountains, where Joshua will build an altar to the Lord according to the law of Moses.

Joshua will write a copy of the law and read it to the whole assembly. It is a solemn process, and one we must prepare our hearts to accept." She touched Rahab's shoulder. "Everyone is to come, even the foreigners among us." She smiled, her gentle eyes warming.

"How does one prepare their heart?" Was not faith in this God enough?

"We ask God to search our hearts for any hidden sins and confess any known sins to Him. The priests will offer sacrifices on the altar on our behalf, and we shall be clean." Eliana's brows knit in a slight frown. "I know this probably does not make much sense to you. It is our way of humbling ourselves before our God and asking Him for mercy. But blood must be shed, the blood of lambs and goats, to cover the wrongs we've done. Otherwise there can be no forgiveness."

"So the innocent animal pays for our guilt."

Eliana nodded. "Yes, in a sense."

Rahab stared at her feet for a long moment. "I doubt even the blood of a lamb could wash away all the things I have done." She turned and walked abruptly away before Eliana could offer her another look of pity.

She hurried to her tent, wondering what she could possibly do to prepare for the upcoming days of sacrifice and atonement. She stopped abruptly near the threshold as Salmon drew near.

"May I speak with you?" He looked slightly nervous, which did nothing to help her own tattered emotions.

"About what?" She was not in the mood to talk of insignificant things. She had questions that needed answers. Answers that went deeper than what Eliana had given her.

He stared at her. "I just want to talk." He looked at her

as though she ought to be able to read his mind—so typical of the men she had known all of her life.

She motioned to the space beneath the awning. "We can talk here. I will get you a cushion if you like." There was no way she was going to invite a man into her tent, no matter how much she wanted to trust him.

"I thought perhaps we could take a short walk."

She glanced around at the crowded camp with people rushing to and fro, where their words could be easily over-heard. She picked up her water jug. "You can accompany me to the Jordan if you like. I need water to attend to the ritual cleansing." Eliana had instructed her on the laws of cleanliness when she first entered her service. She could do at least that much, though her heart was not sure it could do much more.

Salmon nodded and fell into step beside her. Neither spoke as they walked through the camp, and Rahab suddenly realized how alone they were once they passed the last tent and continued to the water's edge. A woman could be waylaid on such a walk if she were not careful. She took a step away from Salmon, suddenly wary.

"You don't need to fear me, Rahab," he said, glancing into her eyes. "I will not let any man hurt you."

She held his gaze, unable to keep the hurt from her tone. "Can you keep me from yourself?" She glanced beyond him. "I've seen you watching me. I know what you want." She continued walking, heat filling her cheeks. How bold she had become! What possessed her to say such things to him?

He caught up with her in two long strides. "You are mistaken," he said softly, the only other sound coming from the buzz of insects and their sandals brushing the grasses as they drew closer to the Jordan. "I will admit you intrigue me. But not because I want to lie with you. I want to understand."

She stopped mid-stride, her heart beating fast within her. "Understand what? Why I became a prostitute? Why I didn't go with my family? It is not a story you would want to hear." Her gaze held challenge. "Even Eliana does not know the things hidden in my heart." She lowered the jar from her shoulder to her arms, her protection between them.

He studied her, lifted a thick dark brow. "Forgive me then. I only meant to show you kindness."

She laughed, surprised at its brittle edge. "Kindness for yourself or for me?" She met his gaze but lowered her voice. "You want to find a reason to stop thinking of me as dung under your foot. You want to understand why your God would save a woman like me and not spare your closest friend." Remorse filled her at the look in his dark eyes. Her words had hit their mark.

When he simply stared at her but did not speak, she straightened, suddenly emboldened. "You judged me from the start, my lord." She studied him, her heart burdened with the sudden death of a longing for this man to care. "And yet you are attracted to me. And you hate yourself for it."

He winced and became suddenly interested in something behind her. She avoided following the direction of his gaze. Silence fell, and the air grew as thick as the insects in the bushes.

"Yes," he said at last, his voice a whisper. He looked up, sorrow in his eyes. "I have despised what you were. But as I have observed you, I know there is a heart of kindness in you, and I don't think you would choose such a life again."

It was her turn to look away. "You do not know me. And the truth of it is, you do not really want to understand. Not in a way that would change anything."

"Did I not say the very opposite only moments ago?" The slightest hint of anger tinged his tone. So typical! "Pardon me, mistress, but you do not know my thoughts either."

She hugged the jar tighter, wishing for the soft fur of the cat rather than the hard press of the jar. "Don't call me that." Her voice was a whisper, and she could not look at him.

"Forgive me. What is wrong with *mistress*? It is a common address among women."

"It is also a profession." She turned a half circle away from him. "It is what I thought mine would be one long-ago day."

"Forgive me. I did not know."

She faced him again. By his look he did not understand a lot of things.

"I am sure as a pure, faithful, God-fearing man, there are many things you do not know." She swallowed, searching her mind. How to make him see. He would want nothing more to do with her once she said it plainly.

"I assure you, Rahab, there are things all men understand. We just keep those things between ourselves." His face seemed to darken as if he were embarrassed by his confession.

"Well then, it will not surprise you," she said, drawing a breath for courage, "to know that I have known more men than I care to remember. I married a fool. Was mistress to another fool. Was used by countless fools. But I played the part of consort well . . . and sometimes . . . I enjoyed it." There. She'd said all she would say to the man. "Now let me retrieve the water and go."

She walked past him to the river, lowered the jar until it

bubbled to the top, and climbed the bank, fully expecting to be alone. But he stood there waiting, watching.

"I am sorry for all that has happened to you," he said as he fell into step beside her.

"I don't need your pity, Salmon." Heat seared her cheeks beneath her headscarf, and she could not hold his gaze. "But thank you for your kindness."

They walked on in silence until they neared the edge of the camp. He touched her arm, bidding her to stop. "I want to explain something to you." He paused until she nodded for him to continue. "Whatever is in your heart is between you and our God. If you have sinned, as all of us do, it is for you to confess it to Him." She watched the Adam's apple move in his neck and felt suddenly sorry to have made him nervous.

"Thank you for telling me," she said, taking a step forward, assuming he had finished.

He stayed her with another touch to her shoulder. The gentle pressure sent the slightest tingling through her, shaking her. How was it possible that this man could both exasperate and attract her? She must have some strange attraction to fools . . . or she was one herself at the very heart.

She looked at him, praying he could not see the way his barest touch had affected her—again.

"The purpose of the sacrifice Joshua is about to offer to Adonai," he said, breaking into her wayward thoughts, "is to bring atonement for the sins of all Israel." He offered her a rueful smile. "I find myself the most in need of this for my anger with God for letting Mishael die through no fault of his own. I question the goodness of our God for allowing hurt and evil and pain in my life, in this world. I don't understand it."

He ran a hand through his hair and released a deep sigh. "Rahab, I loathed myself for my attraction to you because of what you were. But I made excuses for my own pride, which was just as despicable in the eyes of our God."

She did not answer for the space of many breaths. "Even a sacrifice will not wash the memories from my heart." She looked away, too aware of him and the sudden emotion that brought. She was still a prostitute at heart if men could so easily sway her. Repulsion filled her. "I must go."

She hurried ahead of him and fairly ran all the way to her tent.

The journey to Mount Ebal took two days, and the building of the altar was a process such as Rahab had never seen. No iron tool like those used in quarries touched the uncut stones that the men of Israel carted up the hill. Rahab stood with the women, her gaze often straying to Salmon as he hefted heavy stones with apparent ease and put them exactly where Joshua indicated.

At last, the altar completed, the priests came forward with bleating lambs and lowing oxen. Rahab stood beside Eliana, transfixed one moment, stricken the next. Every time a lamb's throat was slit and its blood caught in a bronze basin, she felt the weight of her past, memories she thought long hidden flooding her mind. The blood became each man who knocked on her door, the lambs the babe she had lost.

Her vision blurred as she watched the innocent die for the guilty. Despite Salmon's attempt at explanation, she still did not grasp how this could free her or make her clean. Even if she spent the rest of her life punished for her sins, she would not feel clean. Why should a lamb suffer on her account?

She felt a sudden presence beside her and turned to see Salmon looking down at her. "I did not ask this of you, and you do not have to comply." His hand lightly touched her shoulder. "But Joshua has set aside a lamb for you, Rahab. And if you are willing, I will share in the sacrifice."

Her breath hitched, but no words would come. Would they force this upon her? But no, he said she did not have to comply with it.

"Do not underestimate the power of our God," he said softly, bending close. "A God who can topple Jericho's walls can also offer forgiveness."

Tears came. Rahab nodded and allowed him to lead her to the altar where the priests stood. Smoke from sacrifices already offered rose in a thick column on the burning wood, scorching the stones.

Salmon left her standing near Joshua and the priests, then walked to a makeshift pen where lambs waited. He moved among them, inspecting each one, until at last he lifted a year-old ewe in his arms, carried it toward Rahab, and set it down in the place of the outpouring of blood.

He placed his hands on the lamb's head and glanced at Rahab, his expression telling her to follow his lead. The tears flowed freely now as her fingers explored the soft fur of the glistening white lamb. *Take me instead. Don't make this sweet animal die in my place.*

Joshua's voice interrupted her silent prayer. "Most Holy Adonai, blessed be Your name. We come before You asking for Your great mercy and forgiveness for the sins of this young woman, Rahab, and for the sins of this young man,

Salmon. Fill them with gratitude for Your great kindness to both of them. And when the time is right, bless them both with children to honor You."

Rahab's head snapped up after Joshua's prayer, but she quickly lowered it again as the priest spoke a prayer and blessing over them as well. Why had Joshua included the blessing of children? She was barren and had no desire to wed ever again.

Her fingers rested against the lamb's woolly neck, and she sensed its terror, felt the beating of its heart. She barely heard the last words of the blessing of the priest, but then, too soon, another priest slit the lamb's throat. She felt its heart stop in an instant. A sob escaped her. "Oh God, oh God!" She fell to her knees, rocking back and forth, as the priest caught the lamb's blood and lifted its limp body to place on God's altar.

Why did You spare me? The lamb did nothing wrong. It was I, God of Israel. I alone who sinned against You. Why did the innocent animal have to take her place when she was fully willing to die instead?

You didn't always want to die. You risked your life to save the spies so you could live.

The thought came unbidden, the realization filling her with a sudden, urgent desire to live, to start life anew.

Her tears wet the blood-soaked dirt until she felt Eliana's touch on her arm. Rahab slowly rose, unable to even look Salmon's way. Her gaze instead met Joshua's, whose fatherly kindness told her immediately why he had prayed as he did.

The next day Joshua took a stylus and pushed it against the wet clay to write a copy of the law of Moses on several large stones in the presence of all, from the smallest child to the oldest man. When the task was finally completed several hours later, Joshua stood and faced the group, took the first stone, and began to read.

Rahab listened, her heart stirring with a new desire to follow each of the laws God had given to Moses. *Help me to be worthy.*

Her mind wandered during some of the blessings and curses, but when Joshua spoke about captive brides, her heart beat double time.

"When you go to war against your enemies and the Lord your God delivers them into your hands and you take captives, if you notice among the captives a beautiful woman and are attracted to her, you may take her as your wife. Bring her into your home and have her shave her head, trim her nails, and put aside the clothes she was wearing when captured. After she has lived in your house and mourned her father and mother for a full month, then you may go to her and be her husband, and she shall be your wife. If you are not pleased with her, let her go wherever she wishes. You must not sell her or treat her as a slave, since you have dishonored her."

He continued on about a man having two wives, but Rahab's mind could not get past the previous words. *Shave her head. Trim her nails.* The exact thing Joshua had told Adara she must do to marry an Israelite, what Rahab would not have to do because she had no intention of marrying again. Besides, she had no firm proof that she was truly free of Gamal. What if he still lived in Syria or somewhere else?

And yet . . . She glanced at her hands. The nails, once clean and decorated in colorful henna patterns, were now broken and scarred from turning the millstone and working long hours on her baskets. Someday she hoped to make a small living from the trade.

She touched the scarf covering her head and tucked back a wisp of the silky strands from where it had strayed to her forehead. This God made no sense to her. Even though Joshua had assured her she was not a captive, in a sense she was. A captive who bargained her life for the Israelite spies. But why put a captive woman through such humiliation? And then, after the man had taken her, he could send her away if he wasn't pleased with her? She would never marry!

The words of the law droned on, and Rahab tried to concentrate on the rest. She should be grateful, not angry at such things. But she understood Salmon's frustration better now.

The sun dipped low in the sky, and Joshua ended his reading for the day. Tomorrow they would finish the book of the law and return home. In the meantime, she must seek out Joshua or Eliana and ask if the law of a captive bride applied to her. For if she was Salmon's captive because of his promise to her, then she was not truly free. He could cast her out of Israel on a whim. She could not live with that.

*

The evening meal was simple unleavened bread, herbs, and the fruit of the land. Though it was not Passover, there had been no time to bake normal bread during the lengthy reading of the law. Despite Rahab's desire to speak with Joshua, she found he had retreated early to his tent to pray. She walked to the tent she shared with Joshua's wife and daughters and collapsed on a low mat.

"You look as exhausted as I feel," Eliana said, coming to

sit at Rahab's side. "I'm sorry we have had no chance to talk, but it would be rude to speak during the reading of the law."

Rahab nodded. "I understand. Adonai had much to say to your prophet Moses."

Eliana chuckled. "Yes, and there is more tomorrow."

Rahab sat cross-legged, facing her new friend. "How does one possibly keep such impossible laws? And why are men allowed to give up their wives if they are displeased with them? What if a wife is displeased with her husband? Is there no recourse?"

Eliana pulled the scarf from her head and picked up an ivory comb and started to work it through her long hair. Rahab lifted a hand toward her. "Let me."

Eliana smiled and turned her back to allow Rahab to pull the comb through her thick strands. "The law does have protections for women. A man cannot divorce his wife and then decide he wants her back and marry her again. He also cannot falsely accuse her. It is why the bride's father saves the nuptial sheet, to prove his daughter is a virgin."

Silence followed her remark, and Eliana turned. "Forgive me. I suppose that would not apply to you."

"No. And my father is not here to keep such a thing for me in any case."

Eliana met Rahab's gaze. "That does not mean you cannot marry. Widows marry all the time."

"I am not a widow. At least I do not know if I am."

Eliana swiveled to face her, and Rahab stopped combing. "Perhaps it is time to see if he could be found."

Rahab shook her head. "It would be impossible to find him or what has happened to him now." Not that she cared to marry anyway. Perhaps this was exactly what she needed to keep Salmon and Joshua from pressuring her. Relief filled her at the thought. She would not need to shave her head or do anything else to become some man's captive bride.

"The fact that he abandoned you might mean you are free to marry," Eliana said after a lengthy pause. "Joshua should know." She took the comb from Rahab's slack fingers and quickly finished the job. "We'd best get some sleep now, though. Joshua will begin the reading again as soon as we break our fast at dawn."

Rahab simply nodded, her thoughts once again jumbled, as Eliana made her way to her own pallet. The brief relief she had felt disappeared, replaced by a new fear that she might be free to marry after all.

She wasn't sure what troubled her more—suspecting that Joshua wanted her and Salmon to wed, or knowing Joshua wasn't likely to let her stay as a widow the rest of her days. Which meant she would have to pretend to love a man all over again. And be humiliated as his captive in the process.

Salmon heard Othniel moving inside the darkened tent just before dawn. He groaned, rolling onto his side, longing for a few more moments of blessed sleep. But they had carried few tents with them to Mount Ebal, and only Joshua stayed in one alone.

"Did I wake you?" Othniel stepped closer to Salmon's pallet. "I'm sorry. I meant to keep quiet, but I accidentally kicked my gear in my haste to relieve myself."

Salmon peeked from beneath hooded eyes. "Is dawn upon us already?" He blinked, wanting desperately to find he was mistaken.

"Almost. Joshua is already at the campfire. I think he wants to get an early start on the reading today." Othniel knelt beside his mat, rolled it up, and tied it with leather strings. "We will start back toward camp before the noon repast."

Salmon forced himself awake and ran a hand through his hair. He wasn't much for excessive talking upon first awakening, but Othniel obviously did not notice that fact. Mishael would have. The thought pained him still.

An hour later, their tent disassembled and readied in one of the baggage carts, Salmon joined the rest of the elders near Joshua's campfire. Women and children crowded around, all eager to get started. Joshua rose, straightening to his full height, and held the last of the stones before him.

Laws regarding the festivals they were to keep were followed by laws regarding vows of men and women. Salmon listened even as he glanced across the compound to where Joshua's family stood with Rahab. Confusion and curiosity filled her beautiful face. What thoughts tumbled through her head? Did she realize that Joshua's prayer was like a betrothal blessing on them, in the midst of seeking forgiveness for their sins?

The thought had troubled him most of the night. He stifled a yawn. Definitely not enough sleep once he had finally succumbed. But he could not change what was past or what had been said. Joshua was Adonai's spokesman, and Salmon could not lightly throw his words aside.

"When you cross the Jordan into Canaan," Joshua read, his voice rising, carrying to the farthest reaches of the group, "drive out all the inhabitants of the land before you. Destroy all their carved images and their cast idols, and demolish all their high places. Take possession of the land and settle in it, for I have given you the land to possess. Distribute the land by lot, according to your clans. To a larger group give a larger inheritance, and to a smaller group a smaller one. Whatever falls to them by lot will be theirs. Distribute it according to your ancestral tribes."

He paused in the utter silence, taking in each one closest to him with a grim look. "But if you do not drive out the inhabitants of the land, those you allow to remain will become barbs in your eyes and thorns in your sides. They will give you trouble in the land where you will live. And then I will do to you what I plan to do to them." He stopped and set the stone on the ground beside the others. Levites came quickly and gathered each one up, carefully placing them in leather sacks for the journey back to Gilgal.

"As the Lord commanded His servant Moses, so He commissions us to fulfill those commands." Joshua lifted his hands to the sky. "You have all heard the word of the Lord, and we now know exactly what He wants us to do. Let us return to camp and set out to quickly obey all that our God has commanded us to do."

He dismissed the group then to pack up all that remained. Salmon found his way to Rahab's side. "I have already packed my gear in one of the carts. Is there anything I can do to help you?"

She glanced at him and shook her head. "Thank you, but no. Eliana and I did the same before dawn."

The command went down the line of men and women to head out, and Salmon fell into step with Rahab as they began the long walk.

"Am I a barb in your eye and a thorn in your side?" Rahab asked after they had walked too long in silence.

Salmon glanced at her, sensing confusion behind the question. "Despite the sacrifice, you still do not feel worthy?"

"Is anyone worthy of forgiveness and mercy?" She cinched her cloak carefully around the cat, which slept against her heart, and avoided his gaze.

Salmon studied her, drawn to her protectiveness of the small animal. "No," he said softly. He glanced around. Eliana walked ahead of them, and men and women surrounded them, but thankfully most were engaged in conversations of their own. The buzz of their voices drowned out his own.

"Why did Joshua pray such a prayer over us? Why include the blessing of children? We are not betrothed." She gave him a surreptitious glance, then looked ahead, picking her way along the uneven path.

"Because he wants us to wed. He has said as much to me more than once."

"I can't wed. I am still married to Gamal." She carefully crossed her arms as though warding off a chill.

Her words sank into him, a knife to his gut. "Gamal abandoned you and was sold into slavery. Do you think you are still bound to him?"

"He did not give me a bill of divorcement. If he still lives, I am his wife. I cannot marry another." She lifted her chin as though glad of a reason to push him away.

"Does Joshua know this?" If Joshua had prayed such a blessing, surely he knew.

She looked away. "He knows less than you do."

Salmon searched for something to say, but words would not come.

She looked at him. "Some men in Jericho told me that Gamal was sold to torturers, others told me he was dead. But

I had no proof other than their word, and they were liars." She turned her gaze to the path ahead.

He could not marry her if she was not free. That thought troubled him more than it should. Why should he care? He was not interested in marriage to her any more than she was to him. But he glanced at her anyway, saw the hint of vulnerability in the way she held on to the cat and seemed to draw into herself.

"Where did they take him when he was sold into slavery?" He stopped walking to look at her. "Tell me everything you can recall."

She studied him, a hint of worry creasing her brow. "Why? What good will it do?"

"If I can find him, I can either bring him back to you or bring you a writ of divorcement." He wondered briefly at his own good sense at making such a statement.

Her eyes widened in disbelief, and she started walking again. "All I know is that a merchant from Syria, a man named Qasim of the house of Ratib, paid Dabir a handsome amount for him. What they did with him after that, I do not know. They could have sold him to another kingdom along their travels, or he could be a slave in Damascus somewhere."

The possibility of finding him did not sit well with Salmon. And the chances of doing so were like looking for a single piece of broken flax among an entire field.

"If Gamal had lived in Jericho, he would be dead." Couldn't they just assume such a thing?

"If Gamal had lived in Jericho, I would not have lived as a prostitute. And if by chance you had still found my home and I helped you escape, Gamal would have stayed in our home and been spared. We would not be faced with any of this." Her chin held a defiant tilt, and yet he saw how uneasily she clenched and unclenched the fabric holding the cat.

"Well, the truth is, Gamal is not here. We can presume he is dead, or I can go and look for him."

Silence followed his remark, and he wondered if she would speak again. "I don't want Gamal," she whispered. "I don't want any man ever again."

"You do not want children?" Every woman wanted children. Didn't they?

She looked at the crowd surrounding them, eyed him warily, then took a small step closer. "I cannot bear children. So you see, Joshua is wrong to want you to marry me. And he was wrong to pray such a prayer over me." She clamped her mouth shut, blinked, and looked away from him. Her tears were nearly his undoing.

A sudden urge to protect her from anyone ever hurting her again rose up so strong in him he did not know what to do. His hands were wooden at his sides, and his words seemed to stick in his throat. How could his feelings for her change so quickly, so drastically? She was a prostitute. And yet somehow, hearing her story and seeing her tears as the lamb died to pay for their sins had changed something in him. Childless or not, she mattered.

He breathed deeply. She continued to walk in silence. He swallowed . . . twice. "Rahab." Her name came out like a soft caress. His arms found their ability to move again, and he placed a hand on her shoulder. "If you will have me, I would marry you."

She shook her head and would not look at him.

"You won't have me?"

He could feel her tremble beneath his touch, her tears her only response.

He patted her shoulder and slowly moved his hand away, hating to break the contact. "I will go to Damascus, if Joshua will allow it, and search for Gamal. When I return and can put your mind at ease, then you can answer my question."

She looked at him but did not speak. At last she nodded and wiped the tears from her flushed cheeks. "If Joshua allows it," she whispered.

He wondered if she hoped he wouldn't.

30

Life fell into a pattern once they returned to their camp at Gilgal. Rahab welcomed the sameness, even as she chafed for something she could not quite grasp. What was wrong with her? Salmon's promise to find Gamal, if Joshua thought it wise, had brought all of her past to the forefront of her mind again. She wasn't the same woman Gamal had married, and only Adonai knew whether slavery had changed him. Besides, if he was still living in slavery, there was no way for her to go to him. Her life would end up worse than it was now living alone in Israel.

She hefted her pallet, carried it out of doors, and draped it over a rope she and Eliana had stretched between two trees. A wide flaxen broom provided the exact tool she needed to beat the dust from the mat.

"Be careful where you swing that." She startled at the sound of Salmon's voice, then whirled to face him.

"Be careful you don't sneak up on unsuspecting women. You might find yourself at the end of this broom." Her face heated with her rash words, but his raised brow and quiet chuckle put her strangely at ease.

"Joshua wants to speak to us," he said, smiling down at her.

"Together?" Her heart picked up an unsteady pace, and she gripped the broom tighter between both hands. "I have work to do."

Salmon walked closer, extending a hand. "It can wait."

His commanding tone brooked no argument. She carried the broom to the door of her tent and glanced at her pallet, then at the sky. No sign of rain in the bright blue expanse, so she should be able to finish the job before the noon meal.

She followed Salmon with weighted steps, her fears mounting as they neared Joshua's tent. Eliana met them at the entrance. "Oh good. He's been waiting for you." She ushered them into the receiving room and quickly departed.

Joshua greeted Salmon with a kiss to his cheek, nodded at Rahab, and motioned for them both to sit on cushions along the tent wall. "I will get right to the point." He smiled slightly, but his expression remained serious.

"Rahab," he said, giving her his full attention, "I understand that you have some concerns about the state of your first marriage and whether you are free to marry Salmon."

Rahab folded her hands in her lap, her thoughts whirling like a spindle and distaff. "If it please my lord, I do not believe I have ever suggested that I wish to marry again—ever." She pinned both men with a look, her frustration with their meddling growing with each word. "I merely mentioned to Salmon"—she glanced at him—"that I was never given a writ of divorcement from Gamal when he was sold into slavery and I into prostitution. So according to your God's law, am I not still bound to Gamal?"

Joshua shook his head. "Unfortunately, this type of case is not addressed in our law. Priests are not allowed to marry prostitutes or widows or a divorced woman, but that only applies to the tribe of Levi. And we have been commanded by our God to destroy all of the people of the land of Canaan. If we found Gamal living in one of the Canaanite cities God has commanded we destroy, we would be obligated to put him to death."

"But you spared my family."

"Our God had mercy on you and anyone who willingly stayed with you. Did Gamal willingly stay with you?" Joshua's kind voice mirrored the compassion in his eyes, easing some of her worry.

"Gamal had already been sold to Syrian traders the year before you came."

"And why was he sold?"

She hesitated. The last time he questioned her, Joshua had not pressed her for answers, but now with Salmon requesting permission to find Gamal, of course they would need to understand. Blast their interference! She did not want to revisit those memories.

"I know this is not easy, Rahab. But please, if you can, tell us what happened to your husband."

She drew in a breath, telling herself it did not matter anymore. "Gamal had incurred an enormous debt for his gambling, which the prince forgave. But Gamal's grace was short-lived, as he could not give up his desire for the gaming houses. So he found someone who owed him a pittance and dragged him to debtors' prison to demand payment." Saying the words brought the memories into clearer focus. "Gamal was not a good man."

Joshua cleared his throat. "I do not have this from our law, Rahab, but from what I understand of our God, He is not pleased with greed, or with men who show no mercy. You saw what He required of Achan?"

"Yes, my lord." Achan's greed had brought such dread punishment to many families in Israel. "The punishment seemed a harsh one to the innocents who suffered with him."

"None of us are truly innocent, Rahab." She glanced at Salmon, saw the earnestness in his troubled gaze. What secrets lay behind that handsome brow?

"Salmon is right," Joshua said, drawing her gaze to his once more. "The greed began with Achan, but his family helped him keep his secret. And our spies were overconfident with their proclamation of how easy it would be to take the city. I, in my pride, did not consult the Lord for guidance. I listened to Salmon's and Mishael's advice without question." She watched Salmon's face flush in the dim light. Joshua ran a hand through graying hair. "But even the best counselors cannot replace our reliance on Adonai. He is the leader of our army, and He directs our steps. So you see, Rahab, we have all failed Him."

"There is so much I don't understand." She studied her hands, turning them palms up in her lap, suddenly ashamed of all the things her hands had done.

"Our God is beyond our human understanding." Joshua's voice grew soft, and he glanced from her to Salmon. "The more we read and keep His law, the better we will know Him. But even a lifetime will not give us all of the knowledge we might crave."

Sounds of the camp filtered to them in the quiet room as Rahab pondered Joshua's words.

"What can I do to repay His mercy?" She looked at her sandaled feet.

"Mercy is a gift, child. You cannot pay for what is freely given."

She met Joshua's steady gaze then and slowly nodded.

"As love is a gift," Salmon said, his words like a caress. "You can give and receive it, but you cannot repay it."

She looked at him and felt the soft stirring of appreciation for him growing within her. But love? She was not sure she was capable of loving a man.

"I appreciate all you have done for me—both of you." She looked from one man to the other. "I am grateful you think me worthy of a second chance to be a wife. But I am not ready." She paused, searching for words to help them understand. "You said I could live among you, that I would not have to marry—has that changed? Am I a captive bride who no longer has a choice?"

"You are not a captive, Rahab," Joshua said, pulling her attention back to him. "You are a woman and, if you should want it, a bride of mercy."

"And in this mercy, am I allowed to choose who and when?" She heard the sigh escape Salmon's lips but could not look at him. She looked at Joshua for a response, but it was Salmon's low voice that startled her.

"I will not force you to choose me," he said.

"Nor will I force you to choose marriage," Joshua added. "Our God saved your life, Rahab. We would like to see you a happy mother of children in a loving family, a gift our God can give if you are willing."

"You ask the impossible." The words sent her cheeks to flaming.

"Nothing is impossible with God," Joshua said, his fatherly smile warming her. What would it have been like to grow up in his household? But she would never know.

"I need time to seek your God." She stood, and the men rose with her. "Give me time. Please."

She slipped from the tent, grateful for the reprieve. Salmon would likely change his mind about her as time passed. Besides, he deserved one better than such as she.

⁕

"She is a remarkable woman," Joshua said once Rahab had left the tent, head bowed. "I think once she comes to know us better and the laws of our God, she will want to marry again."

"I'm not sure she wants marriage, my lord." Salmon ran a hand down his neck. "I think she wants release from her guilt, which the sacrifice did not supply. I think she wants time to feel the freedom she's been given. I fear that she wants to earn God's grace."

Joshua lifted a cup of barley water to his lips and drank. "I don't see it that way, my son. I think she wants Adonai to see her heart. What better way to express repentance than through obedience?"

Salmon thought on that a moment. "I will admit, Joshua, I am attracted to her. But I had always thought to marry an untouched woman." He picked up a clay cup of water and studied the contents, though he did not drink.

"God can restore her to be as a virgin to you, my son. A month or two of mourning her family will give her time for her body and heart to heal."

Salmon still studied the cup. "You seem very sure of this.

And yet, could you not allow me to go and search for Gamal? If we know for certain he is gone, she will be freer than she would if she were to always wonder what happened to him. I am used to spy missions, my lord. Give me someone to go with me, and I will search Syria until I find him."

"The next battle is not far off, Salmon. I need you to lead your men." Joshua set his cup down and tugged on his gray beard.

"I will be back to lead them. In the meantime, let Rahab stay as she is, near your tent, which will tell the camp she is bound to your family, but she can also have her time alone without feeling unsettled around me." The desire grew within him as he spoke. He knew the risk. If he found Gamal, could he put him to death? Had the man been living in Jericho, he would have been under God's curse. But if he remained a slave in Syria, the best Salmon could do would be to get him to sign a writ of divorcement. On his life, he could not bring himself to take Rahab to live with Gamal again, slave or free.

The thought brought a kick to his gut. When had he started to feel so strongly about her?

"You are almost as persuasive as Mishael." Joshua's smile was sad.

"I try." His smile felt awkward. "Just say yes, Joshua. You know it's the right thing to do."

Joshua lifted a brow, but his look held a hint of amusement.

"Let Othniel go with me this time. He talks too much, but I promise not to hurt him."

"What will you do if you find Gamal?" Joshua glanced toward the open doorway, where sunlight chased off the shadows of morning.

Kill him. But no. "If he is willing to be circumcised and

294

repent of his ways, I will buy his freedom and return him to his wife." The words did not bring the relief they once would have.

"And if he is not willing?"

"I will seek a writ of divorcement for her."

"And if he will not give it?"

"I don't know. Pray that Adonai grants me wisdom."

Joshua nodded. "Do not risk killing the slave of another man. If we are not at war with the city, we cannot kill without just cause."

"I understand," Salmon said, relieved to have such guidance.

"You must return before month's end. I cannot have the army sitting on their hands while we wait for you to run off on this fruitless errand." Joshua folded his arms in front of him and met Salmon's gaze, unflinching.

"I will leave as soon as Othniel agrees to join me. Do you wish to see him before we go?" Salmon was not so sure the man would appreciate such a mission.

"That is not necessary. Othniel enjoys a challenge." Joshua smiled and walked Salmon to the tent's door.

Salmon followed Joshua from the tent and caught sight of Rahab back at her chore of pounding the dust from her pallet. He approached her, keeping his distance from the swinging broom.

She glanced up and stopped mid-swing. "Interrupting my work again, my lord?" She smiled, though it did not reach her eyes.

He nodded, taking in her dirt-smudged face, which somehow only added to her beauty. "I will be leaving soon to journey to Syria . . . to seek Gamal, or to at least discover his fate."

Her large dark eyes grew wide, and he knew she understood his reasons.

"What will you do if you find him? Will you take me to him then?"

"Not if you do not want to go."

"I don't." She clung to the broom as though it were a staff holding her up. "But I want to obey Adonai. Would He have spared me to send me back?"

Her intelligent questions made his own deepen. "I do not understand all the ways of our God, Rahab," he said at last. "And I do not even know if I will find the man. I just know that I have to try. I will trust Adonai to lead me after that."

She nodded, her gaze moving from him to her feet. "Gamal . . ." she paused, met his gaze, ". . . has a scar along his brow, near his hairline. He got it in the war, saving the prince's life."

He gave her an affirmative smile. "That will help. Thank you." But he could tell by the wariness in her eyes that she gave the information with great hesitation. "I will be back within a month."

She searched his face, her gaze too vulnerable. "Be careful."

Her concern for him lifted his spirits. "If nothing else, it will give you time alone, the time you need to learn more about our God."

───※☖⁂───

Rahab watched Salmon walk with Othniel and head north toward Syria the following morning, her heart heavy within her. Why was he doing this? He could not know the outcome of such a journey. He could be killed along the way. Everyone knew bandits lived in the hills. And if he found

Gamal, what then? Her stomach turned over at the thought of the man.

Oh God, don't let them find him. If they couldn't find him, she would be free of him and free of all men who might come seeking marriage. She would not be bound to Salmon, as Joshua seemed eager for her to be. She need never risk her heart to the untrustworthiness of men again.

She turned back to her tent and gathered the herbs she had found in the fields near their camp. Today she would show Eliana and her daughters how to flavor the flatbread and stews into something other than the bland lentils and barley they had recently reaped from the land. Then perhaps she would take a walk to the Jordan to bathe, though she knew no hyssop or ointments could wash her as clean as she wished to be.

31

Rahab turned the millstone the following week, grinding newly harvested wheat in the company of Eliana and her youngest daughter. She listened as mother and daughter laughed over something they'd overheard as they gathered water that morning. Wistful longing filled her that she would never have a daughter with whom to share the secrets of women. Images of Adara came to mind, and with it homesickness as heavy as the millstone's weight. Why had she stayed here? If she left for Egypt with a passing caravan, could she find her family now?

"You're terribly quiet today, Rahab," Eliana said as she lifted ground grains from the stones and poured them into a thick clay jar. "Does something trouble you?"

Rahab looked up from her work and brushed the flour from her hands. She had spent days in prayer, walking alone among the fields, keeping to herself, her mind turning over the laws of circumcision and captive brides that Joshua had read to them less than a month earlier. If her father and brothers were required to be circumcised to join Israel, how was she released from doing something to show Adonai her allegiance? Was there not some rite for women? Or did everything rest with the men alone?

"I see even now you are struggling to say it." Eliana moved closer and touched Rahab's shoulder. "Can you share what troubles you, my daughter?"

Rahab looked at her friend, suddenly aware of how much the motherly endearment meant to her and how much she missed her own mother. Emotion rose quickly, and she brushed a stray tear from her cheek.

"I . . ." She looked away, her words halted by uncertainty.

"It's all right. You don't have to tell me." Eliana patted her shoulder, then pulled her into a warm embrace. "Let it be enough to know how much we love you and appreciate your presence among us. How grateful we are that Adonai spared your life. Joshua speaks of fondness toward you too."

Rahab looked into Eliana's caring dark eyes. "I miss my family," she said, suddenly realizing just how much that was true.

"Of course you do, dear girl." Eliana touched Rahab's cheek, as her mother had done when she was a small child. "It is natural to grieve so much loss, especially all at once."

Rahab nodded and looked away. "They left without saying goodbye." She could not speak past the lump in her throat.

Eliana drew Rahab into her arms and held her, saying nothing. Rahab stiffened, unaccustomed to such familial closeness. Eliana patted Rahab's back, then released her as if sensing her unease.

"You have suffered much, Rahab. But you are also the strongest woman I have ever known." She smiled. "I hope my daughters will learn such strength from you."

Rahab stared at her, though she kept her expression unreadable. She nodded, considering the woman. For all of Eliana's kind words, could she trust her?

Eliana stood and walked to the stack of threshed wheat to carry another bundle to be ground.

"You are expecting many for the evening meal?" Rahab noted the large jars of already ground grain.

"Joshua always entertains some of the people, usually the elders or Caleb's family." She set some of the wheat beside Rahab's grindstone. Rahab tossed a handful onto the millstone and turned the handle.

"Let me take a turn. Your back must be aching," Eliana said.

Rahab did not deny it. "Thank you." She stood and walked about, rubbing the kinks away, glancing every now and then at her friend. When Eliana's daughters moved toward the cooking tent, Rahab knelt at her friend's side. "I miss my family, but there is more."

At Eliana's curious look, Rahab drew in a breath and slowly released it. "I want to do something to show my allegiance to your God. Your men have circumcision. Surely there is something a woman can do?"

Eliana stopped grinding and studied her in silence for several moments. "You cannot earn a gift, Rahab."

The strength of the morning sun hit Rahab's cheek, and she glanced heavenward into the expanse of bright blue above them. Did Yahweh live in the sky like the moon god did? Or was His home higher, beyond what she could see?

"Joshua read the law to us," Rahab said, meeting Eliana's gaze once more. "He said, 'For the Lord your God is God of gods and Lord of lords, the great, the mighty, and the awesome God, who is not partial and takes no bribe. He executes justice for the fatherless and the widow and loves the sojourner, giving him food and clothing. Love the sojourner, therefore, for you were sojourners in the land of Egypt.'"

"You remember well, my daughter. And we do love you. I hope you know that." Eliana smiled. "You are like a daughter to us. That is why Joshua wants to seek a good husband for you. It is a father's duty."

Rahab glanced away. "I know that." She squatted beside the pile of threshed wheat, sifting it between her fingers. "But if I am a widow, I do not have to marry. Your God will still protect me, yes?"

Eliana nodded. "Our God is very strict about how we treat the widow and orphan and foreigners among us. God cares for the poor, and Joshua remembers what it was like to be a poor slave himself. You have no need to fear lack, Rahab."

Rahab sighed. "Thank you." The words eased some of the questions that had stirred her heart since the reading of God's law. She would be protected whether she married or not. Relief filled her.

"Does this mean you have already made your decision? You will not marry Salmon when he returns?" Eliana's question brought sudden heat to her face. To refuse Salmon would hurt Joshua, who clearly thought them a good match.

Rahab slowly shook her head. But she took a long time answering. "I don't love him, Eliana."

"Well, of course not. You barely know him."

"He despises me."

Eliana turned the grindstone several turns, as though to end the conversation. But a moment later she stopped and looked at Rahab. "He didn't know you, only what you were. He does not despise you now."

"He does not love me." She turned at the sound of voices and waited until the women of the camp passed by. "I would always doubt his sincerity."

Eliana shifted her weight and sighed. "I cannot blame you, dear girl. You have faced much. Why should you risk marriage again?"

Rahab could only nod. "I should probably start kneading some of the bread." Eliana had said it all, and Rahab had no more responses.

But as she kneaded flour and starter and water, she could not help asking herself if she was brave enough to risk such a marriage. If only he would agree to keep the relationship a friendship, not conjugal. She scoffed at her own ridiculous thought. No man on earth would agree to such a thing. Least of all one who seemed haunted by her past from the first day they met until now.

⁓✦⁓

Another week came and went, and still no sign of Salmon and Othniel. Rahab paced the hills near the camp, staying close to the tents but feeling a constant restlessness she could not shake. What if Salmon found Gamal? Gamal would demand her return, would probably try to force her to do things for him so he could continue to gamble away all they had.

If he still lived. And if his owners would allow such a thing. *Oh Adonai, please don't make me face him again.*

But the prayer brought no peace. Perhaps Israel's God did not answer such prayers.

Gamal would probably enjoy seeing her forced into slavery

with him. Or enjoy her earnings as a prostitute, just as Dabir had done. He had not truly been husband to her in years. And hadn't he hinted at giving her to other men for that very purpose—to earn coins to fill his pockets?

If she married Salmon, he could protect her.

The thought made her pause. She would not marry a man she couldn't love, and she would not use him for selfish reasons as others had used her.

Besides, if she was indeed still wed to Gamal, would not marriage to an Israelite anger their God? She shuddered at the thought, remembering Jericho, remembering Achan. She glanced at the camp swarming with women and children she had come to care for. She raised her eyes to the heavens. *I don't want to bring Your wrath on these people.*

She walked to a tributary of the Jordan that fed these hills and sank down among the grasses. She looked at her hands, seeing no sign of the once carefully groomed and hennaed nails. Her nails were chipped in some places, her fingers calloused now. The knowledge brought a small sense of pride. She had changed. Surely she had.

And yet, even the sacrifices did not seem sufficient. Married or not, there must be something she could do to show her alliance with Israel. Her thoughts churned with memories as she prayed in silence for wisdom. At last she stood, determined to seek out Eliana. There was one thing she could do, and before nightfall she would do it.

***

"Will you shave my hair and burn it in the fire in your courtyard?" Rahab asked Eliana later that afternoon before she could change her mind. To cut her hair in public would make her visible to all who passed by. The whole camp would know what she had done. Inside the tent, she could wear a head covering and perhaps none would be the wiser. But then people might never stop seeing her as a prostitute.

"You don't have to do this publicly, Rahab. You don't have to do this at all." Eliana took Rahab's hands in hers, forcing her to meet her gaze.

"Yes, I do." She drew a deep breath. "I want all to know that I am no longer the woman I used to be. I want to be clean."

She walked to one of the large stones near the fire pit in Joshua's courtyard and pulled the scarf from her long tresses, exposing her glory to Eliana and several women who stood nearby.

"Please, get your shears," Rahab said, her pulse drumming fast within her. This was not going to be as easy as she'd thought.

Eliana nodded, retreated into her tent, and returned moments later. Rahab sensed a crowd gathering. What would these women think of her now?

Eliana stood behind her and lifted a thick strand of hair into her hands. Rahab lowered her head and closed her eyes, shutting out the crowd. "Don't hesitate," she said, her voice choked.

Seeming to sense her mood, Eliana quickly cut the long strands until the hair hung just above her ears. She then took a razor used to shear sheep and began to shave the hair close to Rahab's scalp. Whispers of the women floated around her, but Rahab forced her mind to the sins of her past.

Forgive me, Adonai. I know I could have refused the men who made me do such things. I could have chosen imprisonment instead of breaking Your laws. I did not know You then, but I want to know You now. Tears flowed freely down her cheeks, and she let them fall onto her robe as she silently recounted each sin to the Lord.

Eliana set the razor down and came to face her, gently took the headscarf Rahab had removed, and placed it as a covering over her shaved head. She then took Rahab's hands and trimmed each nail short. She tossed the nails and hair into the fire.

"Let it be known this day . . ." Joshua stepped out into the courtyard and placed a hand on Rahab's shoulder. Heat filled her face, and she could not lift her eyes even to look at the men and women now gathered around her. "This woman, Rahab of Jericho, has pledged her life to our God, to Yahweh. As all men of Israel and all foreign men wanting to join the worship of our God must be circumcised, so this foreign woman, though it is not required of her, has chosen to obey the law of captive bride and, despite God's already evident mercy to her, has publicly declared to you all this day that she has put aside her old ways, and from this day forward is one of us."

He cleared his throat, and she heard the rustling of robes in the crowd. More people had joined the few who initially watched.

"Treat Rahab with the respect she deserves as a fellow Israelite. It is because of her faith that our spies were spared. And Jericho fell into our hands in part because of her trust in Adonai. Let us learn from her spirit of humility and obey our God as freely as she has done this day."

Joshua stepped forward and offered Rahab his hand to help her stand. She cinched the scarf tighter about her head, already feeling the loss of her hair's weight and comfort.

At last she placed her smaller hand in Joshua's and stood. "Thank you, my lord," she whispered, not trusting her voice.

He nodded and released her to Eliana. "Do you want some time alone?" Eliana asked quietly against her ear.

Rahab swiped at the tears that still seemed determined to fall. "Yes, thank you." She moved quietly and entered her tent and let the flap fall shut behind her.

32

Salmon tugged at his turban and shook the dust from it away from the fire Othniel had built at the mouth of a small cave. They had been walking with one lone donkey carrying their gear for days, and now camped on the outskirts of Damascus.

"I will be glad when this mission is over," Salmon said, sinking to his knees before the fire. "I must admit, I have asked myself many times why I suggested such a thing." He reached in his pack for a handful of dried beans and set them to soak over the flames. "I'm sorry I dragged you into this."

Othniel pulled a different pot of heated water from the fire and mixed it with crushed ginger. "It's no trouble. Better than sitting around the camp waiting for the next war." He offered a cup of the brew to Salmon, who gratefully took it. "Besides, I would do the same thing for the woman I loved."

Salmon glanced at his new friend. "I don't love her. I'm just doing this to give her peace."

"That so?" Othniel grinned.

"Yes." Salmon stirred the beans, wishing now he had opted for the familiar flatbread and cheese.

"Your silence tells me otherwise." Othniel chuckled as Mishael used to do, garnering Salmon's glare.

"And what woman is it you love who would send you off to follow your own foolishness?" He smiled at Othniel's blush. "Someone I might know?"

Othniel sat cross-legged and sipped his cup. "Probably. She's a cousin, the daughter of my uncle Caleb."

"Which one?" Caleb had had several daughters during his long years on earth, though most were already wed.

"Aksah. She is the youngest and should soon be betrothed." Othniel stared into the distance, his jaw tight.

Salmon blew on the steam from his cup. Their fathers, as all men and women from that unfaithful generation, had died before they crossed the Jordan. Othniel had no one to intercede for him with his uncle, who was one of only two aged men left among them—Joshua being the other. "Have you spoken to Caleb or Joshua about this?"

"Not yet." He shrugged. "Uncle Caleb does not know that I love her."

"And you are afraid to tell him."

Othniel lifted a brow as though considering the thought. "Not afraid." He met Salmon's gaze. "Aksah is the most beautiful of women. I am not sure she would have me."

"What say would she have in it? You should speak to your uncle." Salmon stirred the boiling beans, then tossed in a handful of cumin and raisins. They had not taken the time to snare a bird or small animal, so their meals were mostly cheese and dried fruit and bread without yeast. The beans he had noticed only today. Rahab must have tucked them into his pack. Thoughts of her gave a kick to his heart. Aksah could not possibly be as beautiful as Rahab, and yet Rahab, in her unique situation, had a choice. She could refuse to marry him and leave Israel.

The thought troubled him. Truth be told, he had started to pray every day that they would not find Gamal. But guilt always accompanied that prayer.

Othniel lifted his chin, his grin mischievous as Mishael's used to be. "I will admit this to you, my friend, but you must promise to keep it to yourself. I would not want to be forced to kill you."

Salmon heard the humor in his tone. "Who says you would succeed?" He laughed outright. "So tell me already."

Othniel gave a half shrug. "Aksah does not know that I care for her. She probably sees me as a pest or a brother more than a husband to obey."

"So perhaps you need to do something to change her mind. Prove your worth and earn her respect." Salmon dipped left-over flatbread into the simple stew.

"Is that what this is for you? To earn Rahab's respect?" Othniel swallowed a large mouthful and they both chewed in silence.

"I told you already. I want to give her peace. Other than that, I don't know why I'm doing this. Perhaps I want an excuse to get out of the marriage Joshua seems to want to push me into." Admitting his thoughts only added to his guilt. "Perhaps something will present itself and you will have your answer with Aksah," Salmon said, needing to turn the conversation away from his own troubling predicament.

"Yes, if my uncle doesn't betroth her to someone else before I return." He clenched a fist, then released it. "But I cannot control these things, so there is no sense growing angry or bitter without cause. I would imagine even in this I must place my trust in Adonai's grace."

Salmon nodded. Grace was something he would have to offer to Rahab if indeed he married her. He shook his head, his confusion mounting, one moment wanting her, the next not sure he was capable of such mercy.

"Now, after traveling this far," he said at last, "I truly hope our trip is worth the trouble. But if I find the man, I honestly don't know what I will do with him."

"Perhaps you should hear his side of the story. To prove she has spoken the truth."

"Would God have spared her if she had lied?" Surely not. Not after what he had seen happen to Achan and his family. Even a heathen would not get far lying to God Almighty.

⚜

Rahab ran her fingers along the first soft growth of new hair on her scalp but refused to examine her appearance in the bronze mirror Eliana had given her. Perhaps her avoidance was vain, but she had spent too many years in front of the glass, trying to make herself beautiful for unworthy men.

Her thoughts turned to Salmon's God—her God now—as she drew a plain linen scarf over her head and tucked it securely under her chin, pinning it lest it come loose and expose her. Two weeks had already passed since Salmon left for Syria, and she had submitted her life, her choices, even her future to Yahweh. Already she felt a new connection to her Maker. The brink of dawn each morning had drawn her to the river, not only to gather water before the other women could join her, but to pray. Alone, she felt the pain of her past slowly melting away, as though the sound of the river were washing her clean.

She petted the cat, hefted the jar in her hands, and lifted the tent flap, greeted by the soft gray light that preceded the sunrise. Her feet felt the cold tickle of dew as she made her way barefoot through the camp, down the well-worn path toward the Jordan.

She stopped abruptly at the sound of men's voices and the clop of donkeys' hooves coming her direction. A copse of trees hid her from their immediate view, but she could not cross the road without being noticed. Who were they? Joshua would want to know of strangers passing near their camp.

She whirled about and ran back the way she had come. Most of the camp still lay abed, so her movements went unhindered by women or children blocking the road. She came to Joshua's tent but stopped, uncertain. She couldn't just enter his tent uninvited, a woman alone. Was Eliana with him? She hurried around to the side of the tent where the girls slept and entered without knocking. To her great relief, she found Eliana slowly rising from her pallet.

"Eliana," Rahab whispered, not wanting to wake her daughters. "You must come at once."

She saw the alarm lighten Eliana's dark eyes but did not bother to give an explanation. She ducked from the tent and waited a moment for Eliana to join her.

"What's happened? Is it Joshua?"

Rahab touched Eliana's shoulder and shook her head, sorry she had caused her friend to fear. "No, nothing like that. But I need to warn him that men from a distance are headed to our camp. I heard them talking on my way to the river. I did not get a glimpse of them, so I do not know if they come in peace."

"Praise Adonai that you are an early riser." Eliana gripped Rahab's arm and tugged her outside Joshua's tent. "Wait here."

Rahab nodded, half amused by the comment that she was an early riser, considering that she used to spend most of the daylight hours in bed. But now she longed for the day's newness, when God felt nearest.

Eliana popped her head through the tent's opening. "Come quickly."

Rahab hurried inside the dark interior. Eliana had taken time to light only one lamp. Joshua emerged looking haggard and worn, rubbing a hand over his disheveled hair.

"Rahab, my daughter. What can I do for you?" He motioned for her to sit, but she remained standing.

"Forgive me, my lord, but I come in haste. As I walked to the river to draw water at dawn, I heard men and the hooves of donkeys coming toward our camp. Their accents sounded as though they had come from a distance, but I did not see them, so I could not tell. They could also be neighbors just passing by, but I thought you should know."

Joshua's eyes lost the look of weariness. "Thank you, Rahab. Go with Eliana and prepare the morning meal. I will see to the men." He spoke to a servant boy, sending him to call the elders to his tent.

Rahab went to do Joshua's bidding. Before the bread finished baking on the stones, a crowd of elders had assembled, arriving about the same moment as the foreign men and donkeys entered the camp.

Rahab peered around the corner of the cooking area, finally catching a glimpse of the men she had heard. Their clothes, sacks, and wineskins were worn and mended, and their sandals had patches holding them together. How far had they come?

Joshua emerged, surrounded by the elders.

One of the scraggly men stepped forward. "We have come from a distant country and ask that you make a treaty with us."

Silence followed the remark, but a moment later the elders leaned close to one another and whispered among themselves. At last one of them spoke. "How do we know you have come from a far country? Perhaps you live near us. How then can we make a treaty with you?"

The spokesman looked at Joshua, with only a glance at the speaking elder. "We are your servants."

Joshua stroked his beard, his eyes narrowed as if he were trying to read their thoughts. "Who are you and where do you come from?"

The spokesman cleared his throat, reached for a limp, cracked skin that held only a few drops of water, then shook his head as though pained by his poverty. "Your servants have come from a very distant country because we have heard of the fame of the Lord your God—of all that He did in Egypt, and all that He did to the two kings of the Amorites east of the Jordan. Our elders and all those living in our country said to us, 'Take provisions for your journey. Go and meet them and say to them, "We are your servants. Make a treaty with us."' So we set out and have come to make peace with you."

He pulled a loaf of moldy bread from another sack and held it toward Joshua. "This bread of ours was warm when we packed it at home on the day we left to come to you. But now see how dry and moldy it is. And these wineskins that we filled were new, but see how cracked they are. And our clothes and sandals are worn out by the very long journey."

Rahab felt Eliana's silent presence beside her as she watched. Several of the elders stepped forward, and one of them took the bread, turning it over in his hands. Another lifted the wineskin and examined the cracks. Both turned and nodded at Joshua.

"We will make a treaty of peace with you," Joshua said. "When we wipe out the nations that surround us as the Lord our God has commanded us to do, we will not strike you down to kill you but will let you live."

"May the Lord honor our treaty," said the man who had done most of the speaking. The others spoke their agreement.

"Come, partake of some bread and figs before you return home," Joshua said.

Rahab and Eliana hurried from the place where they watched and enlisted the help of Joshua's daughters and the elders' wives to gather enough food to feed their visitors along with their own men.

Rahab listened to the chatter as she served them and caught the glimpses of amusement in some of their visitors' gazes. Did they think this celebration humorous, or were they merely happy to finally eat a full meal?

A sense of apprehension filled her as she heard the slight change in tone or accent of one or more of the men. Why had these men not named the country from which they came? Which distant country? And why did the elders, did Joshua, not ask the Lord's guidance before they spoke the promise of peace?

The thoughts troubled her until the last donkey and man left Gilgal.

Salmon slung his pack over the donkey's side and secured it with leather strings. He patted the animal's neck and spoke softly to it. "Now the fun begins," he said.

"Are you talking to the donkey?" Othniel chuckled at the scene they must have made as he tied his own sack to the donkey's other side.

"Better than talking to myself." Salmon had seen Rahab talk to that silly cat of all things. "Don't most men speak to their beasts?"

Othniel pointed at himself, then waved a hand toward the Damascus gates. "Not this man. But I can barely talk to the woman I love, so you might as well count me hopeless."

They doused the fire that still lingered from the night before, and Salmon took hold of the animal's reins. They walked to Damascus's gates with Othniel humming a familiar tune, actually managing to put Salmon at ease. They stopped at the guard post to state their business.

"We are in search of a slave," Salmon said, tapping the head of his staff as he spoke. "He was purchased about a year ago in Jericho by a merchant named Qasim, son of Ratib. We have need to see him."

The young guard looked them both up and down, his spear held in front of him like a shield, easily able to block their path. "Jericho? I thought no one came out of there alive after the Israelites attacked them. Where did you say you're from?"

I didn't. "We come from outside of Jericho. We heard what happened to the city. Terrible loss."

The guard's gaze grew skeptical. "We have all kinds of slaves in Damascus," he said at last. "Doubt you'll find one from Jericho, though."

"His name is Gamal," Othniel put in, offering the guard a friendly smile. "I believe his gambling debts got him sold into slavery. Good-looking man, so I'm told."

The guard raised a brow. "Gamal is a common name, even here." He studied them a moment longer, then stepped back. "Enter and search all you like. You can check at the Hall of Records, but I doubt you'll find him."

Salmon nodded at the man as they passed under the wide arches of the stone gate. The streets teemed with turban-clad men and women covered with colorful scarves and flowing robes. Donkeys and camels piled high with goods were unloaded by merchants, while men and women haggled over prices. Salmon glanced at Othniel, then heavenward, his prayers for wisdom silent, urgent.

What other nation is so great as to have their gods near them the way the Lord our God is near us whenever we pray to Him? The memory of Moses' words came to him as though the prophet still spoke.

"Does our God seem near to you when you pray?" Mishael had whispered in his ear that day.

Salmon had not known how to respond. "Sometimes," he'd said. "I guess so."

But he had doubted his own answer. Was God near to those who prayed? He had pondered that question long into that night and beyond. Truth be told, despite all he had witnessed, sometimes he doubted it still.

They moved through the crowd, making inquiries of every male merchant in the area, to no avail. The sun had risen halfway to the sky by the time they finally stopped near a fountain in the center of the city and watched as a crew of workmen raised a mud and brick building across the wide street.

"I wonder how many of those men are slaves?" Othniel pulled a handful of dates from his pack and bit into one.

Salmon focused his attention on the men, whose tanned backs glistened with sweat. Only slaves would work in the heat of the day when others took time for a rest and repast.

"Probably all of them." He studied the group, searching for one who might be in charge. Spotting a man sitting in the shade, fully clothed, he left Othniel with the donkey and walked close to the man. "My lord, may I speak a word with you?"

The man glanced up, startled. He eyed Salmon through a narrowed gaze, his right hand loosely gripping a wooden stick. Probably the supervisor of these men.

"What can I do for you, stranger?" His smile showed uneven gray teeth.

Salmon straightened, feeling the slightest twinge of fear that they had entered a town with little to defend themselves. What if the town leaders decided to hold them against their will, to make them slaves as these men?

"We are looking for a slave from Jericho, a man named Gamal. He was sold to Syrian traders over a year ago." He straightened and lifted his chin, hoping his confidence would keep the man from thinking he could be easily cowed.

"So you say? And what would you want with such a one?" The man ran his tongue over puffy lips, then paused to take a swig from a wineskin. Was the man besotted?

Salmon looked him up and down, then noticed the ring

in his ear. This supervisor was as much a slave as the rest of them. One glance at his feet showed a blackened toe and streaks of purple crawling up his leg. Salmon took a silent step back.

"Do you know this Gamal from Jericho?"

"I might." He took another swig. "What do you want from him?"

Insight dawned on Salmon as he continued to take in the man's appearance. "Are you yourself this Gamal of Jericho, my lord?" A little respect couldn't hurt his chances of finding the truth. And the man seemed about the right age. At one time he was likely a man of handsome looks. But he appeared to suffer some type of sickness, and Salmon had a sense that he was more ill than he had first seemed.

"I asked what you want with him. Any information I give will cost you."

Salmon reached into a pouch in his belt and pulled out a small silver nugget he had recovered from Ai. "If your information proves worthy, there is another like it waiting for you."

The man eyed the nugget, snatched it from Salmon's outstretched hand, and bit down on it with broken gray teeth. Could a man change so much in only a year?

"I know this Gamal from Jericho," the man said.

"Are you him?"

The man shook his head. "No, but I shared a cell with him when they first brought us here." The man's hollow eyes darted to the crew still building the wall. Seemingly satisfied that all continued as it had, he glanced again at Salmon. "He was a good looker, that man. Quick with his tongue too. Tried to talk his way out of slavery, then tried to gamble his way to freedom. He thought the world owed him something, that one did. Turned out to be a good-for-nothing." He spat onto the stones near his feet.

Salmon took another step back and crossed his arms. "What happened to him? Where can I find him?"

"You can find him in one of the pits outside the city, buried with the rest of the scum." He blinked hard, then shrugged one shoulder. "S'pose I'll end up in that pile one of these days. Got the wasting sickness, I do." He pointed to his feet. "Not that I'll miss this life much. But it is a little worrisome not knowing what lies beyond the grave."

"You are telling me that Gamal of Jericho is dead?" Salmon dared not believe the man, though every part of him wanted to do so. "How do I know you tell me the truth? Who can confirm your words?"

The man turned and pointed to a building at the end of the block. "That's the magistrate's office, the Hall of Records. They've got the list of all those sent to debtors' prison or purchased with the king's money. Gamal bragged from the moment he arrived that he would soon be free or at the very least would personally serve the king, but like I said, he talked too much, and his tongue got him in trouble. They cut it out before they killed him."

Salmon's stomach recoiled at the image. "About how long ago did he die?" If it matched Rahab's story of the rumors she had heard, it would be enough.

The man looked thoughtful, as though it took time to pull the memory from his mind. "It was cool in the prison then, so it must have been winter. The walls nearly bake us alive in the heat of summer."

"And you are sure of this?" Surely God did not answer a man's prayers so quickly.

"Said so, didn't I? Check it over there if you don't believe me." He pointed a crooked finger behind him.

Salmon glanced toward the official-looking building. "And they will give this information to anyone who asks?"

The man looked at Salmon as if he had grown feathers. "It's a public building for the people of the city. Are you from Damascus?"

Salmon shook his head. "No. We are travelers passing through. Gamal was related to someone close to us, and we were hoping to locate him. That is all."

"It would be just like Gamal's luck to miss you then. Are you going to give me the rest of that silver now or not?" The man sipped again from his wineskin, and Salmon debated whether to pursue this thing further. Rahab had told him that Gamal had a scar just below his hairline from the battle where he saved the prince's life. But this man wore a turban that covered his forehead.

"I'll give you the silver if you let me buy your turban." He couldn't very well just ask him to remove it.

"Well, that will cost you more than one measly lump."

The turban was filthy, and Salmon didn't even want to go near the man to touch it, but he nodded agreement. He reached in his pouch for three small nuggets. If he was wrong in his guess that the man was lying and that this in fact was Gamal, he would be poorer, though probably no wiser. He drew in a breath and handed the silver to the man.

"The turban, please."

The man tucked the silver into his shirt, his eyes gleaming. He pulled the dirty piece of cloth from his head and tossed it to Salmon. The thing was probably crawling with vermin, and Salmon could not wait to throw it in the gutter. But his quick examination of the man's forehead revealed no scar, only a balding head covered in red splotches.

Salmon looked at the pathetic man and tossed the turban back to him. "Keep the silver, my friend. I believe you."

"Wouldn't lie to a stranger," he said, taking the cloth and wrapping it once more around his head. "Never know when you might be talkin' to an angel."

Salmon startled at the comment but said nothing and slowly backed away.

33

Salmon returned to Othniel's side, gripped the donkey's reins, and turned them toward the city gates without a backward glance. Neither man spoke as they wove their way around the crowds lining the Way of the Merchants, and they simply nodded to the guards as they passed once more beneath the Damascus gates. When they had covered some distance from the towers beside the gate, Salmon at last released a breath he'd held too long.

"I'm going to assume by that sigh you are satisfied with our mission?" Othniel took a turn holding the donkey's reins as Salmon lifted a skin of water to his lips to soothe his parched throat.

Salmon capped the skin and wiped the droplets from his beard. "Not entirely satisfied, no. Let's just say the place put me on edge." He looked at Othniel and took the staff he had draped from the donkey's side to use as he walked. "In Jericho, we were almost caught, if not for Rahab. Though we were not sent to spy out Damascus, I sensed they are not a city that would take kindly to us if they discovered we are

Hebrews. Did you not notice how many slaves worked on those buildings?"

"Hundreds, by the way they swarmed over the place."

"Yes, well, I didn't want us to end up among them." Salmon's heart still beat too fast, and he drew in another breath and slowly released it. "The man I spoke to claims Gamal is dead."

Othniel whistled a victorious tune. "Well then, you have your answer."

"Yes, it would appear so."

Othniel met his gaze. "I say it's the best answer you will get. You could walk from door to door throughout Damascus to see if you could find him or the merchant who purchased him and not do better than what that slave already told you." He batted the thought away as though swatting a pest.

Salmon dug his staff harder into the earth, leaning into its strength as they approached a hill. "For a moment, I wondered if the man was himself Gamal, the way he seemed so eager to take my silver. But he didn't have the scar on his face that Rahab had described to me."

"From where I stood, he looked like he had numerous scars."

"They were blotches." The sound of a river they'd crossed drew close, and Salmon picked up his pace to reach it. "I don't know what disease he had, but I'm going to dunk in the river and hope it carries all contact with the man away from me."

Othniel pulled the donkey to the side of the bank and allowed the animal to drink, but Salmon stepped into the rushing water, sandals and all, and dipped his head under water. He scrubbed his hair and beard with his hands, using the silt from the river's floor to cleanse himself. It wasn't the best way to wash, but he did not want to take the time to do more.

He glanced up at the sound of splashing to see Othniel walk the donkey through the shallow place where the rocks were few and pass over to the other side. Salmon dunked one more time, rinsing the last of the silt from his hair, and picked his way to the opposite bank.

"I have no blanket to give you to dry yourself, unless you wish to sleep without one tonight." Othniel looked at him as though he had lost some of his senses.

Salmon shrugged one shoulder. "It matters little. The sun is warm. I will dry as we walk." He wrung the water from his robe, tunic, and turban as best he could. They walked in silence for a time, but Salmon's thoughts brought him little peace. Should he believe the man, that Gamal was truly dead? What else was he to do?

"So are you going to marry Rahab?" Othniel stopped the donkey near a small cave to let it rest in the shade of a large terebinth tree. He pulled a sack of pistachios and almonds from the pouch and handed some to Salmon.

"I don't know." Salmon accepted the offering, stepping away from the shade to make better use of the sun's rays. He removed his robe and draped it over a rock where the sun hit squarely.

"And you are sure you don't love her?"

Salmon chewed some nuts, pondering the thought. "How do you love a woman who has given herself to so many men?"

Othniel glanced at the donkey, which busily ate from a thick patch of grasses, then met Salmon's gaze. "I suppose the true test of loving someone is forgiveness. Did not even Moses say that our God is a merciful God? If He does not leave us or forget us, how can we be any different? Were we not slaves in Egypt? And yet our God rescued us." He scratched the back of his neck. "Was not Rahab a slave in Jericho?"

Salmon stared at his friend, lifting a curious brow. "I suppose she was. In a certain sense . . . So I should marry her to rescue her, despite her past?"

Othniel shrugged. "Only you can answer such a question, my friend. If you cannot forget her past, you would be better to forget her completely and marry another."

Salmon glanced heavenward, his heart warring with opposite emotions. He had *tried* to forget her! He absolutely could not.

"We should go," Othniel said.

Salmon retrieved his damp robe and donned it again, feeling the sticky wetness of the river still clinging to his skin. What he wouldn't give to remove every stitch of clothing and put on something fresh and clean.

Was that how Rahab felt about her life? Wishing she could start fresh and new?

Suddenly he saw her in a different light, and saw his own heart for its wavering feelings toward her. His heart was as splotched as the head of that man in Damascus, covered with resentment that God would not give him the virgin bride he'd once wanted and instead offered him a blemished bride in Rahab.

"When we get back to camp," Othniel said, interrupting his thoughts, "I think I'm going to approach Uncle Caleb about Aksah."

Salmon glanced at his friend, then looked forward again toward the path leading home. Home. Where Rahab waited. If she would have him. Suddenly the thought that she might choose to remain widowed rather than marry him seemed inconceivable. He wanted her to be his and no one else's.

"When we return to camp," he said, matching Othniel's tone, "I will speak to Rahab and ask her to become my wife."

Othniel smiled, saying nothing. Salmon hid a grin, hoping his nerves would not stop him from saying the right words to convince her that he truly wanted her.

Rahab awoke later than she had hoped, caught in the grip of her monthly cycle. Cramps like she had not experienced since the loss of her babe made her nauseous, and she struggled to rise. The strangers had left camp three days earlier, and nearly a week had passed since she had humbled herself to accept the law of captive bride.

She crawled from her mat and took care of her morning ablution, her steps slow and weighted. She had not had a normal cycle since the loss of her child, one more reason she believed she could never bear another. But now . . . could it be that she was at last truly healed?

Thank You, Adonai. Gratitude seemed the right response. Truly Israel's God had blessed her with grace she didn't deserve. Her heart yearned to understand Him better, and she quickly dressed and lifted the clay water jar to her shoulder, hoping to make it to the river before a crowd of women gathered there.

She met Eliana along the way, realizing that her extra sleep had cost her time alone.

"I didn't expect to see you here," Eliana said, smiling. "You are usually up before the birds."

"I fear my cycle has made me lazy. I only just awoke a few

moments ago." Rahab shifted the jar to her head and held it steady with one hand.

"You haven't heard the news then." Eliana's brows drew down, and a slight scowl appeared on her normally smiling round face.

Rahab tensed, sensing the news was not good. "Has something happened to Salmon?" The thought made her feel suddenly worse than the cramps had that morning. She dared not explore what such feelings meant.

Eliana shook her head. "Nothing like that. Joshua has heard nothing from either Salmon or Othniel yet. It's about those men who came to make a treaty with us."

They had arrived at the river's edge and stepped down the bank to fill their jars. "What's happened?" Rahab felt uncommon relief that the news was not about Salmon, yet she could not help but wonder what awful thing would now affect Israel. Would these strangers prove as big a bane as Achan's sin had been to the whole camp?

They started back, falling into step beside each other. "A large group of our men followed the men to their homes. They reported to Joshua that they did not come from a distance after all. They are neighbors living nearby in Gibeon. Adonai would have wanted us to destroy Gibeon."

Rahab stopped walking to face Eliana. "What does that mean? Is God going to judge Israel for making the treaty?" A shudder worked through her.

"It has caused Joshua nothing but grief from the leaders of our people since they discovered the ruse. Some men want to destroy them, but the leaders cannot go back on their word. They swore an oath before the Lord." Eliana batted a fly from her face, and the two continued walking.

"How is Joshua taking this?" She ached for this new responsibility that rested on him.

"He's blaming himself for not consulting the Lord before making the treaty. He believed what he saw without checking for the truth."

They drew close to the camp now, where a large group of men had gathered in front of Joshua's tent.

"Oh no," Rahab whispered, glancing at her friend. "Will there be trouble?"

Eliana motioned for Rahab to follow her around to the back of her tent.

"Why have you made a treaty with our neighbors? Now we will never be able to take their land as the Lord our God promised to us." A spokesman from the crowd stepped forward and faced Joshua and the elders. Eliana and Rahab stopped to listen.

"We have given them our oath by the Lord, the God of Israel, and we cannot touch them now," one of the elders said. "This is what we will do to them," he continued when the crowd quieted. "We will let them live, so that God's wrath will not fall on us for breaking the oath we swore to them."

Another elder stepped forward. "Let them live, but let them be woodcutters and water carriers in the service of the whole assembly."

"Summon the Gibeonites to return to me," Joshua said to the elders when the crowd dispersed, seemingly satisfied. "I want them here before sundown."

"Yes, my lord," one of the men said, then several hurried off to do Joshua's bidding.

34

Rahab stirred the lentil stew with an olive branch, listening to the heated conversation going on in front of Joshua's tent.

"Why did you deceive us by saying, 'We live a long way from you,' while actually you live near us?" Joshua's voice held uncharacteristic anger. Rahab glanced at Eliana, who met her gaze with a worried one of her own. "You are now under a curse," Joshua said.

Silence followed his comment, and Rahab's heart beat faster. She stretched as far as the stir stick would allow, straining to hear. At last one of the men of Gibeon spoke.

"Your servants were clearly told how the Lord your God had commanded His servant Moses to give you the whole land and to wipe out all its inhabitants from before you. So we feared for our lives because of you, and that is why we did this. We are now in your hands. Do to us whatever seems good and right to you."

The crowd seemed to speak all at once, until one of Israel's men shouted from the back. "They deserve death for their lies. If Achan died for his, how can you allow these heathens to live?"

Joshua held up a hand for silence. "We dare not anger the Lord by breaking our oath to them. It is our sin of trusting them without consulting the Lord that will be judged if we break our word to them now." He addressed the Gibeonites again. "You will not die, but rest assured, you will be wood-cutters and water carriers for the assembly, to provide for the needs of the altar of the Lord at the place the Lord chooses from this day forward."

"May it be as you have said," the Gibeonite spokesman said.

Rahab returned to her stirring, half listening as the men of Israel divided the Gibeonites into groups and assigned them specific work. A contingent of men returned to Gibeon with the foreigners to make sure Joshua's instructions were carried out.

"Will Adonai be angry with us for this?" Rahab asked Eliana some time later, after the men had been fed and the leftover food tucked in baskets to hang from poles in Eliana's tent. "How hard it is to keep His laws. There are so many."

Eliana turned from covering the basket and gave Rahab a thoughtful look. "Keeping the whole law of Moses is impossible. It is why Adonai has allowed us the sacrifices, to cover our sins and our failures."

Rahab nodded. In the distance, she could hear the bleating of lambs kept in pens near the tents when they weren't out foraging in the fields with the shepherds. "A lot of blood must be spilled because of our sins." The image of the spotless lamb Salmon had chosen for them filled her mind. "Why could God not accept a different type of offering? Why must an innocent animal be killed?"

"I do not know," Eliana admitted. "All I know is that from the beginning God expected animal sacrifice. Adam's oldest son Cain tried to bring an offering of the fruit of the ground, as though he could choose which way to worship our great Creator. Elohim did not accept him, and in the end, Cain killed the brother God accepted out of jealousy. I think the blood reminds us of how grievous sin is to God."

Rahab pondered the thought. "I don't suppose a pomegranate or a fig as an offering would have the same effect on our hearts. To see an innocent life taken in our place is much more humbling than offering Adonai fruit."

Eliana laughed, then quickly sobered. "I never thought of it that way."

Rahab smiled. "This God of yours is hard to understand."

"None can. Even our leader Moses, who spoke with God face-to-face, did not always obey Him. We are made in Elohim's image, but we are not to take His place."

Rahab pondered Eliana's words over the next few weeks. Her hair continued to grow, along with her sense of gratitude and peace.

More than a month had passed since Salmon had gone off in search of Gamal. He should return soon, and the thought caused her heart to skip a beat.

She glanced at Eliana, whose presence in her life had become a steadying force. Her friend offered a smile as she lifted a heavy pot of stew and carried it to the central court in front of Joshua's tent.

Dusk had settled over the camp, and the sound of men's voices grew louder. She stepped closer, squinting to see who approached in the gathering darkness.

"Joshua!" the voice called. Rahab's stomach did a soft flip. *Salmon.*

Eliana returned to the cooking area. "Bring the bread and a flask of the new wine," she said, her eyes alight.

Rahab nodded. "He has returned." Her hands shook, and she gripped the edge of her skirt, forcing herself to be still.

Joshua emerged from his tent and gripped first Salmon then Othniel in a fierce hug, kissing each of their cheeks. "Come in at once. Tell me all that you learned." He stepped back and motioned them forward. A servant took the donkey's reins, leading it to one of the pens.

Rahab hung back, feeling suddenly awkward and unsure of what to do. She deposited the food she had gathered at the door of the tent, then followed Eliana to the cooking area once more.

Eliana handed Rahab several clay cups and bowls. "You must come with me."

"But . . . please, not yet. I didn't—that is, I did not expect him today. I am not ready."

Eliana studied her for a brief moment, then nodded. "To-morrow then."

Rahab breathed a sigh of relief. "Thank you." As much as she longed to see the man, surprising herself that she did, she wasn't ready. Not until she had time to seek the Lord alone, to be sure she was truly clean enough to join His people.

She turned to leave when a new thought struck her, and her heart caught in her throat. "Eliana?"

"What is it, dear child?" Eliana put an arm around her, apparently aware of the fear in her tone.

"Will you let me know if they found Gamal?" Why had she not thought of it sooner? He was not with them when they entered the tent, but that did not mean arrangements had not been made for her to return to him. The thought sent shivers down her spine.

"I will tell you as quickly as I hear something." She kissed Rahab's cheek. "Now don't you worry. Things will be all right."

"I hope so." But as she walked to her tent alone, she did not think so, and hope was a long time returning.

⚜

"Tell me everything," Joshua said as he took a seat across from Salmon and Othniel. "Did you find Rahab's husband?"

Salmon accepted a cup of wine from Eliana as his gaze held Joshua's. "No." He looked at the swirling liquid, wishing his answers were more conclusive.

"The man Salmon spoke to told him that Gamal is dead." Othniel nodded at Salmon, then drank deeply from his cup.

"Is this true?" Joshua's gaze could be felt, though Salmon sensed in it intense compassion and hope.

"It is. We spoke to guards at the city gate, but they had not heard of the man. They allowed us to walk the streets, and we spoke to many merchants, winding our way through the city until we came upon a building project being put together by slaves. I approached a man who appeared to be an overseer, though a slave himself, and he said he'd shared a prison cell with Gamal and that Gamal is dead." Salmon ran a hand over his beard, the words taking the last of his energy. "I could have checked the Hall of Records, but something about the man, perhaps, or the city itself made me uneasy. I feared being taken captive and made into slaves like the rest of those men." He hung his head at the admission. Fear was the last thing he should let consume him if he truly trusted Adonai.

"So you left without checking the man's story." It wasn't a question, but Salmon nodded at Joshua anyway. "I don't blame you and, in fact, am glad you had sense enough to leave before something happened. These nations do not like us. They may fear us, but they also hate us. We must always be on our guard against their attack."

Salmon glanced up. "What do we do about Gamal then?"

Joshua sipped from his cup. "There is nothing to be done. The witness told you the man is dead. Did he have a reason to lie to you?"

Salmon thought on that a moment. "No. And I made sure the overseer did not carry the scar Rahab had described. He took plenty of silver to obtain the answer, but he did not have the scar."

"Then though it is only one witness, there is no reason to doubt him. Did not Rahab say she was told of Gamal's death soon after he was sold into slavery?" Joshua folded his hands across his knees.

Salmon nodded. "Yes, she did."

"Well then, there is nothing more to be done. He abandoned his wife long enough ago that he has no right to claim her again. If he were to one day show up looking for her, I will deal with him."

Salmon studied the older man in heavy silence. At last he cleared his throat. "So then, if someone wanted to marry Rahab . . ." He let the thought go unfinished.

"I would give you my blessing, my son." Joshua smiled.

A throat cleared, and the men turned, surprised to see

Eliana step forward from a dark corner of the tent. "My lord, perhaps Salmon should be told of Rahab's choice."

Joshua gave a nod of understanding, while Salmon felt heat rush to his face. "What choice?" The words felt choked. Had she made a vow never to marry while he was away?

"Rahab succumbed to the rite of a captive bride. In sight of all, Eliana shaved her hair and clipped her nails and burned them in the fire. Rahab did this to fully become one of us." Joshua smiled, and Othniel grinned in that annoying way he had. Salmon scowled at him.

"That does not mean she wishes to marry," Joshua added. "She simply wanted to show Adonai her allegiance and repentance."

"Has she chosen not to marry then?" Disappointment coiled in Salmon's middle. He didn't realize until this moment how eagerly he longed to return to her, to make her his.

"She has made no decision at all of which I'm aware." Joshua glanced at his wife, who shook her head.

"She has said nothing to me either, my lord."

"It seems then, my son," Joshua said as he stood to bid them farewell, "that when her time of mourning is past, you must ask her. If you love her, do not hesitate to show her."

⁕

Rahab awoke the next morning to the feel of soft whiskers tickling her cheek. She opened her eyes and could not help but smile at the purring cat. "Well there. Are you here to make sure I don't oversleep today?" She petted his soft fur, awarded by a louder purr and an arched back, as though he was asking for more. She laughed. "You sure are a friendly thing."

She rubbed her eyes and forced her stiff limbs to rise. What she wouldn't give for the plush bed she once owned in Jericho. And yet, no. She would not wish that life back, even with its comforts. She would get used to sleeping on the ground until she could afford to sew a thicker cushion—perhaps one she would share with Salmon. If he still wanted her.

She patted the cat's head once more, rubbed his back, and then stood. She took hyssop, soap, fresh linen, and a clean tunic into her arms and tucked them into the empty water jar, the cat nearly tripping her on her way to the tent's opening.

"What? Are you trying to stop me?" She glanced down at the black and brown striped animal, wondering at how quickly he had become a pet, as though he needed her as much as she needed him. "Well, come along then, if you must. But I'll warn you, the river is fast and wet, and I guarantee you won't like it."

She lifted the flap and left the tent, fully expecting the cat to follow, half disappointed and half surprised when he didn't. She really ought to name the poor thing, but so far, nothing seemed to come to her or stick to him. What did it matter with an animal, after all?

She moved through the quiet camp, passing Joshua's still dark tent, and felt the dew tickle her feet as she padded softly toward the river to greet the pink light of dawn. No other women appeared along the river's edge, the only sound that of mourning doves singing greetings to her from the trees.

Eliana had taught her a woman's purification ritual, but that would come later, after she had washed her whole body in the river. For a brief moment, she wished she had brought Eliana with her to protect her privacy, to hand her the hyssop and soap as needed, but another part of her relished the time alone.

She removed her soiled clothes and left them by the bank, then quickly ducked under the frigid waters, her breath catching from the cold. She lifted her gaze to the brightening sky as she rubbed the soap and hyssop over her skin, her heart yearning heavenward.

Do You find me clean in Your sight, Adonai? After all I have done? Is it possible for one like me to be accepted as one of Your people? You know I believe in You, but my heart is stained by so much wrong. All the hyssop in the valley cannot make it new.

She closed her eyes, feeling the weight of her tears with each heartfelt word. *You are holy, Adonai. You are pure and just and right, whereas I am not. Please forgive Your servant her many sins. Let me find favor in Your eyes.*

She ducked beneath the surface again and opened her eyes to the dark, swirling waters. And in that moment, she sensed the silt and dirt of the river carrying the stains of her soul with them to the bottom and down the river's path to the sea. Carried away from her forever.

She pushed up from under the water and raised her arms overhead, her short hair not long enough to cover her exposed skin, her heart bare before the Lord.

Thank You, Adonai.

Whether Israel ever accepted her or not, she knew she was finally clean before the only One who really mattered. Her Maker.

As she quickly dried her body and donned fresh clothes, she vowed in her heart to do her best to please only Him all of her days.

35

Salmon left his tent before dawn, hyssop and soap and a fresh tunic in hand, so he could give his skin and clothes a proper washing, some of which still carried the river's silt among the folds. If he hurried, he could be done before the camp awoke.

He paused in his walking, his silent prayers for himself, for Rahab, halting at the sound of water splashing and a voice raised in praise.

"Blessed be the Lord, the God of Israel. Great are You, for You do not hold a woman's sins against her. A broken and contrite heart, oh Lord, you will not despise."

The voice was clearly Rahab's, and Salmon's pulse quickened to hear it. Was she in the river? Temptation to see her warred with the fear of what he would find. When she finally came to him, he wanted her to be as a virgin again, a true and pure bride. If he came upon her bathing, he would ruin that first moment.

He stepped back behind a copse of trees and waited, keeping his gaze turned away from the river. He tipped his head, listening, at last aware that she had stepped from the water at the rustling sounds of fabric on skin.

She would surely pass him on the way back to camp. Should he make his presence known, declare his love for her here? But no. She would not believe that he had not spied on her. Even if she wanted to believe it, he would compromise her trust.

He slipped farther into the trees, waiting until he saw the outline of her form pass, the heavy jar of water on her head and her washed clothes draped over one arm. She was humming a soft tune, and his heart lightened to hear it. Perhaps Joshua was right. God had saved Rahab because of her faith, and now He was giving her a future and a hope in Israel.

Starlight danced in the sky overhead, and the fire crackled in Joshua's courtyard. Caleb and his family, including Othniel and his cousin Aksah, Salmon, Rahab, and Joshua's family talked among themselves. They had just come together at the end of the Sabbath. In a few weeks they would celebrate the Feast of Ingathering, if the festival was not interrupted by war. Already threats loomed on the horizon, and Joshua had confided to the elders that he had heard rumors of the Amorite kings preparing to war against them.

Salmon glanced across the court, where the women sat talking quietly. No distaff or spindle moved in their nimble fingers. Joshua had made it clear that the Sabbath was a gift from Yahweh to rest, to worship Him alone. From where he sat, it was clear that Rahab was at rest, at peace with herself, with Adonai. He had never seen such a beautiful smile as she possessed now as she laughed softly at something Aksah said. If Othniel had his wish and married his cousin, perhaps the four of them could remain close friends. They were from the same tribe, after all, so they could live in the same proximity once they secured their land.

"You're terribly quiet for such a talkative man, Salmon," Othniel said, laughing. They both knew it was Othniel, and Mishael before him, who spoke many words. "Or are you just taken with watching a particular maiden?" he said, leaning close to Salmon's ear.

Salmon faced him and lifted a brow. "I could ask you the same thing. Have you spoken yet to Caleb?" he whispered.

Othniel shook his head, but his gaze traveled to Aksah. He barely hid a smile. "Soon, I hope." He looked again into Salmon's eyes. "What about you, my friend? Joshua has already given you his blessing."

Salmon watched Rahab, an uneasy feeling settling in his gut. He needed to speak to her. But where to start? "I have not spoken to her yet," he admitted.

"What are you waiting for?" Othniel's look held challenge. They both knew that war could interrupt any attempt at marriage. And if anything happened to him . . . would she miss him?

"I'm not sure she'll say yes."

"Coward." The word, though said in a lighthearted tone, held too much truth.

Something moved in the shadows, and Salmon straightened, suddenly alert to the sounds of night. Wolves would not come near the fire, but as he looked closer, he saw something small, like a small dog or a large coney, amble into Joshua's courtyard. It approached Rahab.

Salmon jumped up, whipped the dagger from its leather casing, and squinted to see in the darkness. No, not a dog or unclean rodent, but that silly cat. The animal had jumped onto Rahab's lap at the same time that Salmon was nearly upon it before he recognized her pet.

She startled. Looked at him strangely. Glanced from his dagger to the animal now cradled in her arms. "Salmon, are you trying to kill my cat?"

He sheathed the blade and sank to the ground near her feet. "My mistake. I thought it was a wild animal."

Her light laughter lifted his spirits. She stroked the cat's fur and bent to kiss its head. "Well, he *is* an animal and was probably wild sometime in his life. He has followed me everywhere since before Jericho's destruction." She met Salmon's gaze, her smile soft in the hearth's glow. But she quickly turned her attention to the cat again and scratched its ears. "What a little shadow you are," she said to the animal. "You know, when he first showed up, he was so skinny my cook threatened to add him to a stew." Her smile moved him. She seemed more at peace than he had yet seen her.

Salmon sat closer and lifted a hand toward the animal. It turned, faced Salmon, hair on end, and hissed. He withdrew his hand and moved away.

"My protector," Rahab said, leaning close to the cat, whispering comforting words in its raised ears. "It's all right. Salmon is a friend. He didn't really mean you harm." The cat slowly settled again on Rahab's lap.

Salmon rose slowly, taking a step backwards. "Do you suppose this little nemesis will allow me to walk you to your tent?"

Rahab's large eyes widened at his request, and a soft

blush covered her cheeks. She looked at the cat once more. "What do you think, little friend? Shall we let Salmon take us home?"

A loud purr was the only response, and when Rahab stood with the animal still in her arms, it glowered at Salmon but made no attempt to raise its claws. Wooing Rahab was going to be harder than he expected.

***

Rahab sat beneath the shade of a terebinth tree the following afternoon, thinking. Salmon had said little on the walk to her tent. Perhaps he feared angering the cat again. But she sensed he had wanted to speak, and felt the sting of disappointment when he bid her good night without more than a blessing on her sleep. Not that it did any good. She had tossed with fitful dreams.

But before dawn at the riverside during her walk with Adonai, peace had returned. Gamal was dead, and she hoped he had found the peace in Sheol he had not seemed capable of finding in life. Grief had come with the news but did not last. She had mourned her family's move far longer. And Tendaji's protective loss. She had grieved the loss of her innocence and missed Adara's and Cala's closeness. Were they happy in their new home in Egypt? She would never know. The thought made her frown as she worked the flax into a basket.

"Is the work so difficult to bring such a scowl to your beautiful face?" Salmon's voice came from her right. He thought her beautiful? Her hair was still as short as a man's, though it remained hidden beneath her scarf. She looked up.

He glanced about him. "I'm not going to be attacked by your little 'protector,' am I?" He seemed almost worried if not for his smile, and he did not have his dagger or sword at the ready.

"He sleeps during the day. I think you are safe." Rahab's heart skipped a beat. She drew a breath, then focused again on the basket. "Can I help you?"

He squatted beside her. "That depends," he said, his voice gentled. "May I sit beside you?"

She met his gaze but a moment and nodded. "Of course. If you wish."

She sensed him studying her, and she could not keep her concentration. She set the basket aside. "That is," she said, "you may state what you need, but you are distracting me from my work."

His smile was slow and held the slightest hint of amusement. "Am I now?" He settled on the ground more comfortably. "Distracting you?"

His steady look did strange things to her insides. Her stomach did a little flip. She swallowed. "From my work."

"I see." He paused. "Only your work?"

She stared at him, saw the intense interest in his eyes. "Yes." She glanced away, betrayed by the heat filling her face. How was it possible this man could make her blush? She was acting like a new bride—with feelings she should not feel.

Except . . . Yahweh *had* washed her clean. She knew it deep within her. At least in His eyes, she was not what she used to be.

"Unfortunate," Salmon said, his brows drawn in a mild frown. "Which goes to show that I am a terrible judge of character." He studied her.

"Are you?"

He nodded. "I will tell you a story if you will spare the time."

She could only nod in return. His kindness warmed her.

"You see," he began, "I once met this woman, and she proved to be kind and giving. She risked her life for mine, and even bargained for her family to be free when she was only a sword's breadth away from death." He looked at her, and she could not pull away from the earnest gaze. "This woman was beautiful and remarkable and had more faith than I had seen in anyone around me, except Moses and Joshua and Caleb. I had never met a woman like her in all of Israel."

She held too tightly to her breath, but she could not speak. He reached for her hand and turned it palm up in his larger one. "But I disdained this woman despite her character, because of her profession. In the eyes of my God, she was a sinner."

His Adam's apple moved in his neck, and she knew the words were hard to form on his tongue.

"The problem was," he continued at last, "I did not see that my pride and judgment of her were sinful too. If my God found her faithful and saved her, forgave her past, why couldn't I?"

Silence fell between them.

"Whatever happened to this woman?" she asked, no longer able to accept the silence, sensing his need for her to say something.

He looked into her eyes, and it felt as though he had touched her. Not in a physical way, but with warmth to her heart. "She changed. But more importantly, I changed," he said. "I realized that we are all sinners in our God's eyes. But we are saved by faith in Him, in His ability to save us, and by faith we obey His Word as Moses taught us, and as our forefathers did."

344

"I'm happy for you and this woman, whoever she is," she said, pulling her hand from his grasp. "Our God is mighty to save." Her voice barely rose above a whisper. She took a breath and released it. "So what will you do? Is this woman a friend of yours now?"

Salmon's smile was serious. "I am hoping to make her much more than a friend, though a friend is a good place to start."

Rahab's heartbeat quickened. She dare not look at him, and yet, she could not stop herself. "Much more than a friend?"

He nodded, then shifted so that he sat closer. "Rahab?"

"Yes, my lord?"

He extended his hand palm up. "Will you be my wife?"

She studied the hairs on his arms and hands. Beautiful, calloused, yet gentle hands. Her stomach did another flip as a thousand thoughts flitted through her mind. But none caught hold. None condemned her, and she found she no longer wanted to remain alone. She lifted her own calloused hand and placed it in his. Met his ardent gaze.

"Salmon, nothing would please me more."

The week passed too quickly once Rahab went through the ritual purification with Eliana's help. She stood shaking before the bronze mirror in Eliana's tent, not wanting to pull the scarf from her head. "There is nothing to comb, Eliana. No hair to put up for Salmon to undo."

She cringed, not wanting to look, as Eliana gently lifted the veil from her head. A soft sigh from Eliana's lips made Rahab glance in the bronze looking glass. The reflection that stared back at her barely resembled the Rahab she once knew. Soft hairs had grown in thick atop her head, brushed the tops of her ears, and covered the base of her neck.

"You will be the envy of every woman in Israel who wishes she did not have a heavy head of hair to wash each week." Eliana picked up a shell comb and fluffed the edges of Rahab's freshly washed hair. "Enjoy it so short. You will never have it so easy to care for again."

Rahab studied her reflection. The short hair made her look younger than her twenty-one years. She toyed with a slight smile. "Do you think Salmon will think me pretty?"

Eliana came from behind to face her. "I think the man is completely smitten with you and has been since the moment he met you."

Rahab looked at her short, unpainted nails. "I fairly doubt that." But she could not deny the hope that followed Eliana's statement.

"Come," Eliana said, ignoring her comment. "It is time for Joshua to bless your union." She stepped back as Rahab placed the veil over her head and covered half of her face with it. Her heart raced as she moved out of Eliana's tent to the smaller huppa set up in the court area in front of Joshua's tent.

A crowd had gathered, seemingly the entire tribe of Judah. Music drew her under the canopy, and the women joined hands and circled their tent. Salmon stood looking at her, dressed in princely garb, his striped robe rivaling anything she had seen Prince Nahid or Dabir wear.

She swallowed, wishing away such a disturbing memory, silently praying Adonai would keep her mind clear of every man but Salmon. Her knees weakened as he stepped closer and placed the corner of his robe across her shoulders.

Joshua spoke words of blessing she barely heard, and the women took up dancing and singing again. Salmon wove his fingers through hers and leaned close to her ear. "Thank you," he said, squeezing her hand. "I hope you will not find me wanting."

Rahab felt her cheeks blaze beneath the veil. "I hope you will not think I shall compare you to . . . well, I wouldn't think of . . . that is . . ."

He held up a hand. "Forgive me. I only meant that I promise to provide for you all of your days, and you have my word that though you performed the law of a captive bride, you are not captive to me. We both belong to Adonai, and I believe He fashioned us for each other. I will never set you aside, and I hope that my provisions will please you."

She stared at him, undone. "I . . ."

He touched a finger to her lips, as though oblivious to the onlookers and clapping women swirling around them. Suddenly it was like they were alone under the canopy, just the two of them, and he had in essence declared his love. No other man had ever made such a promise.

"I don't know what to say."

"Don't say anything then. But let us leave these festivities and sup in my tent." His gaze grew intent. "If you are willing?"

She nodded, feeling a lump in her throat as he led her past the women and the feasting tribe, past the tent she had called home since she had joined Israel. Salmon lifted the flap to his own tent, and she ducked inside, drawing in a quick breath at the transformation. Candles lit up the room, and the scent of frankincense lightly filled the air.

She turned to face him. "It's beautiful. You did all of this?"

He gave her a sheepish look. "Eliana and some of the elders' wives helped me in their spare time."

"Still, it's lovely." She had never been at a loss for words with a man, but now she found she could not find her voice to say more.

"I know this is not a first marriage for you," he said, gently guiding her to his side of the tent, where more candles and spices greeted her. A white linen sheet lay atop a plush mat—a bridal sheet that fathers kept on behalf of their virgin daughters. Something she would not need.

"Joshua will keep this for you," Salmon said, pointing to the very sheet that stared up at her now.

"He will have no need. I am not a virgin."

Salmon shrugged. "We have prayed for you, and in my eyes, in God's eyes, you are."

"Joshua is very kind to act in place of my father."

Salmon smiled. "He will have my hide if I ever mistreat you. He considers you a daughter to him."

She blinked, aware of the sudden moisture in her eyes.

Salmon touched her veil and slowly undid the clasp. When her shorn head lay visible before him, he knelt at her feet and kissed them. Tears filled her eyes as he slowly untied her sandals, still bowed before her. Something inside her urged her to place both hands on his head, and as she did so, he slowly rose until her arms fell to his shoulders and his came about her waist.

His kiss was slow and gentle, warm and careful, growing ever more possessive, yet never overbearing. He held her, stroking her back, then whispered words of kindness in her ear.

"You are beautiful, my Rahab. Do you even realize how special you are to me? Can you ever forgive the pride I held in my heart against you, a child of Jericho yet also chosen of God?"

"You had every reason to feel as you did, Salmon. I am—was a prostitute. I deserved your condemnation." She looked beyond him, but his gentle fingers under her chin tugged her back to look at him.

"You are a prostitute no more. You are my bride." He kissed her again until her knees grew so weak she needed his strength to remain standing.

He removed her robe and led her to the bridal cushions. He removed his tunic from his lean body and pulled her close. "Now, no more of this talk." His kiss lingered, and she saw the smile in his eyes.

He accepted her. Truly. Completely.

The following morning as they rose from the bed, Rahab stared at the stain of blood in the center of the sheet, something she had not seen since her wedding night with Gamal, a lifetime ago.

She knelt beside it. "This is not possible." She looked up into Salmon's clear dark eyes.

He squatted at her side and pulled the sheet closer. "I must take this to Joshua."

"But . . ."

His finger to her lips silenced her. "Nothing is impossible with God, beloved."

Salmon lifted the sheet with the blood exposed and carried it from the tent to Joshua's door. Men of the city still lay sprawled across the court area. Rahab stood at the outskirts as Salmon called Joshua's name.

"Joshua!"

The man emerged a few moments later, bleary-eyed, and drew a hand over his beard. He looked around at the men, who were slowly rising now. "Salmon, my son." Joshua's voice rang clear above the crowd.

"Here is the bridal sheet to prove my wife's virginity. As leader you have promised to keep it for her." Salmon walked forward and placed it in Joshua's hands.

Joshua examined it, then looked at Salmon. "I accept your pledge, my son. There is nothing to be held against your bride. May God bless your union."

Salmon nodded his thanks, then turned and walked back to her side. He took her hand in his and led her toward the Jordan River, though she carried no jug in her arms.

"My lord, shouldn't I fetch the water jar?"

He shook his head. "This is our time. Eliana's daughters will gather the water today."

She accepted his words and the silence that followed, feeling warmed by the strange comfort of his hand in hers.

When they reached the Jordan's bank, he pulled her onto a grassy spot and cradled her in his arms. "This will be our memory place," he said against her ear. "This is where Mishael and I crossed over to spy out Jericho, where I first met you. And this river is where we were both washed clean of the dark things in our hearts." He leaned around her to glimpse her face and kissed her cheek.

She nestled closer into his embrace, barely daring to believe how blessed she felt. After all of the hurt she had endured, God had taken the years and remade them, giving her hope.

"Thank you," she whispered, listening to the buzz of insects in the foliage around them. "And thank You, Adonai."

Salmon rested his head atop hers.

Rahab's heart felt light at his touch, at the gentle way he held her. Perhaps her future would truly be far better than her past. She glanced toward the skies, her heart full of gratitude.

EPILOGUE

ONE YEAR LATER

The boisterous cry of the babe brought a surge of laughter to Rahab's lips. "Hurry! Let me see him." The midwife handed him off to Eliana while she continued to tend to Rahab.

"You must be patient, my dear girl."

"Is he born?" Salmon poked his head into the birthing tent, an unheard-of action, but Rahab smiled at him.

"He is born. But Eliana seems to think his mother should be the last person to hold him." Rahab stuck her lip into a pout, evoking soft laughter from Salmon.

"Well, perhaps she has good reason." He was teasing her, and she loved him for it.

Love. Until this moment she did not realize how much she truly did love Salmon, the father of her new son. A son who lived and even now lay crying beneath Eliana's ministrations.

"I'm hurrying, I'm hurrying," Eliana said to the boy. "My, my, little one, you are as impatient as your mother!" She tucked the swaddling cloths around the baby and turned, holding him up for Salmon to see.

A moment later, Joshua stepped into the tent behind Salmon. "You men do not belong in here," Eliana scolded. "What will people think?"

Joshua walked over to peer at the boy, while Rahab allowed the midwife to settle her among fresh linens and cushions. "They will think this boy has many people anxious to see him, to bless him."

"Not until his mother gets to hold him." Rahab held out her arms, and this time Eliana placed the babe within them.

Rahab's heart stirred as she looked into the dark liquid eyes of her son. So beautiful. So perfect. She directed his mouth to her breast and covered herself lest she embarrass Salmon in front of Joshua. The pull of his mouth brought such a surge of joy to her heart that she could not stop the tears. She stroked his cheek with one finger beneath the blanket and felt the soft wisp of hair clinging to his head.

"What will you name him?" Salmon asked, tears filling his loving gaze as he knelt at her side. He lifted the blanket to peek beneath the fold. A deep sigh escaped his lips. "He will be a prince in Judah."

"As you are, my son," Joshua said.

"I thought we could name him Boaz." Rahab looked into Salmon's eyes, reading his familiar, kind expression. She had not discussed names with him until now for fear the babe would not be born healthy. But Adonai had shown great mercy in allowing her to keep this child.

"Swiftness. He shall be as fast as a gazelle." Salmon smiled, showing a soft dimple above the hairs of his dark beard.

"And impatient, like his mother," Eliana said.

Rahab laughed softly. Boaz was as anxious to nurse as she had been to hold him. But perhaps both of them would settle into patience like Salmon's in time. She would hold on to these days with him and take none for granted. She already knew how quickly life could change.

"He's a beautiful child, Rahab," Eliana said, taking Joshua's arm. "When he is done nursing, we will let these men bless him." Eliana turned to her husband, and Rahab saw in them the only grandparents her boy would know. How blessed she was to have them in her life. "But for now, we will leave the three of you alone. Let Salmon greet his son."

They turned and left the tent, but Salmon lingered at her side. She was unclean, and he couldn't stay with her long, but he fingered a length of her hair, which had already grown past her shoulders during her pregnancy. He brushed it deftly behind her ear.

"I love you, you know." He pushed the blanket from covering the child's head.

"I know," she said, her smile gentle. "I would kiss you if I could. To thank you for my son."

"Your son?" He lifted a brow.

"Our son." She had to stop thinking so selfishly, so self-preserving. "I'm just feeling rather possessive right now."

He nodded. "But you will allow his father to hold him?" He stroked her cheek, then let his finger trail to the babe's soft skin.

She released the boy's mouth from her breast and lifted him to Salmon's arms. "Don't drop him." She smirked, and his responding smile told her he caught her jest.

He pulled the boy close to his heart, and Rahab thought she could almost hear their hearts' simultaneous beating, in rhythm with her own. They were a family. In eight days, Boaz would be circumcised and join the ranks of Israel. And she would be forever in this royal line of Judah, whether a king ever came from her future grandchildren or not.

"We will raise him to be a good man, a man who obeys Adonai's ways," Salmon said, glancing at her.

She nodded. "When he is grown, he will have to choose for himself what he will do, whom he will obey, just as we did."

His sober look made her heart beat faster. "We will pray he makes the right choices." He handed the boy back to her, then leaned in and kissed her forehead. "I have no doubt, beloved, that you will make the best mother in Israel. And our son will learn the ways of Adonai because of you."

Tears filled her eyes that he had such faith in her, a prostitute.

Former prostitute, she corrected herself.

Forgiven prostitute.

Who had married a prince in Judah.

NOTE FROM THE AUTHOR

I hope you have enjoyed my perspective on Rahab's life. Of course, there are many books written about Rahab and no two are completely alike. There is very little given to us in Scripture on her story. All we know from the Old Testament is that she was a prostitute who saved the spies of Israel and lived in Israel after Jericho was destroyed.

Some Jewish commentaries on Rahab suggest that she married Joshua. Since the Bible does not tell us about Joshua's family (other than his father's name and the fact that he does have a "house," meaning family), it is a conclusion some might make. I don't happen to agree because I see it from a Christian perspective.

In the New Testament, Rahab is mentioned in Hebrews 11 and James 2 for her faith. And she is listed in Matthew's first chapter in the genealogy of Jesus, who is called the Christ (Messiah). In that genealogy, she is listed as married to Salmon, son of Nahshon, of the tribe of Judah, and mother of Boaz. That is why I don't believe she married Joshua.

One interesting note on Salmon's history. His father, Nahshon, is listed several times in Numbers as a leader and commander of his tribe—a prince in Judah (see 1 Chron. 2:10–11 ESV). That this legacy of leadership was passed down from Nahshon to Salmon seems highly plausible to me, which is why I chose to show him as one of the leaders under Joshua's command. Salmon was in the chosen line of Judah to father Israel's future kings—most famously, David and Solomon.

Rahab's story was not an easy one to write, despite these interesting findings in Scripture. Part of the problem came in trying to understand the why. What led Rahab into prostitution? Was she truly a prostitute or just an innkeeper, as some have suggested? If her father had sold her into prostitution (another plausible possibility), would she have wanted so badly to save her family? I tried to imagine myself in her place. What resentments might she have carried against men? What trust issues?

And what kind of man would want to marry a prostitute? In the book of Hosea, God *told* Hosea to marry a prostitute. We have no record of Salmon receiving a similar commission. So was Salmon drawn to Rahab's beauty? Her character? Or something more?

One thing the writing of this book has taught me is this: faith is a gift we can't earn, yet obedience accompanies true belief. I believe Rahab may have struggled with some of the laws of the God of Israel, which were so different from all she had known. But even in her struggles, she pledged her allegiance to Israel and God rewarded her faith, giving her a place in His Book, a lasting legacy.

May God grant each of us faith to believe as Rahab did. Even amidst our doubts.

In His Grace,
Jill Eileen Smith

ACKNOWLEDGMENTS

As with every book, the ideas may be mine, but the help in fleshing them out and making them real on the page comes from many other people. *The Crimson Cord* would not be in your hands without the sacrifice and kindness of those friends and family.

I would like to publicly thank the Revell team—editorial, marketing, publicity, design. I thank God for each one of you! Special thanks to Lonnie Hull DuPont (editor extraordinaire and a woman I am privileged to call friend), Jessica English (I'm not sure I can write a book without your suggestions and support!), Michele Misiak (you are the best!), Cheryl Van Andel (your cover designs make the books come to life for me!), Claudia Marsh (great publicist and so much fun!), Twila Bennett (I love visiting Revell and chatting with you!), Jen Leep (thank you for your innovative ideas!), Robin, Lindsay, Janelle, and the rest of the team—thank you, every one of you!

My agent, Wendy Lawton—thank you for being a prayer warrior as well as a great business partner and friend.

To my two critique buds, Jill Stengl and Kathleen Fuller. I don't know where this book would be without you! Dare I mention that you sent me back to the drawing board three times? But every comment helped me grow, and for that I sincerely thank you. I love you guys!

To the writing groups who allow me to remain among them and put up with too many prayer requests and a lot of questions! You girls have upheld me when my arms grew weak, and I felt your prayers when life took so many difficult turns during the writing of this book. I'm honored to call you friends.

To the readers who tell their friends about these books—I thank you!

To my forever friends—you know who you are.

To my guys and my girls—Jeff, Chris and Molly, Ryan and Carissa—I hope you know how much I love you! I love that we all love the arts in one form or another.

To Randy—how the years change our circumstances, but after nearly thirty-eight years together, the journey just grows richer. What a great God we serve, and I get to do so loving you forever!

Yahweh my Elohim—You are Elohim of heaven and earth. Thank You for giving us Rahab's story and for saving her in one simple act of faith.

Jill Eileen Smith is the bestselling author of the Wives of King David series, the Wives of the Patriarchs series, and the ebook novella *The Desert Princess*, first in the Loves of King Solomon series. Her research has taken her from the Bible to Israel, and she particularly enjoys learning how women lived in Old Testament times.

When she isn't writing, she enjoys spending time with her family and friends. She can often be found reading, testing new recipes, grabbing lunch with friends, or snuggling Tiger, her little writing buddy who chews her fingers as she works. She lives with her family in southeast Michigan. She loves hearing from her readers.

Contact Jill at jill@jilleileensmith.com, or visit her website: http://www.jilleileensmith.com.

Connect with Jill on Facebook: https://www.facebook.com/jilleileensmith

Twitter: https://twitter.com/JillEileenSmith

Pinterest: https://pinterest.com/JillEileenSmith

Goodreads: https://www.goodreads.com/author/show/2799806.Jill_Eileen_Smith

Meet

JILL EILEEN SMITH

at **www.JillEileenSmith.com** to learn interesting facts and read her blog!

Connect with her on

f Jill Eileen Smith

🐦 JillEileenSmith

Solomon captured her heart.
But can she hold on to his?

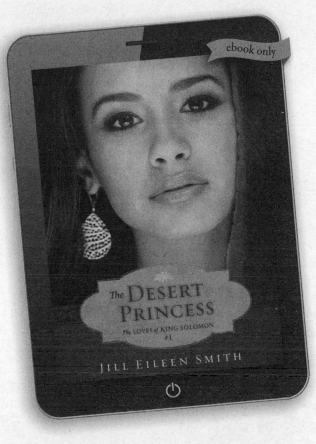

BE SWEPT AWAY with this tale of young love, heartbreaking betrayal, and the power of forgiveness, during one of the most tumultuous times in Israel's history.

"Rich, biblical drama."

—Lyn Cote, author of *Her Abundant Joy*

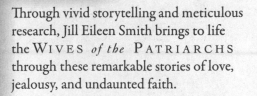

Through vivid storytelling and meticulous
research, Jill Eileen Smith brings to life
the WIVES *of the* PATRIARCHS
through these remarkable stories of love,
jealousy, and undaunted faith.

Praise for bestselling author
Michelle McKinney Hammond

Sassy, Single, and Satisfied...

"Using her fun, tell-it-like-it-is style, Hammond shows how to *get your priorities in order; squeeze the most out of being single; prepare your heart, soul, and mind for a mate;* and have your *deepest desires fulfilled."*

THE CHRISTIAN COURIER

"With thousands of single, dissatisfied women looking for love in wrong places, this book provides encouragement and a refreshing view of singleness...This is the best message on singleness I have read, and *I highly recommend it* for single women of all ages in your church."

CHURCH LIBRARIES

How to Avoid the 10 Mistakes Single Women Make...

"Everyone who reads this book will probably have a few nerves touched by Michelle's raw honesty—I know I certainly did. However, having our beliefs challenged when they are keeping us from God's best is, while not easy, a necessary and good thing. *I look forward to having my thoughts challenged by more of Michelle's refreshing candor* in the future."

ARMCHAIRINTERVIEWS.COM

The Diva Principle...

"Pulling examples of divas from the Bible, Michelle McKinney Hammond shows how each woman can become a diva. But it will take some elbow grease...Becoming a diva is not an easy job. According to Ms. Hammond, a diva is a woman who always *thirsts for knowledge and wisdom.* She is *willing to step out of her comfort zone* to do what needs to be done. A diva encourages others to be all they can be. She *accepts God's higher calling for her life.* A diva knows her strengths and works on her weaknesses. She knows how to handle basic areas of life such as finances, dressing, cooking, and housekeeping. A diva is *confident* in herself and *happy with how God designed her."*

CHRISTIANBOOKPREVIEWS.COM

"Michelle McKinney Hammond has done it again! In her trademark style, she challenges me and others like me to *totally sell out to God* and allow Him to work on us from the inside out. Michelle is definitely a DI-VINE inspiration."

—BABBIE MASON

The Real Deal on Overcoming Heartache: Learning to Live and Love Again

"Michelle Hammond fulfills God's promise of enlightening, freeing, and healing women by sharing her experiences, discoveries, and insights, laced thoroughly with Scripture and sprinkled with modern song fragments. Michelle's writing style is conversational, and easy to read and absorb."

ARMCHAIRINTERVIEWS.COM

101 Ways to Get and Keep His Attention...

"Any woman of God would *benefit from the wealth of knowledge Hammond so skillfully shares. 101 Ways* is truly a labor of love that will *inspire the heart longing for love.* It is a wonderful lesson to women of all ages, shapes, and walks of life on obtaining and maintaining the attention of the opposite sex. God has truly blessed Ms. Hammond with a gift—a gift for teaching and a means of touching the hearts and lives of women looking for love. *I recommend that all single women read this book* and will definitely be sharing it with others."

TEENS4JESUS LIBRARY

The Last Ten Percent (a novel)...

"This is not a sappy, preachy attempt to convey Christian themes to the reader. *The Last Ten Percent* deals with humiliating, ugly things in life and brings the reader to the point where they want to see these ladies find love in Christ alone. *I can't say enough great things about this story.* It's a must-read in my book! Check it out!"

EDGYINSPIRATIONALAUTHOR.BLOGSPOT.COM

"In *The Last Ten Percent* Hammond has done a wonderful job creating characters that the reader will become attached to and care about...*This is one novel that will entertain you while delivering a message of encouragement.*"

RAWSISTAZ LITERARY GROUP,
BLACK BOOK REVIEWS NEWSLETTER

"Her characters are *so real* that they will probably remind you of someone you know or have known! *I definitely recommend* you check this one out!"

FIVE STAR BOOK REVIEWS & MORE